RAGS & HOPE
Hearts Touched by Fire series

Published by *The Bitter End Publishing*

Copyright © 2020 by Gina Danna

This is a work of fiction.
Printed in the USA.

Cover Design and Interior Format

RAGS
AND
HOPE

GINA DANNA

To my mother…

ACKNOWLEDGEMENTS

It takes a team to put together a book. As author, I want to thank my support team in getting Cerisa and Pierce's story published. First, I'd like to thank Cynthia Veldman and Wendy La Capra who helped me iron out plot issues and when I ran off track in the storyline; my editor Louisa Cornell; my strong supporter JJ Jennings, who helped me on resources, even when the odd question was sent for verification and comments as well as putting up with my rantings all the rest of the time. To Bernadette La Manna, who fended off an army of cats to go through this piece for any discrepancies, which always manage to proliferate at a fast pace. And to my fabulous cover designer, Kim Killion and her team of Jennifer Jakes and all the rest of The Killion Group Inc – you guys make my final presentation flawless! I'd also like to the thank The Civil War Trust, an organization that introduced me to the Chickamauga Battlefield and all the intricacies of this complex battle in 1863.

I also want to thank my co-hearts at Southwest, Dallas Love Field, who witnessed me lugging my laptop to work and trying to write during breaks, despite the constant questions on how can I find the time to do so there? And can they be in my book (mostly the men!)? To Tiffany Whitfield, who saved my finishing on deadline by taking my shift.

Thank you to all!

CHAPTER ONE

Let them go. They can take any thing they find, and do any thing
they want, except take the chair I am sitting in.

- Col. Edward Hatch, USA, refusing the pleas of Mrs.
Jacob Thompson to stop his men from looting her house,
Memphis 1864.

❧

New York City
1863

THIS WAS DEFINITELY THE wrong night to be
sober.

Pierce James Duval sat on the green velvet covered settee,
dressed in his customary black trousers, white shirt, and
sapphire blue waistcoat under a black frock coat of fine wool.
He pulled his pocket watch out of his waistcoat pocket for
the fifth time in, as he snapped the lid open, the last twenty
minutes. With a sigh of disgust, he closed the watch and slid it
back into his pocket. He scanned the parlor. It was decorated
with wall hangings and arranged carpets with vases filled
with flowers and whatnot, and nothing changed.

You need to live again, Pierce. Margaret would have wanted you
to go on and not spend each eternal night with a bottle of whiskey!

Edward Brooks meant well by his words, but Pierce
sincerely doubted Margaret's idea of living meant visiting a
brothel.

For all that was holy, what he wouldn't give to be back on

the battlefield and at least find peace in front of a barrage of gunfire…

"Monsieur." The slightly heavy, overly perfumed and gaudily dressed Madame Nikki appeared at his side. He hadn't seen her sidle next to him so he nearly jumped, which only seemed to make her happier. "Perhaps a glass of bourbon would help you relax."

A boy, old enough to need introduction to a straight razor, suddenly came into view, handing him a glass filled with the amber liquor. Pierce eyed the boy. The trained servant wasn't looking at Pierce as he offered the glass. The precision of service made Pierce frown. Kid was too young to be in a place like this.

With a sigh, he took the drink with a nod to the madam. The honey-tasting alcohol slid a path down his throat, leaving a burning trail in its wake—a taste Pierce equated to bliss. It was a good quality stock. But the liquor brought a fierce ire to his mind. Why couldn't Edward just leave him home, with a bottle in hand as he drank Margaret's ghost to oblivion? Why?

"Mr. Brooks has found his match," Madame Nikki stated, breaking Pierce's thoughts. "He told me to send in our finest for you to view." She clapped her hands and, from out of the woodwork or so it seemed, three women walked to the center of the room. They were dressed in nothing other than their chemise, corset, with their laced pantalets showing under the hem of the chemise, stockings and heeled shoes. Their hair was mostly loose, combed but not dressed and it shouldn't be. They were to entertain in bed after all. Two of them wore heavy facial paint along with rouged lips, which they pouted as they posed for his inspection.

The third one, in comparison, was the most modest of

the three, still wearing a silk dressing robe that Madame pulled apart to show off her undergarments. She appeared to have little to none of the face paints. If anything, her cheeks blushed red but there was a defiant gleam to her amber eyes that attracted him. Oh, the rest of her was desirable. She looked slimmer than the other two, her corset of white cotton, trimmed in matching lace, was cleaner and the swell of her breasts inviting. He'd guess she was new and while her hands rested on her hips, her lips were pale and not pursed like the other two.

Madame Nikki caught his attention and smiled as she waved the other two away. "Ahhh, wise choice for the evening, monsieur. Cera is our more sultry dessert, one a man like you should enjoy delving into."

The girl glared at him. Openly glared. Only a glimpse of a smile hinted at her lips. He was enthralled. She stood about average height, probably up to his shoulders, he guessed. Rich golden-brown hair fell in waves over her shoulders and down her back. Those sparkling amber eyes danced under the oiled lamps and candles that lit the room. Her skin was a prized porcelain white except she had a smattering of freckles on her nose—faint but noticeable. She was the very opposite of his fiery Margaret, whose Irish upbringing had set his whole family into panic when he proposed to her. But this girl wasn't without spunk. She hadn't uttered a word, but her gaze let him know she was new, probably untried, scared yet bold.

It was in that instant he recognized her. What the hell was this misplaced Southern belle doing in a New York City brothel?

New York City
Winter 1862

CERISA FONTAINE SHOVED THE last stick of wood into the cast iron stove and slammed the trap door shut. She hoped and prayed to God that Abraham found more wood, but this was the poorer section of the city, where industry ruled. Most of the land was paved and bricked, factories and tenant buildings surrounding them with nothing green anywhere. Hundreds lived in an area unfit for more than one hundred. She shuddered at the thought of another cold night but with him, she'd have some warmth.

The coffee pot on the stove, filled with water, began to heat. She had virtually no coffee to add to it and stale tea, not because of storage but due to lack of funds. To make it last longer, she'd learned from the newspapers how the South was running low of supplies. Stories emerged how they used chicory or walnuts, dried sweet potatoes, just about anything to stretch their coffee supply. These tricks worked, but she'd do just about anything for a taste, even a sniff, of the real stuff.

She waited patiently, warming her hands over the stovetop. A quick study of them made her wince. Once she'd had perfect skin and dainty hands, both of which had dissipated with work in the textile factory. But money was money and to protect her skin by not using her hands in painstaking work wasn't an option.

Unless she went home.

She cringed. She'd never be able to go home, to Bellefontaine, again.

The door to the room slammed open, the wind snatching it from the hand of the tall Black man and whipping it against the wall. Icy winds raced through the room, chilling her further, despite the layers of cotton and woolen clothes she wore. She hissed at the bite of it, and he quickly lowered his bundle and reached for the handle, shutting the wooden door and sliding the latch into place.

She didn't think she'd ever been this cold.

"Sorry, darling," he said, his husky, deep voice warming her nerves as he hugged her tight. He was cool to the touch but within seconds, his presence chased the chill away.

"That wind be somethin' fierce today," she conceded, burying her face in the folds of his shirt.

He chuckled. "Ain't that the truth. Never this cold back home. Be like this there, those poor old magnolias be dyin'." He tipped her chin up off his chest and gave her a brief kiss.

She eyed the man before her and knew she'd made the right choice. With a weak grin, she sighed.

Abraham was a freedman now. Originally a slave on her father's plantation, Bellefontaine, in Louisiana, he had always been her protector. The dark secret of her family's wealth always gnawed the edges of respectability and her sanity after she learned about it. One of her brothers fled once he was initiated into it. The other, she guessed, stayed. All she knew was it ate at her soul and Abraham soothed her until she could figure out what to do. They'd grown up together, like many slave owners' children and slave children did, playing together when toddlers. Friends even, until maturity came and separation to their stations in life became ingrained.

Her brother Jack had stayed friends with Fanny, until…

She shuddered. Abraham held her tighter, thinking it was the cold but this dip in temperature didn't come from nature but from a memory of what she'd witnessed that night. A child herself, she'd snuck off after her brothers, staying in the shadows, virtually undetected. Even to this day, she could hear the screams, the sound of flesh beating flesh, punishment until the job was done, ringing in her ears.

Abraham found her, huddled in the woodpile hours later, shaking, her face tear-stained. Gently he sang a soft melody, washing her face and rocking her off the ledge of insanity. She didn't understand what she saw—oh, the deed was clear but the reasoning escaped her. But Abraham promised he'd protect her from this madness for the rest of her life. A powerful statement coming from a slave only a few months older than her. It had opened her shuttered eyes to the cruelty of slavery. These were not inferior people. They acted like her parents and other adults, had feelings, needs, desires similar to hers and other whites. Scanning the Bible, she found no basis for what the preachers claimed at the Protestant churches. The Catholics, her own denomination, shrugged indifference when she tried to corner her priest during confessional.

How could she continue to live in a world like this?

Her engagement was the final straw...

"I found more wood," Abraham said, interrupting her wayward thoughts. She blinked at his statement and looked at him. He was grinning. It was an infectious smile. It was one of his charms and it was the key to her heart.

"Good," she returned, rubbing her arms. "Because I'm cold."

He chuckled. "I hears ya. Give me a minute. Here," he tossed her a small burlap bag. "Found us a bit of coffee. Why not make some for us?"

She inhaled the beans, and the aroma was like ambrosia, just what she'd been dreaming of just a bit earlier. She eyed him carefully. Abraham was still one of the most handsome men she'd ever seen. Tall, he stood above most men. Broad-shouldered, his arms, chest and stomach rippled with muscles that were solid, like marble, gained from hours in the fields in Louisiana and the manual labor of the docks here. He had a tapered waist and long, strong legs that held up under the strongest of storms. His face was like one of the Roman and Greek statues she'd seen in a picture book at the library, so defined, strong and when he smiled, as alluring as Adonis.

"You did buy this, right?" She needed to know.

"Yes, ma'am. I'd take you to the shop to see but it's closed now."

"Abraham…"

He walked back to her and took her freezing hands in his large callused ones. "Union Navy been keeping us busy. Got paid today. All's good."

Yet the look in his eye told her the truth. It wasn't good. The Proclamation for Emancipation would go into effect in ten days, on the first day of 1863. Its only impact was to be on the rebel states, freeing their slaves. But rumblings here, a free state, let both of them know it changed the atmosphere of the war. Cerisa understood more than she wished. A war started by economics and wealth coiled with domination of international trade and the peculiar institution, the polite phrase for slavery in the South, was twisted by Lincoln to answer the abolitionist supporters and to stop England from recognizing the Confederacy. It also gave Northerners a viable cause to support or despise the war. Many around them here, in New York City, swore they'd not fight to free the slaves because no one wanted them up here, taking their jobs for cheaper pay. Those jobs were the only ones men like Abraham could take and he actually had an education. But the Irish immigrants here, those so hated by the Protestant

Americans, fought to take any job they could, even if it meant cleaning the sewers for low pay. They all knew if freedmen journeyed here, the Irish would be fired, and the job's pay cut in half and filled by ex-slaves.

Protests were verbal now. She expected them to escalate. A sigh escaped her lips before she could stop it. Out of frustration and starvation, she picked up the wooden ladle and went back to the pot on the stove and stirred the stew for dinner.

Abraham came up behind her and wrapped his arms around her waist. He bent forward and kissed her exposed neck.

"I do love you, Mrs. Walker."

She giggled still at his touch and his reference. "And I you. Even if no one will recognize us." The moment those words spilled out, she wished she'd taken them back.

"I like the name Walker," he continued, ignoring her implication. "Walker. Like walking away from the chains of slavery." He hummed, "Abraham Walker has a ring to it."

She snorted. "Out of all the surnames, you chose that one."

"It is my right, as a freedman, to choose the one I like."

In the South, he'd be given her father, his owner's name, Fontaine. But up here, he proclaimed his freedom as a runaway and took another. Not that that would save him under the Fugitive Slave Act, she thought numbly, but the war prevented that law from fulfilling its purpose. On that she was thankful but leery. The Irish would demand its reinstatement if it kept their jobs...

She stared down on her left hand. The indention from the silver wedding band long gone wasn't there. How he'd come up with the ring, she'd never know but she'd sold it two months ago for a bag of potatoes. Her argument with herself for no longer having the wedding ring was it was only a symbol…

His hand grasped her left one to stop her from rubbing the ring's spot. "I'll get you another. Prettier, too."

"Is it a lie? Really?" she asked softly.

"No, we were married in the sight of God…"

"He was the only one present," she murmured. The priest she'd convinced to say the ceremony wouldn't do it in the church for fear of repercussion. New York allowed miscegenation marriages, and she'd heard how the numbers climbed in their area of the Five Points as some Irish lasses had tied to the freedmen, only to cause a ruckus in the community so Abraham thought, for her safety, to say their vows in quiet, audible only to God. To everyone else, they were living in sin. Though, frankly, their tiny hovel, a single roomed flat in the subbasement of the tenant building, was a sin to let anyone live in under any circumstances.

Abraham spun her away from her stew and gazed into her eyes. "He was the only one necessary." He kissed her again, hard, deep and passionately. She melted into his embrace.

A knock at their door interrupted them. "Cerisa? It's me, Annie."

Abraham growled and released her. Cerisa tried to bite back her smile and flattened her hands on her apron before he made it to the door.

"Annie, how great to see you," she greeted her friend. Annie was the only one she had in this ill-begotten city.

The redheaded Irish woman, slender, freckled and always smiling or, when angry, rolling curse words out of her mouth like a sailor, hugged Cerisa tight.

"Tis a cool night out there," Annie stated loudly.

Abraham laughed. "That it be, Miss Annie."

"Glad you came by," Cerisa added, pulling her friend inside further, away from the door that wasn't the tightest seal against the cold.

Lighthearted, earthy giggles filled the air. Annie glanced at Cerisa. "You survived another day."

Cerisa looked down at her chapped hands with their ragged nails. "Yes. Mr. Beatty chose someone else to pick on today." She heard Abraham snarl from across the room, as he pretended to be interested in fixing the chair that'd fallen to pieces yesterday. Second hand goods…

"Beatty is an arse," Annie replied.

They both sat at the table, near the stove. Cerisa handed her a chipped porcelain cup of the freshly brewed coffee before she sat to drink her own. Annie inhaled the drink, closing her eyes and sighed.

"How wonderful! It'd be real coffee?"

Cerisa nodded. "Abraham picked it up today."

Annie looked at the freedman and nodded. He accepted her thanks before he returned to his work. A frown etched across her brow as her gaze slid back to Cerisa. She moved to the edge of her chair and lowered her voice.

"Cera, please. The docks have turned violent. Your man was part of the crew thrown off the pier, chased by a couple of the lads from the Five Points carrying torches. The marshall be havin' a hell of time stopping them from trying to rid the area of the freedmen takin' their jobs."

Cerisa gulped the coffee, the heat scalding down her throat but it didn't hurt as bad as the fear deep inside her, the ugly monster that twisted her stomach tight. Without moving, she slid her view to her husband and quickly back. He hadn't seemed to hear Annie nor did he look back at her. Instead, he studiously worked on the chair. He worked wonders with wood but no one would hire a black man at the furniture factories. Docks were the best he could do.

When she said nothing, her friend became more worried. "Cerisa, you need to find another employer. One who'll pay ya yur worth."

She knew that. "I see no one looking for a companion," she moaned.

"What about a ladies' maid? Or maybe the kitchens?" Annie prodded. "Seamstress?"

She'd been raised on the riches of her family's wealth, educated by the finest tutors, her knowledge of dinner parties, social gatherings and dances was superb. Her escape came quite easily after a year of finishing school in Boston. In addition to all those 'fine' qualities, she knew the French language, spoke it fluently, could read and write it. But darn socks? Sew a dress? Cook? No… She shook her head.

"I know nothing that would qualify me. Best would be a groom in a stable," she answered. She loved horses, spent the better of her childhood in the barnyard, so she knew the chores having helped at home.

Annie snorted. "Cera, no one would take a lady to be a stable lad." She tapped her fingers on the table. "Did you try that sewin' piece I left you?"

A simple task. To embroider the ankle of a stocking, fixing actually the clockwork in the piece. With great reluctance she slid the handkerchief wrapped piece to her under the table. Abraham would not be pleased. He didn't want her waiting on others, like a slave.

Annie looked at it, on her lap, close to the edge of the table.

"It's not as easy to fix a stocking as I thought," she apologized for the semi-ruined length of cotton.

Her friend re-wrapped it, shoved it in her skirt pocket and

withdrew a dollar bill, wadded in her fist. She pushed it into Cerisa's hand. "For work done."

"But I didn't…"

Annie put a finger to her lips. "I might be havin' somethin' easier for you to do but," she paused. "Keep an eye on your man and be careful, ya hear me? Hopefully we won't have to go down that road, but we might. It's a lot more cash but hard."

Cerisa rolled her lip into her mouth, nervous energy requiring her to do something. She nodded as her friend finished her coffee. Annie stood, gave her a kiss on her forehead and yelled at Abraham to keep his wife safe as she slipped out the door.

Cerisa sat for a moment, wondering what Annie hinted at. The girl herself was a housemaid, one of the better jobs the Irish women could get, but it wasn't easy working for the lout who employed her. It was a cleaner job than Cerisa's work in the factory but while they both worked for men they despised, at least hers hadn't made any advances at her like Annie's. Was any of this going to be easier?

CHAPTER TWO

On the authority of Lord God Almighty, have you anything that outranks that?

- "Mother" Mary Ann Ball Bickerdyke, Union army nurse, to a U.S. Army surgeon who questioned the authority upon which she acted.

May 1863

PIERCE ENTERED ST. PATRICK'S Cathedral in Manhattan for the late morning mass. He walked through the doors of the large church, dipped his fingers in the holy water, made the sign of the cross and found a pew, on the left about a two-thirds back from the pulpit. Genuflecting, he slid into the pew, dropped the kneeler and prayed. Margaret was too ill to attend and as her cough rattled roughly through the night, his fear of losing her increased to the point he finally attended mass. A prayer to the Man upstairs for a reprieve of her illness was top in his mind.

Raised Catholic by his Creole mother, whose family moved south of Arcadia once the Protestant British assumed possession of Canada, Pierce was well versed in the protocol of service but often avoided it, even with his Irish Catholic wife. His dismissal of attending mass often was based on work he needed to do but the truth was, growing up in a house with a Catholic mother who ruled over the children more than his overtly Protestant father, the arguments that ensued over religion were enough to make any child veer away from the word of God in either form.

Then he committed the worse offense, according to his father—he married an Irish woman. Margaret O'Mallory carried every essence of her heritage. She was copper haired, freckled, quick-tempered and as Catholic as the day was long. Pierce loved her. The fact his father was barely tolerable at the wedding was duly noted. Add to it that she and her family were against abolition for fear of what it would do to the Irish only added fuel to his father's pro-abolitionist views. The heated arguments he held with his paternal parent drove him away.

But now, only six months after their wedding, Margaret was ill. Last spring, she'd become part of the U.S. Sanitary Commission. The pristine ladies of that organization gladly took Mrs. Pierce Duval into their group because he was an officer of the 40th Regiment, New York Infantry. She devoted her time in his absence to helping the Commission raise funds for the military hospitals and visited them to help on inspections, something the military surgeons hated, having civilians grade their establishments. According to her letters, the surgeons should have been pleased because they lacked so much in equipment and medicines, items the Sanitary Commission could aid them in getting. He'd been so proud of her.

But after the Battle of Chancellorsville, in Virginia, he found himself staring at a letter from her sister, demanding he return and fast. Margaret was dying. Some ailment she'd picked up during their hospital inspections. Fear raced through him and he'd finagled a pass to return home for two weeks. Two weeks. Not enough time…

Out of the corner of his eye, he saw a flash of blue go

down and up in the aisle next to him. He glanced up and
found a woman staring at him. She was stunning. Dressed
in a sapphire blue silk dress trimmed in black and white,
she stood facing him. Chestnut curls cascaded off the side of
her head, brushing her neck delicately. She had shimmering
golden-brown eyes barely visible through the netting draped
over them from the matching blue bonnet. It caressed her
high cheekbones but left her rose-colored lips exposed
and the tie ribbons didn't hide the long graceful neck. Her
white leather gloved hands rested on the side of the torn
and tattered black wool cloak she wore, ready to help her
crinoline skirt squeeze into the pew. She stood impatiently,
waiting for him to realize her politely expected question. It
hit him suddenly, as if he was a school-age boy, and he got off
the kneeler to allow her to take the seat at the end of the pew.

Her look finally registered with him. "Apologies," he
stated and moved to sit on the bench, rolling the kneeler
back upright.

The woman gave a tilt of her head as an answer before she
stepped into the pew.

Closer to him, he noticed her better. The dress was in
excellent condition, the blues startling brilliant in hue but,
he knew from his own wife's discussions and what he saw,
this lady was out of place. The dress was an older one, the
type worn more before the war, before many textile factories
turned to making uniforms and such for the war effort. It was
more expensive than his own wife had worn even married to
him and he made a decent income as an officer. But the cloak
told him another tale – it was used, as if she wore it often, not
able to part with it long enough to wash and air dry.

"Thank you," she replied slowly, clasping her hands before
her she flipped the kneeler back down. "I should'va said

pardon me." A deep Southern accent rolled prettily off her tongue, even in its whispered state.

Surprise rippled through him. He always appreciated a Southern accent as much as he did the Irish lilt. Her drawl was sublime yet strangely out of place. Quickly he looked at her gloved hands and kicked himself for looking to see if a wedding band could be seen, but it was the only explanation for her to be here. Yet she was alone. A Southerner this far north wasn't good. He opened his mouth, waiting to see if her husband or someone arrived but she seemed to be alone. His brows furrowed, worried that with no one to protect her from the fiends loitering the streets, anti the war, anti the slave-holding South, she could be in perilous danger, but the church organ fired up the beginning music of the mass. Attending mass alone wasn't breaking societal rules, but leaving alone wasn't safe. He'd have to watch and see if she had an escort out of here.

When it came time in the service, they filed out of the pews for communion, he walked behind her, still formulating what he could say without sounding obtrusive. At the altar, he took the blessing with the wafer and wine, bending his head to pray for Margaret. When he stood, his pew companion was already gone. He scanned the church on his way back to their row but still nothing.

Then he caught the wisp of blue heading down the side aisle, toward the door. His teeth gritted, wanting the service over, to go find her. As the priest blessed the congregation, Pierce sprung from his seat and strode out the door. In the distance, he saw her. She was talking to a tall black man, dressed in a morning coat of black with black pants. The man towered over her so his hand went to her face, his fingers tipping her face up to see him and he smiled. Pierce saw she returned it and then looped her arm through his bent one before they walked off, the man her buffer against the traffic on the street.

A mixed couple. Pierce frowned. Such a visual display could set off fireworks among the people on the street, even though it was the proper stance, the man stood between her and the street. If they were both white, anywhere it was fine. But despite the diversity here, New York City might be free but not toward a relationship between races.

It was then he caught the trio of youths, standing across the street from him, closer to the couple. The boys were talking and looking after the Southern belle and her companion. Something about the youths irked Pierce and as he crossed the street to find out what they were up to, he saw their expressions didn't look welcoming. They fisted their hands, aiming to go after the couple. Pierce stopped in front of the boys and reached out, his hand landing on the chest of the leader, stopping him completely.

The boy glared at him, defiance written on his face. Pierce guessed the three to be about fifteen, sixteen from their height.

"Let me go," the lad demanded, his voice cracked half way through.

Pierce narrowed his gaze, not moving his hand. "I'm thinking you three missed mass this morning."

"Ain't no damn papist," the shortest of the three, the one standing furthest away, spat.

With a snort, Pierce smiled tightly. "There's plenty of other denominations available. All having sessions with God. If I were you, I'd go find one. You need direction."

"Who do you think you is?" the boy before him asked, tension building beneath Pierce's steady hand.

"I am a servant of God," he replied, pushing the kid back a step. "You will leave here and leave that couple alone."

"Ain't right, those two."

"The decision isn't yours to make," Pierce stated. "Now leave."

The street urchin behind, the short one, turned red with anger. "This is bullshit. He's one against our three. Youth will win over the old!" He bullied forward, right into Pierce.

With one move of his free hand, he grabbed the boy's shirt collar and yanked him off his feet toward him. Fear quickly gripped the boy who lost his footing and would have fallen but Pierce held his shirt too tight. "I said leave."

The remaining boy finally spoke. "Ah, come on Arnie. They ain't worth it."

"Damn right, they ain't," the first one added.

"You agree?" Pierce asked the one in his grasp. The boy nodded. "Good." He released him. "Now get!"

The boys turned and ran down the street away from him. Pierce stood, making sure they were gone then looked to see if he saw the girl. They too were gone. With a sigh, he straightened his waistcoat and coat. His work was done. Time to go home to Margaret.

"I didn't like you standing in the back of the church, like a slave." Cerisa sniffed, annoyed at Abraham. "We go to mass as husband and wife only for you not to assume your place at my side."

He squeezed her hand that rested on his arm as they walked home after service. "Cera, you know I do not want to cause you harm…"

"Ah, but abandonment is perfectly acceptable?"

Abraham sighed. "That is not what I mean and you know

it. While freedmen live here, we are not really accepted, an argument you are familiar with. I do not press for attention at church."

They turned the corner and headed toward the tenement row. Cerisa noted the empty brown liquor bottles on the street, the smell of urine and vomit wafting in the air, not as pungent as earlier but still enough she withdrew her perfumed handkerchief from her reticule and placed it at her nose. The smell filtered by lilacs made it tolerable—barely.

She shook her head and inhaled the lilac. "Still, I'd like it better if we took a seat together."

With a shove, Abraham pushed the door to their residence open. The only windows sat across the room, next to each other. Narrow slits of an opening to the outside, they let only a glimpse of the late morning sun in. Between that and the fireplace, the little hovel was barely lit and Cerisa hated it. That and it reeked of coal…

"Cera, no." He closed the door. "Did you see those boys after mass? You know they weren't going to let us go peaceable if we'd been together."

But they were together when the street urchins saw them. She'd noticed them and chose to ignore them as they were young thugs, beneath her, as odd as that sounded while she stood here in a basement shanty. As she plucked her cuff buttons, she also recalled how that handsome man whom she sat next to at mass had stopped and talked to the boys. He must have diffused their zeal to pursue them as no one followed them here.

"I saw that gentleman you sat next to behind us," Abraham continued. "He was attracted to you."

She scowled, unhooking her bodice. "Really? I never noticed him."

Abraham watched her. He didn't say a word and at the last hook, she looked at him squarely. "I think its time I part with this gown. Maybe it'll raise enough with it to get us through the next month…"

"No, do not."

Her hand ran over the silk fabric, lovingly. The dress was old. At home, it would have been thrown in the rag bin three years ago but she couldn't part with it. "I will miss it. I only kept it because it was my wedding dress—"

Suddenly, Abraham took her hands in his and tilted her chin. "It is a fond reminder of days when survival was never a worry." He gave her a sad grin. "Besides, I love how it makes you smile. And because it is what you wore when we stood before God and said our vows."

The lump in her throat grew so large, she couldn't say a word but nodded as she rolled her lips in tight. Such a nervous habit, one she so badly needed to stop but couldn't.

"Good," he whispered and kissed the tip of her nose. "Dance with me."

She frowned, confused. "Dance? It's a Sunday afternoon."

"The Lord would have us dance," he answered smoothly, pulling her into his embrace.

"But there's no music."

He took the lead and stepped to the right, humming. Reluctantly, stiff at first, she followed. Her husband was a determined man and continued his tune, spinning her on the small floor space until she finally relented, moving more naturally with him. She laughed, making him smile that crooked grin that caught her attention years ago. A time when she shouldn't have noticed, being a good girl and he being her slave.

In the next turn, he fumbled the step and she laughed,

caught in his arms as he corrected himself. But despite his misstep, his tune continued and he didn't release her. Still twirling, he broke his music to speak.

"Now, I do have news."

She looked up at him, curious, but waited as they danced.

"A better means of work."

Cerisa's eyes widened. "Truly?" The docks hadn't paid well and her days at the factory were no doubt numbered—if she could just learn to shut her mouth around that fop who served as her boss...

"Do you remember when I went to the meeting?"

Meeting? She frowned. "The anti-slavers group? Yes, wasn't that where you heard that runaway, what was his name? Mr. Douglass speak?"

"Yes, Frederick Douglass. He was quite inspiring."

"Yes, well, I'm sure he was, but darling, you are free," she said, confused. She hadn't wanted him to go. They did not need to bring any attention to themselves. Being a mixed-race couple was something even the abolitionists didn't abide.

He spun her again. She knew something more was coming because he was trying to distract her with the dance. That made her tremble. He knew she wasn't going to like what he had to say. Heavens, she hoped he hadn't planned to join them in their protests in Washington, to press for the abolition of slavery amendment everyone whispered about.

"I know that and thank you."

"Abraham—"

"Mr. Douglass and others were speaking of Colored troops that are forming. How we can't sit back and let these white boys fight for us. We are more than capable of..."

"No!" She stopped, the blood draining from her face and her ears rang. "You can't be thinking of going to fight!"

"But darling, I need…"

"You need to be taking care of your wife. Not be out on some field being shot at!"

"Cerisa."

When he called her name, she knew the rest before he said it. Fear and anger wrapped around her as she pushed him away. "You've already signed up, haven't you?"

He stood still. There was a tick in his jaw and his brows furrowed. "It is better money."

She laughed. It had a nervous tone to it. "Abraham, darling, do you think they'll pay you what the white men get?"

His hand ran over his short cut hair. "Anything is better than what I've got now." He turned and paced. "Cera, they fired all us darkies at the dock. Every last one of us. That new manager, he be Irish and he wanted us all gone so he could hire his kin. You know, no one will hire us—"

"Have you even looked? They refuse to hire the Irish, not you!" The anger was in every word but the tears started to blur her vision. "Abraham, please, don't. I've read the papers, seen the lists of wounded and dead…they're huge and grow daily! I've seen the weeping widows, the orphans—" She sobbed, despite her attempts not to do so and because she couldn't stop it—or him—it fueled her anger. "I can't live without you."

"Shhh, shhhh," he whispered softly, taking her in his arms. "It is because I love you, because of me, you've had to reduce yourself to this." His free hand swept around the dark, bleak home they lived in. "Because of me, you've had to lower yourself, give it all up. You set me free. I need to do this."

She knew she'd lost before he ever told her. The tears came. He held her until she got a grip on herself and stopped. Sniffling a last sob, she pulled back, tugging her handkerchief from her wrist where she'd tucked it up under her cuff.

"Besides," he smiled at her. "I hear most of time, we ain't close to the firing anyway. Got us clearing roads and such."

She knew he'd hate that, but if that was true, she'd be able to handle it. He'd live. But they both knew the truth. Death of a freedman for the life of a white man. "Truly?"

A rattled chuckle came from his lips. "What I was hearin', from the white boys at the recruiters." He looked her in the eye. "I need to do this. For us."

With a deep breath, she realized she had no choice. She nodded and he kissed her, deeply.

He made love to her. It was Sunday, the beginning of June. Passion took her to the highest place, making her complete but it didn't stop the fear that it'd be the last time she'd see him alive.

CHAPTER THREE

Now those Yankees were whipped, fairly whipped and according to all the rules of war they ought to have retreated. But they didn't.

- Sam Watkins, 1ˢᵗ Tennessee Regiment, April 6, 1862 Battle of Shiloh

July 1863

PIERCE PLACED THE WHITE lilies on the mound of earth, his thoughts still muddled despite the reality of the situation. It still felt like it was only yesterday. Margaret had finally succumbed to the arms of Death four weeks ago at exactly five minutes after nine in the morning. Odd that he actually checked the clock at the time but something drove him to glance at it. He'd ignored the doctor's advice and sat next to her, cradling her in his arms, rocking slightly, so in her fevered state, she'd know he was there. The fever that reoccurred over and over again, the one the doctor claimed ate at her will to survive. Somehow, Pierce knew when she gave up fighting, worn out by weeks of battling the disease that devoured her. He'd bent down and gently kissed her goodbye, hearing her mother wailing in the background for him not to. Margaret's eyes opened briefly, as if using her last effort to see him before she left this world.

For the three days of the wake, he'd remained stoic, unmoving. Her family had wanted longer. The coffin sat in the parlor. The glass frame on the top showed Margaret's angelic face, encased in a bed of flowers—tulips, lilies, forget-me-nots, roses and violets. It was June and the heat climbed steadily. He knew as much as he wanted to see her, the flowers would wilt, the incense would run itself dry and the stench of a decaying body would permeate the house. It was a scent that he'd encountered on the battlefield and it'd turn anyone's stomach. Margaret would have been horrified if he let her get that far and for that reason, he'd pushed the funeral forward.

His hand caressed the raised mound of dirt over her grave, still finding it hard to believe she was gone. He wanted to stay here and find his peace with his new status as a widower, but duty called, his leave over, in fact, over by ten days but he didn't care. The only thing his father did for him, with his political connections, was to get his son an extension. Pierce knew his father hoped this favor would help to redirect him to lead one of the forming Colored troops. His father was a politician, always aiming for office. The bastard! Right now, all Pierce wanted was to crawl into his wife's grave.

An equine snort followed by a jingle of tack from the horse drawn carriage waiting for him snapped Pierce out of his sinking melancholy. He had a war to return to, and it was the one place he could take his anger for losing her and direct it out on the battlefield. In an odd twist, there he might find a level of peace.

"Margaret Duval, we will meet again," he whispered, kissed his fingertips and touched the top of the grave. He stood and walked back to the carriage, leaving the shade of the trees to the curbside. The driver moved the conveyance closer, jumped off his seat and held the door open.

The sun beat down hard once he stepped clear of the tree shade that covered most of the cemetery. Instantly, the wool of his navy wool uniform became stifling in the July heat. He tugged at his shirt collar.

"Another hot one," he groaned to the driver.

"Yes, sir. It is July."

He sat on the seat. July 13. Well into summer. It was muggy and he feared it'd get worse. With a clear blue sky, it appeared no rain was coming to cool things off. With a deep sigh, he focused on today. It was time to return to the war. He tapped the roof. "677 Third Avenue."

"Yes sir."

The carriage rumbled down the streets from St. Joseph's Cemetery to the city's Manhattan side. Even with the air entering the open windows, Pierce squirmed as the temperature climbed so he shrugged the frock coat off, leaving him in his shirtsleeves and waistcoat. Instant relief washed over him, despite being 'undressed'. He'd not leave the carriage without dressing, he swore though the area he was headed to was on the outskirts, bordering the Five Points, if he didn't, no one would bother him. The Irish dominant area held the working class, not the stock market side.

Before he left to return to his unit stationed in Virginia, he had one final task. He was to assist the officials as they drew the names for the first official draft to fill the 1,500 vacant slots in the army New York needed to fill. Pierce sighed. In this part of the city, the names would be of men who didn't want to go to war nor could afford to pay someone to take their place for $300, like the rich could.

These people were Irish and he dreaded that some of the names pulled could be from Margaret's family. What a terrible way to drag them out of mourning…

The perspiration was forming on her forehead. A droplet

escaped and landed on the threads in the loom machine beneath her. Cerisa sat back and wiped her forehead again. It was only a little after ten that morning and she was soaking. She dabbed at the drop on the material, quickly glancing at the other women at their machines, hoping no one noticed her. From her perusal, no one had but she wasn't the only one sopping and that somehow was comforting. The rattling noise of the peddle-driven machines filled the air as the large looms functioned back and forth with the weaving of threads. Windows along the one wall were propped open, allowing the mugginess to invade a room already hot from treadled machines and the ladies working them.

Cerisa glanced down at her hands as she set the final bobbin up and cringed. Not only had she perspired on the fabric threads but she was going to have to watch what she touched as her knuckles were cracked, her fingers dry from working constantly with cotton threads and blood threatened to spill over onto the material. She pulled them back and wiped them across her apron, glad for once the piece was dingy tea-colored from dirt and dust.

"Can ya hear all that ruckus out there?" Lila, the girl standing at the next machine muttered, nudging Cerisa.

Forcing her hands flat against her apron, Cerisa frowned as she looked toward the windows. Above all the rumblings of spindles and mechanical looms, the yells from the street could be heard at times, high-pitched voices, like squawking birds.

"I hear them. Saw a crowd forming when I got here."

Lila leaned closer. "All here about the lottery." She snickered. "Ya see them brutes of me brother's group, them Black Joke company blokes? All here cuz heard their chief's name be in that lottery-barrel the Yankees got."

"Won't do them any good. The draft is law—"

"Back to work Walker!"

She glared to her left and found the pot-bellied bearded beast who was her boss returning her stare at full force. Thoughts of strangling him flashed before her eyes and quickly she quelled the image because she doubted she'd be able get a decent grip on that flabby flesh.

Bang!

The loud explosion of a gun being fired, followed by the volume of cries from the crowds outside the windows caught everyone's attention. Lila grabbed Cerisa's hand and pulled her as she, along with the others, ran to the windows. Out of the corner of her eye, Cerisa saw her boss also raced to see what was happening.

Below them bedlam took over on the streets. The crowd reacted violently to whoever, probably one of the police officers who formed a thin line in front of the building the mob lunged at, had fired a pistol in the air. But to Cerisa, through the mayhem forming, she only saw wooden clubs in the policemen's hands, not weapons. The numerous civilians picked up stones, sticks and whatever they could find to throw at the building to break the glass windows as their cries against the lottery grew.

"Look," Lila whispered hoarsely, her finger pointing out the window. "The Black Joke firefighers be lookin' to take fisticuffs to them."

The volunteer firefighters called the Black Joke Company were made of tall men, all bulky and not overly bright Cerisa thought, having bumped into one of them with Abraham one spring day. That man was an ogre, larger than Abraham in thickness. The group below were exact duplicates and it made her lips curdle.

"They don't look intelligent enough to be here, unless

there's a fire," she muttered.

"Ain't looking to stop a fire," her friend countered. "More like add fuel to it."

The firefighters surged toward the building. The policemen rallied. Their commander blew his whistle loud and clear but that only seemed to incite the crowd. Glass shattered and the mob howled as they pushed forward. It was a nightmare, surreal in Cerisa's mind, to realize this was actually happening. People fell in the crowd as screams bantered with the roar of the masses.

The problem in her mind wasn't who yelled but where because she feared she, along with some of the other workers, were the ones adding to the sounding fury. Caught in the stream of the other women, she was moving towards the door, the one her boss normally stood before, barring any from leaving but he wasn't there and no one listened as he bellowed orders to return to work. Lila guided her in the herd that fled down the stairs and out the doors into the onslaught they'd just witnessed above.

"Come on!" Lila tugged.

Cerisa got jostled and run into as they inched closer. She stumbled and almost lost her footing, looking down to see what she ran into and found it was a man, sprawled on the cobblestone. With a shriek, she jumped over him and right into another man who pushed her out of his way. Panic spread through her as her heartbeat throbbed. She was caught in a riot and everything turned to hell.

The carriage skidded to a stop just two blocks from its destination. Pierce heard the rumblings in the distance and looked out of his window in time to see a wave of people teeming before the building he was headed to.

The driver bent over, his face strained. "Mister, I ain't driving into that. You gotta walk from here."

Shrugging his coat back on, Pierce frowned. He dug into his pocket to pay the man when the air rang with a gunshot followed by a roar from the surge of people he'd seen. In one swift move, he shoved the coins into the man's hand as he flung the door wide, leapt out and ran toward the building.

What unfolded before him was a madhouse. He'd been on the battlefield, witnessed men who attacked with a vengeance, others who trembled with fear. This though, was hate and chaos the like he'd never seen. The people protesting included men, women and children. The closer he got, the more the scene turned red.

The bulky firefighters charged through the thin veil of a police line, charging at the building itself, stomping on the fallen cops to attack the building.

"You're not goin' wanna go there," a man nearby said, panting in between each word.

Pierce glanced at him. The broken policeman stood, holding his right arm at an odd angle, blood splattered on the blue wool jacket and white shirt. The blood of his forearm wound poured through the rip in the sleeve. It was obvious the man had just escaped the crowd and as he leaned against a tree, his face paled with each second.

Pierce yanked off his jacket again and wrapped it inside out around the injured policeman as he slid down to the ground. Tugging his necktie off, he bound the wound. "What the hell is this all about? The damn draft?"

The man nodded. "Them Irish firefighters. Their captain got drafted. They're like a wall, cain't stop them."

Pierce stood and turned to go.

"Here, you'll want this," the policeman pushed his handgun

at him. "It's loaded."

Taking the gun would leave the man defenseless but the cop muttered what he was about to do was more mad if he didn't take it. Shoving the gun into the waistband of his trousers, thankful that his dress uniform fit better around the waist than most so it could hold the gun, Pierce took off.

As he got closer, he approached from the side, seeing the mob had broken open the doors but the back of the building was empty and the rear door swung wide.

"Duval!"

He glanced and saw the commander at the door, pushing staff out. "Yes, sir."

"Get the hell out of here!"

The sound of more glass breaking and bangs from inside filled the air. Along with the smell of turpentine followed with smoke. The commander turned to take a look back inside.

"Damn, they started a fire! Run!"

Cerisa hugged her arms tight, trying desperately to stand still for a moment. It had been a big mistake to venture out into this. Once out of the building, they had been swamped by the crowds, all the workers separated and the few she saw were at a distance, wrapped up in the commotion. Lila was nowhere to be seen.

Bottlenecked with the mob, she stumbled onward, taking precarious steps as the ground was uneven, crunching even beneath her worn boots. One step and she gasped at a stabbing pain in the ball of her foot. She couldn't even stop to find the culprit. After a few more agonizing steps, the sharp pain dulled, though inside her shoe, she knew she was bleeding. By the time she realized that, she was in the middle of the front hall of the building, her nostrils flaring from the smell of turpentine. A roar erupted up ahead and the mass of people broke in two, one section racing forward, her section pushing back.

Fear rose inside her. She was injured and the pain ate at her. She didn't want to retreat. Quickly she turned, sidestepping to reach the outer walls, venturing around to the door and freedom. Everyone around her chanted and ranted about the draft, the inequality of it. She'd shudder from the violence if she wasn't nearby.

"They claim this be fair! Ain't fair! They be taken our boys and not their own!" a man bellowed loudly, standing on top of a desk, pounding his chest as the air filled with smoke.

"Hear, hear!" and other confirmations sounded just as loudly.

"And all for the sake of freeing them nigras…"

"Yeah!!!" rang through the crowd.

"…and the fact'ries fire us to hire 'em 'cause we know they'd work for nothin'!"

The smoke was building, making the room opaque and stifling. Cerisa couldn't breath as she tried to make it to the door.

"We ain't dying for that!"

The roar of agreement instantly turned into yells of fear as one of the cross beams in the ceiling picked up sparks and lit into flames. The crowd turned to panic and quickly switched direction, stamping toward the door right as Cerisa made the threshold. The mob of people, her skirts and injured foot made her vulnerable to being run over. Fear threatened to grow out of control but she worked to dampen it and stay standing, pushing with all her might to get outside the room that grew hotter by the moment.

A crack in the ceiling resounded, magnifying the screams behind her to a deafening tone. Stuck in the doorway with too many trying to push into it and leave, with terror seizing control, she couldn't breathe. Suddenly, the people to her sides loosened as the crowd's strength tore at the walls and they fell, bricks pouring out.

Cerisa fell from the push along with the people around her and as she stumbled, a fear that she'd be trampled to death loomed before her. She screamed.

CHAPTER FOUR

Strange as it may seem to you, but the more men I saw killed the more reckless I became.

- Private Oliver Wilcox Norton, 83rd Pennsylvania Volunteers, in 1863

PIERCE ROUNDED THE BLOCK, trying to find a passageway out of the area. The chaos was escalating. The streets filled with angry and scared people—a disaster on the verge of explosion. The madness he'd seen in some of the people's eyes as he wove through the crowds harkened to days during the Peninsular Campaign and Bull Run. Soldiers in their first battle often lingered between terrified and overwhelmed which, unless they were trained well and under watch, could erupt into a strange madness that ate at their souls, compelling them to do the most outrageous things.

Here, in these civilians, that type of insanity meant destruction, as if the devil walked among them, laughing. The evil he'd seen at one point inside him…he shook at the thought, knowing he had to get to the police station or army command to get help. And from the looks of the cut telegraph wires, he'd have to go further to find it.

A loud roar spewed to his right and he turned to find a crowd chasing a man. It caused Pierce to narrow his gaze because he saw no reason for them to attack a single white man dressed in civilian clothes until one of them yelled it was the police superintendent, John Kennedy. That one recognition set the mob into motion. Pierce glanced down at the pistol caught in his suspender strap and knew he'd never win with only six shots against the mass before him. Their numbers sealed the man's fate.

Pierce realized divine providence had given him grace by giving that man his frock earlier because now, he didn't appear as army and had moved so far without any issues. That and a few he recognized in the streets knew him, knowing who his wife had been. Another level of protection.

The need to help and perhaps save his in-laws kept him there. The angry mob took vengeance out on storefronts, tenement houses, factories and anything they felt would rule against them. They'd even attacked an orphanage for freedmen's children, burning the structure down and word passed one of the children as well. The air filled with smoke from it and other fires.

He turned the street corner and found a new level of hell. Before him, a freedman was hanging from a tree limb, his body covered in lacerations as if whipped, the wounds open but the blood stilled because his body had been torched at one point. Pierce's mouth fell open at the sight. War had exposed him to grotesque wounds, fatal and not, yet these were not from the enemy, not from a secesh looking to assert their rights but from a mob that held no thoughts other than revenge. Revenge for something that had not happened yet. The runaways and freedmen hadn't surged north for the low-paying jobs the Irish held.

Suddenly the body quivered. Pierce looked straight across and found the culprits. Children. White children—two boys and a girl, couldn't be older than eight, he thought—stood, one boy holding a stick. He poked at the dead man's foot, shaking the corpse. Of course, the man didn't move, death had claimed him but what haunted Pierce was the kids' laughter.

"Back off!"

Pierce turned at the high-pitch demand. A crowd was starting at the end of the next street, close to a tenement building. He couldn't see who was in distress but the voice was feminine and her fear made the hair on his neck bristle. Slowly he started toward her, his mind gauging the massing people. He counted about fifteen, mostly men.

"No, I know you're the one, fucking that supposed 'freedman'!" The man spat.

"How dare you insult me!" the woman threw back. Pierce couldn't see her but the Southern drawl curled the end of her offense. His heart skipped a beat. He wondered if it was that woman from mass...

As he stepped closer, he saw her. The comb that held her hair up was askew, her chestnut curls coming free, partially falling strands and her eyes intense, a glare of defiance and fear wrapped in one. She faced a group of ten from what he could count with another man joining them. Pierce glanced around. If she attracted more...he pulled the pistol, pushing the chamber out and counting what he feared was the case. He only had one round left. *Hell and damnation!*

"You ain't nothin' more than Southern piece of trash," an elderly woman snarled. "The type lookin' for trouble."

Another man laughed. "Honey, I ain't fightin' for you to screw some darky but if it'd make you feel better, I'd fuck you just as hard."

She stiffened. "Abraham is out there, fightin', as you should be, you low-lying swine. You who think you are above him and his kind know nothing about what is right or wrong."

Her attack on them raised Pierce's brows. She had a fighting spirit, the type he'd never seen in a woman. Truly surprised, he stood still—and realized so did the mob. They hadn't expected her to fight back.

It was then she shifted weight and he glimpsed the flash of pain in her face along with the unsteady balance that she quickly remedied by leaning to the other side again. She was injured. Nothing like a wounded animal, cornered, he thought. On that idea, he sprung forward.

"Darling," he stated as casually as he could, slowing his gait to a walk. At the edge of the crowd, he heard a gasp from the majority and knew that won him the element of surprise. She glanced at him, a glint of confusion in her eyes. "I got here as soon as I could." He butted his way through to her and took her hand in his. The fact that her bare skin was exposed, her palm and fingertips torn, was noted in his mind.

"Who the hell are you?" A voice from the group demanded.

Pierce held her gaze, offering her his safety right as he snorted in a snobbish way toward the crowd. "I'm her husband." At least she held herself steady at that announcement. He winked at her before turning his head toward the crowd. "Don't you think you've done enough damage than to attack a lady on the streets?"

"Lady?" the older woman, middle of the front row, the one with the large freckle on her cheek, sneered. "One of ill-repute I'd reckon."

Half the group nodded in agreement within the half second it took him to turn and place himself between her and the crowd. "Unless you speak of yourself," his gaze raked the accuser with a disgusted grunt. "I suggest you withdraw that statement or find yourself answering to me."

Everyone grumbled, the back few flittering away.

"Why I never…" the elder one began when he interrupted her.

"No, that is highly conceivable." He let that statement stand, accusing her of jealousy of the lady's good looks and how she was probably untried in bed.

Half the remainder of the group snorted, chuckled or tried to cover their laugh, the other half split between disbelief and hatred but when Pierce leaned to the side, knowing full well the pistol's grip was in view, they left.

"Thank you, I suppose is in order."

He snapped his head around to the girl, astounded she'd bite back at him for rescuing her. She was straightening her skirt, leaning slightly, her loose strands blowing with the wind. Her bonnet. With a scan to his left, he caught the piece, stayed from the winds by a barrel on the corner. He reached for it and handed to her.

"Thank you—again." She took the hat and jammed it on her head. With one hand, she grabbed her skirts as if to leave. He stood astounded. She'd just been attacked, publically ridiculed and now, in the mist of all this chaos, with smoke from the fires burning through this section of the city, she'd walk herself home?

It suddenly hit him he didn't even know her name. "My lady," he started. "Let me escort you home."

She laughed. It was a brittle tone. "You don't take gratitude well, now, do you?" Her eyes scanned his dress. "You no doubt will be needed to subdue this mess. Not worrying about me."

"But—"

As she took a step to get out of his reach, she placed the foot she'd been favoring out first, and almost fell with a shriek escaping her lips. Thank the heavens he'd remained, he thought, as he caught her around the waist, one hand supporting the arm nearest him.

"You are injured."

"No, it's nothing," she stated, wiggling her stiff corseted body away from him. But as she tried to stand, she faltered again.

This time, he simply scooped her up into his arms. Despite the stays, one of which jabbed his arm, she was very light. Without the crinoline, she wore a roped petticoat to make her skirts wider—it was the poorer girl's answer to the wired hoop petticoat for factory workers and from where they were, she worked in one of those hellholes, he reckoned. Pierce was thankful she wore it because it made it easier for him. She gasped as he settled her into his arms.

"Put me down!"

"Tell me where you live." He smiled.

With a groan of protest, she directed him down the block to her building. He snuck her in without the mob that ran past them, carrying torches and chains, even looking in their direction. He shuddered at what might have happened because the madness was growing. There was no way he was leaving her here.

Quickly, he pushed opened the door to her rooms and half expected to see that black man waiting but he recalled she said he was off to the fight. That's where he should be too.

He set her on a chair and knelt before her, pulling the injured foot forward. She hissed when he touched her foot, gripping the sides of the chair seat.

"Just leave it. I'll be fine."

"Right," he muttered, loosening the lacing and pulling the boot off. The leather looked well worn, the lacing worn to just threads. Cared for at one point but now, she must have not polished it to fit in. He wanted to yell, particularly when he saw the tear in the stocking gouged into her sole. "What the hell did you step on?"

"I don't believe vulgar words are needed," she countered.

"I apologize." His hands reached under her skirts to her garter and nimbly untied it to inch the rough cotton stocking down, yanking it off her. He looked at the wound. The ball of her foot was red, chaffed and the cut small but right on the muscle. But before he could say a word or do anything, she slipped her foot free, hiding it beneath her skirts.

"That was unnecessary." Her voice trembled.

He shrugged as he went to the metal kettle sitting on the trivet near the fireplace. "Let me introduce myself. I'm Pierce Duval, at your service." He bowed briefly before discovering the cast iron container that sat in the embers. It was still warm. He snatched a rag off the rack nearby and doused it in the liquid before he returned to her. Holding the wet rag, Pierce glanced at her as his hand went beneath her skirts to get the injured foot. Her face held a look of intrigue and irritation with a touch of timidity. The last was the one he expected and the one she tried to hide the best.

"How dare you, Mr. Duval, or whoever you claim to be …"

"We could play this game of coquettish lady all day," he said, his hand finding her naked heel. "Or you could cooperate and let me cleanse this. If infection sets in, you'll be in worse shape."

She grunted but let him take her foot. Slowly, trying to be as gentle as he could, he wiped the skin. Her foot was so dainty. It was made of ivory, her skin alabaster in color, and like satin to the touch. As worn as the boot was, neither her heel or toes looked rough. It was a marvel, considering where she lived. A spur shot through him—he could buy her better shoes. Instantly, he dampened that thought. If he recalled, she was married. He needed to focus.

"There's a strip of linen wrap over there," she said, pointing to the lonely shelf on the distant wall.

He walked over and got it but as he turned to her, he saw her sitting there, her bare foot resting on a stool, her ankle exposed. Even in her faded blue dress, the ruffle of her petticoat was a pristine white. Her brunette hair was straying from her hairpins, the locks curled loosely around her, and in the dim light struggling through the dirty panes of the window, she looked angelic. So unfit for the rough and tumble world that lurked outside her door. He immediately wanted to whisk her away to safety.

She glanced up at him, a questioning brow raised. The look snapped him back. He was a widower and not to be searching for another, at least for him. He raised his chin and sat before her, once more taking her foot.

"Can you stay off it, at least for the rest of today?" he asked. "And elevate it?"

She frowned, her lips pursed. "I don't suppose returning to work is feasible."

Pierce smiled. "Probably not advised."

The door burst open, banging against the wall and they both jumped. Another woman stood there, her coppery colored hair and freckled nose reminded him of Margaret.

"Cerisa, I couldn't find you and heard..." her voice faded as her eyes locked onto Pierce. "I beg pardon, but who the hell are you?"

The lilt of her tongue, even in the brash words, made him smile. Another Irish lass. "I'm Major Pierce Duval, at your service," he bowed slightly.

The lass' mouth dropped open. Even the angel, Cerisa, sat speechless. No doubt he must look like a vagrant, in just his shirtsleeves, playing with the girl's foot but…

"Ye don't look like no soldier."

He expected that. "No, I expect not. Today apparently isn't the day to wear a uniform and expect to be walking." He returned to Cerisa's injury, wrapping the linen around her foot and anchoring it around her ankle. The heat in the room rose, despite the coolness of the shade of a basement flat. The dead silence though was cold. "I'm with Sickles Excelsior Brigade, home on leave, to return shortly."

"You've seen the war?" Cerisa asked calmly. Her tone threw him. This woman was ready to fight an irate and irrational mob outside, to do something women were considered too frail to do, and yet here, at her home, she asked a simple question edged with fear. He frowned.

"Yes." He shifted, suddenly feeling the Irish girl's stare, as if jabbing him with knives with her frank look. In fact, she made him edgy, as if today's hell outside wasn't enough. But she probably had justifiable cause. He was here, alone with Cerisa—nice to know her name—in her flat, caressing her bare ankle. No, no, bandaging an injured foot. Dear God, he needed to leave. Propping her foot on the stool, he stood. "Try to leave it elevated. It'll help the wound seal better if you're not stepping on it."

She tilted her head. "I will."

The silence returned. He knew she'd cut off the rest of her concern, that she couldn't afford a doctor if it got worse. That needled him. From the looks of the place, it appeared she skirted medical care and any convenience in order to survive. She was way too beautiful to be stuck in this muck. The freedman he'd seen her with certainly hadn't done his role as protector well.

He strode to her table, finding a few sheets of the newspaper, mostly talking about the War of the Rebellion, probably trying to find if the man's name was on a casualty list. If she'd foregone food for it…. anger built inside him at the thought. Next to the paper was a pencil. He took it and wrote in the column of the paper.

"This is my street address. If you need anything, anything at all, do not hesitate to send word." He shoved the sheet into her hands and stared at her hard, trying to drive the message home.

"I thought you said you were in the army. You'll be leaving soon," she stated but he caught the hesitation in her voice.

"Send word. If I've left, which won't be for a couple more days, I will leave instructions with my man servant to cover whatever assistance you need." He should leave but he found his feet were firmly planted and his will begged him to stay. Something told him she needed him and, hopefully, wanted him to stay. The pause was pregnant with anticipation.

"I'm sure I can take care of her, Yankee," the sarcastic friend bluntly stated.

Cerisa extended her hand, a gesture of a properly raised lady, especially one of the wealthier Southern planter class. "Thank you for your aid. It was," she swallowed. "Appreciated."

He gave her a smile and a nod before he spun and left. It took him a moment to realize the pain on his heart had flitted away and for once, he wished he could stay, if only for his own sanity.

CHAPTER FIVE

On Monday evening, a large number of marauders paid a visit to the extensive clothing store of Messrs Brooks Brothers [and] helped themselves to such articles as they wanted.

- *Harper's Weekly*, reported July 13, 1863 New York City Draft Riots

"**D**O YA KNOW WHAT the hell your doin'?"

Cerisa flinched. "Annie, please…"

"Do not be Annie-me anything o'er this." The Irish woman stomped over to the table, lifting the newsprint, twisting the page to the markings. "Here I be, worrying about you in all this mess and find ya here, with that man, him playin' with ya—"

"He was not 'playing' with me or my foot," she snapped back. "I got caught up in that crowd around the lottery-pulling. It turned into a riot, with me in the middle. A lot of glass breaking, yelling and pushing. I stepped on some glass, ripped through my boot." A chill rippled through her, as if the impact of what she'd witnessed slammed into her. The mob that cornered her grew in her mind to become monsters and she began to shiver. Her ears started to ring.

"Cera, are you all right?"

She blinked hard, realizing Annie was at her side, forcing a cup into her hands.

"Drink," Annie ordered.

With the first sip, the buzzing lightened. The next one dampened it further. Her friend ran her hand over Cerisa's forehead.

"What happened out there? Did Mr. Pierce Duval," his name rolled sarcastically off Annie's tongue. "Do something he shouldn't have? 'Cause I know some good Irish lads that'll take 'im down a might—"

"He did nothing wrong," Cerisa stated, putting her cup down and standing up. The injured foot tingled but with the bandage it wasn't hard to stand. She took a tentative step. Outside her toes registering she needed to sweep the floor, her balance worked and she could walk. "He actually saved me from the mob. They cornered me at the end of Monroe Street, throwing all sorts of insults at me."

"Insults? Because of Abraham?"

She hated when Annie came to the right conclusion. "Yes," she whispered.

"Oh, Cerisa, I'm so sorry. But ya knew you're walking a dangerous line being hooked to that darky."

"He's my husband, Annie, of course I'll stick by him."

Annie narrowed her gaze. "A husband, ha. He canna take care of ya."

"Annie…" She'd yet to see anything of Abraham's pay. He'd assured her he'd have the funds sent home to her, for their future, but he'd been gone for close to two months and nothing came.

"No, Cera. I was there, with you, last week when you went to the paymaster of that local tribe of Yankees." She spat, barely making the cuspidor. It was a habit Cerisa despised but there was no stopping Annie. "That Captain whoever—"

"He was a sergeant," Cerisa corrected.

"It don't matter. The fact was he refused ta turn over

Abraham's money, stood there like an idiot when ya proclaimed spousal rank and he nearly kicked ya out. Apparently, you'll need a stinkin' piece of paper claiming your marriage before they might, I mean might, turn the funds o'er to ya, but we know you'll never get that e'en then."

It had been a disaster. The sergeant was polite, but she saw the scrutiny he gave her, as if condemning her for her claim to being Abraham's wife. Her own funds were dwindling. She'd counted on him following through with his statement he'd send money home, but outside the last letter she'd received, five weeks ago, that his unit was heading south to meet up with troops fighting, nothing came. No mail. Nothing. She had no choice but to go find out. All she could get out of the sergeant was that pay hit the end of the month and for those sending home the pay, it'd be sent. She got the hint not to return scurrying around for a freedman's crumbs.

"I'll write to him about it."

"Ya sent him a letter last week." Annie stepped closer, her voice sounded sympathetic as she said, "He's at war. I doubt the mail is up to snuff headin' down there."

Cerisa's brows fretted. No, she wrote him after her rejection at the army's post. It was posted last week. Patience. She needed patience—something that had gone missing lately.

"That dashing army officer might be of aid."

Cerisa's head snapped to her right, anger coursing through her veins. "I'm a married woman. Besides, he didn't say he was a wealthy man."

"Oh, please," Annie laughed. "Didn't you see the clothes he wore? The way he walked? No, he's one by Jove. And well to do also."

Of course she'd noticed that. Who wouldn't notice him? Dark hair, almost black in color, his eyes a vibrant blue, very classical look to his face. Broad shouldered, without a frock coat on, the navy wool waistcoat and matching trousers showed his back narrowed to his waist and he was surefooted carrying her here. Also, something she noticed while in his arms—the man was all muscles and frame, the contours of his arms and the rock-solid chest and stomach she rested against sent a thrill through her. She'd tried not to notice and failed miserably.

"Yes, well, he knows of my marital status, thanks to the horde that accosted me so," she snapped.

"Which means he knows Abraham ain't white," Annie concluded. "And at war. Look, Cera, there may be other concerns. The factory emptied because of the crowds. You know Mr. Beatty, probably pulling what's left of his hair out, his anger climbing everyone left for the draft pick. Don't be surprised he don't fire everyone for newcomers."

Cerisa groaned. "We'll find out, tomorrow." If she lost her job, she'd be doomed.

July 1863, New York City

Pierce sat at his desk, his hand cramping. He leaned back with a deep sigh.

Five weeks ago, he'd been prepared to return to the beast, to the war. His gear packed, the last couple of letters from Margaret and her picture stored away for when he returned—if he returned. As he picked up his bag to leave, a note arrived, reassigning him to headquarters in the city. At first, he was confused. He'd longed to return to the war, to fight and put all the anger over losing his wife to proper use. He was told his expertise was needed as his unit, the 40th, would be acquiring other regiments, like the 38th, the 37th and parts of the 101st Infantries as these men's three-year contract quickly came close to expiring and the 40th needed those troops to fill their ranks.

A desk job with a promotion to colonel. As it sank in, he seethed. This was no doubt his father's maneuvering. Senator Timothy Duval had the connections. What amazed Pierce was he hadn't interfered before, so why now?

The door swung open and in walked a tall black man, his longer hair slightly greyed, as was part of his goatee. He stood in front of Pierce's desk, just walking straight through the door to the desk without greeting. This man stood proud and arrogant, Pierce decided, but then Frederick Douglass was like that. A runaway slave turned abolitionist champion. Pierce admired and disliked the man, the dislike growing every second the man stood before him.

"Good afternoon, Mr. Douglass." Pierce emotions toned his voice tight. He didn't stand to offer his hand to shake, instead, he dropped his pencil and leaned back in his chair, schooling his features. Looming in the back of his mind was his father and his abolitionist leanings. If he'd sent the man here to convince him to lead Colored troops... He bit back his anger. "How can I be of service?"

For a second, Pierce caught the freedman raising his brows slightly at the lack of manners on Pierce's part, but that faded quickly as the former slave slid on the mask he wore for the master when he spoke. Interesting. It also made Pierce maybe like him a bit—but not by much. Perhaps he'd spent too much time listening to Margaret's family's quarrels over abolition that made his thoughts sway.

"As you know, many of our Colored boys have joined in the fight for freedom."

Pierce's mind wanted to close his ears to this, but he gritted his teeth to keep attention.

"We've had to fight for our right to join, to get equal pay and even equal training."

They had the same training, Pierce wanted to argue. Just because the sergeants who were placed to do so hated the Coloreds as inferior was hardly inferior training, just harsh. Welcome to the army, he wanted to spit out. It often was a bitter pill for any man. Why they should have it any better than other recruits eluded Pierce.

"And we've welcomed the chance to pay for our freedom but," Douglass stopped.

"But?"

The black man stared at him a moment, his gaze enough to make Pierce think the man would reprimand him for something he'd done or hadn't, like take charge of a Colored troop.

"You've made a good start in your career, joining the Mozart Regiment."

Pierce opened his mouth, but the man shook his head and waved his hand, gesturing he hadn't finished. "You've also progressed through the ranks well. I also know several of the volunteer regiments are disbanding, the three-year contracts are up. Your regiment is close to the same problem and you've been stuck here, deskbound, over heading back to see the elephant. Perhaps, I could convince you to take charge of one of the Colored units. They are in the thick of it and sorely need strong officers."

He fought hard to contain the sigh of frustration that beckoned to escape his lips. Carefully, he considered his thoughts and how to word his refusal. His teeth sank into the inside of his cheeks, an old habit of his when thinking hard. Damn his father for pushing this! Unable to hold his breath a second longer, he released it as he stood.

"Mr. Douglass, I appreciate you dropping in to see if you could persuade me to consider this offer, but I assure you, the Mozart Regiment is hardly close to ending service. In fact, many of the other units have had their men who re-enlist become one with us—"

"And a fine military force it is," Douglass stated. He still stood tall and proud, as if he commanded a win here. "I understand, though, that moving higher in rank becomes more difficult with more men and more experience."

Definitely his father at work here. "Sir, by chance did you happen to meet with Senator Duval before coming here?"

Douglass gave him a half smile. It was warm, not cold and calculating like Senator Duval's tended to be. "I have met your father. Strong man, good for the cause of abolition. He believes in you and we both agree if you continue your career in the army, you might consider a higher rank with the Colored units."

Pierce snorted as he walked around his desk and opened the door to his office. "Certainly something I shall consider. I thank you for stopping by, Mr. Douglass."

The freedman gave a tight grin as he walked to the door. "Good luck to you, Colonel. And condolences on your loss. Good day."

Pierce stood, staring at the closed door, the clicking of Douglass' shoes on the wood floor grew more distant. The constant beat was slower than his heart, which thudded loudly as the anger surged through him. His father had pushed the former slave to come here, hoping to persuade him to take up the cause for Colored men. He'd spit if could but his mouth was so dry, it couldn't form a drop to shoot. Grinding his teeth, he reached for his frock coat, shrugging it on as he left his office. To hell with this! He stormed down the hallway to the office of the U.S. Army and strode right in, stopping at the clerk at the front desk. The clerk looked up at him, eyebrows raised above his spectacles.

"I'm here to enlist."

The man frowned, staring at the frock Pierce wore. It was navy wool with colonel shoulder straps and US-emblem shank buttons. "But colonel, you are in the army."

"Colonel Duval, what seems to be the problem?"

Pierce half-smiled as he glanced beyond the clerk to the hallway behind the desk. "Major General Mueller, I'd like to discuss a transfer with you." Mueller had badgered him at first to leave the volunteers behind and join the real force. A slight of hand—both the volunteers and most of the US regulars were new enlistees. Just the bulk of the experienced officers were in the army and not volunteer groups.

Mueller eyed him, not saying a word for a couple of minutes. Pierce started counting inside his head, his patience growing thin. He was tired of having to put up with what was being pushed down his throat. Granted, joining the regular army might very well put him in charge of a Colored unit, but not if he could help it.

Mueller nodded and stepped back, Pierce not far behind. They went to the officer's office and sat.

"So, after three years, now you want to leave your pristine position in the Mozart Regiment and join us? Why?"

Pierce's gaze narrowed. "You're well aware the three-year contracts will be expiring. Regiments are falling apart and reforming. I've been working on the papers to arrange this, joining several under the 40th. New orders, new bravados to deal with. I'd like to stay on course, know the game and who's in charge versus the volunteer political appointees."

"Ah, but are you not one of those political appointees, son

of Senator Duval?" The man rested his chin on the tips of his fingers as his hands formed a pinnacle underneath.

"You know I've had the connections to rise in rank, but I am a graduate of the Point."

"Yes, but you didn't stay in service," Mueller pointed out.

"Granted. I gave my allotted time but personal matters detained me from reenlisting." Once more, his father interfering with his life and having him join his office staff, to groom him for political office. One week at the capital was all it took. He came home to work in his father's New York office and find a way to escape. Looking for a new venture west, Pierce met the woman of his dreams at the bank. The memory now made him smile.

"I see. And will there be another 'personal reason' for you to leave?" Mueller prodded.

Bastard! After all those months begging him... "No, sir."

Mueller shuffled pages on his desk until he found a few he pulled and scanned. He frowned, searching for another report. "Let me find where to stick you. We've New York troops spread through the South—"

"I wasn't aware you stayed to the states, like the volunteers," Pierce prodded.

This time, Mueller glared, the heat in his eyes grew, as if he'd bury Pierce first before transferring him. "No, but you've gained rank. Your graduation and experience indicate you require rank. I will find you a spot. Go see my man at the desk for the formalities to start your request."

Pierce nodded, rose and left. In his head, he began to count the days to escape New York, his father and memories of Margaret.

CHAPTER SIX

We are Americans, speaking the same language, adopting the same customs, holding the same general opinions…and shall rise and fall with Americans.

—Frederick Douglass, 1862

July 1863

A FLURRY OF EMOTIONS WHIRLED inside Cerisa's head as she stood at the door to her place, listening to the well-dressed sergeant and his aide standing before her. Pain was the easy one to place, shock, dismay, surprise and disbelief fought for control inside her.

The sergeant, whatever his name was because she couldn't remember at this second, eyed her precariously. She realized he stared down at her clenched fists so she forced herself to open and flatten them against the fabric of her hoopless skirt.

They had come to deliver the news to Mrs. Walker and wanted to know if she knew where the woman was. She'd gulped hard. Behind her, Annie gasped. Thank God Annie was here—she was much needed support. When she opened her mouth to claim that title, Annie scooted her chair loudly, which was a hard task on a packed hard dirt floor. Cerisa shot her a glance and met a stern look with a slight, miniscule shake *no*. Pursing her lips in defiance, she turned back to the Union officer, forcing herself to control her features.

"Mrs. Walker came down with consumption shortly ago," she managed to reply. "Is there something from Mr. Walker? I can take her the message." Her insides clenched, twisted, bracing for the news. She knew of only one reason she might get a visit. But the Fugitive Slave Law shouldn't reach into the army.

The army official's eyes narrowed as she spoke. The years of trying to suppress her Southern drawl evaporated as she bordered on the edge of hysteria. Silence filled the air and choked her.

With a disgruntled sigh, he reached into his pocket and presented her a letter. It was sealed and address to Mrs. Walker. She recognized the handwriting by its crooked letters and the hitch in the 'k' that Abraham made. His hand had been damaged on the docks, making it hard to hold a writing utensil for long periods.

The letter made a fact loud and clear to her. Abraham was dead.

Cerisa's blood turned cold as the knowledge, unsaid, slithered down her spine. A buzz started in her ears. Her hands shook as she reached for the envelope. Trembling, she couldn't take it and Annie jumped up behind her, helping her with an arm around her as she took the letter.

"He is dead?" The words came from her but she didn't recall really saying them.

The man's head tilted and he looked confused. Apparently, Cerisa concluded, he still didn't understand that she was Mrs. Walker.

"He is presumed so, we have witnesses who claim it. The battle left large numbers of the Coloreds dead, many maimed from shrapnel. It was his unit. His belongings should arrive within a day. Please forward them as well to the family."

Cerisa could barely nod, her body frozen in place.

"Thank ye, for coming by," Annie said, shuffling them towards the door. Even through her pounding heart and dizziness, Cerisa could hear Annie add softly, "Miss W herself ain't been well. Pardon me, but we'll see this gets ta where it needs."

He glared at her. "She sounds like a Southerner. What's she here for? Sergeant Walker her slave?"

"No, no, she's been in New York for long time, long before fightin' began. But ye know, canna be hard to forget one's upbringin'," the Irish girl replied, emphasizing her own native tongue.

The army sergeant mumbled something Cerisa couldn't hear, but she flared with anger. How dare that man act as if she was nothing better than white trash!

"His final pay will be delivered as well," the officer added, his tone more polite. "Please send our condolences."

As the door closed, Cerisa spun toward her friend. "How dare he speak to me like that!"

Annie shook her head. "Cera, I'm so sorry."

That final word struck the wall she'd built around her, to not believe why they'd been here. Her insides shattered and her vision blurred. She saw Annie held the sealed letter before her, and she saw Abraham's handwriting again. The realization slammed into her chest, breaking her heart before she'd even broken the seal. With a huge sob, she collapsed to the floor.

Abraham Walker, her husband, was dead.

It was evening and Pierce found himself at his parents' house, mansion really, sitting at the dining room table, staring at the fancy gold rimmed decorated porcelain plates, silverware set around each place setting and crystal wine glasses that shimmered under the candelabra. His mother rambled about the latest gossip, he assumed, because he'd hardly listened. His cousins, Edna and Marguerite, bobbed their heads at what must be the appropriate times because his mother continued her stories despite the fact they watched his every move. His uncle, Matthew, just ate. But there was tension in the air and he knew it was directed at him. It came from his father, who glared at him, and he knew exactly why.

His orders were being processed to be part of the Army of the Potomac. He'd keep his rank of Colonel but beyond that, he didn't know. The final papers had yet to arrive. But from the looks of things, his father knew.

As if his father's glance didn't burn a big enough hole in him, the loss of who should be across the table from him did. Margaret's absence was keenly felt and especially at times like this, for she was his only ally in a family fighting for control. In response, he reached for his wine glass and downed the contents. When the servant promptly came to refill the glass, Pierce caught his father's glare turn to the man, as if daring him to do his job. Infuriated, his father would deem he'd had too much to drink, Pierce brought the glass closer to the servant and nodded to fill it. The troubled servant took a second but filled the glass and quickly stepped back. Pierce lifted the goblet and as he brought it slowly towards his lips, he turned his head toward his patriarch and gave him a small smile of satisfaction.

He saw the fire in the man's eyes and inwardly laughed. No one was going to control his life, not any more.

"Wouldn't you agree, my son?"

He whipped his head back toward his mother. Whatever she'd been discussing, he hadn't paid one notion to, so he was lost. "I beg your pardon, mother?"

Madeleine Duval was a striking woman. Her dark, almost black hair was pulled back, with curls dangling, held in place by tortoise shell combs and a fancy headpiece of lace and ribbon. Her dark brown eyes were warm, but she had minor wrinkles, crow's feet, around them. Her lips gave a faint smile, one that bordered on amusement to aggravated that he hadn't paid attention.

"Edna and Marguerite were listening to me discuss the Sanitary Commission meeting that will be here next week. They are trying to decide how they can help our troops and I believe this to be a fairly appropriate venue for them to join. You have a better prospective on the army, but I believe we do help the wounded men."

The U.S. Sanitary Commission. The do-gooders who raised funds, inspected the military hospitals and donated supplies were hated and liked. To him, though, they were nothing more than vindictive because they at first refused Margaret once they learned she was Irish and a Catholic. Though once it was discovered she was a Duval, they quickly gushed to invite her in. And that work exposed her to the illness that carried her to death. Through the haze of mourning and the wall he built to keep from falling prey to it, he remained always amazed how his mother could barge through such barriers but not help his wife. He gritted his teeth, biting back the words he wanted to say.

"Mother," he began, picking his words carefully, which was hard to do when his cousins stared at him. It reminded him of a child looking into a candy store only here, he was the candy. He bristled and fought against it. "I've little exposure to the army medical surgeons—"

"For which, I'm entirely grateful," she interceded.

He smiled. "But I'm sure the help is greatly needed."

His mother nodded. "I know how hard this must be for you," she said softly. "Margaret was a fine woman."

Those words hit him hard, cracking just a little the hard shell he'd been trying to build around him. His mother was a good woman and had accepted his wife after they'd wed. A lump formed in his throat, making breathing difficult as well as speech but he did manage a few words, "Thank you, Mother."

She smiled sympathetically. The impact of her comfort twisted his gut and without him realizing it at first, he clenched his glass so tight wine spilled over the top. As the red liquor seeped out, drenching his fingers to fall to the white linen tablecloth, mayhem broke loose. The ladies began chattering at him, his uncle raised his brows, his father called his name and the servant raced forward with a damp cloth, but his mother never broke her gaze. In fact, it turned sad.

Christ, he needed out of here.

"Let us adjourn to the parlor," Madeleine said, breaking the gaze with her son. That said, chairs scooted back, his cousins and uncle heading out first. His mother came and took his hand. "Pierce, I am sorry. It is time you consider taking another wife, to soothe the pain. Marguerite or Edna would make you a charming wife."

Pierce frowned. His cousins were once removed, if even that. He often questioned whether their father was truly a blood uncle but it was a subject avoided when he tried to inquire. "They are kin—"

"Far removed from being too close to cause concern," she assured him. "Think on it." She kissed his cheek and left.

His father remained. "Pierce, let us go to my study."

Inside the dark wood paneled room, a truly masculine

chamber, holding just a whiff of his father's cigar in the air and linseed oil mixed with leather. Pierce cringed when his father lit the lamp and sat in the big leather backed armchair behind his massive mahogany desk. Apparently, it was to be one of his infamous father-to-son speeches. Pierce planted his feet firmly on the ground, waiting for the first volley and wished for another drink.

"Stop looking for the decanters. I believe you've had enough for the evening."

First shot. Pierce stood still and sighed. "By your command." It was his only return and he got the response he wanted. His father's cold demeanor turned harsh under the oil lamp he'd just lit.

"Your behavior tonight is reprehensible." Timothy Duval sat straight, a tick in his cheek let Pierce know this wasn't going to be quick. "Your mother is correct. You need to remarry and push that memory to the back of your mind."

"She. Was. My. Wife." His own anger flared. Just forget Margaret, as if she never lived?

"One you chose without consideration," his father stated.

"I loved her."

"You married beneath you." Timothy Duval stared at his son as the air between them remained still.

Pierce breathed heavily, trying to control the building fire within him. Of course his father would think that. Margaret was Irish. That in itself was damning enough. "You had no right to decide who I should wed."

"Perhaps, while Gabriel lived, you were correct. But," the man leaned forward. "Since his death last summer at that God-forsaken town in Pennsylvania, you now are the heir and I will have you readied to take your place."

Pierce snorted. Gabriel was the eldest son. His father still played by the old rules of oldest son gets it all. That played a part in Pierce's venture to West Point and the military since. As much as he loved Gabe, a line of resentment filtered through him because as the heir, Gabe got everything. Everything. Mostly, his father's love. Now? The second-hand son moves to the head—well to hell with him being groomed to follow his father.

"I'm leaving for the army. I have no time for another wife to lose while I'm at the front."

His father's eyes narrowed. "Yes, I heard you've requested a transfer to the IX Corps. I at first thought to deny that."

Pierce had turned to look at the books on his father's shelves that lined the back wall of the office but that statement made him turn on his heel to face the man. "You've no jurisdiction over the Federal   army."

"But I do." Timothy Duval stood, leaning forward over his desk, propping himself with clenched hands on the desktop. "I am the chair for the Committee on the War, established by the President himself."

Pierce's mind raced. There was no such committee… or was there? This was New York, not Washington. But his father seldom lied openly, for a political career like his, part of his abilities to remain stayed with his upfront, direct attack using the truth.

"While I can't stop the transfer, there are always the particulars."

Pierce met him at the desk. He gripped the edge tight. "I will not command Colored troops. Sending Douglass to convince me did not work."

Timothy stood silent. Pierce tried to gauge his thoughts but the man's face was too blank, covered in a shield. Absently, he wondered if the man had learned that trait from

Douglass. His father sat in his chair, a look of satisfaction now registering. "Perhaps. Let us see what happens when the orders arrive. Unless you care to reconsider your marriage status."

"You'd make sure I wasn't assigned to one of those units if I marry?" That made absolutely no sense to him. "I am mourning the loss of my wife. You'd have me cut my time of mourning for the sake of marrying again? It's too soon and I won't do it!"

"With your brother gone, you must take up the reins to be the heir. I will not allow you to waste your life, standing in front of a Secesh gun. At least," he sighed. "Not without an heir of your own."

Pierce stared, absolutely speechless. But when his father wouldn't retract that statement, Pierce laughed in ridicule. "Let me see if I understand this. Forget the love of my life and my chance to grieve my loss—an honor no one else would deny me, all for the 'family'?" he slurred the end with anger. "All so I can marry, get her with child *then* I can do what I feel I must, which is return to the War. Am I correct?"

His father said nothing.

He really needed a drink. A strong one, or three. His greatest fear was while the US Army didn't take father's orders about their sons, it did bend to the President. And his father was highly influential in Congress. He could do what he threatened. Hatred coursed his veins.

"I am in mourning for my wife. When I feel it is necessary, I might, and I mean this severely, might reconsider marriage. But, I do intend to report and find my orders. Until then, good night." He headed toward the door.

Fury poured through his body, down to his bones. He'd see hell first before giving in to Senator Duval.

CHAPTER SEVEN

"That man [Grant] will fight us every day and every hour till the end of the war."

– Abraham Longstreet, Battle of the Wilderness, May 1864

THE KNOCK ON THE door at dawn completely surprised Cerisa. She'd stirred the embers of her fire, mixing in the new shreds of wood, a pot of water warming when the tapping came. Putting the poker down, she opened the door and found her landlord, a sour-faced old man with wrinkles, thinning greasy grey hair and clothes that looked as if he'd been raked through the mud thrice over. Tobacco juice stained his lips and whiskers.

The old man shoved a page into her hand. "I gives ya til tomorrow, supper time. I's through with you, nigger-lover." He spat tobacco just inside her doorway before he grunted and spun, walking away.

Rude wasn't the word she wanted to use. The colorful metaphor she wanted wasn't in her nature to give. She slammed the door, thankful he missed her skirt with his mess. With a deep sigh, she ran her fingers through her hair. The war that was to have ended in three months was close to ending its third year with no end in sight. It had become a living nightmare of endless battles, an endless list of casualties with a lack of supplies and growing mistrust. A wave of cold and disgust washed over her. She emptied her teacup, put in the remains of the coffee Abraham had brought home oh so many months ago, the coffee she had hidden and brought out on special occasions, which had been never with his death. But today, she needed it to fortify herself.

She knew what that folded page was and refused to open it until she had a sip. Carefully, she got her tin coffee pot, something Abraham had also found for them, dented but serviceable, and put her drink together. It was the end of the bag, just like the end of the life she knew. The bitter smell of the coffee filled the air as she poured it and sat.

The door again rattled with a knock and then swung open. She didn't have to look to know who it was. Annie. She was the only person she knew who instantly made herself at home wherever she was.

"Did that ole troll bang on your door this morning?"

Cerisa smiled as the cup touched her lips. Annie was one of a kind—no manners but she loved her anyway. The Irish girl had been with her during her darkest days after learning of Abraham's death and had covered for her at work. Which had been for naught because yesterday, that fat slug she worked for fired her for being 'secesh'—as if he hadn't noticed her accent before.

"Oh, I see he did," her friend continued. "Do you care?" she asked, holding the folded sheet in her hand.

Cerisa stopped caring last month when the news of Abraham arrived. She motioned with her hand that Annie could open it. The hot coffee was bland, almost closer to coffee favored water but it was hot and it took the chill off her. The scalding of her throat was minor to the shards that had been figuratively flung at her since those riots. She closed her eyes, trying to block out the visions of the people who gave her odd looks, their rude behavior, and the whispers about her. They might have existed before but she ignored them with Abraham to protect her.

"Cera, you'd better be lookin' at this."

With great reluctance she opened her eyes only to find her friend's serious face. Deathly serious. She reached for the paper.

"It's an eviction notice? That white trash is evicting me, told me so, but I'm amazed he can write. Kicking me out of this rat's den." Her arm swept around the dark, dingy room. The dark veil she'd hid under, mourning Abraham lifted as reality struck deep. "Just who does he think he is?"

Annie's brows arched. "The owner. That's who he is, and yes, he can throw you out."

"I won't put up with it!" She was Cerisa Fontaine. No one threw out a Fontaine! A voice in the back of her head nagged about her lost job. She shut it up. That slug would get his come-uppance.

"Just how much are you late in rent?"

That inquiry faltered her step. Of course, Annie would cut to the quick. The rent. "I'll make a payment soon."

Her friend tilted her head and stepped closer. "Cera, how? Did Abraham's money arrive?"

His pay. Thirteen dollars for the span of two months. That was all that came. He'd been in for twice that. She'd paid Mr. White Trash immediately but that was two weeks ago. They owed ten dollars a week. She barely squeaked by on that and her own measly income but now, without it, what would she do? The reality slammed into her hard, hitting her gut like a sledgehammer and she sank into the chair.

"Oh, Annie, what will I do? Mr. Miteneur sent me off yesterday." A sob escaped her before she could stop it.

"He what? Oh, dear Cera, I'm so sorry," her friend cajoled,

taking one of Cerisa's hands in her own and squeezing.

All the bravado left her in one fell swoop. Where she'd been enraged over eviction, the truth was, he had his rights to do so, and she doubted her being a Southerner was the only cause. He'd made a futile attempt to make a trade of her body for rent but the mere thought made her furious and later, the thought of him touching her made her want to retch. Of course, he snorted and left, yelling loudly that she was a slattern for letting Abraham touch her.

In just the last hour, her remaining shreds of strength seem to leave her. She was alone and penniless. "What should I do, Annie? What am I going to do?" Her vision blurred. "It took me too long to find the job there. I've tried not to sound so southern but that shouldn't be held against me. I'm here, up in Yankeedom," the word curled off her tongue sarcastically. "It's just not warm up here, in the North." That sounded like a whimper and she hated it. But she did feel at loose ends. Even in her mind, she counted her supplies. There was enough for the rest of the week…maybe. But she'd be without a bed before then.

Annie didn't answer at first. Her face tightened and Cerisa saw the tick in her cheek. Annie had left her job as a maid. She had another job, though what exactly, Cerisa hadn't bothered to ask, which now she realized was very rude on her part. But her friend looked clean, her clothes, simple but well made. What was she doing?

"Cera, there's someone I know who would love to hire you."

"Pierce, snap out of it."

The voice was distant, wavering but it was getting louder. His muddled thoughts refused to focus, but he forced them since the sound didn't go away, despite him waving his hand to send it off. Still fighting sleep deprivation, Pierce's eyes shot open when he was shoved and he teetered on falling off his chair.

"What?!" He snapped and glared at the man next to him. It was his friend, Edward, dressed in his finest black frock coat and trousers. His emerald green waistcoat was startling bright to Pierce's tired gaze and it hurt to look at it so he closed his eyes only to quickly open them, hearing his friend move to push him again.

"I'm awake, dammit!"

Edward chuckled. "Well, it didn't appear as such, leaning on your papers."

Pierce yawned, rubbing the sleep from his eyes. "Fuck you. I've been busy."

"Burning the candle from both ends, yes, I know." The man took the poker and prodded at the embers in the fireplace, making them reignite on the fresh kindling he threw in. He picked up the empty bourbon bottle at the edge of the desk and the glass. "Of course, you wouldn't be in such a predicament if you didn't consume one of these every night."

Pierce's gaze narrowed on his friend. Drinking a bottle a night or close to it, helped him sleep without the memories of his wife or his family flooding his mind. Nothing came to him, and he slept or so he called it. The throbbing headache made him regret it every morning, enough he swore off it until the late afternoon arrived, with the skies darkening and him returning to an empty house.

"We have plans for this evening, if you'll recall," Edward stated, throwing the curtains wide and opening the window. A quick cool breeze swooshed in and hit Pierce hard.

"Good God, man, must you?" he muttered, shrugging his

jacket back on.

"Yes, I must. I need you awake," Edward stated cheerfully.

Pierce's thoughts darkened. He so wanted to wipe the grin off his friend's face.

"I believe your plans are to take me out drinking," he stated grimly as he stood, walked past Edward and slammed the window shut. "Hardly a reason to rudely awaken me."

"No, the idea was to get you out of this drunken stupor you've been hiding in—"

"I've not been hiding. I've been here," he countered, slumping back into his chair and grabbing the bottle to yank the cork out.

"Exactly, so that is why we are going out for some rest and relaxation." Edward's smile vanished and his brows furrowed as he leaned across the desk and pulled the glass from his friend. "Margaret is gone. Outside of the army, you've shut yourself off from the world—"

Pierce glared. "That will change quickly. My orders have finally arrived to reassign me to the IXth. I'll be heading back to the war within a week and out of everyone's concern."

"Good. Because if I remember your wife well, she'd be very unhappy you've stayed here in a drunken state all under the pretense of mourning her. And now, we have an even better reason for us to go out on the town and celebrate." His friend's grin returned.

Relieved, Pierce reached for the glass, but Edward scooted it further out of his reach. "Tsk, tsk, tsk. The town is calling us. Change so we can leave. I've got just the thing to cheer you up."

Cerisa pulled the brush through her hair one more time, staring into the looking glass across the vanity from her without seeing a thing. A loud crash outside her room snapped her back to the present, enough so she virtually jumped off her seat. It took another moment to register what she was doing, and what she was getting ready for.

Another night. Another opportunity to lose her mind.

The door to her room opened and Annie barged right in.

"Cera, you need to move faster," she stated, standing right behind her and taking over doing Cerisa's hair.

"Thank you, Annie," she said quietly. "I just can't seem to get it right."

Her friend laughed. "No, I think you like it if someone else does it for you. Ain't no slaves up here so you dawdle, waiting for me." Her fingers separated the strands, pinning a few up in sweeping strokes, the rest she pinned so the curls fell in cascading patterns.

Cerisa watched her, her own mind playing the coming hours over and over in her head. When she'd been evicted and jobless, Annie said she knew a place where they'd get paid well. What she didn't tell Cerisa was that the employer was a brothel. Finding out that this was Annie's new career hadn't surprised her, but she didn't think it was a good one. A week of looking for new employment in New York City, though, changed Cerisa's mind. No one would hire a Southern lady. It didn't seem to matter how much she fought to speak without a hint of an accent, something triggered a word or three to come out in a Louisiana drawl and she'd be out the door, no job offered.

With no prospect of work, she turned to her friend. The madam of the house instantly hired her, exclaiming that with her looks, her accent and, when she discovered via Annie her 'previous lover' had been a freedman, the woman almost swooned. It made Cerisa's stomach churn but somehow it made sense to be here. She got a room, meals, and clothes for the evening, though they were not the type to wear anywhere else. And she got paid. Paid by those men who bought her service.

"There. Done. Isn't she grand?"

Cerisa blinked, refocusing on now and looked in the mirror. What had been loose and straight now was pinned and curled. "It is beautiful," she sighed. It was and all just to attract a man.

"You're doing it again."

She frowned and looked at her. "I beg your pardon."

"Oh, Cera," Annie sighed, plopping down on the edge of the bed. "You give this look as if you've died or worse."

She bit the inside of her bottom lip. "No, I don't," she decided to deny vehemently. "I just worry I won't be picked, that's all." Actually, she prayed she wasn't but then, if not, she'd not get any money.

Annie's gaze narrowed and the room was deathly silent for a minute. Cerisa wasn't sure what Annie was thinking. She looked great, this type of flamboyant lifestyle appeared to suit her better than any factory job. Not that manual labor at the mill had been Cerisa's life pursuit either, but she'd always thought she'd be a wife and mother with her own house, not working in a factory nor lowering herself to selling her body.

Annie snorted as she stood, her hands quickly smoothing the fine lawn robe into place, and shifting her hips to adjust the red satin corset. Cerisa still marveled over that piece. Only for a brothel would one think of it but for her, she'd stay clear of red. It wasn't her color—of course, wearing only stockings, pantalets, corset and a fancy silk wrapper wasn't exactly normal decorum either. When Annie tilted her chin, the question in her eyes, Cerisa shook her head.

"One more minute," she pleaded. Still needing to dress, she wanted to finish it alone. She wanted that time with no other soul around. It'd take her more than that to mentally prepare herself to do what she was raised not to do.

"Well, don't waste time. You know she'll be calling for us shortly."

"Yes, I know. Do not worry. Go." She pushed Annie out the door and then shut it, not breathing until she heard the click of the latch.

With a gulp of air, she straightened her shoulders and shook off her apprehensions. She eased the corset on, fastened the busk and reached for the ribbon in the back to tighten it. This was the tenth time she'd walk down those stairs, on display, for the waiting clients. Her first two nights, she panicked and the madam let her just walk through the throng of visitors, chatting a minute or two but not have to accept any. The third night, she had to take a client or she was out. When that white-collared clerk took her hand, she felt doomed. Nerves on fire when they entered her chamber, she was shocked to find the man only wanted to be with her and talk. Odd, but she gladly accepted it.

The next two nights equaled the first. One wanted her to walk on his back as he laid nose first to the floor. The second one just wanted her to talk, his head tilted and a crazy smile on his face. He apparently loved her Louisiana accent.

The fourth one scared her. He wanted her to treat him like he was a slave and to whip him as he kneeled. When he left, a happy grin on his face, she closed the door and promptly retched in her chamber pot. The worst was he came the next two nights.

It wasn't until the eighth client that she had to do anything intimate. She'd taken all the precautions and thankfully he couldn't stay hard enough to enter her but she hated herself once he left. Immediately she sent for a bath and scrubbed her skin till it turned pink from all the scouring.

So far, she'd been lucky. But what about tonight? She pulled her wrapper on and tied it. One last glance in her looking glass, she sighed, figuring she was as ready as she'd ever be. She turned the doorknob and with a deep breath, she walked out and braced herself.

The Southern belle of the Fontaine dynasty found a way to reinvent herself. That horrendous comparison made her jaw tighten and anger race through her. It gave her strength to bolster herself and step out of her room to the stairs that would lead her to the man who'd buy her body tonight.

CHAPTER EIGHT

"This war must go on till the last of this generation falls in his tracks, and his children seize his musket and fight our battle, unless you acknowledge our right to self-government. We are not fighting for slavery; we are fighting for independence, and that or extermination we will have."

—Jefferson Davis

THE DESSERT FACTORY WAS the perfect name for the den of sin Cerisa worked in and the steps down to the second floor of the townhouse seemed to burn, reminding her to be on her toes. The true clients came to the upper salon for more intimate entertainment than the salon on the first floor. These men were the supposed better part of society. She snorted over the thought of better part because they were here, to have sex with a prostitute. But they had money. During war, that was a scarce commodity. The going price to be paid was what she had to turn in, but Annie confided, if they paid more, it was for her.

As if giving them access to her body wasn't worth far more than the price…

She shoved that thought aside and tried to paste a smile on her face. It failed to materialize and she abandoned the idea by the last step. At the doorway to the front room, she ran into Annie who stopped before her. Annie smiled, fixing the opening to her wrapper to expose a bit more of Cerisa's cleavage.

"Walk out there like you own him," Annie prompted her. "Of course, he'll choose me but try." She laughed as she sauntered forward.

They caught up to the third girl, sneaking up to her before Madame Nikki caught them. Cerisa turned to her friend, who glimpsed at her and they both smiled. Perhaps tonight wouldn't be so bad, Cerisa imagined. The city was bustling. With everyone so busy, she expected few attendees here tonight —or so she hoped.

As they walked into the parlor and she glanced at the man sitting on the settee, her heart skipped a beat before it began to thud wildly.

It was him, that man from the riot. Her rescuer. What was his name? More importantly, why was he here?

As Madame Nikki talked to him, pimping the three standing before him, Cerisa dropped her gaze, praying he didn't recognize her. Fear slithered down her spine. Despite his handsome look, she couldn't take him. There was something about him that unnerved her.

"Please, sur," Madame Nikki drawled. It drove Cerisa crazy that the woman tried to talk in a Southern drawl at this time, considering the fact that she did it miserably. "Do step closer, inspect them to decide."

Cerisa tensed when he took a step toward them. She stared at the floor, thoughts of it opening and swallowing her whole played in her mind until the toes of his shoes were in her line of sight. He reached forward and tipped her chin up. She refused to meet his eyes at first but his fingers ignited a flame in her jawline and as it spread inside her, she lifted her chin to barely off his touch, which upswept her vision so she looked into his eyes. He was staring at her so intently she tightened and looked at him, their gaze locked.

His lips curved in a lopsided grin.

Madame Nikki must have seen this interplay, because Cerisa heard her clap and send the other two away.

"A perfect choice, monsieur. Our lovely Cera will show you just how wicked a Southern belle can be."

Cerisa wanted to scream. One day, Madame Nikki would discover just how true her words were.

Never breaking his eyes off her, he murmured, "I can hardly wait."

Cerisa exhaled the breath she'd been absently holding. There was no choice remaining. She didn't take his hand but motioned toward the stairs. Time for the games to begin. She'd get him to release before she took a stitch off. She smiled. "This way."

Pierce followed her up the stairs, intrigued. He'd been so stunned to find her here, selling herself, that he stood speechless for a minute. Out of the three girls, she was by far the most beautiful. Dressed in fancy undergarments, she was delectable. Watching her take the steps before him, her short-heeled mule slippers, all decked in embroidered silk and lace, he found his mouth watering.

At the top, she looked over her shoulder at him and her lips, rosy pink and plump, smiled before she led him down the hallway. The candle sconces gave a soft light that gave her an even more sultry look, her cascading curls glowed in the light, angelic and that thought made him want to chuckle. She was here, dressed like sin, not a heavenly body.

She opened the door to a room and motioned for him to enter. He walked into a bedchamber. The fireplace burned a low steady flame. The dark green wall-papered walls gave the room a rich, dark, luxuriant flavor. The centerpiece to the room was a large four-poster bed with a canopied top and the dark crimson curtains, tied back to the pillars at the four corners, matched the satin coverlet on the bed.

The presentation sent the message loud and clear—it was decadent like she was and he was here to enjoy every last morsel of her body. His cock twitched at the mere hint. As the girl spun before him, the diaphanous wrapper floating with her, he stood bewitched. Was she blushing? Her cheeks looked reddish but not by face paints. There was a sparkle in her eyes and her lips gave a hint of a smile. For some odd reason, he refused to let his gaze drop and rove over her body. It didn't seem right. Was Margaret's ghost pressing on him not to? Or was it the faint memory of this woman being verbally accosted by those vagrants last summer?

Why the hell was a lady here? Had things really gone that bad? Or had his judgment of character become that flawed?

The ghost of a grin vacated her face when he stood and did nothing.

"How can I help you fill your desires tonight?"

Her words were like a whisper in the night, but he heard them and the fear that mixed with them. No doubt Madame Nikki would punish her if he left not satiated. While not sure what the outcome of that would be, he imagined a woman here not making clients happy soon found herself on the streets.

"How did you end up here?" Considering the hovel he'd seen her in last, money was an issue. But to do this?

She startled. He couldn't help but watch her gulp, the movement of throat muscles so seductive to him, his balls tightened in anticipation. But she soon steeled her shoulders, her chin lifted in defiance.

"I'm here to please you." There wasn't a seductive tone to that sentence but more like fact.

Pierce snorted. She had to be a virgin at this. Not a virgin sexually, he decided, for he knew she lived with that freedman.

Good Lord, this was the last thing he wanted or needed. Not that he didn't find her appealing. It'd been not that long ago he'd seen the shape of her long legs and that memory, the mere thought of plowing between her thighs definitely stirred him. But this wasn't right, a thought he just could not shake.

When he didn't move, she quickly poured him a glass of wine and shoved it into his hands. Wine. His lips touched the rim and he welcomed the taste. It was a red vintage, thankfully not a madeira or port, though the kick of a port would've been welcomed. No, the acidly smooth blend of fermented grapes slid down his throat with ease.

She sat on the edge of the bed, her legs crossing at the ankle as she gripped the edge of the mattress. It was obvious to him she was trying to appear relaxed but the whites of her knuckles gave her away.

"Perhaps my pleasure would be to hear how you went from living in that hellish basement, your man in the army, to here."

He watched the hurt and pain flash across her eyes, a tug at the corner of her mouth before she slid a mask into place, hiding her emotions. There was a stab at his heart at the convicted torture he just witnessed because he too could understand but he didn't back down. She was too beautiful, too vulnerable to be here. Of course, he could be wrong about her, but he doubted it.

In a graceful move, she leaped off the bed and took his empty glass to refill it. Before he released the stemware, he said, "Pour one for yourself, as well. It is my wish for you to." He grinned, twisting her *desire* to please him in a way to make her not so tense.

She shot him a look but he knew she'd do it. He was, after all, the paying customer. A quick turn, she refilled his glass and poured a little for herself.

"If you must know," she started, handing him his glass before she stepped back. "I was turned out from my job at the factory and with no funds, I was evicted from my room." She sipped but never took her eyes off him.

Silence filled the next several minutes as he waited, but she said nothing more.

"And? Why not return home?"

"I have no home I can return to." There was a deadness to her words that made him want to cringe but he didn't.

"I can't believe you don't have family in…." He waited.

Her gaze hardened. "Louisiana."

"Yes, there. Why not return?"

"There is a war, if you'll recall. If I remember correctly, you told me you were returning to it." She glimpsed him up and down. "I don't see you hurt. Why aren't you fightin'?"

Ah, she fought back. He liked that.

"I report to the front by next week," he spilled out. Why he told her that when he'd not said a word to anyone else surprised him. Inside, his gut twisted. There was something about her, about the blood and death and his leaving that made him raw, hungry and vacant. Perhaps it was too many months of mourning, of lashing out at the world, at his father mainly, that ate at his soul. He glanced at her. "I want to see you again."

She gasped.

In the two weeks she'd been here, this request scared her the most.

He stood there, dressed in his fine black frock coat and trousers, the candlelight made his sapphire waistcoat the perfect match to his eyes. She remembered him so well, how polite he was and the man to have his way in carrying her home and mending her wound. One lock of his dark ebony hair curled down on his forehead, giving her the impression of how he was like that piece, unwilling to stay in place.

He was handsome, alluring and dangerous. And he wanted to see her again, which confused her more because here they stood, in her bedchamber, and nothing had happened. He hadn't requested much other than to ask her a couple of questions. No demanding her to undress, to undress him, nor to do anything. So why want her again? Her wine wasn't that good.

The intensity of his glare made her uncomfortable. She bit her bottom lip, taking her own gaze off him and that's when she saw it. It was her turn to return the attention onto him.

"To be with me? And what of your wife?" she pointed to the thin gold band on his ring-finger. Not that he was the only married man through the doors here or the first for her, but it burned her none the less. There was a draw to him she couldn't find a way to stop and to discover he was married marred him for her. Forgetting her position as a lady of the night, her voice turned hard, rancid even. "I think you should spend your time with her, before our boys send you straight to hell."

Instead of looking surprised or even chagrin, he gave her a lopsided grin. "I think you leap before you look—"

"Ha! You will deny that's a wedding ring?" Her anger escalated.

He put the wineglass down and stepped closer to her. "No, it is." He took her glass and set it down, which was pretty good for him because she was on the verge of throwing it at him. "My wife died last spring," he added softly.

Her gaze widened and she was about to apologize when he pulled her to him and sealed her lips with his. The kiss stunned her. She froze instantly, her mind racing as he pressed into her. As he wrapped his arms around her, she reminded herself she'd lashed out at him when she was to please him. Madame Nikki throwing her out echoed in her mind, so she worked to calm the firestorm inside her. But as the kiss deepened, she wondered if those flames came from anger or desire?

Slowly her icy wall melted, her arms sluggish at first but they moved to encircle his neck. He moaned against her mouth when she did that and it made her hug him back. At that moment, his tongue traced along the seam of her lips, begging them to part. It was that intimacy that made her shut down inside, reminding herself it was only her body he wanted, not her. That acknowledgement made her relax and her lips gave in to his push. He invaded her mouth, his tongue touching hers, dancing. He tasted like wine and tobacco, combined with the sandalwood scent he wore mixed with leather and the wool frock coat.

He lifted her without breaking the kiss and carried her to the bed. Her breasts smashed against his chest, still both of them fully clothed, sent tingles through her. Her ears pounded with her thudding heart. Once the bed hit the back of her legs, he lowered her to a seated position on the edge, still refusing to leave the kiss. Instinctively, her legs wrapped around his firmly planted legs. The whole position was evocative—the bulge at his groin pushed against her nether lips that were exposed in this position thanks to the split pantalets. In a swift move, he bent her back on the mattress without moving his legs.

The thick hard cock behind the wool trousers pressed against her and in response, she rocked a little, unaware of what she was doing until it was done. It hit her at her core. Without realizing it, she exposed herself to a man she did not know. His hand skimming down her side to her hips and squeezed.

She mewled in response. If he'd just take her and finish this, it'd be so much better…

It was at that exact moment he broke the kiss. A look of confusion filled his eyes and he frowned, as if as surprised as she was by the heat of their touch. It took a second and then she wanted to laugh—they were in a brothel, for heavens sake! But the lost gaze in his eyes cleared and he stood silent.

Fear snaked through her veins. Was she too forward or not enough? Had he stopped because she did nothing for him? Despite the bulge she saw, she worried he'd leave and complain how she'd failed.

Pierce's head and heart thudded, one in pain and the other in excitement. The two conflicted, wanting to tear him in two.

What the hell was he doing?

She was halfway laying on the mattress, her hair no longer an organized mess but mussed because of him. Her lips were swollen and slightly redder from his kiss. The problem and the promise was the woman before him, gorgeous, and desirable, but his conscience nagged him. He hadn't quite come to grips that for a man, his grieving was to be over, that he should marry again, something Margaret would have expected. While she didn't plague his dreams as she had, this still felt awkward, particularly with this girl, though of all here, she was the one that drew him. He credited that to having saved her from the riots and she was beautiful, though was she here because she had no where else to go after the disaster that day? Had she lost her income and forced to sell herself to be able to live? He'd given her his card to call if she needed anything. Why hadn't she? What was he thinking?

He stood back and ran his fingers through his hair, trying to come to grips with what had happened. She sat upright, watching him. When she bit her bottom lip, he was lost.

"I'd apologize," he began then chuckled. "But then I remember where I am. Please excuse me. It's been a long time."

She released the injured tissue and stood. "Your wife. You must have loved her very much."

He did, didn't he? What a strange thought to surface now. Of course, he did. In fact, he should leave. "This was a ridiculous idea," he muttered but didn't move.

She tilted her head. Doing so sent the cascade of curls falling down that shoulder, mesmerizing him.

"I don't understand. Ridiculous?"

Without knowing, he stepped closer and reached to pull the two hairpins that held the waterfall of coiled hair up. He wanted to see it loose, to run his fingers through it...

"Yes. I have a friend who insisted I go out with him this evening instead of remaining home, as I have been. I didn't know his destination for us was here." The hair fell onto her shoulder. He decided he wanted to run his fingers ran through the strands. A tremble passed through her, he could see it, feel it as his hand touched her hair and missed a pin because of it.

She gulped again. *Exquisite.*

The room suddenly became too warm. He struggled for a breath. Quickly, he shrugged out of his coat, throwing it on the chest at the foot of the bed as his free hand came to his neck, fingers squeezing between the collar and tie. As he struggled to unknot the tie, Cerisa reached up and undid it for him, yanking it off.

Free of the coat, the waistcoat she unbuttoned and shoved off with the necktie. Pierce scooped her up and placed her on her back. She was still clothed in the few garments she wore. The fact that she aided him without removing hers indicated to him that she was a reluctant whore, or one that demanded to be waited on but so far, her mannerism didn't denote that. At the moment, he decided it was unimportant, as he climbed onto the bed with her.

She flinched when he went to pull her near.

He nuzzled her neck, spooning her in the curve of his body. For the first time in months, he relaxed. Being with her put him at ease, better than the liquor he'd consumed, better than the physical exertion he did to wear himself out. Her scent was one of roses and lilies—sweet but he'd remember that roses also had thorns. The tightness in her shoulders told him she had thorns. Good, he decided. He inhaled her fragrance again, snuggling next to her.

Who would have guessed that a beautiful whore, one he'd paid a pretty price for, was the one thing that made him forget everything and let the evasive sleep come?

Vacantly, he heard a raspy breath and knew it came from him. Then everything went black.

CHAPTER NINE

You cannot make soldiers of slaves, or slaves of soldiers. The day you make a soldier of them is the beginning of the end of the revolution. And if slaves seem good soldiers, then our whole theory of slavery is wrong.

- Confederate General Howell Cobb, a former U.S. Congressman, on Robert E. Lee's late-war proposal of enlisting slaves in the Confederate army.

August 1863

PIERCE READ THE NOTE one more time, not sure if he wanted to moan in frustration or joy. Either way, he still wadded the note and threw it onto his desk. He walked over to the sideboard and poured some bourbon into a glass, downing a large gulp before he slammed it back down. With a deep sigh as he ran his fingers through his hair, he walked over and yanked his satchel from under the bed.

"New orders?"

He shoved a shirt into the bag without looking up at Edward. "Yes."

"Isn't that what you've been wanting? To get back to the elephant?"

It was, wasn't it? "Of course. I have to get to Washington by tomorrow afternoon." It left him little time to get his affairs into order. Not that he had a lot but something was niggling at the back of his mind.

Cerisa.

Why the hell did that whore tug at strings he'd cut when he'd watched them lower Margaret's casket into the earth? He shoved another article into the bag.

"Let's get out of here, Pierce," Edward started. "Go grab a drink of farewell and all that."

Pierce eyed his friend. The man avoided confronting the enemy by remaining here, running the ironworks just to the west of the city. His family's business, now with him in charge. Heir to the company, he didn't have Pierce's slanted eye stare at progenitor practice nor was he a West Point graduate like Pierce. Times like this made him wonder how he became friends with the man in the first place.

Pierce stood, a pair of drawers in his hands to shove in the satchel when Edward made that remark. That was how they'd made friends. They understood each other, offering support when needed. Edward remained close even though Pierce went to war, married a Catholic Irish girl, stood even as his best man, even though his own family and upbringing would have agreed with Senator Duval.

"You're right. My last night in this God-forsaken city." He slapped Edward on the shoulder. "Let's go."

Somehow, he knew he'd end up here. He took a sip from the champagne flute as he scanned the room. Madame Nikki's house had once again pulled him back and he stood in the front room with other men among the ladies fluttering about in fanciful undergarments and loosely tied filmy wraps. The women tried to entice him but he barely paid attention, looking for her.

"Lookin' fer someone in particula'?"

The Irish lilt on the words grabbed his attention and he

glanced down at the redhead. Her shiny brown eyes held a speculative glare and the smile on her coral lips lacked the seductive appeal the others had. She was serious on the question and, if his memory served him right, this woman knew where Cerisa was.

"Actually, now that you mentioned it, I am." He turned to give her his full attention, a wave of relief that someone noticed the mood sweeping through him. "I'm looking for that beautiful temptress, Cera. As I recall, you are friends with her…"

The girl rolled her bottom lip through her teeth and her hooded gaze gave a judgmental assessment of him. She didn't speak for a moment. The splatter of freckles on her nose seemed to darken as he waited.

"If she's already occupied," he gulped. That was an unpleasant thought, her in another man's arms. A truly ridiculous thought, considering her current occupation, but he could not shake that dismal idea. "I mean, I'd have to understand, of course, but I had hopes of seeing her. Before I return to the war." He added the last in, not only because it was true, but hopefully a prod to get her to open up.

With a deep sigh, as if she didn't want to tell him but felt she had to, she hooked her arm in the bend of his and led him toward the staircase. "She is here. Upstairs and in her room, but not entertaining. She hasn't since—," she glanced up the staircase and around the base of it. "Since two nights ago. Madame Nikki will be after her soon to return to the floor, so perhaps a visit from a soldier would satisfy both Madam and Cera. She's the third door from the right at the top."

"Thank—" But he never finished as she scampered back into the growing crowd of men. He stood there for a moment, trying to decipher what she had been hinting at. Maybe Cera had been sick. In this house, that wouldn't surprise him, considering the clientele had one thought on their minds and health wasn't one of them.

Now knowing where she was, he turned and leapt up the staircase and went to the third door. He paused as he stood there, righting his frock coat and tugging on the waistcoat beneath. Unsure why he hesitated, he finally knocked at the door and waited. It seemed like an eternity before she opened it, her profile silhouetted by the faint candlelight behind her. At her invitation, he bolted into the room, the excitement of just seeing her lifted his spirits that had been dragging all day.

He spun on his heels to pull her into his arms but what he saw made him stop. She stood in the shadows and he didn't think it was because of him. "Cera, come here please." He held out his hand to her but she stood, shaking her head. It looked like she tried to take a step back but the wall was behind her. He frowned. This wasn't how whores got business, his inner voice mused. He frowned and took a step toward her, reaching out for her and grabbing her hand to pull her close. The candlelight shimmered off her sheer white organza wrap that was open down the front. Trimmed in pale lace, it flowed loosely and revealed the white lace-trimmed corset beneath with pantalets hinting at the secrets beneath. She had no stockings on and her toes curled on the floor as he gave her a pull to him.

But when she came a footstep closer, he saw why she hid in the dark. One of her eyes showed traces of bruising that trailed down her cheek. The dangling chestnut curl from the upswept hair danced near the motley-colored skin, as if she tried to conceal the damage. Her rose-color lips looked muted, as if the blood there had pooled on the mark of her jawline and the corner of her mouth looked puffed with a crack in those luscious petals. His eyes widened in shock at her appearance and the signs of her abuse made the anger inside him grow, wanting to beat the daylights out of anyone who hit her.

"Who the hell did this?"

She frowned and tried to retreat but he resisted letting her go. "You're hurting me."

He blinked and looked down. His fingers wound tight around her hands and he instantly released them. "Apologies." He put his hand around her, placing it on her lower back, hoping she wasn't hurt there. When she didn't flinch, he guided her to the upright chair near the fireplace. "Cera, what happened?"

She gave a short laugh. "So dear Annie told you where to find me? That doesn't surprise me. Madame Nikki has been kind and let me off the floor, so to speak, trying to get this to pass but I fear my time is short."

That hit him hard. She'd be forced to submit to another man in this state? Instantly, he wanted to wrap her in his arms and protect her. "Tell me what happened."

She looked at him with a guarded gaze. It was the second time he'd been so judged and he wasn't happy. Considering where he was, he bit his tongue from saying anything. He wanted her to be able to trust him, which was asking a lot, considering what he knew of her. The ridicule of being with that freedman, of factory work, of the riots, of that hovel she lived in and being employed here no doubt jaded her views on men.

"There's not much to tell," she replied. He noticed she wasn't looking at him and had actually drawn the wrapper tighter. The primal male in him objected loudly but he quelled the voice.

"But something did." She didn't reply so he continued. "Who was he? I shall have words." The anger in him still broiled.

"No!" her hands came flying up in a stopping gesture. "Please. That'd only serve to thwart my work here. Madame Nikki says this house does well by remaining silent of her patrons."

He inhaled deep, trying to keep himself from exploding. Someone had hurt her. Some lowlife had dared to touch her and that someone would pay! His fists clenched and it took some hard effort to uncurl them.

"No names. Charming." He ran his fingers through his hair.

"I look much better today. Nikki says I'm over the worst of it."

He spun back around. "Over the worst?" he stated in a mocking tone. "Just what prompted this prig to strike out at a lady?"

She cringed when he said lady. Damn, she took that either wrong as he was referring to her lady of the night situation, or the fact he knew, by all her actions, that she was a true lady on hard times.

Cera sat up straighter, he could see her bracing her shoulders as she swallowed hard. "He is involved in the war, soldier perhaps? Seen too much blood, he said, and as our discussion continued, he got madder and madder, only to change into the most gentle creature I've had the chance to meet in ages." She blinked hard and he saw her Adam's apple swing up and down as she gulped her fear. "Then he hit me, claiming I was his to do with as he pleased." She shuddered. "So he, he…" Tears rolled down her cheeks as she let her hand sweep down her body.

Pierce's eyes widened. Instantly he was at her side, cooing in her ear sweet nothings to try to distract her. Up close, he saw the bruises. The villain had hit her everywhere. His blood boiled.

"That's enough. You need to get out of here!"

She looked at him, a sad grin on her lips. "I can't afford to. I need an income. The factories won't take me, considering…" She shrugged. He knew she referred to her relationship with the freedman and her cadence. "You know they all talk. If they don't block me due to Abraham, it's because I'm Southern. I've tried to adopt the Yankee way of speakin' but…" Another shrug, but he caught a hint of a smile tugging on her lips. This lady was a little rebel and it fit her well.

He pulled her up to her feet and saw her wince by the movement. That irritated him more. "Well, I'm going to go have a talk with Madame Nikki."

"Pierce, please."

"What?" His mind was racing. He had to get her out of here. If one blowhard did this, there would be more. The war was pressing against everyone's sensibilities and working girls like her could see the worst side of the men who fought it. "I won't have you hurt again."

She cocked her head. "And how would you stop it? This is my job, to take men as they want." She shuddered despite steeling herself. "Come, take a seat." She patted the mattress next to her. Her voice was soft and alluring, making him bend to her.

"I don't like this."

She gave him a half smile and a kiss on his cheek. "Let it pass."

Her fingers interlocked with his. He squeezed her hand, with a deep sigh while his mind continued its race to find a way to protect her.

"You came to spend the evening with me?" she asked.

He gave her a nod and lifted her chin to look straight into her golden-brown eyes. "Yes. I leave tomorrow to report to my command. Apparently, all paths to keep me here have dried up and the war calls." He shrugged, but the ache inside his chest widened. The loss of his dear wife had opened the crevice where his heart used to be, making him feel numb, but this girl sparked some dying ember. It was a whisper of what had been and enough to drive him to come here tonight. Knowing his departure was on the horizon, the mere thought of leaving her drove a spike through him, and he wasn't sure if he could.

"So, you're returning to the fight?" Her words held a tremor to them, as if she was fighting back her own tears.

He couldn't take it if she cried. His insides tightened and he squeezed her hand as he kissed her temple. "Yes."

"Then don't let my appearance drive you away. Stay."

Her request, not made by a shaky voice but as a woman wanting a man, washed through him with warmth and affection. There was a small glimmer of hope that she wanted him as more than just a   client who was to leave for war and possible death. It was a farce to allow that idea to pass through him but it did, and he knew better. But she was here with him, and as she stood, never releasing his hand, she spun to stand before him and pulled the corset tie at her waist. The contraption's tie unraveled and as the ribbon pooled at her toes, he put his hands on her waist and pushed. The busk unclasped and fell to the floor.

The chemise was scant, not the type he'd seen on women outside this house. It took him only seconds to scoop the piece off over her head and throw it to the floor. Still sitting on the bed, he was at the right height for her standing and he snaked his arm around her middle, pulling her closer, his mouth finding her nipple when she stepped forward. He pulled her pearled tip into his mouth, and being as gentle as he could, his teeth scraped across her and his hand on her back felt the shimmer down her spine. A smile hinted at him, pleased that he got her mind off the injuries. When he tugged at the pearled point, she shivered and mewled. Despite the discomfort as his member hardened and his position put him at an angle that gave him no room, he'd gladly put up with that if he pleased her enough to make her forget where she was...

There was something about his touch that erased her gut-ripping pain, the anxious notion of being here, in her room, with a man, after what that one did last week. As her inner fear started to boil, he suckled harder on her nipple, as if he read her mind. She melted against him, arching her back and actually pushing into him.

The attention he gave her, very gentle but urgent, made her tension yield as her body built in anticipation. She couldn't imagine being without him so the thought of him being gone to the war made her shudder. Not that she expected him here. His few visits had been like a glimpse to her past, when things were easier to take. Surprisingly, he hadn't taken her sexually. He kissed her, caressed her but never pushed to complete, which at first broke her tension only to leave her wanting more. They always ended up wrapped in each other's arms, fast asleep. Nights with him made her existence here easier. Simple. Easy. If only they could all be like this always.

Instantly, she felt a pang of guilt. After all, she had been a married woman. Which also made her cringe considering what she had turned to to make money in order to survive. Despite being with this man, who held her in his arms, his steady breath blowing on the back of her neck, she shuddered.

She wondered if he watched her because his arm around her waist tightened, as if reassuring her he was there. The mere suggestion of that made her snuggle against him and find herself drifting to dreams of a life that she barely remembered.

CHAPTER TEN

*"It appears certain that General McClellan's force has escaped
us. I feel greatly mortified…He ought not to have got off so easily."*

~General Lee to President Davis, August 17, 1862 after
Harrison's Landing

PIERCE STRAIGHTENED HIS JACKET and
took a deep breath before he knocked on the office
door.

"Come in."

He stepped into the office. Madame Nikki sat at the large
mahogany desk, a stack of papers before her and a pair of
spectacles on. Dressed in the elaborate gown she wore for
her guests, she glanced above the rim of the glasses, a pen in
her hand. It was so unusual to see a woman like her doing
paperwork. He'd assumed she hired an accountant to handle
this, but apparently, he was wrong.

"How can I help you, Colonel?" She motioned to the
chair before her. When he hesitated, she pushed the glasses
down and snorted. "I run a tight establishment and learned
a long time ago to never trust a man with numbers. Now,
please sit and state to what I owe this visit. Was it one of my
girls? Did she not please you?" Her tone wasn't harsh but he
could see why this place held an appeal. She wanted the men
to be pleased and therefore, spread the word and hence the
wealth by spending their dollars here. He was amused. But

the thought of another woman spurred him to move forward to the chair.

"I've come on behalf of your lovely nymph, Cera. Her condition is upsetting, to say the least."

The madam pushed herself from the papers and raised an eyebrow. "True, it is a tragedy when clients believe they are allowed to harm one of my girls. He was addressed accordingly, rest assured."

He doubted that. Brothels that demanded justice for a woman of ill-repute would have little in clientele if word got out.

"'Tis good to hear the culprit was righted, but I fear for her safety."

"Thank you, sir." The woman tilted her head, a slow smile forming at her lips. "You've seen her what? A handful of times and she moves you so?"

That remark on the number of times he'd visited here and requested Cera specifically made his stomach lurch. He'd enjoyed her company, the way she listened to him and his babbling about the war, and so much more, without judging him, or not so verbally. A relief against fighting his father's political game.

Now, there was a voice in the back of his head. It was Margaret, he was sure, or perhaps he'd been around her Irish clan too much with their premotions, telling him God had put Cera in his path and he was to protect her. It was a notion he couldn't shake and that was typical of anything Margaret set her mind to, particularly if she believed God was behind it. So, despite all the perils of his future and the struggle he had to keep living and avoid his father's machinations, he found himself here, talking to a madam about one of her girls.

"Yes, she does. In fact, I'd like to pay her contract, or whatever agreement you have with her, to release her from this place."

Madame Nikki's brows furrowed as she put the end of the pen to her lips, the look of confusion plainly on her face. "You, sir, mean to tell me you want to whisk my darling Southern belle away from this house of the flesh to protect her from men?"

At his nod, she leaned forward and added, "And who will protect her from you? Oh, I know of your plight, Colonel. With a name like Duval, your family is always in the news. Your father's fight for the future of my race is admirable, though from what I hear, you are not fully with him, am I not right? And further, I know you're a military man and that means, you will return to the beast. What will she do then?"

He gritted his teeth. She wasn't ignorant. It would have been so much better if she had been.

"I fully intend to return her to her family. The bonds of loved ones often heal wounds of the past."

"And what of your wounds?" She leaned forward. "I know you lost your wife. And don't try that look of innocence. With a senator father, gossip is the game here. You'll return to the war. So how will you achieve your goal?"

That he hadn't figured out yet. "Madame, please. I cannot bring myself to leave her here and find she is hurt again. My conscience won't allow it, plus I do have connections to aid me."

Her eyes widened at the insinuation that she caused the abuse. After a tense moment, he watched the myriad of colors in her eyes finally settle as a smile came to her face. "Certainly. Well, her room this month will be the equivalent of one night with her."

To him, that was letting her off lightly, but then again, he never knew what they had agreed on. Instead of pushing it, he reached inside his coat and withdrew his pocketbook.

Cerisa vaguely heard the light rap on her door and really wanted to ignore it. She was too tired and for the first time in several nights, she finally was able to sleep.

"Cerisa! Psst. Cerisa!"

Annie. She knew Annie would not go away, so she slowly opened her eyes. She looked at the space next to her on the bed and found it cold and empty. He was gone. Inside, a small pang hit her stomach. Pierce had left and she found the ache immeasurable. When did that happen? All it took was to get up and pull at one of her injuries doing so to remind her that she felt safe when he was here. Deep inside, she knew he'd protect her. He'd saved her before and she'd wager he would again and with her being all alone, she realized she had started to rely on his presence. In her heart, she knew Abraham would have wanted her to, but did he want to?

The knock continued, interrupting her thoughts, so with a slow reluctance, she pulled herself out of the bed, tied her wrapper on and padded to the door.

Annie barged right on in and strode right over to the window.

"You will not believe what has happened!" She yanked the drapes aside and fished through the gauze fabric beneath to the expose the room to the sun streaming in.

Cerisa hooded her eyes, the light too bright. She must've slept in very late and no doubt well past breakfast. Her stomach rumbled. Running her fingers through her hair, she stifled a yawn.

"I have no idea what you're referring to."

"Your man, tha' officer," Annie answered, now pulling Cerisa's torn carpetbag out of the trunk at the foot of the bed. "He's done rescued ye." The redhead was smiling, as she started to pull the clothes from the armoire—what few pieces she still possessed—and began folding them for the bag.

Cerisa frowned. "He did what?"

"He's done rescued ye. Paid Miss Nikki rest o' what ye owed her. Done see 'im leavin' her lair nigh on minutes ago."

Cerisa didn't hear her right, she was sure. Pierce had left her to go pay for what she owed, which meant clothes and boarding? But why?

"'O stop tha' way of thinkin' and go wash yer face. I'd expect him to be here right soon," Annie stated as she whipped another petticoat into the air to fluff it before she folded.

"But I don't—" Confusion seemed to sap the energy she had on rising.

A blue dress hit her in the stomach and automatically, she grabbed the piece. Next came a petticoat and she turned, taking the pieces to the bed.

"All right, I get it." She shook the skirt and bodice out. This was the dressiest piece she owned, dating back years prior to the war. Slightly worn but still neat, it was a nicer outfit than her one of late that consisted of corset and pantalets and greedy men.

With Annie's help, she was dressed and her hair coiffed above her ears in a roll with tendrils of trim cascading down her neck with the wisps' that strayed, giving a softer appearance, one that was badly needed, when the reflection in the looking glass wore a purplish mar on the cheek and jawline. She fretted over the bruises, wondering if he'd regret saving her when another knock came. Had to be Pierce, she thought, and her heart fluttered a beat. But before she could say a word, Annie pounded for the door and flung it open.

"Major, mighty fine to see ya this morn!"

"It Colonel, Annie. I'm here to see Cera."

Cerisa drank him in, noticing the determination etched in his face, as well as the clenching of his hat's brim in the clutch of his hands. He fought around the overly talkative Annie to get into the room, while her friend continued to prattle about something that Cerisa didn't hear due the buzz in her ears, and he found her.

He came straight to her, a lazy smile on his lips. "I've come for you."

She bit her bottom lip, a shiver running down her spine. "You had me last night," she whispered, hoping beyond hope what her friend had said was true but then, again, wasn't sure what to expect from him.

He chuckled. "I know, love. But this is a tad different. You need to pack your things because you're leaving with me." He kissed the top of her head.

She squinted at him. "Annie here hinted at that. That and how you managed to get me out of Madame Nikki's care. It that true?"

He stopped and looked at her. A puzzled look washed over him for a second, or perhaps she thought it did, until he gave her a lop-sided grin. "Your friend is right. I am getting you out of this elaborate hellhole."

On cue, Annie handed him Cerisa's carpetbag, packed with her few belongings.

"Colonel, take good care of her. She's a special lady." She smiled at her friend and slipped out the door.

Cerisa's stomach flipped and she raced to follow Annie for a proper farewell but knew the Irish lass disappeared on purpose, claiming to her days ago that she couldn't take farewells. But she'd miss that girl… Her eyes blurred.

"Cera…"

She blinked and gave him another look. Pierce Duval looked dashing in his military uniform, dressed up to whisk her away. His dark hair and piercing blue eyes added to the aura around him that spoke of his strong-will and determination. As she thought before, this was a man who could protect her but the real question was would she let him?

It must have been her slight hesitancy that made him take her hand and pull her close.

"Shhh, all will be well. I promise," he whispered.

"Cerisa."

He cocked his head.

"If you're to take me with you, at least you should call me correctly. Cera is a nickname I took to here, but my full name is Cerisa."

He smiled and pulled her hand to his lips. "Cerisa. As beautiful as the woman herself."

This man seduced her by his soft words and the light touch of his lips against her skin, a way that made her insides turn molten, making her want him to continue. The mere suggestion in her head of that turned her cheeks hot.

"You flatter when you know you don't have to." Nor did he ever, as he had paid to be with her so flattery, while soothing to her ears, was so unnecessary.

He handed her her wrap and scooped up her satchel. Still sporting a grin, he opened the door and gestured. "After you, my lady."

As if she was in a fairy tale, no matter how distorted since they were leaving a whorehouse, she floated out the door with her Prince Charming behind her. But a voice in the back of her head wondered if her prince was really a toad in disguise.

CHAPTER ELEVEN

"Well, if you see the President, tell him from me that whatever happens, there will be no turning back."

~ General U.S. Grant to Henry Wing, young reporter for the New York Tribune, 1864

Washington D.C., August 1863

TIMOTHY DUVAL SAT IN the leather chair, every nerve inside him on fire. He stared at the Secretary of War. "She said *what?*"

Edward Stanton peered above his report, his brows arching upward, widening his eyes behind the glasses perched on his nose. Duval thought it gave him an owl-look but the lawyer didn't move, a look of amusement on his face.

"We have pushed for less but it does not give them what they want," Stanton replied.

"She skirted the issue," Duval shot back. "Gave those rebels the chance to hope."

The tall dark figure sitting at the head of the table stared at the map of the United States on the wall. He had a stern expression but managed to chuckle. "Belligerent status is exactly what they are. Perhaps Jefferson Davis and his staff could preclude that as recognition but I severely doubt it."

Duval turned toward his president and scowled. "There was no need to give them any hope." His fists balanced him on the tabletop as he leaned forward. "That Emancipation Proclamation should have closed off any opportunity for recognition!"

Lincoln tilted his head, the look of a patriarch soothing his child schooled his face. "Senator, we have made an impact with our status." He leaned back in his chair. Duval could see the lines around his eyes, the greying of his hair and the ink stains on his shirtsleeves. The man who held the highest office of the land appeared more like a law clerk than leader of a democratic republic. He rubbed his eyes.

"Senator Duval, England had taken our proclamation with serious mind. She, too, has freed the slaves in her lands but rumor has surfaced that even the mighty queen has had problems with those former slaves. Some there have even petitioned to re-instate slavery, to control those 'unruly' souls."

"Education, Mr. President, is the key," the other attendant to this meeting interjected. Duval had included Frederick Douglass in hopes of persuading Lincoln to his cause, one that might be diverted with England's quasi-recognition of the South's independence.

Lincoln gave a lop-sided grin. "Indeed, Mr. Douglass, indeed."

"Education of the freedmen will be addressed once the war has concluded," Stanton blared.

"My people hunger for knowledge," Douglass continued, then added, "And the right to fight for the freedom to do so."

"Precisely, which is the reason for my, our, visit," Duval stated. "The use of negroes as 'contraband' is demeaning. Giving them only manual labor as a way to help our troops equally so. The 54th Massachusetts demonstrated how well men of color can do in battle. We need to increase those numbers, and in that sense, prevent another uprising in our midst, like the riots in New York."

Stanton snarled, "Irish are a contemptible lot. Them and their damnable papal ways—"

"They feared the certainty of death, Secretary Stanton, just like many mothers and wives across this land," Lincoln said softly. "Loss of lives and their jobs to the freed slaves can push people beyond reason."

"Still no cause to lynch men because of their color." Duval was furious. Anytime the Irish raised their bloody hands, the mere thoughts that his son had been pulled into their lair by that slattern always sent his anger to boil.

"It is something men of color have been exposed to throughout their lives as slaves. What we need is more troops to show how we are willing to die for our right to be free."

"Which is precisely why we need to enlist more." Duval slammed the tabletop to emphasis his statement but Stanton only glared and Lincoln smiled.

"Senator, I appreciate your enthusiasm and Mr. Douglass's reverence, all of which I will take under consideration. Enlistments are high among the blacks but I also must adhere to the law, for while the Emancipation Proclamation is a step toward correction of the travesty slavery has wrought, do keep in mind that it does not affect those under chain in states still holding loyalty to the Union. Therefore, any enlistments must be allowed by their owners or their freedom proven."

That rattled the senator and he opened his mouth to object when the runaway slave-turned-abolitionist put his hand on his sleeve as a calming gesture.

"Of course, Mr. President." Douglass bowed his head.

Duval bit his tongue but added, "Yes, Mr. President. I will push for more officers to lead these men to glorious victories and end this conflict once and for all!"

Stanton stood, placing himself as almost a wall between the senator and the president. "Gentlemen, it is time for you to go."

Duval bit his inner lip but knew he pressed too hard. He said his thanks and farewells and wheeled out of the office fast, leaving Douglass behind.

Pierce pulled his horse to a stop in front of the multi-storied building and jumped out of the saddle in time to grab the reins of Cerisa's beast. His insides were tight, as what he'd done was hitting him hard, like a cannonball that hadn't exploded. Within seconds, he tied the two horses to the hitching post and lifted her off her saddle to the ground. It took her a moment to regain her balance and she looked too hot, he decided, kicking himself for driving them for the past day toward the nation's capital when it was late July and the heat kicked. She looked wilted and he only had himself to blame.

"Are you all right?"

She blinked and took a step out of his reach. "Yes, just been a while since I've ridden."

He smiled, biting back a grimace. It never occurred to him that considering the hovel he'd seen her live in and her latest employment that she even knew how to ride. "Apologies. My haste in getting you out of that place drove me harder than was necessary."

"It is all right. I thought you had to get to the army and fast."

He laughed. "Granted, you are correct but still, I am trained to be an officer and gentleman."

She gave him a smile and its splendor took his breath

away. She was as beautiful as Aphrodite, or so he imagined the goddess of love would be. Just what had he done? He'd rescued her from hell only to throw himself into one. He was mourning, despite society telling him to find another as it had been long enough. Long enough? Only God would be this spiteful and throw an angel at him. He had to force himself to breath.

"Where are we?"

The moment she asked, a team of horses came racing down the street, their driver whipping them faster. Pierce barely had time to scoot out of the way before being trampled. After they smoked past them, he looked up and down the street and answered, "Washington, D.C."

Her eyes widened and he mentally swore she paled.

"I have to report to the War Office, confirming my orders." And make sure his father hadn't pressured them to change his status. He wasn't sure how far Senator Duval could go. He took a deep breath and offered her his arm. "Come, let me get you settled in your room first. Then we can find dinner."

Gingerly, she placed her hand on his arm and let him guide her up the stairs to the grand hotel. The Jefferson Hotel was one of Pierce's favorites and whenever he was in Washington, he stayed here instead of his father's capital residence. The stone façade hinted at an austere establishment but it was a welcoming place, with help that surpassed many in warmth and elegance.

He steered her to the front desk. The staff instantly recognized him yet gave the lady on his arm a stern look. He grinned.

"Colonel Duval, what a pleasure to have you with us again," the desk clerk greeted, turning the guest book toward Pierce to sign.

"Always a pleasure to be here," he returned. "May I introduce my wife, Cerisa."

The clerk gave a short smile and a quick bow of his head. "Always delight to meet one of the Colonel's guests."

Despite the lighthearted tone of the clerk, Pierce felt the stabbing glare of Cerisa's gaze. Her brows rose in a questioning gesture and he guessed he'd hear all about this later. He just couldn't decide if he objected to it or rather enjoyed the attention she'd give him over it.

"My key, if you would Joseph," he answered, putting his hand out for the piece.

"Of course, of course, please pardon me," the clerk sputtered, fumbling about the counter for the key. As he placed it in Pierce's hand, he added, "Please excuse me, Mrs. Duval. Manners, at times, appear inept in the presence of a beautiful lady."

"Thank you," she murmured. Her voice hit a cord deep inside Pierce, making his insides tighten. The smile that graced her lips was demure and alluring, at least to him. He prayed the clerk wasn't drawn to her, because his inner soul claimed her as his and his alone. And watching her glide across the marble floor to the stairs, he lost his ability to breath. She was a siren, and to heed to her call might kill him.

Their beginning was rather lackluster, Cerisa decided as she finally took a seat and stared into the looking glass poised above the vanity. Pierce had whisked her away from selling her body for money and the risk imposed on her, being naked with a perfect stranger, but their trip here was rather quiet. Once here, at this fine hotel, he'd escorted her to this room, dropped her baggage and promptly left. Odd indeed…

He'd called her his wife. The title made her shake. A

couple traveling alone was often questioned, if not by words, definitely by look, for only familial or martial couples were socially condoned. He could have said sister though she wondered if that would have implied two rooms. If that was the case, probably not available here. Washington seemed to be bustling with people, thanks to the war. At Madame Nikki's, thoughts surfaced of men who visited, probably the same as stayed here. Made her wonder if they beat women as well...

She closed her eyes and forced the memory from her thoughts. Here was a new beginning and one she needed to use. Perhaps Pierce could help her find her husband's body. The man deserved a proper burial.

A knock at the door interrupted her musings and she jumped. "Yes?"

"Ma'am, it's the porter here. Colonel ordered some food for you," came the response through the paneled door.

As if on cue, her stomach rumbled. They hadn't had much on the road. The hardtack was barely edible and the apple he'd pulled from his haversack didn't go far. After all, she hadn't really eaten anything before leaving Madame Nikki's, since her jaw had hurt too much until the morning Pierce arrived. She eyed the dishes when the servant entered, her mouth watering as she sniffed the aroma of roast beef, cooked vegetables and seasoning. As he put the tray down on the table, she realized just how hungry she was.

"The colonel wanted me to inform you that he had to report to the War Department and would return as soon as he can."

She only vaguely heard him but nodded, wanting him to leave so she could devour it all. The only way to deal with this situation, of being with a man not her husband and not a client, still rubbed her wrong but until she ate and assessed, she could not think. She lifted a cover and found biscuits, which she instantly took one and bit into it, savoring every crumb. What was he going to do with her? The possibilities, if she allowed herself to think about it, could drive her to insanity.

Washington had never been far from becoming a cesspool, thanks to the politicians that inhabited the town, but now, it was worse. The coat of slime and muck seemed to cover him and he hated it even more. It was hard to believe that he once thought the capital was a place of adventure and intrigue but he was young and in his child's eyes, his father loomed from a pinnacle of power and might. Pierce grimaced. The man's ability to forge forward during war hadn't decreased, he hoped it hadn't dragged him along with the senator into the final rims of hell…

Pierce weaved through the mass of people on the streets and up the stairs to the War Department. The air inside was stale and the area deathly quiet. People still amassed in the halls but the tone was dark and ominous. This building and its inhabitants were part of the old school of generals and political posturing. War was schemed and designed here, not a welcoming place when the prime objective was conquering the rebels.

The click of his heels seemed to echo loud despite the mass of people. He turned the corner and found the room he was looking for. With a deep breath and a yank on his frock coat to straighten it, he pushed through the door to the office of General William Halleck.

"Lt. Erickson, if I could have a moment," he started but the General's assistant raised his hand to stop him.

"Colonel, I am amazed to see you here. You have been unaccountable in the ranks for some time. General Halleck has little time to spend with an officer who decides personal loss takes precedence over your duty, after the allotted time given."

Pierce's jaw twitched. "You, sir, are not a married man, I take it."

Erikson flinched. "Perhaps not yet but that has little to do with it. You were given a month and instead of conveying a message, you simply refrained from returning. That could be considered desertion."

"Sir, I did not come to simply present myself to the mercy of the tribunal. No, I have appeared for my orders and to make an inquiry." Blast the man on chiding him!

Erikson gave him a half smile. "You always do take reprimands badly."

Pierce sat in the chair and eyed the man. "I'd say you take liberties, here, protected by position and walls that do not speak back."

Silence followed as both looked at the other then they laughed.

"Good to hear a laugh, old man." Erikson's own grin was infectious and made Pierce chuckle.

"Good to see you, too, though," Pierce took a glance about the spacious office. "I had feared you'd turned to stone, sitting stagnant among the reports and demands of…" He nodded toward the closed office door of the general.

Erikson shook his head. "He's off to see Lincoln again. I should let you know that your father's been stalking the halls, that ex-slave in his wake. He's stirring the pot on more Colored troops." He shrugged. "Of course, your name has been bantered about."

Pierce groaned. "I've no intention to lead the Coloreds into anything."

"The word goes it'd be a path to promotion…"

"Colonel suits me well." He circled the desk, looking at the documents on top of it. "I plan to return to the fight."

"Well, you may not appreciate this," Erikson muttered. "Heading west hasn't been the most desired position."

Pierce fought the first inclination to grimace. The western theater was nothing but a seesaw of troop movements. "Who do I report to?"

"Rosecrans."

"*Sheesh!*" He started to pace. His mind held a whirlwind of thoughts and emotions. That meant he'd be heading west, to the Army of the Cumberland and in the battle against the Confederate Army of Tennessee. "Against Bragg, I'd take it?"

Erikson nodded.

He ran his fingers through his hair. "And what of the other?"

The clerk rummaged through his papers and pulled a sheet. "According to all accounts, all of the 54th were obliterated at Fort Wagner. They're still cataloging and informing families. You know the War Department—nothing races through the casualty lists."

Pierce gritted his teeth. "I know the numbers. They were posted. But I'm well aware they do not take this long in listing the casualties."

Erikson shrugged. "They are the Colored troops. Standards are," he paused. "Adjusted, with those in the power justifying it with the 'true' casualties are among the main army."

The white man's army. That statement rubbed him wrong and from the agitated shuffle of the clerk's hands and darting of his eyes, Pierce knew the man was well aware it wouldn't. It should be a simple task, to find out if Cera's 'husband', a title he realized he had a hard time wrapping his thoughts around, if the man was still alive. From what little he had heard of the 54th's attack, the possibility was exceedingly small. The forward assault, up the bare sandy hill to the Confederate fort, situated in a prime spot to repel any attack, was an out and out disaster for those soldiers who were nailed by rebel guns. He shook his head at the mere hint of a vision of it, even if it was only in his mind.

"Why do you care, anyway?" Erikson asked. "Influence from your father, the senator, prompt this move toward the Coloreds? I know he's been busy pushing his plan to increase the black soldiers, pushing that freedman's bureau and the like."

Pierce stared out the window, his mind racing. "I have a lady who has ties to one of the soldiers of that regiment. As a wife, she's has rights, does she not? She had received monies from him but they'd stopped coming, long before this ill-fated assault."

"Well, I do believe that answers the question on his fate. Army's not far off stopping money leaving here anyway."

Pierce frowned. The army had also been known to be wrong, as well. But with a quick nod, he left, his heart thudding. He had to tell her. *But how?*

CHAPTER TWELVE

"To hear this child tell about the thrashing he has received from a brutal master and the chains and weights he has carried in the field, is enough to make a man feel like it would be God's service to shoot them down like buzzards."

~A soldier of the 70ᵗʰ Indiana Infantry on story runaway slave told them.

THE BATH WAS LUXURIOUS. So much so Cerisa feared if she closed her eyes for too long, she'd wake to find it missing. Madame Nikki required hot soaks prior to the evening's entertainment, claiming she had a reputation to uphold regarding clean and healthy girls but the baths were not as hot nor alone. Plus, the assessment they all did on the others, vying to reach out for the most money in an evening, even if it meant stealing another's client for the night…She closed her eyes and sunk a little lower in the small brass tub, working furiously inside to forget that whorehouse in New York.

The warmth of the sun radiated in the room, making it far warmer, and a tad more friendly than New York had been—at any time. That hiccup in her thoughts turned to be Abraham. Her darling Abe. She closed her eyes tightly, fighting the tears that threatened to fall. The man had fled with her from her parents' home in Louisiana. Doing so made him a runaway slave, but he wouldn't let her flee into the night without his protection. They had grown up together and as children, played in the same fields until they were parted by their stations in life. She had kept him from the fields as long as she could, utilizing her position to assign him duties in the big house under her control, but it grew harder and harder to do.

But Abe knew one thing more than she did, something more dramatic and compelling than how to follow orders and remember his lot in life. When her family's deep dark secret burst out of the closets around her, drenching her in their wickedness, she panicked. How could her father and brothers condone this? And her mother? But the evidence was too plain to ignore. Her father and brothers were there, witnessing the act that degraded all just that much more. Overwhelmed by grief and despair, she threw some of her belongings into her satchel and ran.

The memory made her heart race and breathing difficult. Even sitting in the tin ware tub, the water cooling by the second, did not help her to relax. The intense desire to get out of it grew by the moment so she reached for the linen sheet and rose from the water, encasing herself in the material to dry. Trying to calm her erratic nerves, rationalizing to herself that that scene was from the past, over four years, before this war started. She grabbed her pantalets and chemise and started to dress when it hit her, she truly had nothing left to wear. The undergarments were in sufficient numbers, though she could tell this set was old and the cloth bare. Dresses, though, were another matter. She owned two and one was already fit for washing. Both were outdated. She cringed. At Madame Nikki's, Pierce had only seen her in the fancy lace underthings. That was unacceptable here.

With a frown, she pulled the dress over her head and began to button the bodice when she heard the twist of the room's door handle. It had to be Pierce, but regardless, she turned her back toward the entryway and called, "Who's there?"

She heard a chuckle. Pierce.

"'tis only I, my lady." He came up behind her and took her hand, spinning her on her heels right as she connected the last button. "You look stunning." He kissed the back of her hand.

She smiled but shook her head. "I doubt that."

He tipped her chin up. "Smile for me. Yes, like that. All will be well. I promise you."

With a slight twist, she freed herself from his grasp and took a step away. "What are we doing here?" The words sounded shaky to her ears and she sensed he'd take it bad.

He raised his brows in a look of surprise but controlled his facial expression other than that. "I needed to get you away from that position you had. You're too beautiful to be plying that trade. Men will push and can take out their weakness on the fairer sex, particularly ones they pay to play with. I could not see your beauty marred again. And I had the means to secure your release."

She bit her bottom lip, curtailing a stream of emotions that raced through her. His words moved her more than they should and while she was grateful to him, she couldn't stay. "Colonel, I appreciate what you've done. But if what you say is true, did you not buy me in your attempt to free me of selling myself? You paid good dollar, Yankee dollars, for a tainted, soiled woman. Despite my deep gratitude, is this not exactly what you Unionists are fighting against? Doesn't that make me a slave, in a matter of speaking, considering your transaction and now, bringing me here with you, sharing accommodations?"

As her words spilled out of her mouth, their meaning

surprised even her. She watched his expression and saw the storm clouds that filled his eyes along with the grit of his jawline.

"You know that was not my intention."

She tilted her head when he offered no more. "Know that I truly appreciate you being my white knight, but for what purpose?"

He closed his eyes tightly and ran his fingers through his hair.

Suddenly, she wanted to run her fingertips through his hair and then over the rest of him. The motion itself sent a tingle down from her shoulders and ignited a fire in her loins.

"I have made inquiries into your," he faltered. She knew he had a hard time with the title he was about to say. He grunted and continued. "Husband's whereabouts."

Inside her heart, a flare of pain and sorrow fought for control. Biting her lip, she waited.

"The outcome for the 54th at Fort Wagner isn't good. The whole attack strategy was a death sentence." His eyes softened. "I am sorry, Cerisa."

Tears pooled in her eyes but she refused to blink, which was hard. She clenched her fists and turned away from looking at him. Instead, she picked up the linen and shook it hard.

"So, have they found his body? As a widow, what means do I have?" Her heart stuttered. "I haven't enough for even widow's weeds," she whispered as her stomach twisted. She should've known the outcome wasn't going to be good. The paper's version of what happened alone was brutal to take. To hear it from Pierce only drove the nail into the coffin.

His sapphire blue eyes turned harsh and the look seemed to drill right into her soul.

"I will get you what you need."

The words were far from comforting in his tone but she still felt that he would take care of her. A shudder raced through her as ice spiraled down her spine. She gasped as if it finally stuck her in the gut. Abraham was gone. She knew that before but hope hadn't died. Now, coming from this man, it evaporated. As a cold air wrapped around her, she began to shake and she wrapped her arm around her middle.

He pulled her toward him and gave her a hug. There was a certain hesitancy in his motion, a stiffness in his arms, causing her to tense further, but once against his chest, she shivered as the tension seemed to wash away. His body seemed to relax also and the warmth from him encompassed her. It was a comfort and that support made her sight blurred as a sniffle escaped her lips.

"*Shhhh.*" He kissed the top of her head lightly. "Let it go. It will be all right."

The tears slowly dripped down her face, wetting the front of his shirt and waistcoat. It took a moment for her to realize that and she rubbed her cheeks to stop the flow. In response, he gave her his handkerchief.

"Thank you." She dabbed her cheeks and straightened her shoulders, lifting her chin, pasting a smile on her face. "I appreciate you for helping me."

He returned her smile, but it was bigger and deep. "Let us go and get supper. I know a great restaurant we can go to. It is also a place we can talk."

She didn't necessarily feel like stepping out. She was sure her face was marred with her tears and heated cheeks. Dressed in an old dress, she looked as she felt, miserable, and her manners in polite society no doubt rusty. But he looked so sincere, she couldn't turn him down. Forcing a smile onto her lips, she put her hand in his offered one and let him lead her away.

Pierce couldn't take the pain he saw so clearly in her eyes. He'd do whatever it'd take to make her smile. Once, he caught a glimpse of it and it took his breath away. He knew it would take a lot to correct all she'd endured, all the heartache, to make those lips curl upwards again but it was a goal he'd make, he swore. One step toward that end was dinner and that would be one at a nice place. Anything to erase the memory of the grit and grime of the New York Five Points and that whorehouse.

Sitting in the armchair, near the fireplace, he took a sip out of his whiskey glass as memories of the evening played in his head. She had been stiff, for lack of a better phrase. As if the simple act of going out to eat was foreign to her. He'd bet more like a distant memory, because once at Gerard's, as they sat at the table and looked at the menu, he saw her easing, as if testing the waters of social graces. Her manners were impeccable, no doubt ingrained as his were from growing up in a proper house. An odd thought, he mused, but living in the lower areas had made her box up polite society in order to survive.

The truth was, he admired her. She was beauty and grace, forced to endure hardships he knew most ladies he was acquainted with would find beyond their capabilities. Except for Margaret. She knew those hardships, as the Irish were pushed down, yet they kept moving forward, settling in a land that despised their presence, lumping them all as drunkards and papists. He bit back a smile. Margaret had more grit than the upper crust of New York. From what he could tell, Cerisa was of the same make.

Her Southern accent, more French creole style than straight

Southern he determined from traveling there before the war, played in her speech and at first, the wait staff here and at Gerard's had a flash of surprise that they all quickly washed when he glared at them. Nothing like his Federal uniform to persuade them that any doubts of her were unfounded.

Yet when they returned after dinner, she was apprehensive. So was he, he admitted to himself. He had whisked her away from Madame Nikki's and her place of bought flesh, only to bring her here, to a hotel room shared with him without the monetary exchange. The air became thick as they busied themselves in the room, as if trying to find some common ground. It was obvious she was apprehensive that he'd demand sex from her in exchange for her freedom. That latter thought sent a pang of anger and sympathy down his spine and irritated, he'd turned and left her for a drink at the bar in the lounge. The look of surprise, a mixture of relief and shock drove him out of the room, slamming the door shut behind him.

The lounge below was filled with politicians and war hotheads. He downed two whiskeys rather quickly, his gaze darting about the room, as if anticipating his father's arrival, and the need to return to the room. Margaret's voice inside his head told him to make sure Cerisa was okay, or perhaps that's what he imagined, but whatever the case was, he bolted up the stairs to their room and quietly snuck in. And, here in the dark, he sat with his glass of whiskey, studying her as she slept. She looked like an angel and a seductress all wrapped in one. He wanted to protect her and to make love to her. The two images seemed to fit and yet be at cross-purposes, perhaps the reason he couldn't sleep.

He was set to leave for the Army of Tennessee and report to Rosecrans. It left him but only two days to arrange his travel and to find a place for her with arrangements to pay for it. Was it enough time?

The angel stirred and he refocused on her. She turned and opened her eyes to find him. He caught a whisper of a smile as she sat up, stretched and threw her long legs over the side of the bed. Her nightgown inched its way down as she stood, hiding those luscious limbs. He tightened, his blood starting to boil.

Temptation…

Cerisa wasn't sure what woke her but once she turned in the empty bed, a part of her felt incomplete without Pierce next to her. It was an odd longing, no doubt pushed by being in a strange place without any semblance of what her life had become except for him. When she rolled over, she opened her eyes and found him, sitting there with a drink in his hand, watching her. She couldn't help but smile. It'd been so long since she'd seen anything as peaceful. Not demanding like Madame Nikki's. If nothing else, he kind of looked like a kid caught taking a pie off the windowsill. Unable to stop a grin herself, she stood and padded over to him, well aware that his eyes were fixated on her naked shins when she put her legs over the side of the bed.

With a grin, she bent over and kissed him. It wasn't a chaste kiss but one she beckoned for him to respond to. Her lips pressed against his and with the slightest hint of temptation, she traced the seam between his, tasting the liquor that coated them. He took the hint and kissed her deep, sending a thrill through her body. The real taste of him, laced with the whiskey, was an enticing aroma, very masculine and smooth like the liquor. With a deep groan that she felt vibrate through him and into her, he wrapped his arms around her as he stood.

This man had saved her, on more than one occasion, and now she relished being in his arms. Without a corset on, she could mold against him, every muscle of his chest and stomach burning a trace into her skin. She pushed a little harder against his rock-hard chest, her hips and thighs meeting his with only the thin lawn fabric of her gown and the wool of his trousers between them. At the apex of her thighs, she cradled his hardened member. His reaction to her made him devour her and she melted.

He scooped her up into his arms and at first, just held her. His arms were muscular and the tendons flexed under her weight. He stared into her eyes. She noticed his were dark and the hunger was evident, but so was the hint of hesitation. Deep inside her, a longing grew, one that made her tongue lick her upper lip. The move she hadn't really realized she'd done but it prompted a flicker in his eyes.

"Back to bed," he growled and he carried her straight to the bed she'd just crawled out of.

As he laid her on the mattress and stepped back, she tensed for a second, feeling more vulnerable than she had in ages. The look of a lion about to take his mate never left his face and that reassured her he still wanted her. The other let her know all of him was in tune with her. She got on her knees and began to unbutton the two buttons at the top of his shirt and slowly pulled its tails out of his pants and raised them up, over his shoulders and head to be flipped to the side. The result was the exposure of his corded abdomen and chiseled chest. His chest held a slight dusting of dark curls and she ran her fingers through the strands, reveling in their softness.

As she played, he grabbed the sides of her gown and pulled, making her wiggle off her knees a tad to free the material and stopped her fingers from roaming when he pulled it off over her head, tossing it to the floor. She was naked before him and a nervous streak sent a cool shot down her spine. Here, all was different. It was simply them, without money exchanged. It was true passion.

He put his finger under her chin and lifted it up so she could see his face.

"It is just you and me."

She swallowed the knot in her throat. Her mouth was dry and the fire burned low in her abdomen. She gave him a slight nod—it was all she could do.

He didn't smile but instead, bent over and kissed her. The invasion of her mouth was hard and deep, as he took possession of her lips. His hands went to her sides and lifted her off her knees as he joined her on the bed, all without breaking the kiss. Gently, he lowered them to the mattress and pulled her close.

It was luxurious to be next to him. He was warm and hard and demanding yet teased her with his devouring kiss. The flutter touch of his fingers across her naked body was so tempting. As she tried to return the favor of caressing him, the lower she went, she ran into a barrier of his pants. Tracing his waistband, she found the button closure and tugged, freeing it. There was a grunt from him as he twisted his hips and aided her in removing them.

She marveled at the sight of him. Pierce was a man accustomed to riding and being physical, as his lean, hard body revealed., of how she imagined Apollo and other ancient Greek gods would be. It truly was amazing that when he held her, she was comfortable at all but there was a gentleness to him that surprised her. She started to explore the contours of him, her lips following her fingertips, even as she traveled lower.

"Be careful, darling," he warned huskily.

She gave him a short gaze upward and smiled before she continued. She truly wanted to please him, this man who had saved her, though that wasn't the only reason. Her own body craved his touch.

Suddenly, his fingers which he had laced through her hair, locked tight and tilted her back to the mattress, twisting her so she beneath him as he wiggled between her thighs.

The fire within her, the one that opened her and made her almost desperate for him, grew out of control. She couldn't breath or say a word but her body pleaded with him to take her now!

Pierce watched her. She was withering beneath him. He could smell her musk, tasted her essence and the pleading look in her eyes made him joyous. When she mewled to his touch, he blew the devil aside.

"You are mine," he stated and slid into her.

She moaned as she tilted her hips to be able to take him all inside her. Her sheath welcomed every inch and he joined her in the moan, never realizing just how badly he needed her. When she tightened around him, he plunged forward, relishing in the connection and longing for more.

Slowly, he rocked his hips with each thrust, her meeting his rhythm.

The tempo increased. She groaned and he realized he loved that. As he pressed further, he began to lose himself. He couldn't move as the stars exploded before his eyes. It was marvelous as the fire burned like a firecracker and in the end, he felt complete.

As they both gulped for air, the guilt slammed into him

like a cannonball. He was a widower. And she a widow. By societal rules, he should be taking another wife by now, but for a woman, mourning was longer. He stifled the groan that threatened, but he was a wretch for taking her. The only way he could rest was to try to put it all into perspective. He posed them as married to protect her. Now, he had to protect her from himself. *Damn!*

CHAPTER THIRTEEN

"I don't feel like dying yet."
—General Chatham Roberdeau "Rob" Wheat to his surgeon at First Manassas 1861, after he was seriously wounded at the battlefront.

SLOWLY SHE STIRRED THE black liquid, steam raising off the top. Despite the fact they sat at the hotel's restaurant for breakfast, a room filled with people and the aroma of edible delights that made her stomach rumble, Cerisa was anything but relaxed. She should be enjoying this, sitting in a nice place, ordering food, most of which she hadn't tasted in years, and enjoying a true cup of coffee, but her nerves were still rattled over last night.

Pierce had made love to her. She hadn't felt compelled to please him for fear he'd complain to Madame Nikki about her or worse, strike her for not making him moan. No, instead she wanted him. And that made her curse herself, for that was not a nice way to think when Abraham was gone. But the voice in the back of her head reminded her how Abraham would not frown. He had remarked that 'that soldier' watched her and how he'd be a better match for her. Despite her denying that, Abraham always seem to understand the situation and reminded her that married to a white man would be safer for her.

Oh, how her head pounded.

"Are you all right?"

She glanced up at him. Pierce sat across the table, a frown on his face. She painted a smile on her lips. "Yes, apologies. It's been ages since I've had such niceties and I do not want to disappoint you with some ill-forgotten manners."

He smiled as he took her hand. "You'll be fine. I promise. Besides," his gaze darted around the room. "Most of these people have their own business they're worried about. Washington and her politics often breed not only contempt but all self-centeredness." He winked as he took a sip of his own coffee.

Her grin turned real at his very suggestion. As she took the coffee cup to her lips, the hot drink poured easily down her throat and she relished in it.

"I take it Madame Nikki's coffee was not of par?"

She laughed. "By the time I awoke, what little was served was long gone."

His brows furrowed and she took another sip, trying not to squirm. That casual and honest answer spoke volumes, of which he'd no doubt interpret as she entertained clients so late, she slept all morning. It was her own disappointment of her situation that kept her in bed with only sheer survival peeling her off the sheets.

"I have a surprise for you."

That caught her off guard. "Truly? What?" There was an edge of excitement in her voice. At least, she believed it was and not fear.

Pierce nodded. "I've arranged for one of the dressmakers to stop by and take your measurements to have a new wardrobe made."

She quickly withdrew her hand from his grasp. The knot in her throat was growing. So he had noticed the frayed hemline, battered lace and backdated dress she was wearing and despite his politeness, it had bothered him.

"That is most kind of you, but truly unnecessary."

"No, I insist. I want you to have it." He took her hand again and squeezed. "I have the rest of the money owed to you by Madame Nikki. I do not want you to use it for clothes and other necessities but for other things you might enjoy. The wardrobe will be a gift."

A flutter curled down her spine. "I thank you for retrieving that. She kept that under lock and key—extremely frustrating, since she said it was to keep us from vice and some of the ladies did have some, in liquor or other methods." She shuddered. The use of laudanum, to hide the pains of rudeful men, or the pain of ending an unwanted pregnancy, and so much more, was extensive. It was enough to keep her from using it after that client abused her, despite the urging of the other girls.

"But I still prefer to purchase my own gowns."

Pierce gave her a sympathetic look. "It is better to accept a gift, my dear, than refuse. Particularly in this case."

It took her a moment to grasp his meaning. The sum lacked enough for such a venture. She murmured a quiet *Oh* and took another sip of her coffee, hoping to hide the sudden abyss that threatened to take over, curving her lips downward and causing her vision to blur. Yet that made another emotional thread start inside her, one that she hadn't heard from in too long a time—anger. Anger at being caught like this, penniless. After all, she was a Fontaine, of a long-established family, well respected. She would not let this set her back! It would take time, though, for her to rediscover her footing, even if that meant the last thing she wanted and that was to return home.

Pierce recalled breakfast and even now, at the mid-afternoon on a busy Thursday, he again thanked God for surviving. Cerisa was a temptress. He knew that and last night was a prime example of how dangerous she was to him, for he had only planned to unwind, watching her sleep before hitting the pillow himself. But when she woke from slumber and stretched, the moment her legs went over the bedside and he saw her dainty feet and shapely ankles and calves, his whole body seemed to wake, sending heat unfurling through him and pooling in his loins. The firelight only added to the flames for the sheer lawn nightgown she wore hid nothing in its light. She was a siren sent to break the hard shell he had made around him, to not be taken so easily by a pretty woman. Despite everything, he was returning to the war, where his life, along with all the soldiers, was in jeopardy, so another relationship was iffy.

"Sir."

He glanced up and found his clerk standing before him with an envelop in his hand. Pierce read it was from the War Department and thankfully not his father. He hoped to escape the city long before that man tried to pressure him again to lead a Colored regiment.

"Well, do you want the good or the bad, first?"

Pierce glanced up and found First Lieutenant Jordan leaning in his doorway, a half-cocked grin on the man's face. With a deep sigh, he motioned the man in and to the chair before his desk.

"What did you find for me?"

Jordan fell into the leather padded chair and gave him a comical look. "As you might guess, most of the boarding houses here are filled. Busy city. But think there's one, east side, which might accommodate. Owner demands interviewing you two."

Pierce frowned. "I've no time for this. I must leave with the 22nd day after tomorrow."

Jordan shrugged. "She ain't takin' my word about your missus or finances. Done all I could do, outside filling your orders for the army."

He pinched the bridge of his nose, disgusted. "What type of establishment is this?"

"Looks pretty fancy, to me, but then, I know nothing about boarding houses. Considering, sir, I ain't married."

East side of the city, farther than the respectable part of town he wanted. He wouldn't leave her any place that wasn't safe. "No place else?"

"No, sir. Not till maybe spring time, when most of these warbirds fly home for the summer."

He threw his orders down in frustration and ran his fingers through his hair as he stood and stared out the dirty window onto the streets of Washington. "Thank you, Lt. Jordan. I've pulled you too far away from your duties for this errand. Please leave the address of the house and I'll see to the owner."

There was a pause when Jordan didn't leave right away, and Pierce turned, his eyebrow raised in question.

"Well, sir, if I can be frank here, you could take her with you, you being an officer and all, rather than leave her to this muck and mire. Word is, streets out there are turning into a brutal lot, the longer this war rages. And if word leaked on her previous association…" he left the sentence hang and he shrugged.

Pierce's temper began to broil. He'd sent this clerk on two errands. One was a boarding house for Cerisa and the other was to double check on the 54th Massachusetts casualty count. If he could offer her any glimmer of hope, any better clarity on her man, he would but calling her the wife of such was still difficult. Especially after last night. He'd claimed her for his own when he took her but to be sure, he wanted to know for certain he didn't face a ghost.

"I do believe you reported no findings on survivors of the Fort Wagner's assault."

"Yes sir, last report I read."

He exhaled, trying to school his thoughts. With the administration as it sat, getting her his pension would be nigh on impossible as marriage between blacks and whites was frowned on or even outlawed and most certainly ignored, despite the legality issue. She'd be left penniless again. His ground his teeth. There was no way he'd allow her to fall back into the clutches of a lady of the night.

"Thank you, Lieutenant. That is all."

Cerisa would need him and he would not fail her!

"Thank you." Cerisa handed the hotel restaurant's waiter coins for her tea and pastry. It was a decadent moment, ordering something so lush when she knew the money could be used for something more important…she stopped her thoughts. Pierce had told her to indulge herself with some of the amenities of the hotel, like the hot bath with scented oils this morning and the tea this afternoon. So she sat back after stirring the sugar—true, refined sugar, something she hadn't seen in years—in her tea cup and taking a sip.

Casually, she glanced about the room. There were but three other ladies, two sitting at a table and one with a gentleman off to the left. Other tables that had occupants were men. She settled into the surroundings, relaxing and for once, no longer feeling as if scrutinized by hooligans when she was with Abraham or by men looking to buy her services for the night. It was an uplifting emotion and she closed her eyes to let it settle as she took another sip of the tea.

Unfortunately, the bliss didn't last long. She opened her eyes with an edginess that she couldn't place. She shivered and took a sip of the cooling tea to try to settle her nerves and found trying to keep the cup steady was difficult. Looking over the brim of her cup, she found the two men across the room staring at her. The intensity of their glare and the slight smile they gave her made her squirm, making her uncomfortable. Her skin crawled. How did they know she had been a whore? Was there a sign on her head that pointed to her and sex on demand? Or the way she carried herself? Discouraged, she focused on her plate on the table and silently prayed they'd go away and leave her alone.

Then she caught the women. One was openly glaring at her, as if accusing her of vile behavior. Between them and the men's leery smiles, she began to feel like she was suffocating. She frowned and tried to swallow, but the lump in her throat was lodged in place. It was a panicking moment, as if the whole world judged her as wanton. Her past crept up and began to encircle her. She needed to get out of here. Where was Pierce now?

"Mrs. Duval, are you all right?"

The voice startled her and all of the haunting images faded as she re-focused and tried to concentrate on the question. She glanced up and found the front desk clerk above her, a worried frown on his forehead. He was a like a beacon for calmer waters and she found she could now breath.

With a swallow of that worrisome lump in her throat, she nodded. "Yes, Frank, thank you." She prayed she got his name correct. "Has my husband, by chance, sent word?"

"No, ma'am."

She tried to smile. "Thank you again."

He nodded and left.

Breathing easier, she took a sip and decided to look out the window and away from the troubling guests. But it was in the moment of what she thought was a momentary escape of her past, as she looked at the scenery, that she missed the man coming to her table. There was a click on the wooden tabletop that startled her. She glanced down at the object and bit her tongue—it was a brass key. And standing next to her was a tall, dark haired man, one of the two from the table across the way. He smiled at her but it was the dark, blatant hunger in his eyes that made her heart sink.

"I'm in room 12, if you so desire." He gave a slight nod and left.

It took everything she had not to scream.

CHAPTER FOURTEEN

"I am tired and sick of war. Its glory is all moonshine. It is only those who have neither fired a shot nor heard the shrieks and groans of the wounded who cry aloud for blood, for vengeance, for desolation. War is hell."

— William Tecumseh Sherman

SENATOR DUVAL THREW HIS pen across his desk, any sound muffled by the stack of papers that never seemed to diminish. He shook his head and pulled at the collar that seemed to tighten around his neck.

"Bobby, where is the latest on Fort Wagner's casualties?"

His law clerk peaked around the doorway. "The third pile to your right, senator."

"Ah, yes, I see." He picked up the report. The Colored troops had been devastated by the attack of a fort that sat uphill on a beachfront. Despite the bomb blasts of cannon fire from the land and ships, the fort still remained in Confederate hands and a frontal assault, led by the Colored 54th Massachusetts, had met deadly blows. The smile couldn't escape Duval's lips, for that bold move by that unit had escalated Congress's growing approval of Colored troops and using them as a true fighting force and not as laborers for the army. Granted, the white officers of that famed unit had demanded their troops equal pay to white troops and that had hit a wall in Congress, for the bulk still viewed blacks as under whites, yet they also threw the Irish in that pool of lower equality as well, though Duval knew the Irish raised Union troops also faired as well as the whites did. Still, if he could get those last couple of diehards to push the pay to forever equal the whites, then the ranks would swell and this war would be done.

Duval sat back in his leather chair and despite the heat sweltering in his office, pouring in through the open windows from the better part of Washington, he felt an innate pride. He had seen the errors of the slavery system when he was young, spending winters in the Tidewater area with his uncle. Those poor wretches, working the fields for cotton, looking haggard and lean, made a lasting impression on the young Yankee. He had witnessed the whipping one young hand received for supposedly breaking a rake to avoid work and that had ripped his soul to the marrow, making him vow to work against this peculiar institution, as the Southerners referred to it. It went against God's will, as far as Duval was concerned.

Granted, he considered the Irish not much above that and any papists of similar note. How his son had become so involved in that was beyond his understanding. Thank heavens, that Irish harlot and her papist propaganda was gone. Now if he could just get Pierce to get beyond his grief, and to Duval, a way to re-learn his son was to get him involved with the Colored troops. The normal army was too encumbered with officers that simply didn't leave or die for the underlings to advance and many saw the Colored troops as a quick way to move up, but Pierce fought him at every angle in this regard. Why, eluded him.

His inner thoughts stopped abruptly by his clerk, Norman, who raced into the office and skidded to a halt at the desk.

"Your son is here, Senator! In Washington!"

"Pierce?"

"Yes sir!"

Duval frowned, pleased and yet surprised. "Where is he?" Great news, he thought. He could press the boy for field command instead of returning to a regiment stuck in the mire of the West, for he had seen the upcoming lists of troops and knew he'd been assigned to Tennessee. The glory of service would be here, in the East, where the true battles took place.

"He's at Jefferson Hotel." The clerk leaned forward. "He's rooming with a woman, so the word goes."

Senator Duval's thoughts came to a scattering halt. "A woman? Who?"

His aide gave a snide smile. "Said she's his wife, though rumor has it she may be nothing other than a mistress he dragged with him."

That would not go well with the future he had designed for his son. He didn't need to sully his reputation when he ran for office later. Duval tapped his desktop with his writing instrument, trying to decide his course of action.

Pierce put the key into the door slot and twisted it, with the tumbling of the lock following. With a push, he opened the door. "Cerisa," he called.

He heard a slosh of water coming from the bedroom and he strode through the sitting room to find her. The moment he entered the room, he discovered the slip of the girl dripping in water, clenching the linen sheet tightly around her. The look of surprise was on her face.

"I apologize," he started in an attempt to calm the frightened deer before him. "I did not know you chose to bathe in the middle of the day."

She went to the three-panel partition in the corner, picking up a dress on her way. "I felt the need to wash the stench of my past from me, after the afternoon I had."

He stood, mesmerized, as she tossed the towel over the partition. What he wouldn't give to be able to see through the curtained inserts of the panel, he thought, as his body tightened, his thoughts swirling, craving more until her words registered in his head.

"What happened today to prompt such action?" He did his best to concentrate on what she said and not what his primitive self wanted.

"I was a fool to believe that my past would not come back to haunt me." The words were edged in pain that even he could hear. "I decided to have a tea below and try to relax but found the sitting room filled with people who noticed me."

Still struggling to control the lust that boiled inside, he frowned. "Of course. Who wouldn't notice a lovely lady like yourself?"

She peered around the panel and glared at him. "That wasn't the impression I took. No, they appeared to know what I had done."

He still wasn't following her and now, as he devoured the sight of her as she emerged from behind the screen, his libido took a hit as she was now fully dressed. She whizzed past him to the vanity where she took a seat and picked up the hairbrush, stroking her hair. Her chestnut hair glowed by the sunlight streaming through the window, mesmerizing him but he couldn't help but notice the violent motion of her hands. It was like she attacked her hair out of sheer frustration. Why?

"Tell me what happened."

Her hand slowed as she bit her lower lip.

"I had two gentlemen give me the look I used to receive when I was under Madame Nikki's tutelage. One," she swallowed. "Even left his room key on my table with his room number."

Instantly, Pierce's temper ignited. "He did what?!"

She rolled her lips inward and her cheeks blushed with a nod.

"How dare he! What was the room? I will go and correct his insolence!" His anger rolled through him as he stormed to the door. He'd throttle the man!

"Pierce, please, stop."

He did but spun. "Why? He insulted my wife, my family and his own!"

"But I'm not your wife. I had been a whore. He just saw through the disguise." She shrugged but he saw her tremble. He'd give anything to make her not but she wasn't helping it by withholding information on this vermin.

"Then you must marry me and truly carry my name and that of my family."

She gave him a sorrowful look. "No. This is not a good reason to be burdened with me."

Within a second, he was at her feet and took her hands into his. "You are not a burden. You are a treasure."

That made her smile a little. What he wouldn't give to broaden that more. But she hadn't spilled it all, he reckoned, so he pushed. "Is that all?"

She shuddered but shook her head. "A pair of ladies looked at me as if I was a slattern, barging into polite society." She gave a harsh, short laugh. "I've been part of that society. Those looks can be more damaging than a man's inappropriate proposition."

Pierce stood and ran his fingers through his hair as he

began to pace. Apparently, to leave her here was not a good idea, for if casual guests in a hotel took one look at her and pursued her as wanton woman, how would she fair without him here to protect her? He growled. And the interview at the boarding house wasn't any better. The charming Mrs. Culpepper seemed pleased at his inquiry until he explained the room was for his new wife while he returned to the war.

"A new bride? Colonel, congratulations!" Mrs. Culpepper smiled, making her stony, upright frame, the type of build he'd witnessed most of his life by the upper society of New York wear. The snotty posture, he used to sneer in a whisper when he pointed them out to Margaret, with their noses pointed so high in the air, made them the most unbearable of ladies to be around. So to find the same creatures here in the capital did not surprise him.

"Thank you, Mrs. Culpepper. But the War Department demands my return, so I fear I must return to the front, making my concern for my wife of high importance." He spoke the truth. The need to protect Cerisa ate at his gut, more so since last night...

"But of course." The woman nodded. "Yet I fail to understand why you do not send her back to your home. New York City, if I heard you correctly? Surely, it'd be a better place than here, in all the muck and mire of politics." She paused. "And if I may, are you not the son of Senator Duval? I'm willing to wager he'd agree..."

That comment caused his stomach to flip. Of course, she was right and had this been Margaret, he would have thought the same. Though, at the mention of his father's name, his ancestral home was no better than a snake pit when it came to anything not fitting their approval, like an Irish Catholic wife. He bit back the memory and pushed his thoughts back to today. He forced a smile.

"Ever so true, Mrs. Culpepper, but I feel the need to chaperone her there and the army will not grant me leave so I must find another way." He swept his arm across the room before him. "My clerk

found your place of high note, and with my father in residence for Congressional session, I believe I have what I need for my new bride."

The landlady actually blushed, though he bet it was an art form she had mastered when needed, like now.

"I would be honored, then, Colonel, to have Mrs. Duval stay with us." She went to her ledger and opened it, grabbing a pencil and began to write. "Tell me, is Mrs. Duval of New York as well? Or perhaps Washington?"

Her question caught him off guard. Instantly, Cerisa's lyrical Southern accent echoed in his head. Did he tell Mrs. Culpepper of her true home? Part of him told him not to but he also knew the moment Cerisa spoke, the proverbial cat would be out of the bag.

"No, ma'am." He steeled himself, though kept the grin. "She is from Louisiana."

The woman's mouth dropped open in a state of shock. "You married a rebel lady?"

The worried look on Cerisa's face answered all his questions. Especially since Mrs. Culpepper's demeanor changed to one of righteous attitude, informing him that she'd have no slave owner in her house. That raised a thought in his own mind, that he missed ever hearing of Cerisa's past and if she had ever owned a slave. He figured she must have, considering the darky she was 'married' to, yet he wasn't sure.

Now was not the time to ask, from appearance sake…She looked too shaken by the incident.

"Who was this cad? For I shall promptly put him in his place."

She swallowed and slid a piece of paper his direction with the number 12 on it. "His room number, or so the key flop read."

He picked it up, crumpling it in his hand as he spun to the door. "I shall have a conversation with this man. Remain here. I shall return shortly." And with that, he left, well aware the Jefferson housed dignitaries, politicians and military officers. With his upbringing, he knew a slew of these types and how they always figured they were right and so privileged to do what they wanted. What he prayed was it wasn't anyone he knew, for this required he'd be the answer for any insult to Cerisa. And if the culprit was his father, he'd kill him.

The door slammed and that noise seemed to break through Cerisa's befuddled thinking, snapping her back to what had just occurred. Instantly, she thought to leap up and stop him but another voice inside her told her to stay and let the Colonel fix this. Her whole body felt on fire and her mind was still fuzzy but as she sat at the vanity, she found herself in the looking glass and thought how odd she looked. Like a ghost, even through the marred glass, she assessed she looked too pale, too thin and not herself. What had happened to the Cerisa Fontaine Walker she knew?

Reality was, she could dig and discover that woman, who'd shown such fortitude to survive her family, to survive her and Abraham's trek north, to survive the ridicule of being part of the lower class to be able to stay with the man she'd turned to love, only to let the world consume her. The result of that was evident in today's circumstance. She'd allowed her inner self-doubt, her fear of the unknown, to make her vulnerable to outsiders, particularly men. Pierce had saved her from falling further down the rabbit hole of whoredom but keeping her with him, under this pretense of this false marriage, just allowed another man to control her.

As she sat there contemplating her fate, she noticed a

twinkle in her eyes that wasn't there a moment ago. She straightened, her shoulders level, her chin higher. If Abraham was here, he would have smiled. He loved her, that she was sure. Not just for letting him escape with her, and not for freeing him or even marrying him but because he believed in her. She'd make him happier yet. For it was time to flee this Yankee invested part of the country. It was time to head home and face the demons, because there was family and families stayed together. Life without him made being up here dangerous for a widow hailing from the South. Absolutely, she had to go.

The war. It would be more hazardous now than running north had been. Pierce was her key to safety. She'd play the game of his wife. It wouldn't be a hard role. He was handsome and debonair and she suspected, not one to always follow the rules. He had saved her from having to sell her soul for money. Now, she'd have to convince him to take her home.

With a smile, she found herself....

CHAPTER FIFTEEN

"The fact that one army was fighting for union and the other for disunion is a political expression; the actual fact on the battlefield, in the face of cannon and musket, was that Federal troops came as invaders, and the Southern troops stood as defenders of their homes, and further than this we need not go."

—Pierre Gustave Toutant Beauregard, Confederate General

PIERCE SHIFTED IN HIS seat, subconsciously pulling his frockcoat straight and once he realized what he was doing, he stopped and promptly put his hand down. As subtly as he believed he could, he glanced at Cerisa, who sat across the table from him. He couldn't help but drink in her beauty. He swore she even ate gracefully. Her neck was arched, her shoulders slightly rounded and her porcelain skin glowed in the oil light from the chandelier above them. A sudden thought raced through his mind that she might be his undoing.

She glanced up at him, a quizzical look in her gorgeous amber colored eyes that made the fire inside his veins flare. What he wouldn't give to sweep her up into his arms and promise her the world.

"One wonders what is running through your thoughts," she commented, her lips curving with a smile. She looked delicious. The drop of sauce that perched on her bottom lip made his hunger roar.

He chuckled, finding himself uncomfortable. In an attempt to curb his libido, one that seemed so ill-fitting considering her past and how the thought of seducing her, which was strong, needed to be culled. Some protector he'd be, if he let it go rampant. He coughed to clear his dry throat. "Just admiring your beauty, my dear."

Her eyes narrowed. "And did you find that vermin that abused me?"

The anger for that incident kindled. "Yes. He has been duly corrected." He'd go no further. He'd found the culprit, sitting in the lounge near the stairs. The words he used made his point clear—if the man approached her again, or if any of his companions did, Pierce would send them to the dark hell of the battlefield and face death on a face-to-face encounter. The man was a politician to the core and retreated, vowing he knew of no woman.

"You appear unscathed from the interview," she remarked with a lilt to it, as if making it a question.

"Scalawags like him are easily set on a correct path." He chewed another bite though the beef held no taste since his distraction had waned. Considering the price of this meal, that irritated him. It would be one of the last civilized meals he'd have, since his departure was imminent. He swallowed hard and pushed his mind forward.

"So, Cerisa, I have to report back to the war, as you know." He paused to take a sip of his wine, trying to figure out how to put this without causing a scene. "Yet, I have a dilemma on my hands."

She paused with her fork in hand, a tiny morsel of meat in its prongs. With her gaze locked on him, she showed no emotion other than attentiveness as she guided the tool toward her mouth. Slowly, daintily, she pulled the morsel into her mouth in the slowest, most seductive way he could imagine, causing his discomfort level to heighten. *Damn!*

"What pray tell might that be?"

He swallowed hard. "You."

Her eyes widened. "Me?"

"Yes. What to do with you? I have given this much thought of late. Perhaps my white knight in rescuing you might have been a bit much, though I simply could not leave you to the fate of staying in the house of ill-repute much longer. The mere thoughts of another man striking you or, or, anything else." The words seemed to jumble. It was not the place to say the thought of another man taking her filled him with rage. "I have taken an advantage by introducing you as my wife here and at command, hence now I must find a safe place for you—"

"Worry no more," she stated plainly. "I have my own plans in case this occurred."

He raised an eyebrow in an unspoken question.

"I will go home."

Curious and immediately livid, for heading anywhere south was dangerous at best, he spat, "And how do you intend on doing that, during war?"

She flinched at his tone but quickly her eyes turned hard. "By whatever means I can."

Instantly, images of her at Madame Nikki's, of her lying on a bed, her legs parted, shot through his mind and his hand clenched his wine glass. "No."

Strangely, she looked relaxed as she took a sip of her own wine. "I beg to differ."

"You are my wife!"

"In ruse only!" she shot back. "You have no hold over me."

Pierce bit his tongue, darting a glance about the restaurant to see if they had been heard. The tone was tense but from what he could tell, no one appeared to notice. His own blood raced, appalled that she would fight him on this but she was right.

With a set determination, he lowered his voice. "That we must correct."

"*Harrumph.*" She straightened. "I am a married woman."

At that, he gave her a slanted look. "Ma'am, I do believe you are a widow. And a lady needing protection."

Her lips tightened. "And you're the man to take care of me? A Yankee? You'd take vows with a Southerner? A 'Secesh'? A whore?"

"Don't talk like that," he growled.

She leaned forward, a glint to her eyes. It threw his thinking off balance. Was she now cajoling him or angry, or worse, both?

"Why? Because I'm all that."

"You are not a whore," were the first words that stumbled out of his mouth before he could catch himself.

She laughed. It was a hollow sound. "That would be nice to hear, if it wasn't the truth."

He reached and took her hand in his. "Marry me. Let my name protect you."

A frown marred her face. "Would your family appreciate my addition? I am the enemy on many fronts to a Northerner."

"Cerisa, please," he begged. This was getting exasperating. The pressure of time was weighing on him. He had to return to the war but he had to get her situated before he left. "Darling, according to all reports, your," his voice stuttered, "husband did not survive the attack on Fort Wagner. He died an honorable death, waging war on the side of the Federal army. But, considering the circumstances, the possibility of you receiving a widow's pension are little to none, since your marriage was not legal, according to the laws of the land."

She opened her mouth to object but he raised his hand to stop her.

"No, hear me out. You know this as well as I. I've made inquiries but so far, you will gain nothing. Now, I have to return to the battle lines, but I won't leave you alone in this muck and mire of Washington."

Her lips thinned and he witnessed the blood draining from her face. "You'd marry me but leave me? How much better is that?"

He bit his lower lip, frustration rising. "With my family's name, you'd be respected and in an honorable position. I have found a boarding house you can reside at, unless you wanted to return to New York and await my return with my family." Even that made him cringe, but he fought to retain a stoic face.

Her gaze widened. "A boarding house? Here? In Washington? No. You will not leave me in this vile place. Name or not, men will seek distraction at any cost, and in this asylum for lunatics, who wage war, plundering their kinsman's land, what makes you think your name and wages can keep some sorry excuse of a man from thinking I'm a lonely bride needing to be fulfilled?" The look in her eyes showed him blood, as the hatred against men seemed to gain hold of her. "And no, I will not return to that cesspit of New York."

He took a glance at his plate, realizing he had absently shoved the peas on his plate around in a circle as she spoke. No, he could understand her contempt for the North and New York in particular.

"I want to return home."

His head snapped up. "Home? As in the South?"

She raised her chin, determination written across her face. "Yes. To Bellefontaine, in Louis'ana." Her southern drawl curled around the state's name with a lilt that mesmerized him.

The realization of her conviction and the location hit him with a full force. "There's a war! I can't allow it!"

"Again, you do not own me," she stated quietly yet firmly. "Without Abraham, I am at a loss. Even if I allow myself to marry you, you too shall return to the beast that devoured him and once more, I am alone. No, I need the comfort of my family, despite our past."

That was something he didn't know—whatever had happened that pushed her to run away with a slave. Whatever it was, it had kept her in the poorest area of New York, so it had to be big because what he had discovered was her family held a fortune. Her father's name was prominent in the Confederate government and Jefferson Davis had not filled his government with poor men.

"I still offer the protection of my family name and my body, because nowhere does a woman alone fend well."

He caught the twitch in her cheek as the realization stuck home. Her silence, measured with the darkening of her eyes, gave hint she was weighing the proposal. Of course, he was right and he knew she had no choice but to realize that. She paused before inhaling and sitting straight.

"Then I will accept your proposal."

All at once, he smiled. He was elated and doomed.

Had she just agreed to marry him? Inside, her stomach flipped. What was she doing? Here sat another man, he claimed for her protection, but what did he want in return?

"I'll talk to the priest tomorrow. Perhaps a quick exchange of vows can be arranged—" The rest of his words faded to the buzzing in her ears.

"I see." She cringed. It was like she was a task to accomplish, like packing his uniforms, instead of a mate to join in wedlock. That rubbed her wrong.

Quickly, he took her hands in his, a stricken look on his face. "Cerisa, please. I promise with all my soul to take care of you."

Take care of her. The comfort those words should have held now made her want to shudder. She stared at him, trying to figure his motives out. He had saved her from selling herself to other men but was he now claiming exclusive rights strictly for the bedroom? And was that a bad thing? Had being at Madame Nikki's slanted her view on men? His gaze reflected a begging glance, as if he was trying sincerely to convince her he wasn't a bad man. Bad men…The thought made her head hurt. She'd been raised that respectful women got married, ran their homes properly and raised their children in a Christian manner.

It was also enforced that proper ladies did not live with their partner in sin without the matrimonial yoke, because to do so made her no better than a lady of ill-repute and that she refused to return to. Her only option it seemed was to marry him.

Now, another thought crossed her mind. "How will you do so, heading back to the army and this despicable war?"

He didn't answer but seemed to favor the cake he was eating. His silence made her wonder if he was trying to find the way to let her know he'd changed his mind but she quickly dismissed that idea.

"I'll find a solution to that," he muttered, swallowing the bite in his mouth. "We need to finish and go pack. Roll out is early in the morning."

"You're taking me with you now?"

He frowned. "Of course. I would not leave my wife here nor have we time to buy a home for you to stay, since you decided against the boarding house and my boyhood home."

She grimaced. Her refusal of staying with his parents must have been a bit crass on her part. Biting her lower lip, she gave him a slight nod as she stared down at her half-eaten dinner.

Marriage. Again, Abraham's ghost returned, the wide, enticing smile shining across his face. He was her best friend, she'd known him for years and the shift to being his wife had been so easy, once they made it north. All the hardships they had weathered, with the warm comfort of just each other her only relief, the times spent laughing because crying did no good and the return home not an option, flashed before her eyes. She loved him, but Pierce was right. All evidence pointed towards his death, one the army had confirmed when they appeared at her doorstep with those awful words. So, she was a widow and alone, in a world where men ruled.

Swallowing the lump in her throat that had formed in the last few seconds, she took her wine glass and took a sip, glancing at the officer across from her. He, too, was a widower and from what little he said, he'd loved his wife. The tension over the woman seemed to haunt him. Even in bed, when he touched Cerisa, it was with a driving need, as if he had demons that possessed him or an urgency to take another who only filled the place of his dead wife in a way. Though close, he kept a distance, perhaps, she mused, the same type she used to keep her sanity at the brothel. Yet, could she allow herself to be with him, as a wife should? Could he let her past his grieving soul? Would she do the favor in return?

Taking a bite of the cake, the flavor lost to her as her mind mulled the issue of marriage, she knew she had little choice. *Dear God, save them both!*

CHAPTER SIXTEEN

"Colonel Sorrel, it was splendid; we shall smash them now."
—General Micah Jenkins, Confederate staff officer May 6,
1864 at the Battle of the Wilderness

Baltimore, August 27th, 1863

THE SMOKE WAS CHOKING. The sound of the people chatting and the engines chugging all around her made Cerisa believe she would suffocate soon if they didn't move. As she stood on the platform, she was at a loss as to what to do. She glanced at her cuffs and flattened the front of her skirt again, her temper slowly starting to rise. It still made no sense to her. Pierce woke her early, pressing her to get ready, that their train was leaving shortly. It did. But it took them north, toward Baltimore, not into the belly of the beast raging on the battlefields.

Thankfully the ride itself was uneventful. Yet the whole ordeal was, for lack of a better term, way too grimy, and she felt like a layer of filth covered her. First, she sat in a passenger car that had seen better times. Its seat upholstery was now stained, some cushions torn, and the windows carried a film of dirt, making any clear view impossible. When they arrived in Baltimore, Pierce kissed her cheek and sped off, claiming he'd be back soon. Suffocating inside the cabin, she walked out to the platform to breath, though it wasn't much better with the churning train engine still rolling.

She turned slightly, adjusting her parasol just to keep the sun from burning her cheeks. Her thoughts, though, stayed on Pierce. Last night, if it showed how the future was to be with him, would make her question her sanity. She realized she didn't understand the man who had saved her from the road to complete ruin.

After dinner, she'd left for the room but he'd stayed behind, saying he craved a good cigar and whiskey. With her thoughts still whirling with her acquiescence to marrying him, she nodded and left. She'd sat in the room, brushing her hair over and over, part of her wanting to scream, the other to cry. A little voice deep inside kept repeating that Abraham was dead. With her head pounding, and tired of waiting for him, she'd gone to sleep.

It took time for sleep to come but in the depths of it, she found her body responding to a quiet need, deep in her core. It had not taken long for her to wake in a fully aroused state. Pierce hadn't said a word. He had slipped into bed with her, touching her in ways he knew would bring her to the pinnacle of pleasure. Panting slowly, trying to contain herself, she'd veered at him and found he appeared like a wolf, about to devour her. His gaze was dark and hooded, his hands working magic on her, setting off the need to have him to the point of explosion. And it was a gift he'd given her as she'd started to tremble, on the verge of ecstasy when he thrust home.

Their lovemaking was intense, like they were animals in heat. He took her again and again and every time, she matched him, making him shudder deep inside her. It took her breath away and she shattered, the stars in her eyes exploding in an array of lights. The air was thick with musk, wrapping around them and she relished it. She fell into deep slumber in his arms, only vaguely noticing no words had been exchanged.

The bliss, though, quickly vanished this morning as she was pulled from sleep, hearing him up. She remembered the surprise as he had had breakfast brought to the room, the aroma of coffee drifting up in the air, the fresh baked goods, eggs and fruit making her stomach rumble. He told her to get up and ready. It was time to leave. With virtually no time to inhale, Cerisa dressed, packed and downed a cup of the black gold before he whisked her away.

After the short trip to Baltimore, they now waited for another train. She simply didn't understand why.

"You look lost."

She smiled. Pierce had returned. "I thought we were heading toward your army. I hadn't realized the war was up north."

He chuckled, tucking her hand in the bend of his arm and turning them toward another set of rail cars. "Unfortunately, to head south, we had to go north to switch lines. The normal route to our destination falls across a section of the conflict, where it could get involved in the melee and I won't put you in harm's way." He kissed her cheek ever so lightly. Then he whispered softly, "Besides, we have a stop to make, picking up more soldiers."

She hummed in acknowledgement as they crossed the yard to another platform. The train sitting there looked similar to the one they'd traveled on except there was a car that looked out of place with the rest. It was too brightly painted in red and green with gold accents. She marveled at the sight. No doubt it was the car of a wealthy man, she decided. But as Pierce steered her toward it, she frowned, all the way to the steward who stood near its stairs, extending his gloved hand toward her.

"Surely, this isn't the car for us," she murmured, as Pierce placed her hand in the servant's.

She climbed the stairs and went into the car, only to gasp at the inside. It was filled with velvet-designed wallpaper, plush sitting couches and ornate table and chairs. A section in back was blocked off but a glimpse through the partially opened door showed a double bed covered in fine counterpane.

"Colonel Duval, is there anything else I can get for you?" the steward asked.

Pierce shook his head and walked into the room, clearly at ease. As the cabin door closed, he turned to her and smiled. "What do you think? Better accommodations for a lady?"

Cerisa smiled as she slowly traced the back of one of the chairs. Her fingers circled the scroll at the top of the frame till it got to the peak and there she found the source of the car. The letter "D" was embossed in gold. "D" for Duval.

She turned to ask when there was a knock at the cabin's door.

"Colonel."

Pierce opened it and two soldiers carried in a large traveling trunk. Cerisa was puzzled. She hadn't seen this piece before. It looked new and similar to a trunk she used to have; when she lived at home with all the privileges of wealth and status. That was years ago…The memory struck an emotional chord deep inside her, one that she had buried.

"Very good, Corporal Prasse. Make sure all is loaded. We roll in fifteen minutes."

"Yes, Colonel." The soldier saluted before he and the other one left.

"Is this more to your standards, my lady?" he finally asked after the silence filled the air.

She bit the inside of her cheek, mulling for a moment. "It is very nice." She turned towards him. "D for Duval? And let me guess, for Senator Duval, since I doubt army wages even for a colonel afford a detailed railcar for personal use."

Pierce snorted. "Rank does have its privileges, though you are correct. It is my father's car. I found he has no need of it presently, so I borrowed it, to get you the traveling accommodations a wife of a Duval should have."

Another glimpse of her past. Her father, too, would have seen her and her mother treated like this. It seemed truly too expensive to the woman she had become, struggling the past four years just to get food. How she had ever allowed such costly living before when so many suffered, she couldn't imagine.

"Why don't you take a look in the trunk," he prodded, his tone soft yet inviting.

She twisted the key in the lock and the tumblers fell into place, pushing the latch free. She lifted the lid and before her, she found layers of neatly folded silks with trim of folded dresses, a stack of white cotton undergarments and a new cage crinoline coiled to one side. Her eyes widened. "For me?"

Pierce nodded. "Take one of the dresses out and let's see."

She pulled the top one out. It was a muted golden yellow and cream striped piece, with jacket sleeves, and ivory trim down the front of the bodice. Unfolded, the dress was gorgeous, elegant and looked the right size for her. The silk draped off her fingertips, so soft and smooth, with the lacing matching it. It was a taste from a life she had years ago, when everything was prim, proper and fashionable. The dress resembled one she'd seen in the storefront on Jefferson Avenue in Washington, near their hotel, and she had mentally drooled over it but knew it was well out of her price range. She turned the bodice, sizing it up to her and knew it would fit.

"This is the size for me," she murmured dreamily and then glanced at him. "Are these all for me?"

He nodded.

"That seamstress of the hotel was able to do all this so fast?"

His brows shot up in feigned surprise as a know it all smile showed how pleased he was she noticed. "It took a bit of negotiating, but yes."

A thrill of excitement race through her, at the mere suggestion she had a new wardrobe, but also made her ask, "There are several dresses here and I see more intimate apparel. It's a wonderful gift, but why?" She figured she'd get one or two dresses but this was an entire wardrobe.

"Cerisa, think of this as a wedding gift. A wife of an officer should dress accordingly, to the rank and privilege that position demands." He came closer and stood behind her as she held the new dress up in front of her. With a feather-light kiss on her neck, he said in a hush tone, "Frankly, I'd rather see you with nothing on, but it's hard to attend balls and the like in such a state."

She giggled. "Yes, I would be a bit underdressed. Thank you."

Pierce smiled and inwardly thanked the Almighty that she'd taken it well. His purpose for the garments was exactly as he stated, and, as a Duval, she'd need more. He was in the position to get them. She could've refused them but thankfully, she didn't.

As Cerisa rummaged through the trunk, carefully, he observed, there was a joyful look on her face, her cheeks rosy and a surprise on her lips as she examined each piece. It was like Christmas morning and he was pleased. She was a beautiful woman, a true Southern belle, who should be honored and cherished, dressed in the finest and gracing his arm, not toiling in a factory with second best clothes, or worse. The mere idea made his blood boil. He tried to bury the little voice inside him that reminded him he had been one of those miscreants who had spent money for the latter.

Suddenly, she looked up at him, a new ivory fan in her hand with a fancy tortoise hair comb in the other. "I have nothing for you in return."

He caught the sadness curling around her words and it irked him. "My dear, you are to be my wife. Your gift to me is your beauty." He gently took the pieces out of her hands and brought one of them to his lips for a kiss. "All I want from you, is you with me." *Did he?* It was the right thing to say and the words fell from him as easy as holding her in his arms. The brief catch in Cerisa's eyes told him she wondered the same and he was, after all, competing with a man who held title of her husband before him. Could he fight with that? Anger flared deep inside, at the mere suggestion of her with another and he fought to control that. He had no right to judge her so, for she could easily turn on him for marrying an Irish woman. The irony of their previous relationships was almost laughable, considering.

A glorious smile curved her lips at his compliment. "This is very generous of you. And yet, we are not wed. What happened to finding a priest to ensure that?"

Yes, a priest. He had promised to wed her. "Washington is not full of papists, nor many other available clerics, not with the war raging, funerals rising and souls needing help." He sighed. "I will marry you, have no doubt. At the very least, there is a clergyman with the army, and we'll enlist his aid."

She nodded and stepped from the traveling trunk, having to grab the back of the chair she had traced the initial of as the train started to roll. Her fingers traced the D again.

With a deep inhale, he grimaced. He had a lady, his future wife, to transport. In the long run, his goal was to get her home, even if it was way down in the deep South, yet to do so hit a chord that ran deep inside him. A driving need to protect her and the best way he could think of was as his wife, with all the connections his family name could bring her, from Yankee wealth to political and societal connections. Either way, he'd make sure she was safe. It was a desire that consumed him from the first time he met her, in that church back in New York, and from those vermin who chose to zero her and her man out, all due to the color of their skin. The man, who shunned his father's abolitionist ambitions for his progeny, wanted to keep safe a woman who had shared a bed with a freedman. It made no sense...why did he want her?

CHAPTER SEVENTEEN

*"I would not push you to any rashness, but I am very anxious
that you do your utmost, short of rashness, to keep Bragg from getting
off to help Johnston against Grant."*

—President Lincoln to General Rosecrans, May 28, 1863

*September 10ᵗʰ, Rosecrans's camp
North of Elk River, Tennessee*

BRIGADIER GENERAL JAMES A. Garfield
yawned. It was mid-morning and he couldn't help
himself. Just one night of true sleep was all he wanted.
One. But that wasn't to happen, as long as Major General
Rosecrans remained in charge. The commanding general
rarely slept and wanted others up with him during his long,
often abstract, 'discussions', which continued usually until
the wee hours of the morning. Garfield many times couldn't
remember one word, his body exhausted, his mind numb
due to the lack of rest, particularly since Rosecrans had
chosen him to be his tentmate. What was a political step up,
colluding as it was with the commanding officer, Garfield
argued with himself, if the goal would never get awarded?
But as he wrote his wife, he got no sleep and could barely
function during the day.

"General."

He refocused at the soldier who stood dutifully before

him, a scrap of papers in his hand. Garfield took the bundle and motioned to the man to leave.

"So did Lincoln and Halleck approve my demands?" Rosecrans asked, walking up to the cherry wood table they had appropriated, no, Garfield mentally corrected, stolen, from a secessionist Tennessean house just down the river. The shine of the polish furniture bordered on the line of blinding any who stood close to the reflection as the sun beamed down from above.

"General Halleck still demands daily reports on movements and the President," Garfield coughed. Where did he pick up a cough? "Lends support on an increase in men." He folded the missive up and gave it to his commander when another cough erupted. How annoying!

Rosecrans halfway snarled, but it was only a minor upcurl in his lip that caught Garfield's attention. The general had a temper and too easily flew off the handle. He had written a sharp rebuttal to Halleck's demand he receive daily reports on the army's movements after Confederate forces. Garfield decided the letter was out of line, perhaps too curt, ending with his resignation if the Secretary of War felt it necessary, with all the backing of Garfield and the other generals here if that were the case, to prevent it. The attack on Halleck issued another terse reply still demanding the report, but Lincoln conceded and allowed him more troops.

All in the name of the Union. Garfield choked and tugged at his collar. It seemed intensely warm today.

"Did you release that lieutenant?"

Garfield mentally shook his head, refocusing. "The rebel you filled with lies about our attack strategy?"

Rosecrans smiled. "Who said those plans are false? I intend to play them out. But its doubtful Bragg and his command will believe it. Bragg will expect another way, despite it and therefore they will not follow through." He slapped Garfield on his shoulder. "It will make taking Chattanooga and the pursuit that much better."

Garfield could only nod, the pain shooting down his arm from the general's excitement made speaking coherently hard. His ears started to ring. He could only pray the new troops would arrive and with all that excitement, he could slip away, because he was starting to feel miserable.

Rosecrans shuffled through the papers on the top of his desk, his gaze intense, as if he was looking for something, which he found. Yanking the folded sheet out of the stack, he threw it at Garfield. "The ladies have sent another demand. I need you to take care of this. I cannot have problems here that could spread to their men and all the troops. This army must operate like a well-oiled wheel to take those Confederates on."

Blinking, Garfield tried to clear his eyes of the film that covered them. The feminine cursive screamed for the general to address this situation. He grimaced. Not what he wanted to take on but with a sigh, he nodded to Rosecrans and sent the aide next to him off.

The general applauded his quick manners on it and took off to review troops as Garfield waited. He hated domestic issues and abhorred the fact that there were ladies near the camps in the first place. But he had no control over officers and their wives. He inhaled deeply, straightened his shoulders and took a seat at the table, facing the camp. It wouldn't take long. Around the corner of a wall-tent six down the row, the soldier returned, the culprit in his wake. He walked straight up to the desk and saluted.

"Yes, sir!"

Garfield looked up, fighting the shot of ice that raced down his spine and the cotton texture of his mouth. "Colonel Duval, please explain why you brought your whore to camp."

Three days earlier

THE LONG ARDUOUS JOURNEY down into Tennessee finally came to a halt in northern part of the state, at the remains of some small town Pierce failed to notice, having to supervise the soldiers on the train, being the senior officer, while having one of them find a carriage suitable for a lady to travel in. Private Smith seemed overly enthusiastic to take that task, perhaps he wanted to make an impression, Pierce pondered. Or an opportunity to put off leaving for the big elephant, the soldiers' euphemism for the war. But it didn't matter, for by the time all had disembarked the train, gathered supplies and lined up, the man returned with a rather nice carriage, its fringed canopy top firmly attached. He couldn't refrain from asking where he'd gotten it, in such small amount of time. The boy looked down and shuffled his feet for a moment before he looked at the boy and sighed. Obviously, he'd purloined it from a 'secesh.' Swallowing the thought, he found Cerisa and whisked her away in the carriage, following the line of marching soldiers and cavalry on their way to the Army of the Cumberland. He sat on his horse, allowing his eyes to keep the men in his view yet still be close to his soon-to-be wife.

She sat in the carriage, her posture straight as a lady, etiquette of her upbringing totally on display. Silence between them had only escalated as their trip south began. He wasn't sure what prompted that, outside his absence for much of the train trip, having to coordinate all military aspects of the men who joined them and their equipment, correspondence and reports the currier had delivered before they left plus the ones he received en route. But he did make sure her accommodations were good and did join her every night. Memories of being with her, even just in her presence on the tucked away bed in the train car, ignited the flame that hadn't dimmed, to flare slightly, enough to make him shift in the saddle. He had to refocus on what he was doing.

As they got closer to the camp, Pierce saw the beginnings of a large army installation, with tents littering the countryside, some coming down as he watched. Surrounded by horses and mules, the low noises of soldiers filled the air. He inhaled and halfway closed his eyes, a feeling of excitement seeping into his bones. The familiar scent of dirt, campfire smoke, horse dung, filthy wool and gunpowder swirled around him as the horse plodded closer. The leather of his saddle, the sound of the hooves hitting hard ground was like the icing on a dessert before him. He was home. Strangely enough, after an upbringing of wealth and power, he craved for the need to be counted, to pulling off a maneuver only brothers in arms could accomplish. It was home and he smiled.

Corporal Prasse appeared at his side. "Sir, the ladies camp is over to the left, close to those trees the boys left standing."

Pierce took a glance. The area had a set of walled tents up with small fires burning. It was late afternoon and dinner no doubt cooking. The civilian camp was a good distance from the military one—no reason to sully the women's thinking of their men, seeing the mess men can make. Slowly he nodded and Prasse took off, pulling the livery wagon that carried Cerisa's new trunk of clothes, with him. Cerisa's head tilted, watching the wagon take off as the carriage halted. With a swallow, knowing this news probably would not be what she wanted to hear, he got up to the carriage right before it turned.

"Cerisa, the civilian camp is over there. They'll take you there and I'll meet you after I check in with command."

She inhaled deeply, her shoulders setting rigid as she finally looked at him. There was a distant look in her eyes, bordering on hatred. "So, we stop here? In the fields of Tennessee?"

"It is where my assignment is."

"I fail to see how you can fulfill your promise to return me to my family—who reside in Lou's'ana, some three states away." Her Southern drawl was unraveling in her speech more and more the further South they went. It was a beautiful accent to his ears, but one that would not be welcomed here, in the Union Army camp.

"Cerisa, I have no choice at the moment. You would not return to New York to wait at my family home and that, I understand," he paused. He'd sooner wish death than return to the rantings of his father, and his push to get Pierce assigned to one of the Colored units. "And not remaining in Washington, that pit of mongers and thieves, that too I understand but I cannot abandon my position simply to take you back. Married or not."

She glared at him. "Marriage. You convinced me marriage to you would save me. 'Protect' me, was your argument, yet here I sit, in a camp full of men, unencumbered with title of wife to an officer. To God, I'm still a widow, not wife."

He winced. She was right. He'd failed to get a preacher in time. And he knew the train lacked one. Nor did they stop at a town along their way, at least not long enough for inquiries. Well, actually for him to remember to look and that was his fault. He'd have to find the company chaplain as soon as he could, but he had his job to do first.

"You are my fiancée. Be nice to the ladies and I'll be back as soon as I can." He tipped his hat at the half-smile she mustered for him. With a quick nudge with his knees, he got his horse to take off towards camp and an atmosphere he understood, leaving the fiery, beautiful and upset lady, knowing he'd better fix their situation and soon.

Cerisa shook the blanket out again as the soldiers came into her tent, the large traveling trunk in their hands. The lovely wood framed and leather piece looked so out of place here. She skimmed her palm across the top of it, a vague thought flittered through her mind of when would she have a place to wear such pieces?

"Ma'am, where you want us to put it?"

She blinked and pulled her hand back. "Over there would be mighty fine."

The two took it to the side and placed it near the tent wall, on top of a stack of wood slats that were on the ground. "Anything else, ma'am?"

They were so polite, she decided, and way too young to be out here, firing weapons at people they didn't even know for a cause she highly suspected neither of them understood. "No, private. Thank you."

She unlatched the lid and raised it, admiring the fine linen undergarments that appeared first, the silks further beneath. As if a reminder was needed on how such beautiful pieces needed to remain packed, a small trickle of perspiration dripped down her temple as a fly buzzed right in front of her face. A frustrated yet strangled growl fought to be heard but she slammed the trunk's lid to wipe the offending sweat away. It was hot, reminding her of home yet after the last few years in New York City, she soon discovered her tolerance had dropped along with her patience. *Where was Pierce and how in the world was she to live under these circumstances?*

"Knock, knock!"

Cerisa spun to the opening tent flap right as it flew open to the young lady standing right before her.

"Why, how are you doing?" the woman asked. "Moving into a tent isn't always the easiest for us ladies. All the muck and mess the soldiers make." she shuddered.

Cerisa just stood, her hand receding back from the trunk as she looked at the woman before her. She was taller than Cerisa, with dark brown hair pulled up and pinned in the back, her dress a green and gold plaid trimmed in black on the skirt and the coat sleeves. She wore a large smile but her gaze gave it all away. The woman was here, spying on her, seeing who the new girl was. Cerisa returned the grin. It'd been years since it was this subtle.

"Oh, please, pardon me," she added with a surprise. "I should introduce myself. I'm Abby Gaines, my husband is Major Thomas Gaines, of the 79th Pennsylvania. And I have the honor of…."

It took a moment for Cerisa to understand she was expected to return the favor. "Apologies. I'm Cerisa Walker," she stumbled as her thoughts collided. She needed to slow her speech and correct that Southern drawl. She'd been able to bury it when she worked at the factory, at Abraham's suggestion, but Madame Nikki begged her to resume using it, to increase her 'allure' as a 'Southern belle'. Struggling to reign it back in, she added, "Duval." She tried to smile brightly, hoping that momentary slip wasn't too damning. "My husband is—"

"Yes, well, we all know who Colonel Duval is. Last we'd

heard, his wife was gravely ill…." She let her voice fade yet her gaze hardened.

A chill breezed across Cerisa. If she recalled correctly, Pierce told her of his wife's demise and it was last spring, she guessed, realizing she was aware of that detail. It was a reason to worry, for it was uncommon for gentlemen to remarry so quickly, unless there were children involved. He'd never mentioned any and she had none, so why would they marry? Even she'd started to wonder what her argument would be if this turned badly.

She pulled herself up straighter. "Mrs. Duval did not recover." She added nothing more, realizing the last word curled with a touch of Southern creole.

Abby's face tightened but her expression remained set as pleasant appearing. The silence deepened. Why this woman irked her Cerisa couldn't pin except that she was tired of others judging her. It took every ounce of energy for her to keep up as a perfect lady.

"Well," Abby finally started. "I've come to invite you to tea. We do try to retain some civility during these trying times and a good afternoon tea has been just the key." She gave a tight smile, her tone sounded like it was a Sunday afternoon, cordial and polite, not near an army camp that was stirring for battle.

It took Cerisa a moment to recover. "That sounds lovely," she answered, carefully pronouncing her words to not sound like a drawl. "I gladly accept your invitation."

Abby nodded, her appearance relaxed, except for the tight hold on the back of the camp chair she stood behind. "We'll be pleased to have you." She spun on her heel and headed to the tent flap. "We'll see you at tea time, in Mrs. Macgruder's tent, at the end of the row on the left." And she left.

Cerisa closed her eyes, her energy evaporating fast. The woman made her skin prickle, just as her abrupt departure was an exclamation point to her 'invitation.' Polite, yes, but far from warm. She had read all the reports in the newspapers she could about the war when Abraham was alive. After his death, she'd only scan the words, still hoping her brother wasn't also dead. All the while still trying to fathom the depth of despair her world had become. But never, ever, in that dialogue on the pages of print had she heard of wives being here, on the battlefield, holding tea, as if nothing else was happening. She closed her eyes and pinched the bridge of her nose. What in the name of the Blessed Mary was going on here?

Pierce shifted in his seat, trying to find a way to stay awake during this officers meeting Rosecrans had called. If he had to hear one more time how General Halleck was wrong, he'd probably leave.

"Bragg won't see us!" Rosecrans slammed his fist down, the smack on the tabletop made Pierce wince.

"Sir, this army is too big not to be noticed by the rebs," another officer interjected. Some buffoon from Ohio, Pierce gathered. Those Utopian types produced by that state often failed to see the whole picture, he decided.

"Perhaps, and thanks to the arrival of the New York contingent," the general looked right at Pierce, "Thank you, Colonel Duval." He spun back to the other, continuing his rant. "Halleck has delayed our plans long enough, though now that cretin wants reports on our movements and that is daily!"

Pierce sat, staring right at Rosecrans. The man's face was mottled with fury. In certain respects, he was correct. Halleck's dislike of the general was as plain as the bluing on a rifle and just as dark. The President had pushed Rosecrans through and for that, Halleck balked but he ran out of diversions, thus the latest ruse here. Made Pierce's stomach flip, his desire to return to his future wife burning deep inside him over being here, talking politics and war— two items that didn't mix well at the commanding general's desk.

"General, perhaps if our design was strictly to gain Chattanooga," Pierce began in a desperate attempt to turn Rosecrans's attention back onto the war. "We will defeat Bragg by control of his supply base."

Rosecrans frowned, though his lips curled in a satisfied grin. "Duval, that would stand as a well practiced stratum of the Point, and I know as a student thereof, you are still schooled by that way of thinking, but the point is, we need to defeat Bragg to strip away his army."

Pierce bristled at the remark. Behind him, he heard a low rumble amidst a shuffling in the chairs and from the group standing past them. The one to his immediate left muttered, "His honor demands a head on a platter."

Pierce refused to retreat. He, as well as most of the North, had heard the praises of Grant's victory at Vicksburg and even the groan at Meade's loss of whipping Lee fully at Gettysburg. Rosecrans maintained Tennessee but the lack of bloody battles put his pushing Bragg south as little more than military maneuvers. But to chase Bragg only, to put him at the level of Grant, at the cost of lives, supplies and larger military advantage was ill-planned. Pierce would bet his rank on that.

"Sir, if we take Chattanooga, we've cut their supplies off," Pierce argued. "The impact on the rebels will be harder for them to swallow. Then we can use it as the supply depot for our attack on Bragg."

Rosecrans shot him a look, his facial features giving a myriad of emotions, ranging from deep concern to aggravation to mild amusement. Pierce stood his ground, absently noticing the rest of the officers in the tent shifting, either physically or subtly. The Army of the Cumberland was indeed filled with the miscreants of the east, he inwardly swore.

The awkward silence grew until the general motioned to the junior officer who sat at the side, pen and paper at his command.

"Perhaps, Brevet General Duval, perhaps," Rosecrans started.

The rank caught Pierce off guard and he double blinked. Had the general just promoted him? For arguing with him? A murmur rose from the attendees, each no doubt equally surprised as Pierce, though he fought to retain his composure, despite the increased pounding of his heart. A brevet, he mused.

"Bravo, sir. Washington has seen the value and honor of your service." Rosecrans smiled.

A murmur of thanks echoed behind him, but Pierce frowned. He'd been gone on leave for his wife's illness and death, subjects that were honorable by society, he supposed, yet of a personal nature, not militarily so. No, what he feared was the promotion came from another political source. He gritted his teeth.

"…But Bragg is the ultimate objective here," the general concluded. He rubbed his temples, a look of exhaustion taking control. "Sir, I'm aware of your recent loss and to that, my condolences, but for now, let us look at the primary goal. Taking the commanders halts the soldiers and in essence, stops the war. Elementary rule of warfare and one we shall act on." He rose from the table, the rest of the men in the tent coming to attention. "That is all gentlemen."

Pierce turned on his heel and followed the rest of the men out, his mind still tumbling over the name only promotion in rank, knowing it was a name only when suddenly, Prasse skidded before him, panting, his abrupt stop kicking up dust around them.

"Sir, you wanted me to inform you if anything was amiss with your wife." He near choked on the dust as he spat the words out.

Pierce's heart skipped a beat. Cerisa. "What happened corporal?"

"She's at Major Macgruder's wife's tent for tea."

The civilian camp. He started to laugh but caught himself. The ladies there no doubt invited Cerisa out of an act of kindness but he knew one of them all too well and if she was there, Cerisa had just entered a snakepit of vipers. On that threat, he took off at run.

CHAPTER EIGHTEEN

"[T]he contest is really for empire on the side of the North, and for independence on that of the South, and in this respect, we recognize an exact analogy between the North and the Gov't of George III, and in the South and the Thirteen Revolted Provinces. These opinions…are the general opinions of the English nation."

—London Times, November 7, 1861

CERISA TOOK ANOTHER SIP of her tea, allowing the motion to give her a break and a look away from the Yankee women sitting before her. They had been very polite, a mask of warmth on their faces but the endearments were far from tepid. These women were far too calculating in their questions and inquiries, enough so that a timid woman would faint, but not Cerisa. It'd been years since she'd been home but her memories on manners and decorum crowded her mind now, as did the proper way to handle such vipers.

"Dear Mrs. Duval, please don't think we are judgmental," started the woman to her left. Mrs. Macgruder, Cerisa recalled. "But your husband left us in a rush, right before the fights in Tennessee, over his wife's ailment. The question is, who are you really? The late wife come back to haunt all, or his latest conquest?"

Conquest. That could be used in several ways, including wife and whore, Cerisa thought. A shot of rage raced through her at the mere suggestion he was a womanizer. She'd have to save his reputation, after all, wasn't that what a wife would do?

"I met him in New York City, not long after the death of my husband," she said carefully, slowly stirring her tea as she concentrated on the annunciation of her words to curb her accent. "We got along famously. He found I was a widow, my husband died at the front like so many brave lads, and with his loss, he suggested marriage to protect me and soothe his aching heart." She glanced up at them and smiled.

Abby halfway glared at her while the rest of the group nodded in understanding.

"Still," Abby started. "Rules require mourning a husband—"

"Abby, please. It is wartime," another one of wives interjected. "Surely the rules are not unbending."

"Of course not. Please forgive me," Abby replied, her look one of regret, except for her eyes. She still held a cold gaze toward her, enough that if Cerisa wasn't a strong woman, she would've cringed. "You had no children? I saw none when you two arrived."

The woman was a gossip as well as a judge. Cerisa steamed. "No." She inhaled and met Abby's look head on. "I had no where to turn when I ran into my darlin' Pierce, after mass. He protected me from some street urchins who were reeking mischief. He corrected their mistake and it made me fall for him." She smiled at the memory before she realized at the end of the sentence, her southern lilt whispered in the words. A faint hope glimmered no one heard it but a view of the others showed it didn't escape notice. Of course, any mention of her Catholicism also could raise an eyebrow in these Protestant-minded Yankees, she thought, biting back the notion to roll her eyes at their narrow-mindedness, so typical of what she saw outside home. Except in the Five Points, where the Irish-Catholics resided.

In an attempt to avoid glancing up, she stared at the silver platter on the center table that held an assortment of sweets. Her stomach rumbled. Her first inclination was to snatch a couple of the cakes. The hunger and fear that lit deep inside her belly brought back the days after Abraham left for war and when she lost her job, leaving her to starve. And Madame Nikki's wasn't much better…

"Your husband was in the army?"

She blinked the memories away. "Yes."

The ladies stirred as Abby asked, "We're sorry for your loss. Where did he serve?"

"He was at the battle of—" she began when the tent flaps whipped open and Pierce appeared. He held a stern look for a second, bordering on panic, when his gaze found her and he suddenly grinned—a warm and welcoming smile of a gentleman.

"Good afternoon, ladies. I apologize for interrupting your afternoon of the decadent indulgence of tea," he stated.

"Colonel Duval, you are more than welcome to join us," one of the wives off to the right of Cerisa added.

Had the woman's voice trembled at the end? As if, she hoped he'd stay? Cerisa did a double blink, realizing many of the ladies here looked pleased her soon-to-be husband had stopped in. While she enjoyed Pierce and appreciated him, she didn't think she'd fallen for him, yet the green snake that slithered up her spine, making her want to hiss, surprised her. She couldn't tame the jealousy that raised her hackles.

"My dear ladies," Pierce began, his tone soothing but slightly flirtatious, Cerisa thought. "As much as I would love to, I truly need to take my wife from your soiree." And he winked.

Cerisa fought to keep her mouth closed, despite the fact that statement made it clear his intentions with her were not vertical. Yet when he extended his hand to her, she slowly gathered her shawl before she rose. And in that movement, she leaned forward a bit more to snatch up one of the tea cakes, hiding it in the folds of her bishop's sleeve, covered by her shawl, as she straightened. With control she fought to contain, she put her hand on Pierce's arm and smiled at him.

"Darling, how pleasant to see you," she murmured as she squeezed a touch closer. His appearance was exactly what she needed as these ladies were about to push her too far.

He smiled at her as he spoke their goodbyes and escorted her out of the tent. Within a minute, they were at the one he'd appointed as hers and safely inside.

With a grateful sigh, she reached up to kiss his cheek before she slumped into the tapestry cloth folding camp chair. "You'll never know how deeply thrilled I was for you to arrive."

He chuckled as he watched her shed her shawl. "Yes, when word reached me you had been ensconced with the ladies of the camp, I figured you might need a little help extricating yourself."

Unlacing her boots, she glanced up at him. "They seemed to know you quite well, considering their words and looks."

With a snort, he took his frock coat off. "Yes, well, in a camp like this, the ladies get to know the officers well."

She glared at him, but he didn't appear to notice as he shed his frock coat and put it on top of the wooden chest at the foot of the roped bed in their tent. Irritated, she went to put her shawl down, careful to keep the food hidden. With a swallow to shake the anger, she threw out, "So you like to flirt with them? What else, pray tell, have you done, might I ask?"

That prompted him to turn his head, a surprised look in his eyes. "You think I have taken liberties with one of them? Cerisa, I am a gentleman…"

"Yes, I'm familiar with the type. They visit brothels as easily as the cads and rogues."

Shocked at her sneer, Pierce pulled in his look, closing his mouth and gave her a frown as a better response. Perhaps Madame Nikki's and Five Points had left a less than pleasant experience on her mind. "Cerisa, I promise you the ladies here are…." He paused and walked over to the washbasin as he tried to form the right words. "They are no doubt bored. Shoved to the side of the camp, not with their husbands, and most assuredly kept clear of the tents because of the all the men here, they have a tendency to soak up any visitation, even by an officer who is not their husband." He splashed water on his face, in a feeble attempt to cool not only his face but the temper that escalated inside the tent. What surprised him was his own anger slowly coming to flame that she would think him unfaithful.

But why wouldn't she? He was a man, who met her in a brothel…

He pushed that thought away as he dried his face, sneaking a peek at her reaction from beneath the folds of the linen. She carefully pulled her handkerchief out of her shawl, placed the wadded piece on the cot and slowly opened it. Inside, there was a pastry. A pastry? Still patting his face, he watched with amazement as she gently picked it up and slowly moved, her garment in the other hand, to her travel stand, a moveable vanity he had picked up for her, and opened the right-side drawer to put her food in.

Why the hell did she take a cake from the tea? Did she miss proper society that badly? Or was this a habit from years of being poor in New York? He growled, low and defensively. While he didn't know her 'husband,' Pierce now considered the man lower than a garden snake if he couldn't support her.

Her shoulders stiffened at his disgruntled grunt, as she slid the cake to the side, out of his view.

Inwardly, he stifled his anger and cleared his throat. He needed to redirect her dastardly thoughts of him. "Did you enjoy your time?"

"As much as I could, considering they find me not much better than a harlot, taking vows with you so quickly after your wife's death." Her gaze narrowed. "Why didn't you tell me about her?"

He gritted his teeth. "I did not think it appropriate to discuss my *wife* when I was in…" he stumbled, fighting to find the right words to say. He didn't have to.

"When you were in a *whore*'s bed?" she blurted with anger.

"In your room was what I was going to say," he corrected, while inwardly cursing.

"Harrumph!" She stormed to the other side of the tent's space, yanking the hair combs out to brush her mane furiously.

He bit back a snarl and closed his eyes. She simply didn't understand. After all, Margaret's grave was still too fresh and he should have been deep in mourning, not with Cerisa, not under any circumstance! Even now, guilt seeped in and he swore his necktie was tightening around his neck. Between the war, General Rosecrans, those women and now this, he might go mad. He tugged at his collar, wanting to shed the tie, the shirt, the waistcoat and shirt but he couldn't. Duty still called for his attention. Irritated, he yanked his coat back and snapped.

"I apologize for any offense, my dear. My leave was to tend to my dying wife. Her funeral was several weeks ago, and by all rights, my official 'mourning' period was through before Edward insisted we head to the clubs and his first stop was Madame Nikki's. To my way of thinking, I shouldn't have been there." He looked at her, her face schooled perfectly well but her eyes gave away the emotions she held in check. Hatred and anger reflected loudly, along with the tears that managed to not fall. It hit him hard, like a rifle butt slammed into his gut.

"I'm sorry she died," she whispered. "I can see you miss her still...."

He nodded. It was true. And made him question bringing her here but the lion inside him roared. She too had paid for this war and he could not stop the urge to protect her at all costs.

"...just like I miss my Abraham."

That struck a chord at his core. It was like lightning, fast and hard. He wasn't expecting it and to acknowledge it could set off a myriad of emotions he didn't have the time or patience for. Angry at himself and at her, he grabbed his feathered hat.

"I have to go to dine with the command staff at General Rosecran's section."

"You'd leave me again, to forage in a camp I know nothing of except for the vipers I met?"

"I've no choice, Cerisa. I've been promoted to Brevet General—"

"You're a general?" She jumped, grinning ear to ear. "How wonderful! I'm so proud of you!" She ran up and kissed his cheek, all the fire in her eyes gone, replaced with cheerfulness.

He chuckled, befuddled by her flip in attitude. "It's Brevet rank, only a temporary position."

"Still, I think that is great." Her smile was reflected in her eyes. "After all the bad news we've both endured, it is nice to have something wonderful happen."

She was right, he decided and her enthusiasm for his promotion gained hold in him. He picked her up, hugging her tightly and inhaled the faint scent of lavender on her skin—a fragrance that was the exact opposite of the wool and men and the sulfur and gunpowder of war. He buried his nose in her hair, close to her neck and drank it in, imprinting it in his memory. A growl of the hungry wolf escaped his lips and she giggled. With great reluctance, he put her down. It also registered in his head that she was as light as a feather, like most ladies were, but he could tell now her face looked a little more gaunt and even fully dressed, she was too thin. Had she always been so thin? How had that look skipped his notice? His mind raced, trying to recall when perhaps she wasn't well or had he failed his duty in caring for her? Another guilt….

"Cerisa, I'll do my best to get out of there at a decent hour and will bring you dinner. Army cooking isn't the best, but for officers, it is a bit more bearable." And he prayed Rosecrans brought his cook with him, because hardtack and beef fat was hardly edible by a private's standards.

She pulled herself upright. "Yes, sir, I'll look forward to it."

Pierce snorted. "Don't get too excited. It's hardly Delmonico's." Once the words were out, he wished he could bring them back for he doubted she'd ever been to any of the City's finest establishments. He shook the worry and kissed her on her lips, so wanting more, especially when he tasted the sugar from one of the pastries she had eaten at the tea.

And the succulent nectar of her, mixed with the sugar, acted as an aphrodisiac. He groaned as his loins started to heat up. "I must go. I'll be back soon. I promise."

And he darted out of the tent before he threw her on the cot and devoured her instead. *Damn war!*

Squinting, Pierce tried to focus, but his eyes itched, like sand was in them, no doubt a result of the dry, hot summer air and the late hour. Last time he looked, it was midnight and heavens only knew how long ago that was. He fought the yawn that threatened. Not with Rosecrans in the middle of his latest oratory on a subject Pierce couldn't recall. How did he get tricked into this punishment?

With exacting clarity, it all came rushing back to him. A dinner that was exquisite for army regimes. Staff reports, congratulations on latest promotions, himself in this lot, and battle plans, a debate over methods, mostly led by Rosecrans, continuing on into hours. As the sky darkened, and the bugle called for lights out, Rosecrans took a break—with the majority in the room scurrying out the tent, as if the plague loomed over it. He stood to snatch his hat and follow them when Garfield grabbed his arm with a desperate look on his face.

"General, sir," the officer started. "May I beg on you to stay? The general has more to discuss," his gaze darted back to Rosecrans. He coughed. It was a rattling sound, enough to make Pierce really give the man a once over. Garfield looked half-past death with a pale complexion, red nose, watery eyes and that hacking cough he could barely contain through the meeting. "I need my bed and sleep if I'm to be of any service to the general." His grip tightened. "Please."

Pierce agreed and right now, could see how the general's 'discussion' could linger too long. He'd heard the rumors, very vague rumors, on the late-night discussions Rosecrans launched, but Pierce thought they were a joke. Sneaking a peek at the clock on the general's desk, with the hands indicating it was an hour past midnight, Pierce gritted his teeth. He needed to get back and check on Cerisa. He did promise her dinner. From the looks of the table, he'd failed in that as the plate he'd set aside for her was no longer there, no doubt picked up by the privates who cleaned off the table. Pierce couldn't stop them due to the attention he had to give the commander. Anger boiled deeper.

"Have I lost you, General?"

Pierce looked up. Rosecrans was staring at him. The interruption in the dialogue spilling from the general's mouth jarred Pierce's train of thought—that is, if there was one. Fatigue raced through him as he slowly stood and stretched. His thinking scattered, when he tried to form an answer to a question he couldn't recall now.

"Apologies, General," he sputtered, stifling a yawn. "It's late, sir, well past my bed time."

Rosecrans snorted. "I do, at times, go on rather late. Usually, Garfield is here, and he's accustomed to staying up late himself, so we keep our conversation going. But you," he eyed Pierce. "You've been through a lot, with the death of your wife and acquiring another, so quickly."

Pierce struggled to contain his schooled look. Yes, another accusation this 'marriage' was too soon, but the general's views and those of others were neither welcome nor needed. He had to save Cerisa or she'd be crushed by the onslaught of 'patrons' who thought their money bought them all their desires, including beating her.

"The situation I found myself in required a shorter mourning period for my beloved, but I am sure she would give her blessing here, sir." That had to be sufficient because that was as far as he would go.

Rosecrans's gaze narrowed before he stood and stretched himself. "Let us call it a night, Duval. We've got the enemy scurrying, I'm sure, because they know we're at their door." He gave a curt smile. "That is all, General."

"Yes, sir." Pierce had to hold himself in check, thrilled to be free. He'd strangle Garfield tomorrow, or actually later today he thought, because he was sure the man wrangled him to stay, knowing full well how Rosecrans worked, whereas Pierce didn't. He bolted from the tent and headed back to Cerisa.

The camp was quiet, with the sounds of nocturnal life and sentries manning the camp's perimeters. As quietly as he could, he headed back to her, realizing he'd failed to fetch her dinner. He'd check on her and then find something to eat.

The civilian camp was silent and dark, not even the sound of buzzing insects or grazing horses. It was eerie, as he turned to the end of a row and then on to the tent of his charge. No light was lit, and he cursed himself for being stuck under a rambling commander but there was nothing he could've done. Silently, he slipped into the tent.

Cerisa was asleep, sprawled as it was on her cot, dressed in her chemise. In the heat of the night, her cotton cover was askew and one leg was exposed. The garment had inched up her thigh and even in the darkness, he could admire the feminine shape and ivory skin of her slender leg. He gritted his teeth and quietly covered the limb before taking his own clothing off. Not wanting to wake her, he slid under the cover of the heavy wool blanket on the ground, thankful to finally collapse. He'd need the sleep because he had no doubt he'd get an earful tomorrow over his tardiness.

The wool beneath him scratched at his skin. Damn the War and the men who lead it, he wanted to yell, but knew it was times like this and his dampened longings, was what they were fighting for.

Oh, hell, why did he bring her here? To torture himself? He could make all the excuses he wanted, but the truth fought to be heard. Not yet, not yet...

CHAPTER NINETEEN

"Right on they move, as with one soul, in perfect order, without impediment of ditch, or wall or stream, over ridge and slope, through orchard and meadow, and cornfield, magnificent, grim, irresistible."

—Col. Frank Haskell, aide to Union Gen. John Gibbon, on description of Pickett's Charge at Gettysburg, July 3, 1863.

WITH A STRONG BREATH, Cerisa blew the stray lock out of her eyes, wiped the perspiration off her forehead and inhaled deeply. It was a warm August morning in Tennessee and the air was heavy with humidity, making a simple task like scrubbing laundry just that more difficult. With a glance down at her undergarments in the basin she'd found, off to the side of the civilian camp, near the servants, she surmised her talents for this task, while improved over her first attempt years ago when they'd arrived in New York City, probably would still get a scoff from Jenny. As her father's house matron slave, Jenny, with her tall stance, broad shoulders and readable expressions, had always run Bellefontaine, her parent's home, and her rule on household chores reigned high. Cerisa and her brothers, Jack and Francois, were under her watchful eye when they were children. Following her around, Cerisa saw how the house was run and was exposed to some of the slaves' chores, like cooking and laundry, both of which Cerisa had tried when she and Abraham made it north. Apparently, watching had not taught her anything. She'd failed miserably. Abraham had chuckled and told her she'd improve, as he tried to eat her rock-hard biscuits. Out of necessity, she did, though she'd love a meal where she didn't have to lift a finger.

And laundry? She picked up the soaking chemise and the sliver of lye soap, wiped it across the fabric and plunged the piece into the murky wash water. No, she decided, while she had improved, she was far from perfect. As she scrubbed the cotton cloth against the washboard, her mind returned to the reason she'd turned to domestic jobs today—Pierce.

That man could drive anyone to extremes! Last night, he'd failed to bring her dinner. Not that she truly believed he would do so. After all, he was now a high-ranking officer in a meeting of like-minded men, plotting the overthrow of her part of the country. Frankly, she hadn't allowed herself to be absorbed in the conflict like so many of the inhabitants of the Five Points. The Irish abhorred the mere whisper of the Emancipation Proclamation, because they feared that if the 'freedmen' came north, they'd be thrown out on the streets. She understood their terror. The Irish were lumped together by Protestant Americans as papists and drunks, neither trait desired by society. Her Catholicism was sneered at but from her part of the country, her denomination ranked high, Louisiana being settled by the French and Spanish. Her family's summer retreat in New York exposed her early on to this hatred that grew as more Irish arrived, and soon became a reason to not hire the immigrants, even though they were white and spoke English, hence they took whatever jobs they could, which were usually the worst. The idea of freedmen swarming the area if freed made the Irish fear for their jobs.

Yet, her first encounter with Pierce was in a Catholic church, long before the riots. Considering he sat through the mass, she concurred he too was one of the dreaded papists, which gave another odd quirk to the man who'd bought her services and ended up saving her. She couldn't quite figure him out. He'd seemed most adamant about securing her freedom from Madame Nikki and pressed for marriage to protect her yet, in the speed to leave Washington and get to the front, vows had yet to be exchanged.

Had his interest waned? She recalled the Yankee women fawning over his appearance at the tea yesterday. Did he have a mistress among them? It seemed too unlikely to her that they swooned over a man just because he was handsome and debonair. Pierce Duval, general or citizen, was a striking man. Tall, broad shouldered, he was lean but not sickly, with a rock-hard chest, narrow waist and muscular arms and thighs. In uniform or civilian clothes, he was handsome. But here, these ladies were also wives so their sighs over him should be nothing. However when he didn't return till pre-dawn, jacket thrown over his shoulder, his white shirt unbuttoned at the neck, his tie-strings limp around the collar and a worn out look on his face, as if he'd been too physically challenged, seducing another, she wondered.

Of course, he might have had to endure a long-winded meeting as well, a voice inside her argued. She dampened that sound, for here, these officers were in camp all day, surely their nights were not consumed with war as well.

Thank heavens, she'd taken the tea cakes. While not enough to fill her, they did curb her appetite until today when surely, she'd find a cook to wrangle a plate from. Though she couldn't help but be mad. He had saved her from being a slattern, but outside saving her from that, he left her to her own devices? In a male world of war? She swallowed the cussword that threatened to fall from her lips.

It wasn't ladylike—though after the last few years, when was the last time she was a lady?

Pierce faintly heard the bugle sounding off rollcall. He wanted to fight against the noise, to stay in the dark bliss of sleep when reality slammed into him hard and he bolted upright. It was a military camp and time to haul his ass out of bed!

Despite the reality, he was still sluggish to move. As an officer, he should be there before the bugle called but then again, he would have been in bed long before he was last night. With a push, he was up and grabbed his pants to put them on when it hit him that Cerisa wasn't there. He frowned, trying to wipe the rest of sleep cobwebs from his mind as he glanced around the tent. *Where the hell did she go?*

Corporal Prasse appeared. "Good morning, sir." He handed Pierce his shirt.

Still frowning, he looked at his aide as he took the garment. "Did you see Mrs. Duval this morning?"

"Yes, sir." Prasse gave him his boots. "She headed toward the laundry, sir, with her arms full of clothes. Ladies stuff, she told me, and refused my aid."

He cocked his head. "She's at the laundry? Doesn't take long to leave clothes with those women," he snapped. The women the army employed, on a loose term of employed, were mostly the wives of the lower rank, privates and such, whose families trailed the army because to stay home left them with nothing. Many times, they didn't own the land they resided on, nor could they afford to live without the man home to provide. Pierce scowled, because these types were like those who inhabited the Points—poor, uneducated, with a passel of children and a quantity of odds and ends of dogs, goats and sheep. The army tried their best to *shoo* them away so often these camp followers stayed back, though sometimes, the army hired a few to fill spots needed, like laundresses.

And, he had to admit, they were not much better off than the officers' wives that set up near the war camp, just to be close to their husbands.

He shook his head. "Show me the way." He shrugged the wool frock officer's coat on without buttoning his blouse.

In a matter of minutes, he stormed through the camp, to the outer skirts, near a creek where the laundry had set up shop. The slovenly matron, halfway soaked in wash water, glared at him before giving him a 'yes, sir' and pointing to the right when asked where Cerisa was. When he got to the location, what he found was the Southern belle bent over a washbasin, her bodice sleeves pushed high and her hands and bare arms submerged in the tub with a wad of white cloth in her hands. Her long chestnut hair was pulled back and tied with one of his neckties—the one he couldn't find this morning. She didn't appear to see him when he walked up, and that irritated him more.

"And what the hell are you doing?"

She sighed loudly. "Good morning to you as well, General." She scrubbed the piece against the washboard. Her hands looked red and rough. A growl escaped his lips.

"The army has people who do this, Cera," he snarled.

"I'm perfectly capable of laundry," she countered.

She had yet to look at him so he moved in front of her and the washtub, tipping her chin up. "No lady would wash her clothes, especially not here."

With a tilt of her chin, she was free of his touch. "Perhaps Yankee ladies, but those of us from the South, we can handle anything thrown at us."

The determination in her voice surprised him. He figured she'd be upset about last night but not this much. He lowered his tone. "I apologize about last night. General Garfield begged me to stay with General Rosecrans after the meeting, because he felt too ill to continue. I had no idea that he condemned me to listen to ramblings, both intelligent and somewhat wandering, until the wee hours of the dawn. If I had had any clue, I would have declined, though Garfield sounded dreadful." He dropped lower, to be level with her in her bent over form. "I plan to make the man pay for that, except I fear that'd result in my repeating last night so I'm thinking of deserting."

She looked up at him wide-eyed and saw his mischievous grin. She snorted. "You'll do no such thing. Instead, let me make a tonic that will revive this ailing general."

"Perhaps it could be poisonous? It'd be only right and fittin'…"

She rinsed the piece in her hands and twisted it, her lips waggling. "No. True tonic, I learned from—"

If she said that freedman, it'd take a herd of horses to contain his anger.

"—Jenny, back home. She'd give it to all the ailing. Not just the darkies, mind you, but even I have downed a spoonful. Made me feel right as rain."

Her grin took his breath away. It made her amber eyes sparkle with fire and seemed to brighten her cheeks. It had him so caught in her web of attraction, like a moth to flames because he had no doubt he'd burn if he got too close. He mentally shook his head. Close to her was exactly what he wanted and so what she didn't need. When he was in bed with her, he couldn't keep away, like a starving man, who wanted to devour her whole before he realized what he was doing. Perhaps that was why there was a closeness but still space between them. Guilt still hung over him about Margaret, yet she was gone and Cerisa was here. The irony was, to protect her, he'd brought her to the worst place in the world to be—a military camp, full of men who hadn't seen a woman to speak of in months, men teetered on the verge of death daily at the hands of the enemy. Whatever was he thinking?

"Then it's settled," he stated. "We'll forward some to him, *then* I'll throttle him for it!" At her giggle, he gave her a look. "But, please, the army hires these laundresses. Let them do their jobs. Otherwise, they might get upset, and then I'll have some sergeant yelling at me for some insult I've surely thrown at them."

Her gaze narrowed. "I see. And what, then, would you have me do? Cook? I'm sure that would also be against the rules, considering."

He frowned, frustration growing because she was right. What did the women do? "What do the other ladies do?"

"Do? Probably drink tea and plan the next social engagement." She wrung out the cloth and put it into the basket along with the rest of the washed pieces. All in, she picked it up and walked to the line in the trees and promptly started to hang them to dry.

"What are you doing?" he asked.

"Hanging them to dry." The slight breeze, ever so slight, blew the two hung pieces in the sunlight. Pantalets now hung from the line.

When she didn't continue, he tensed, feeling backed against a wall with the pressure building.

"What about the priest? We can't maintain this presentation of a married couple without the truth coming out." She snapped the wet chemise out and hung it from the line.

Pierce flinched slightly. Even at the corner of his eyes, he saw the women washers and a couple of the men bringing them firewood were now watching them. He figured they had to be making quite a scene. Cerisa was in her older dress, one slightly too frilly for laundry, even without her hoops, and him, standing before her, dressed in his officer's uniform and no bundle of dirty clothes in his hands, adding more curiosity to the scene. Why would a high-ranking officer come to the wash to talk to a woman who could easily be thrown into the pile of soiled doves, with her hair tasseled on her head so as not to get in her washwater, her sleeves pushed high, the neckline unbuttoned and the skirt pulled up by ties, exposing her naked calves.

Her statement hit the mark. "I'll find him today. We will be wed shortly."

A bugle call blared through the camp. Mess call. Pierce swallowed.

"Cerisa, will you please return to the civilian camp? I'll have breakfast sent and report about the priest. Rosecrans is Catholic, so I know there is a proper clergyman here. But," he stepped closer and lowered his voice. "Please try to refrain from venturing too far afoot. This is a military camp, filled with men who haven't had the luxury of seeing proper lady, or frankly, a woman outside these behind you, in months. War can make one act out of character and I can't be there to protect you all the time, so please stay still. Perhaps, you'll give the other ladies another visit?" He raised his brows, hoping.

She inhaled and tilted her chin up. "I was raised to be a proper Southern lady. Yes, I will do as you request."

He smiled. It'd be all right, he thought, as he bent to kiss her cheek. With a whispered good-bye, he darted to the officer's mess and thanked God, Cerisa would follow his orders or so he fervently prayed.

Cerisa threaded her way back to the tent, her empty basket in tow. The old woman, Mrs. O'Leary, she had drawled with an Irish lilt, said she would make sure the hanging pieces would be fine. O'Leary touched a chord inside Cerisa, one that hinted of warmth and security. She had to be as old as Cerisa's mother but held a jovial spirit like the elderly slaves on her father's plantation did.

Mrs. O'Leary, though, seemed to be slightly more gifted. She'd peered at Cerisa and calmly asked, "That man of yours. You aimin' to keep 'im?"

The question surprised Cerisa. Despite his honor, one that made him swear to protect her, she knew a job like that didn't really require marriage. After all, what if he tired of a rebel who had sold her body? She had had no choice if she wanted to keep herself alive and fed. He said he believed her, but did he?

Swallowing the bile that had inched up her throat, she forced a smile and replied, "Yes, ma'am, I do, with the help of the Lord." A round of gunfire roared behind her and she jumped.

The old lady snorted. "They be drillin', missy. Part o' the army way." She leaned forward from her perch on the makeshift stool she sat on. "Thinkin' you might be needing a bite and a prayer. Food I got, but the fathers here, they congregate over that way," she pointed to the left. "That General Rosecrans even brought a priest to preach. So unexpected but we all be lovin' it." She laughed.

Cerisa spun around and found in the distance a tent with a cross above the flap entrance. "Yes," she murmured, walking around to take another shot of the property. If the priest was here, perhaps she'd be the one arranging this marriage. On that thought, she stopped. In all the turmoil of her life in the last few weeks, she never felt she'd mourned Abraham properly. yet now was not the time, nor the place. How would she explain this if anyone stopped to console her? The fact was, she couldn't, not rightfully so, not with Pierce here. Inhaling deep, forcing herself to stop the dam of tears that threatened to drench her, she steeled her shoulders and marched to the devotional tent.

Inside the makeshift church were four rows of benches facing a simple wooden pulpit with a wooden cross hung from the tent pole behind it. A soldier sat on the bench, his head bent in prayer, but no one else was there. She scrunched her brows and blew a hiss, anger building. *Where in the world would the man be?* An exasperated sigh escaped her lips before she could stop it.

The soldier looked up. "May I be of service, ma'am?"

Startled, she stood straighter as she gazed at the officer. The man stood, and she looked him over, eyes widening at how debonair he was. He appeared to be about Pierce's height, sporting a clean-cut mustache and beard, his long wavy hair combed to the side. His uniform, deep navy wool with shoulder boards of two gold stars each and trimmed in gold, adorned him like a man of power and prestige. His youthful face, too young to see all the bloodshed of the last three years, was beautiful while his eyes held the wisdom of experience, far beyond his youth. He rattled her thoughts, because she didn't think anyone would be here, which was a silly thought. No doubt many prayed daily, mostly not to die…

"Pardon me," she finally answered. "I didn't mean to bother you. I was looking for the priest. I heard there is one amongst us."

The officer smiled. "Father Treacy, I believe, is detained. At the hospital, tending those who are in need of his services." He stepped closer and took her hand. With a delicate kiss to the back of it, he looked at her, a twinkle in his gaze. "I was unaware there was another in need of his services. Despite my many exonerations of his expertise, many here still believe we 'papists' are worse than the Confederates."

She laughed. *If he only knew.* "Yes, well, there are some Southerners that are of the same persuasion."

He gave her a guarded smile as he bowed. "Let me introduce myself. Major General Rosecrans, at your service, my dear lady."

She bit back a gasp. Pierce's commander. She gave a slight curtsey in return. "Mrs. Duval, sir."

"Ah, the newly promoted General Duval. I was surprised at his return, not so much for his presence, for oftentimes, men will go to fight to fill the void of a love one's demise. But to return with a new wife was most intriguing."

She knew the tension in the camp, despite Pierce's attempt to wipe it aside. "Yes. I, too, lost my husband, due to this, this nightmare." She swallowed. But Rosecrans' raised brows prodded for more information. "We were two lost souls, mourning our mates, and God led us to each other." She hoped the Christian reference would work. After all, admitting she was a Southerner who turned whore to survive and Pierce was a client probably wouldn't sound right. Before he could say anything, she added, "Sorry to have interrupted your prayers," and gathered her skirts to turn to leave.

"No, ma'am. I am finished." He gave her another friendly grin. "I'll inform the Father of your need of his services." He nodded and left.

Cerisa stood, not sure if it had been a good or bad interview. At least, she appeared to placate him on her and Pierce's rapid marriage. A marriage that had yet to happen…

CHAPTER TWENTY

"Arm the negroes. I am perfectly satisfied it must be done."
—George S. Denison to Salmon P Chase, Union Secretary
of the Treasury, January 8, 1863

ABBY GAINES STARED AT her reflection in the cheval, or what fragment of looking glass she deemed was one, and decided her dress was showing signs of Tennessee mud above the hemline. She sighed with disgust and shook the fabric again. At least she'd brought mostly cotton and gingham gowns, with her silks only for special occasions, which Thomas had snickered at. He told her out in the fields, there were no balls to attend, nor any other societal event. She knew it was his way of telling her not to come, but how could she leave him and stay in glorious Philadelphia, knowing he'd need her presence here? Especially when she heard of the other wives packing, she had to come.

In the long run, she was sure he was pleased. What man wouldn't, knowing his wife was here to comfort him during the long days on the field?

Another shake and the folds of the skirt seemed to crease over that spot and she smiled. She'd have it laundered better next time. A simple tie to her bonnet, she grabbed her shawl and gloves, and left her tent. It was time for breakfast and she was sure Jermaine, the cook for the Major General Rosecrans, would have a fine fair for her and the ladies.

"Good day, Abby," her friend Sarah greeted, falling in step with her. "Another hot day here in paradise." She giggled, making Abby join in with her.

"We truly shouldn't call an army war camp paradise, my dear," Abby tried to correct but the girl continued to giggle.

"If we can smile and look happy, that should inspire our men to do the same, don't you think?"

Abby glanced at her. Sarah was a newlywed, recently married to Lieutenant Prescott, a young officer she'd met at a US Sanitary Fair earlier this spring, before he was assigned to return to duty here. Abby figured the young man was very insecure about returning to a war that had wounded him but Sarah had nursed him back to health and without her, Abby would've bet Prescott might have fled.

As they turned the corner in the camp, Abby saw Duval's wife walking a few tent rows ahead. Her skirt was anchored up off the ground and she was barefoot, carrying a large basket.

"Heavens above!" She nodded to Cerisa.

Sarah looked. "Why, I do declare, isn't that Colonel, I mean General Duval's new wife? My, o' my, she's rather inappropriately attired to be in public," she gasped.

Abby frowned. The woman was walking from the laundry. Her gaze narrowed. It was way too early to be up for such an adventure, she thought. "Looks like she went to the laundresses. Not appropriate at all! Hmmm," she paused. She'd seen Corporal Prasse with them recently and he was Duval's aide de camp, so she'd have to look further into this woman, who's accent had a slight Southern drawl to it, one Abby had heard but it was so faint, she doubted the others had discerned it. Just something wasn't right about Duval's wife and she meant to find it out what the woman was all about.

Cerisa drudged her way back to the tent. The mugginess of the morning was hinting in the air. Of course, the coarse cotton dress she'd worn to the wash was damp itself from the ordeal and that wasn't helping her any. She'd gone without stockings or shoes because she didn't have a pair she'd wear there, her work boots long since gone to shreds and she'd not ruin a new pair nor her stockings doing laundry. Besides, with her skirts low, no one would know. Granted, she'd pulled the skirt off the ground a few inches by tucking some up under the waistband in an attempt not to soak the skirt and she'd been too involved in her argument with Pierce to drop it. When she heard the gasp off to her right as she returned to camp carrying her basket, she silently swore. The busy-bodies were out, she growled softly, though she hoped they didn't recognize her, not dressed like this with her hair all tangled up, held by two hairpins and she wouldn't stop to see.

Quickly she made it around the turn, away from the ladies, and closer to her tent, still looking downward to avoid stepping in any horse dung or mess and hopefully, no more women. But her concentration that way also kept her from seeing the man who stepped before her and she ran right into him, her basket falling to the ground.

"Oh, dear, please, sir, excuse me." She was so startled as she dropped to pick up her basket and its clean linens and stockings, that her Southern drawl spilled out on every syllable.

"Please excuse me, my lady, the fault is mine, I fear."

Cerisa stopped and felt her heart skip a beat. She recognized that voice. A slow glance up confirmed what she feared. Eugene Smitherton, an officer for the Union from

New York, his Yankee accent from that city ringing in her ears. Memories of her sully days instantly filled her head. *Oh, dear Lord....* Prayers upward spewed in her thoughts, begging that he didn't recognize her. He hadn't paid for her that evening but she recalled him from the parlor, talking to her and others. His distinctive voice and the odd-colored eyes, ones that looked blue only to turn green or brown, made him stand out in a crowd. He'd been in New York for the draft rally and, according to him, barely escaped with his life from those 'dreadful black Irish', adding a limp to his walk as if on command.

"No, sir, it is truly mine. I was too hurried to return to see where I was headed." He was holding her basket and she took it back. "Thank you."

"Let me be more polite. Lt. Eugene Smitherton, at your service."

She couldn't say a word as he stared at her with his funny gaze. Her stomach flipped. She averted her eyes. "Thank you, sir. I must be going."

She tried to turn away when she heard, "You look familiar. Have you ever been to New York? Your dialect says not, but I swear I've seen you before."

With a deep swallow, she answered over her shoulder, not wanting to give him another full take of her because what if he did recognize her? From a whore house, no less. "I have made the city my home of late."

"Really? Where—"

"Truly, sir, if you'll be so kind as to let me go." She couldn't stay another moment and when she saw him step aside, as if offering her an escape, she nearly ran.

What would she do if he remembered her? And what if he told others a whore was here? Her heart fell to her stomach because her whole world might explode.

Pierce ran his fingers through his hair before shoving the hat back on. The feathered plume stuck in the brim curled down the back of the brim and tickled his neckline. Add to that, rolling sweat and he squirmed, fighting the compulsion to rip his necktie off, unbutton his shirt and breath. The promotion sounded grand, the no increase in pay was an insult and the multiplied responsibility would make any man a roiling inferno but he tempered himself. Maturity had to win over impulsiveness.

"General Duval, you need to…."

Damn it all to hell, what did Rosecrans just say?

"Apologies, sir, could you repeat that?" He looked like a fool.

Rosecrans's brows furrowed and the rest of the group shuffled on horseback, saddle leather creaking. There was a very low mutter among them as the commander edged his mount closer, the menacing look on his face darkened.

"General Duval, we understand the death of your wife, the acquisition of a new one and a promotion may have put your thinking into a whirlwind of distraction, but sir," he leaned forward, still ramrod straight, the leather bending to the pressure. "This battle requires your immediate and forthwith attention. While myself, and the War Department, have deemed you fit for command at some point, that future, along with your rank, are highly disposable if this mistreatment continues. Am I understood, General?"

Pierce wasn't sure what felt the discomfort of the moment more—his pride or the reprimand, threatening his position. He fought to bury that emotion while he answered affirmative to Rosecrans. The general, in reply, gave a tight nod then returned to the front of the column and repeated his objectives.

Another soldier sidled his mount closer and whispered, "Better to watch yourself, Duval. Old Rosey ain't for dick over victory, if'n you get my meaning."

Pierce held a low chuckle. "Thank you, Captain Blackburn. Well noted."

The junior officer gave a short single nod and silently moved his horse back. Pierce inhaled and adjusted his seat as he re-adjusted his thinking. His top priority at this moment was the War and following orders to defeat Bragg, not bedding his soon to be wife. With new perspective, he opened his ears and focused on Rosecrans's direction for the Army of the Cumberland.

Cerisa rummaged through the dresses Pierce gifted her with, looking for one she could wear here, in the heat and humidity of a male dominated camp, one that was serviceable, attractive for him since he got them, and would not be too badly damaged by tears or dirtied by filth or sweat. She roved through the silks, admiring just the fluid, cool feel of the fabric through her fingertips, knowing these were not the type she sought, till she hit the cotton dresses. A quick check and she pulled a striped blue one out, shook it out and put it on, adjusting the skirts over the corded petticoat, putting the cage crinoline aside for now as the multi-rung cage contraption seemed too formal in a military camp in a land of red clay.

"Pardon me, Missus Duval?"

Twisting the braid of her hair up and pinning it in place, Cerisa replied, "Yes. Do come in."

Through the opening, a young lady slipped in. "Good

morning. I'm Melody, Captain Brown's wife. Nice to meet you." She curtsied.

Cerisa smiled. She remembered seeing this very young, brunette lady, sitting near the back of the tent at yesterday's tea. The lady's petite youthful appearance made her seem very spritely for this early in the morning, or perhaps, it was Cerisa's lack of coffee that made her feel sluggish in comparison.

"Good morning, Mrs. Brown. How may I help you?"

The girl took a bouncing step closer. "Well, the main core of the ladies are busy, but I had one of the orderlies from the hospital come and beg for help. Apparently, they got a supply shipment in but with the latest round of sun-sickness and food issues, most of the staff is tied up in patients so they could use the help in unpacking. As you might guess, the lovely Miss Abby had projects to do, along with several others. So I've come to beg for your help."

Cerisa frowned. Helping she had no issue with, but Pierce had made her swear she'd participate with the ladies. But then again, the ladies were helping the hospital to deal with the future wounded and the current illnesses. It would occupy her time, which was exactly what she needed at this moment.

She walked up to Melody and took her hand on her arm. "Why of course, I'd be more than happy to help."

Walking out, she couldn't help but pick up on Melody's excitement as the girl rambled about the camp and her husband and the ladies. Cerisa laughed, appreciating the comradeship while learning more about her situation.

"…and General Rosecrans is so dapper!"

Cerisa blinked. She remembered the man. "Yes, he is rather so."

"Of course, my Thomas is my dream," she sighed with a

dreamy look in her eyes.

Cerisa gave a lopsided grin.

"And so is your husband," Melody added quietly. She touched Cerisa's arm and leaned closer, her voice dropping to a whisper. "Don't you worry none about those women. Word came he'd lost his wife whilst he was home, and they'd set their hats to come to his aid, providing any comfort he needed. I mean, a shoulder to weep on, or clothes mended, not anything else," she patted her, as if to offer assurances.

Cerisa gave her a proper nod while thinking Melody was way too young to understand women like Abby and her ilk. But she wasn't about to ruin this friendship that quickly by correcting her. "Thank you. It has caused me some concern."

Melody had the radiant bounce and glee of youth, of an innocent in love, in the middle of a war. Cerisa tensed. Had she ever been that way, after that night at home? The night that sent her running? She was afraid the answer was no.

They turned the corner to come to a large wall-tent where the sounds of men coughing and rustling escaped through the flaps. The hospital. A soldier near the front directed them to go to the rear of the tent and Melody virtually skipped back there, making Cerisa realize the girl had never been exposed to illness and men. It wasn't a course of instruction a mother readily gave a growing young lady. Pity, for the scene inside would probably be too much for her.

"Oh, here, Mr. Olsen!" Melody waved to a young man standing among a pile of crates and barrels with papers in his hand. He waved back and she raced over to him.

Cerisa sighed, taking a minute before she followed. The scene before her was a mess. The supplies far outranked the workers and she had to wonder just how she and any women could help since all she saw was crates being moved, not unpacked. As if to answer that question, she saw another soldier pry open a crate and Melody was right there. Cerisa decided she needed to jump in, so she unbuttoned her cuffs, starting to roll up her sleeves and start over when she heard a yell from the wall tent and a flurry of noise. She spun and hurried back.

At the tent, she drew back the flap and saw mayhem unfolding. The patient on the stretcher was flaying, fighting against the young man and doctor trying to keep him from hurting himself, which was not going to be easy. The patient was missing his lower leg and the amputation site was purple and bleeding. He was yelling incoherent phrases, his eyes wild with fever.

"Oh, my!" a feminine voice sputtered in surprise right behind Cerisa.

Melody. *Of course, this would cause any proper, young, inexperienced lady to swoon.* Cerisa spun and grabbed her friend by her elbow, escorting her out of the tent.

"This is not a place for your delicate eyes," she whispered. "Help with the supplies out here, all right?" She left the girl in the midst of the crates and hurried back inside, hearing Melody cry, "Cerisa!" Thankfully, she didn't venture back in.

Inside the tent, the orderly got the man stable as the doctor came up with a bottle and spoon in hand.

"No, no! I won't take that poison again!" he screeched when he saw the bottle. "All rot-gut, I tell you!" He started to struggle again.

Cerisa raced to the bed, maneuvering her skirt out of the way. The patient's face was turning red. She grabbed his hands and clutched them tightly, appalled at how the skin was rough and hot. He had a fever.

"Shh….," she murmured. "Let them help you."

"No, that man is the devil!" He nodded to the surgeon, who was busy pouring the medicine from the bottle into a cup.

Cerisa kept her hold on him but glanced up at the doctor. The man raised his brows and mouthed the word *laudanum,* a common pain killer made of opium delivered by whiskey. It was highly effective but, from seeing some of the women in New York, who took it as a cure for their monthly pain, it could be a little too good and they took it all the time. As the patient struggled, it would do his sutured wound no good and she knew it could make it much worse than it already looked. Knowing the drug would calm him and let the doctor take a look at the inflammation, she soothed, "Shhh, darlin', I won't let them poison you. It'll help you sleep and get better, all right?"

His reluctance waned enough the doctor was able to pour the vile concoction down his throat. As she felt the man in her embrace relax, she took a breath, not realizing she had held her breath during it all. The steward took over, helping the man lay down and started to expose the wound as the doctor came forward.

"Thank you, Miss?" he asked.

"Miss Fontaine," she started then stumbled out, "No, Mrs. Duval. Apologies. Still getting used to it," she whispered, hoping that sounded sincere.

The doctor frowned. "General Duval's wife? Well, thank you again. Major Richard Eugene Peregoy, at your service," he bowed. "Most of the ladies here rarely check on the wounded men, which at the moment we have few, but still." He smiled. It was a warm smile. "Frankly, I believe most of this here is not for a proper lady to see, so your assistance and strength to withstand the horrors are gratefully welcomed."

He paused. "I detected a southern drawl?"

She nodded but didn't add anything else.

"Well, I'm originally from Philadelphia myself, though I've got kin in Virginia." He gave a gaze at the patient's wound, a concerned look flittered across his face before he looked back at her. "Sometimes, I think, the men appreciate the soft tone ladies like you give to them in their moment of dire need."

"Thank you. It appears you have need of such help at times?"

He gave a soft chuckle. "Your help will always be gladly accepted, if you would be so inclined. I have little help with the numbers I can get, particularly from battle."

"I'd be more than happy to help you."

"Cerisa!" The flap flew open as Melody called for her. She paled upon seeing the man on the cot and his exposed amputation. "Oh, dear!"

Cerisa got up and went to her. "Are you done? Shall we see if they need us anymore?" She turned the girl around before she fainted but added over her shoulder, "I'll be back later."

The doctor nodded.

As they walked away, Melody chatted nonstop about the unpacking, no doubt, Cerisa decided, to avoid hearing about that gruesome scene at hospital tent. Cerisa smiled. Now, she had a purpose, a meaning to be here and it was not to put up with snobby Yankee women nor being abandoned by her newly appointed general/husband. Helping with the wounded was a salve to her soul, a way to heal, she thought. Perhaps to aid others who had been in Abraham's position, though she never knew if he died of wounds in a hospital or on the battlefield. But here, she could help those on the

mend. So with that, she finally found a way to fit and that
wasn't legally attached to another man, even if he was her
handsome guardian angel who saved her from prostitution.
She owed Pierce for that but outside of using his name and
money to return home, she feared owing him anymore...

Abby was shocked, no, she was stunned at the news. "She's
a whore? He brought a whore, to a military camp? Why
would he do that?"

Her friend shook her head. "Simply appalling! And to have
her dine with us, no less, and giving her his name! As if that
would wash her sins away!"

Abby would have been more disgusted if the mere
suggestion didn't make her wonder how a woman could
degrade herself so. "Well, I'm sure General Duval will receive
his halo in heaven for saving her, but to try to make her part
of our level of society is just wrong." She paced. "I sincerely
doubt they are married. If I were the type to bet, I'd lay coin
he's got her here simply for his, his...," she couldn't say the
word. Heat spread to her cheeks at the mere suggestion of
that woman spreading her legs for him. Why would he need
her when Abby could help him that way? Her cheeks heated
further.

"I do say, we must report her! How dare he! And when the
men find out, the General will have trouble controlling those
wolves in sheep's clothing!" Mary argued. Abby noticed her
friend wasn't flushed like she knew she was. Mary was too
innocent to think such immoral thoughts...

"I think you're right, Mary. It is our Christian duty to
have her removed from our presence." And from that lovely
Duval's bed, Abby wanted to add. She'd be more than happy
to help him recover from this harlot.... Abby adjusted. Her

feminine parts began to throb with desire at the mere thought of Pierce touching her.

Yes, report her they must!

CHAPTER TWENTY-ONE

"I sincerely hope that the people of the north may take the sober second thoughts and that none of us will ever be called on to witness another such a day."

—Letter from a Confederate soldier to his sister after the Battle of Wilson's Creek, where outnumbered, out-gunned, poorly equipped Confederates killed over 1,300 Union soldiers & lost 1,230 of their own. August 1861

PIERCE RETURNED TO ROSECRANS'S headquarters after a ride through the troops he'd be in command of during the attack on General Bragg and his Confederate Army. He should've been pleased with what he saw, and by the military manual they professed to follow, they were ready, but the tension amongst the soldiers leveled high and not with the feeling of fear and bravado that was normal, more of the results of being lax for too long in a war that seemed to continue on and on. He promptly had their immediate commanders put them to drill, to refocus on what was coming. It wasn't the report he wanted to give.

As he dismounted, he saw Garfield sitting at the table outside with a stack of papers before him. Whereas he wanted to simply collapse, lack of sleep making him cross, he found him appearing rested and, from the look of things, looking much better. That wouldn't last, not after Pierce put him to rights for dumping his guard-dog status to another last night. That was what he determined Garfield was, only he wasn't a fearsome sleeping monster, no, he was on-duty, to answer to Rosecrans's wants, even if that meant putting up with a raving lunatic at the wee hours of the morning. So he stormed over to the commander, the words slicing him in two at the forefront of Pierce's thinking.

"Yes, sir," he said, salute in hand as he stood before the man. He ignored the signs that up close, Garfield wasn't any better.

"Colonel Duval, please explain why you brought your whore to camp," he stated as he slowly looked up from his paperwork.

Pierce stood, frozen to the scorched ground. It took every ounce of strength for him to appear calm and focused. *What the hell happened?*

"It is *General* Duval," he quietly corrected. "That is a rather bold accusation. For what purpose do you throw a red shirt?"

Garfield leaned forward on the table. "Rosey has no patience for complaints or disruption in his command. Surely you were made well aware of this. And while I do owe you a debt of gratitude for letting me get out of his stranglehold last night, since you now bear witness to what I'm subjected to *every* night, I can't hide what the general has been made aware of. Somehow, those ladies," he used the term like it was a curse. "Claim they discovered your wife is not wife at all, but a New York prostitute you dragged down here to service you and that, *General*, Rosey will not tolerate."

Pierce stood, fuming. How the hell had these gossips found out about Cerisa's history? He'd expected maybe a sneer at her being Southern or even at his sudden remarriage but not this. In fact, he hadn't seen her in a day, so to speak, because when he finally arrived to the tent last night, he was too exhausted to say more than hello before he collapsed on the cot, deep asleep, the depravation from the night before overwhelming him. And the whole bit of her doing laundry hadn't set the few moments they had in good standing. He yanked his hat off his head and ran his fingers through his sweat-soaked hair when it hit him he still hadn't seen about the chaplain either. *Damn!*

"Cerisa is my wife," he stated. "Her only fault, I see, is having to put up with me. She's a true Southern belle, misplaced by the war. I saved her from the miscreants in New York City who wanted nothing more than to taunt a 'rebel'." That was putting the riots mildly. They had wanted to slice her up and feed her to the dogs. "She deserves no such insult as these ladies press."

Garfield sat back with a sigh. "I'm sure she doesn't. You know Abby, once she gets that bee in her bonnet, she is determined, to say the least. Perhaps if you could get knowledge out about the wedding?"

Pierce raised his brows. "What? Say a rag story? Not worthy on the news front when there's a war taking the main draw." Though he did think. Cerisa didn't wear a wedding ring, or really any jewelry. Dammit! And there was no need to send announcements for he would've eloped with her. What was he thinking? The only way he could protect Cerisa from other vermin was to marry her, but he hadn't pressed how. It was an elopement by circumstance, not over love.

Love. What a dreadful concept, he muttered inside. What the hell was he doing?

"Well, take care of it," Garfield stated, turning back to his reports. "Because if the general discovers a ruse, hell won't be below but right here."

Pierce growled low and left with fury building. He'd find the chaplain and end this slander now.

Cerisa brought the washbasin outside the tent and dumped its murky water to the ground as she inhaled deeply the Tennessee air. Saltpeter and sulfur lingered in the air but the heat amplified it. Summer in the South. She smiled. How long she had missed it.

"What is that smile about? Can't be from the work."

She spun on her heel and found Major Peregoy perched against a stack of crates. With a swipe at her brow, she fully turned, dragging the empty enameled bowl with her.

"I was just thinkin' how the heat reminds me of home."

The surgeon chuckled. "I bet. Of course, summers in Philadelphia are not like this."

She nodded, giving him a better glance. Peregoy was dressed in a navy-colored wool uniform, which she imagined would be rather warm here. The white coat he wore over it all was dirty and stained, some of the colors a muted red and it made her shudder to think how that had to be blood. He was a solid man, she thought, with no better term for his build other than it was slim, broad-shouldered, but never frayed or weak looking. His grin was easy to get and his warm brown eyes were inviting, with reddish-brown hair that had a little bit of gray to it. Frankly, he was the only man here who made her feel welcomed. Those women certainly had not.

As they entered the hospital tent, she returned the basin and gave the ward a look over. The men were resting as best as one could despite the heat.

"Your aid is most appreciated."

She turned back around. "Thank you, doctor. I would have thought you'd be more staffed than I can see."

"It is the fate of the Medical Department, to fail in getting us the supplies or means to make this a fully functional

hospital but with what I've got, I'd say it runs smoothly."
He poured her a cup of water. It was tepid but she greedily
downed the contents with as much grace as she could muster.
He tilted his head and asked, "Have you taken care of the ill
before, Mrs. Duval?"

"In a matter of speaking, yes. I used to follow my momma
and Aunt Jenny around the slave shacks, helping where I
could."

"Yes, indeed. Southern slaves. I tend to forget."

She snorted with amusement. "You forgot my Louisiana
accent? I'm not sure that'd be possible."

Peregoy shrugged. "My energy is spent mostly here. Lately,
it's been light, though I expect that's to change. Now, most
of the ladies here put on airs of caring, and perhaps in their
own way they do, but when push comes to shove, I'm bettin'
none of those wives will give a thought to the wounded and
sick. So for you to volunteer, even being here as early as you
were, just surprises me. A welcomed surprise, but one none
the same."

He did look tired.

"Thank you for the breakfast. And lunch. It was much
appreciated."

He gave her a nod. "Well, lady, you looked like you were
about to drop. As much as I appreciate the help, next time,
ma'am, eat breakfast, you hear me?"

She'd awakened and found herself alone. No Pierce.
Anger had started to boil. Not even so much as a by-your-
leave, good morning, nothing. He'd banned her from doing
laundry, in a discussion that turned vicious. Furious, she got
up, stormed about the tent, and finally, decided to forget
him and forget those women. She'd find a way to spend her
time and headed to the hospital tent without thinking of

food. Peregoy appeared pleased she'd come and offered her coffee with a list of items she could help with. But as the day dragged on, her empty stomach grumbled, despite being bound by her corset. The surgeon heard it, too, and pulled her to his office, sat her at his desk and found her food.

"Yes, sir!" She tried to give him a salute but she was no good at it and they both laughed.

"My lady, you've no need to salute a simple country doctor," he stated, trying to contain his laughter.

"Simple? Somehow I doubt that." There was something about this man. He was warm and kind to her, thankful for her help, yet he was hardly simply. The way he walked and how he acted, he gave every indication of professionalism and, to her, great intelligence. She'd trust him to treat any injury she had. Conversations with him were comfortable. Almost made her want to stay a while longer. That thought startled her and shook her back to where she was.

"Well," she started, as she ran her hands down, flattening her corded skirt. "I should be returning to camp." She stumbled over that last word. She was about to say home, but it wasn't—this was a military camp, on the edge of battled ground—yet it was. Though a tent sounded anything but ideal.

"Shall I escort you? To protect you from all the eye-hungry soldiers, who love to spend time with a lovely lady."

She smiled. "No, as I am a general's wife, I think I will be fine." She tipped her chin down, giving him a nod as she grabbed her shawl. "Good night, sir."

Pierce was angry. He was exactly where he'd prayed he'd be—back at the battlefield, on the verge of having a barrage of gunfire hailing around him and men as determined as he was to take over the other side and end this war. But, before he could have his cannon fire and blazing attack, a woman demanded his attention and that was his future wife. Over and over in his head, he tried to find out how her previous situation had been discovered. He could think of several ways and none suited him.

Stomping through the tent lanes, his boot heels kicked up Tennessee dust, adding another coat to the layers he wore on his uniform. Sweat, dirt and the smell of wool mixed with leather clouded around him. It was the scent of the army and he usually never noticed it, but with Cerisa here, it was far too obvious. He'd take time to wash only Garfield was right. Damn! He'd have to find that minister and quick, to finish this marriage before he could return to business. He had no doubt Rosey, as Garfield's nickname for the General stuck in his mind, would raise holy hell if he knew the situation.

As he rounded the corner toward their tent, on the edge of the military camp, he found Cerisa walking towards the same destination but not coming from the side of the civilian camp. Nor was she dressed like the ladies did, from what he'd seen. In fact, she wore a simple gown without the structured bell crinoline and her upswept hair was slightly askew. In fact, she looked just like the factory workers in New York. Every aspect of her outfit and composure indicated absolutely no contact with the other officers' wives, he suspected and that irritated him. Rumors would fly if she rummaged through an army camp, especially one where the wolves appeared as soldiers.

He stepped into her path, making her come to a sudden halt.

"Pierce, you startled me." She looked at him all wide-eyed and shocked. Had he truly surprised her or was she lost in thought of what she'd been doing? Something he feared he wouldn't like.

He forced a chuckle. "I just returned, my dear, from reporting to the general and am equally pleased to run into you." Controlling his anger might be difficult, he absently thought. "I'd thought you'd be here already, perhaps waiting for me?"

She swallowed. "I was intending to do just that. I had hoped for a chance to clean a bit but guess I'm running behind."

Yes, indeed you were. He eyed her carefully. "I had thought for the ladies, you might be a tad underdressed, unless you all were grooming the horses."

She snorted as she tried to get around him for the tent. "No, I missed the vipers, I mean, ladies today." When he maneuvered in front of her again, she glanced at him. "If you don't mind, sir, let me pass."

"And just what, pray tell, did you do today?"

Her shoulders jerked before she frowned. "I was busy."

"Yes, I can see the muss of your gown. It would make one wonder how that might have happened to a *lady*, in a military camp." He was pushing it, his inner self struggled to keep the anger from showing, but from the glare on her face, he was losing the battle.

With her fists at her hips, she snipped back, "Yes, of course. You'll always consider me a scarlet woman." She spun away from him, facing the tent.

"What else would you have me think?!" Once the words flew out, he instantly regretted the volume, as other soldiers in the area, no doubt noticing their turmoil, now at the tone, turned to see and hear more. *Damn! But she provoked him so!*

She stopped but didn't turn. His little rebel was glowing and shaking from her anger. He needed to stop this. This wasn't the place or the time.

Cerisa couldn't hear well, her blood raced, pounding in her ears, madder than a hornet at him. How dare he! But the last remark tipped her over the edge. Where she'd been reared to respect her husband and provider, at the moment, Pierce truly wasn't that, not before God or the law. She turned so fast, it amazed her but she refused to be belittled by a damned Yankee!

"How dare you," she snarled at him, her voice extremely low. "Unless you found the priest, which I know you have not, you have *no* right to question me!"

"Ah, but there is your error," he countered, stepping closer. "I do demand obedience from my—" He stopped and she caught the look of anger in his eyes change to something she couldn't tell.

"From your whore?" she finished, her Louisiana drawl curled around every letter. "So you brought me here, just for your pleasure?"

The men around them, standing back enough to almost not be there but she caught them and so did Pierce. They had an audience, one that was eating every word.

Again, he came closer, his tone lower. "You know better than that."

"Truly? How? I see no priest at your side, not anything that indicates that you've even tried, from the looks of you! Out gallivanting through the rebel countryside, I'd wager, from the smell of you! Looking for the enemy? You'd better look closer, darlin', I'm not that far away!"

She stared him and he returned it, his glare matching her own. Fury burned a circle around them and outside the ring, stood a growing number of soldiers. By all rights, she should try to reconcile with him, as a lady would, but he'd virtually called her a whore in public and she'd be damned if she'd let some Yankee, no matter how handsome he was or how he'd saved her from the throes of the trade! But her mother's lessons in civility rang through her bones.

"I was assisting Major Peregoy at the hospital if you must know." She stood straighter, pulling her chin up and her shoulders steeled.

"You ignored a simple request to abide my wishes and ignored the wives for menial work?"

"I did go with one of the wives to help them with their supplies that just arrived. The doctor needed help with a patient," she said calmly, fighting every nerve to tell him where he could go with that attitude. It wasn't ladylike to behave so, she could hear her mother say. So to win over herself, she looked at everything but him.

"I see," he countered. At least he wasn't yelling. Then he added, "So cleaning men's asses is more acceptable than spreading your legs?"

Slap!

William S Rosecrans, the commanding general of the Army of the Cumberland, had had it with all the officers playing off him, looking for advancement, catering to him for whatever he could do for them and from all the news contrary to what he wanted. He still roiled when he thought of that westerner who deemed him incompetent. So what if the man won Vicksburg and Meade claimed victory in the east, Rosecrans bickered. He had kept Tennessee from falling into enemy hands, at the same time they claimed victory, but he knew his blood loss was minimal, his casualties not substantial and the newsmen ignored his triumph just like

Washington did, as if nothing had happened since the losses didn't even come close to Meade or Grant. Even now, at the mere suggestion of the eastern or western part of the front set his anger off. *Braggarts, both of them!*

So he took off through the camp, to be with the soldiers who he knew loved him and he them. They called him Old Rosey and, while he considered himself anything but old, he thoroughly adored them for it. His officers, though, tried him thoroughly, except for Garfield. He appreciated that man. Good soldier, he'd keep up with his general's demands, for Rosecrans knew his orders would have his army make General Braxton Bragg and his rebels fall. With them gone, the west was won and who'd get that honor? That drunkard from Ohio, Grant? No, not him, but William S. Rosecrans would, by all God's mercy! Settled he'd win, he strode off, to be with his men who'd help him turn this war for the North.

The soldiers, for the most part, gave him a nod and a salute, mentioning "general" or "sir" in preference to his rank. The few who didn't were tied up in something. As he walked, he soaked up the spirit going through camp, of the restless men, some of which twitched for the fight, as well as the few who'd do anything to avoid it. It was relatively quiet and steady, with the occasional loud burst and crackle of fire popping up.

A splintering noise echoed, its source just before him. It was a painful sound, like flesh being flayed. He flinched before he caught himself. That type of punishment was not for his camp unless he ordered it! Heel to the ground and fast, he stormed ahead to stop this tempest before the whole war erupted here.

But rounding the next corner in the square-shaped lanes, he saw a gathering of soldiers and an argument so fierce

Rosecrans feared Bragg was here. Quickly, he bullied through the soldier-spectators to see the culprits and immediately stopped when he saw his newly appointed general spatting words at a woman. *What the hell was going on?*

"Do not do that again!" Pierce roared, his cheek brilliantly red and slightly swollen.

"Then do not insult me with your vulgarities! You Yankees are all ready to belittle my kind, well now, you've hit a wall, mister, because I will not be humiliated by your accusations!"

Rosecrans stared, suddenly realizing he was immobile by the storm before him. Domestic fights could turn ugly, heaven knows he'd seen enough of that, but this was his camp and he was their leader. He racked his brain, trying to wrap his mind around this scene when he noticed his men whispering. Gossip was not just a woman's vice, he groaned. Men could be worse and this scene just painted the perfect cyclone. He ran his fingers along the edge of his beard as he tried to think of what to say to cool them down before he found himself having to evict a good soldier. With a deep breath, he took a step forward.

"General Duval, if you please, sir."

Pierce's anger had hit a point that he no longer knew why it was provoked, but he was on fire and from the look in her eyes, she matched him, word for word. This Southern belle had turned into a hurricane, steeling herself and ready to blow right through him. Strangely, it was that magnitude of her conviction, of those flames in her eyes that burned through his core and shot like a bolt to his loins. She was vivacious, steaming and so alive. It made him hungry, because she wouldn't back down nor cower at him, whether he was right or wrong.

But when his name and rank rang in the air, his anger dissipated fast and he pulled himself upright, automatically, at attention for his commanding officer. Out of the corner of his eye, he caught Cerisa also straighten, her palms on her skirt as she panted softly. Her cheeks were still pinked from their argument.

"General, sir," he saluted.

Rosecrans offered Cerisa his arm. "Mrs. Duval." He tipped the corner of his hat with a smile.

"Pardon us, sir," Cerisa intervened, her Southern tones muted.

"Of course." The general patted her hand and shot over his shoulder to Pierce, "If I could have a word."

Pierce acknowledged the command and fell into line behind them as the general led them to a tent on the side. They entered a large wall-tent, one that appeared to serve as a meeting place perhaps, he thought, for it was too big for a normal soldier's tent and lacked the cots and rolls the men used. It did have a large table and numerous crates, barrels and assorted goods. Then he saw it. HOSPITAL was stenciled on the crates.

Rosecrans turned and offered Cerisa a box to sit on, near Pierce, as he faced them.

"General, you and the missus were having a rather," he paused, as if thinking of the right word. "Loud discussion. Now, while I'm aware the situation here can make martial relationships difficult, perhaps we could come to a resolution?"

Pierce's total being relaxed a bit. The man seemed to have a practical request. Just as he opened his mouth to state there's wasn't anything wrong, Cerisa jumped right in.

"Your priest, sir, what did you call him? Father Treacy? Perhaps you could help us find him or direct him to us for a little spiritual discussion."

Rosecran's mouth dropped open with a look of surprise crossing his brow. Pierce, inwardly, wanted to laugh. After putting up with the man's ravings til the wee hours of the morning, on subjects not always military in nature, the general had maintained an air of total control, as if he ran the entire Union army, but now? His 'wife's' request was direct, with a touch of humor Pierce decided was aimed at him, not the commander. But the fire in her eyes told him her temper hadn't abated.

"Father Patrick Treacy, ah yes. I apologize for not forwarding your previous request for his presence. He is at the local township, on a mission from God." Rosecrans's coughed. That uncomfortable statement made even Pierce raise a brow. "But I'm sure Corporal Prasse could go collect him and correct any mishaps that might have taken place? Erasing, of course, any sordid rumors."

Now Cerisa's face paled under the blazing August sun. Those damn women, Pierce swore, led by Abby Gaines. He had long suspected she was attempting to lure him into a misguided tryst, guised as a visit to comfort a mourning husband. He just wasn't interested enough to address it, and didn't really want to, mainly because he didn't trust her.

As Prasse saluted and took off at a fast military pace to find the priest, Rosecrans stepped closer. Pierce frowned. Where the hell had his aid been to suddenly be here? He shook his head as Rosey continued.

"General, my lady," he nodded to them lightly. "A possible situation has come to my attention that might cause an uproar that could, perhaps, allow General Bragg and his men to become aware of our position and, possibly, our plans. Now, I understand that the rumor is wrong, but I think, for all rights and purposes, we could revisit your union and thus silence the wolves."

Pierce's world flipped. He'd let Cerisa down and buried himself in his work, thus neglecting to find the priest to marry them, but then again, when did he have time? There was an attack to be made. He guessed he should be pleased Rosecrans happened along when he did, so this could be righted. However, a glance at her made him wonder. Was that surprise or regret? The big gulp she took led him to suspect she might reject him, an idea that, at this moment, would devastate him.

Cerisa's stomach lurched. She had been so riled up at Pierce's accusations, she frankly hadn't paid attention to the growing crowd around them nor had she cared. The man who had saved her from a life of sin only made her feel more like a whore than she had when she was one. Everything inside her screamed and all the pent-up anger and frustration fueled her argument. And in the long run, what was the result? Those vipers apparently called her a lady of ill-repute to the general. Pierce, in his absence 'working,' also launched into the same complaint when she'd spent the day helping the medical ward that could some day house him if he was injured! *How dare he!*

So all that now led to the priest being called to marry them. In a Northern army camp. It irked her to find herself now beginning to see the war this way. She'd spent the last two years doing her best to avoid thinking too much about the 'War of the Rebellion' the newspapers blasted across their front pages. She had family that lived in the South and despite her hasty running away, memories of them surfaced and made her wonder how her mamma faired and if Francois had joined up or not. Her father, she'd suspected, was a powerful man and no doubt took advantage of any road to more power and status. Of course, her brother, Jack, was a soldier for the US Army. So her family was torn, just like her.

The heat from not only the sun beat down on her. It was Pierce, giving her a look that outwardly appeared placid but she'd learned his façade to trouble. No, his eyes reflected his own confusion. She squirmed, realizing she had no choice. A marriage it would be.

"General Rosecrans, you called for me?"

She turned to see an officer peak through the tent flap.

"Yes, Father Patrick, do come in."

In stepped the man, dressed in full navy wool uniform, plucking a feathered Hardee hat from his head. He looked like no priest she'd ever seen.

The priest smiled big. "Sir, I fear dear Prasse neared medical help, the way he raced to retrieve me, so I take it the Devil has arrived, and you're in need of my assistance to rid us of him?"

"The Devil, Father, is on the other side of that river—"

"Rosey, you know as well as myself, God doesn't take sides." He stood, firm and bold, arguing against the general. "Now, tell me, what is the spiritual emergency?" He eyed her and Pierce and held a questioning look at Rosecrans.

"Yes, indeed, I think General Duval and Miss…." He looked at Cerisa and she shuddered as he continued. "Or Mrs. Duval are in need of an exchange."

The cleric rocked back on his heels. "Exchange? What type might you be suggesting? Because only one I can think of requires a priest."

"An exchange of marriage vows." Pierce's voice was tight, even she could hear the anger seeping through. Treacy gave a questionable frown.

"Yes, Father. We had been seeking your guidance to give us a union under the grace of the Church," Cerisa answered. The air was getting thick in the tent as tension rose around them. She wasn't sure why she had so quickly jumped except that's what proper ladies did, to protect their husbands and families and to waylay the uneasiness of the four. "Since my darling had to return to the War," she continued, her drawl curling each word. "And he couldn't leave me in that pit of politicians—" She heard Rosecrans smirk softly and it made her smile. "He whisked me away to the justice of the peace. Not quite the wedding I had dreamed of as a little girl."

She bit her tongue as she tried to smile brighter and gaze at Pierce lovingly. Now he wore a puzzled face. What was she to tell him? She and Abraham had bartered a reluctant, and drunk priest to marry them, but the man proved to be not much better than the gutter they'd found him in. He gave them a quick ceremony, a foolscap with his name and message he served at their marriage, took their coin and, after a sorry glance, wished them luck. Mixed marriages did exist but were hardly tolerated, particularly by the Irish as it was their women who took to the black man, she found out later. Their marriage was real as the priest was true to his faith but the clerk at the city hall barely looked at them when they entered to have it recorded by the state. It was a marriage that was bound to fail, she remembered, because only Abraham believed it was a real marriage, one the state would recognize. To her, the priest wasn't honest nor, as the city clerk declared, competent.

But as she wandered down memory lane, the group around her exploded with a way to arrange a 'wedding', for her sake she mused, and she managed to smile at the right time, but truth be told, she couldn't help but feel sad, as if this was wrong. Quickly, she found herself in front of Father Treacy, with Pierce holding her hand, and Rosecrans and Pierce's aide in attendance. She stared at the odd assortment of wildflowers and greens tied in a fast bouquet, which floored her since where did one find flowers in a military camp? She was simply amazed. The vows were said and the blessings made in one of the fastest wedding ceremonies she'd seen.

"And now you may kiss your bride."

Those words hit her hard. On her left hand was a milled narrow gold band where before there was none. Pierce had a Cheshire-cat grin on his face. It was this handsome, boyish way that always made her laugh.

Pierce stood before her, his gaze dancing with joy. "My darling wife." He raised her hand and kissed it.

She managed to smile, gritting her teeth behind closed lips. Despite his debonair looks and the fact she adored his kisses, he was truly her husband. The man before her was a good catch, the type any woman wanted and her family would adore. She cringed. It was her family that struck home. All the secrets roiled in her stomach.

What had she just done?

CHAPTER TWENTY-TWO

"You infernal s. of B.! You came to see the fun did you?"
—CSA Col. Cash cornered New York congressman, Alfred
Ely, who came to picnic to watch of the battle at the First
Bull Run, July 21, 1861

IT HAD TURNED INTO one helluva day. Pierce's
head swam. Between the heat and the flies, the dirt and
horses, the stench of wool and grungy men, he was about
done in. But to be abruptly accused of bringing his personal
whore to camp and belittling his Cerisa, set off an explosion
and he wanted to strangle someone. But the moment his lips
touched hers, his insides fell a notch. Warm wasn't the feeling
he got in return. Oh, she kissed him like a proper wife should
and that was the problem. He didn't need a high society frigid
wife. But right now, the woman he'd just exchanged vows
with, acted like she'd just been attached to a monster. Maybe
she was right, he pondered vacantly. Hadn't he messed up
this marriage, by never getting the priest himself when she
wanted, and having to follow orders to see this through by
the man whose prime objective was to crush General Bragg?

With his thoughts still tied up trying to comprehend what
just happened, Rosecrans and Father Treacy waved them
over. The priest was scrawling on a piece of paper. Rosecrans
was beaming, which looked odd to Pierce. Taking his wife by
her arm, he led her to the table, thinking how cold her hand

was, considering the temperature in the tent was growing by each second.

"General and Mrs. Duval, the registry," the priest stated, his smile brilliant. "Mrs. Duval, if you would please sign your name first."

She took the pen with a moment of hesitation, her lips thinned and her brows furrowed. A shiver of uneasiness inched down Pierce's back. Why would she be timid about a name? But with a sudden flourish, she scribbled her name and handed him the writing instrument, her lips curved in a lopsided grin. He looked down at the page and saw her full name – Cerisa Marie Fontaine Walker. Walker had to be the Colored man's name. It was right and he gave her a wink before he added his own signature. As he held her gaze, he heard the priest, general and his corporal congratulating them and probably a sigh of relief from Rosecrans. Garfield had mentioned the man was harsh on his officers and if he had one who had sneaked a whore into camp, or so said Abby Gaines, he was told, then this squashed that woman's voice.

Another thought crossed his mind. How Margaret might giggle at the thought of him taking a rebel to wife…

Shoving that aside, he pulled Cerisa closer, her hand in the crook of his arm, her face flushed with a tint of red on her cheeks.

"Father, thank you for coming to our dire need," he stated and turned to the general. "Sir, if you will, excuse me from—"

"Heavens, General Duval. I will release you from our meeting this evening. I'm sure you might have a lady here, demanding some attention." Rosecrans gave a wink. "But only this evening. Report in tomorrow morning. We have a battle to move forward."

"Yes, sir."

Cerisa moved forward and added softly, "Thank you, General. Nice way to end the day."

Rosecrans nodded, spun on his heel and left. The priest gave them another blessing, giving them their signed marriage document and followed the general, with Prasse on his heel out the flap door.

The mood was silent. Trying to give her a more warm, complacent look, he took her arm and pulled her closer.

"Please forgive me," he murmured, nuzzling along her neckline, inhaling her scent. She was complete woman, seductive, even in an old work dress. She was his wife. The idea made him growl. "I failed you on the promise I made, to keep you safe with my name and all that entails."

She gave a small laugh, causing a flash of desire to race through him, making his body tighten.

"Perhaps I did the same."

Those words cut through his lustful thoughts. A flash of that surgeon at the camp hospital went through his mind. Mere suggestion of that man made Pierce want to plant his fist in his face, but he struggled to maintain control. "How do you mean?"

She fidgeted with her shawl. "I went to the camp church, looking for the father. I didn't find him, but I met your General Rosecrans. Had a lovely but short conversation with the man. I didn't realize he was Catholic but found him practicing the same as me and he knew of Father Treacy. Told me he'd let the father know I was looking for him. I never told him why. Perhaps, if I had, we could have been a bit more discreet about this."

He led her out of the tent, leading her back to theirs. "It was pretty quiet…"

"Only after he interrupted our squabble." Inside the tent,

she turned to face him. "I cannot sit idly by, in a camp where I feel uncomfortable."

"There's no reason for that."

"Oh, truly? Those wives see me as a threat to their pursuit of you." He opened his mouth to protest but she raised her hands to quiet him. "Now, don't start with the fact they are wives. I know the looks they gave you, particularly that one, and she let me know I'm not wanted here."

He pulled her closer. "But you are." He kissed the back of her hand. "It appears, Mrs. Duval, we have one night to celebrate our marriage. Let us leave Abby Gaines and the rest outside our tent." He kissed her other hand. There was a slight shudder that even he could feel and he glanced up. Her eyes were darker and those delectable coral lips trembled, slightly open and begging for him to kiss her. He leaned forward and kissed her. Hard. Like a thirsty man led to stream, he drank every bit of her in. She locked her hands around his neck, standing on her toes to reach him. Desire swirled around them and he swooped her upright as there was a pounding on the tent pole near the door.

Quelling the drive to kill whoever interrupted him, Pierce set Cerisa back down and went to the doorway. "What?!"

Prasse handed him a bottle and a basket and quickly backed away. "Sorry, sir. General Rosecrans's sent these."

It was a bottle of wine and the basket gave the scent of beef stew. He inhaled the flavor, his mouth watering. A quick rush of hot air on his cheek with the weight of her leaning over his shoulder while he put the repast down made him chuckle.

"That smells heavenly." She sighed rather loudly. "I can't believe that is camp fare."

"It is for a general."

"You're now of that rank. Is that what you've had the last two nights while I try to down tasteless, watered stew and hard biscuits?"

"Hardtack, darling, hardtack and no. Though my meals might have been a bit more, thanks to the same general." He looked at the wine. "Sometimes, being in charge allows one better than others." He wheedled the cork clear and inhaled a sniff out of the bottle. It was robust, with a hint of berries. Pleased, he grabbed two tin cups and poured. Handing her one, he raised his. "To my wife, the rebel."

She gave him a half smile. "To my husband, Yankee to the core."

He couldn't help but laugh. It was so fitting. As they took a sip, he saw her swallow her sip and the animal inside him roared. All it took was a look, and perhaps he had growled but he wasn't sure, and they were in each other's arms again.

This time, he drank from her lips, rolling in the pleasure of her taste mixed with the wine. She was decadent and seductive. He had no doubt she'd out do him in the end and he'd go with a smile plastered on his face. Quickly he invaded her lips, his tongue at odds with hers, before he left there to trace down her neckline with the tip of his tongue. Her skin had its own taste. It was so soft, so smooth. Perhaps it held a trace of glistening from the sun, the result of work in a hot climate or the essence of cotton against skin, he wasn't sure but the one thing he did know was he wanted more of her.

Tracing a finger around her dress collar, he found the closures and started to unlatch every hook and eye down the front of her bodice. At the moment, he despised women's clothes, because the snug bodices were closed so tightly that it took every ounce of stamina he possessed not to just rip the top open and let the fabric rent as it would. At the waistline, there was one closure then an open split that opened the dress enough he could peel it off her. Once freed of the dress, the fabric, combined with the loosened petticoat fell to the ground and she stood in her undergarments.

She laughed. "Not exactly the same sheer outfit you first saw me in at Madame Nikki's, is it?"

Frankly, his only thought was she was still too overdressed. He lifted her chin and found a strange look in her eyes, as if he judged her by that brief moment she had fallen, in an attempt to stay alive. His earlier accusation of it hung heavy over him and made him grimace. He'd spend the rest of his life if needed to get her to forget that place.

"Shhh," he whispered. "Truth be told, all I notice is you're still way too dressed. I want my wife." He kissed her lips then her neck, down to her shoulder and then on the skin just above her breast.

Kissing across the mounds above the chemise, he pulled the ties to the corset and in a split second, gave her a nudge so he could unhook the busk of it and once undone, he flipped it off. The chemise followed, with the under petticoat and pantalets next. He hummed. "Much more to my liking."

She had waited for him to finish then started to unbutton his shirt and the waist of his trousers. He stood, amazed how quickly her hands worked. Her nipples were hard and red, as if begging him to suckle. She had him down to his drawers but he couldn't take it any longer. Those pearled tips called his name and he had to answer.

When he took the first one into his mouth, she shuddered, the shiver passing into his arms. He suckled just a little harder and heard her mewl in response. He wouldn't give in just yet. Tracing up her leg, he hit the lips to her feminine core and inside he roared. Instantly, he felt the heat as the musk wrapped around them. Inwardly, he smiled. He glanced at her as he laid her down on the roped cot and saw the same hunger in her that he felt deep inside. The buttons at his crotch opened, his throbbing member sprang free and in seconds, slid deep into her.

As they rocked, matching each other's thrusts, he put his fingers over her mouth when she released an anguished sigh. Last thing he wanted was for the soldiers outside their tent, even though they were on the edge of camp, to be alerted to them. The quiet sent him to a higher plane, because he saw her giving in deeper, concentrating more on the motions than reacting. He moved faster. The pulsing of her sheath seemed to tighten with every move and he tried to keep it going longer, for he so wanted to please her in this first time as a truly married couple. With the next thrust, she shattered, igniting the ebbs of uncontrolled passion to pull him in and within that split second, the stars exploded in his head.

They stopped in motion, never moving as each tried to regain their bearing. Pierce couldn't help but smile and when he opened his eyes to see her, he expected joy. What he saw were tears.

CHAPTER TWENTY-THREE

"I tell you now, sir, that you are standing over a crater, whose smothered fires in a moment may burst forth."

—Rose O'Neill Greenhow letter to US Secretary of State William Seward, November 17, 1861

September 18, 1863

SLOWLY AND WITH GREAT reluctance, Cerisa allowed the buzzing noise to pull her from sleep. The heat of the morning was picking up and the sun forced its way into the tent, along with the sound of boots on packed earth, the grunts of soldiers along with the nicker of a horse or two. One of the equine's tails batted the canvas wall and the slapping sound made her eyes shoot wide open. With a blink to clear the sleep from her eyes, she focused, sitting up on the roped bed, noticing she was the only one there. She shook her head and groaned.

She had married him, to save her reputation, which was a disgrace by any means, and then he ran from her as she slept. The whole idea made her stomach twist. Well, he did suggest she put her chemise on last night, after they were spent from making love, so she wasn't nude. A flash of anger instantly shot through her and she threw her legs over the cot's edge, gripped the sides of the make-shift bed, and stood. So he wedded her, bedded her, then left with no word. Nothing better than Madame Nikki's…

Crash! The sound of falling wood, rifle barrels and horses neighing with stomping hooves clamored outside her tent and she jumped, startled, quickly grabbing the scratching woolen blanket at the foot of the cot to cover herself with. She heard the soldiers cooing as well as scolding the horses and someone named Ted about the disaster as they picked up whatever it was that fell. No one came to the tent and the canvas wall backing up to the accident remained intact so she had that to be thankful for. It surprised her anything was going on here. Pierce's officer's tent was at the edge of the officers' section, closer to the civilian camp. She too had a 'house' so to speak with the other ladies but she'd never stayed there. Despite their discontent, she preferred to stay with him and he wanted her there. In a way, she believed it and it fulfilled their newlywed status, despite what those vipers said. She exhaled the breath she had held and released the blanket. The horses and soldiers walked away.

She poured water into the washbasin and splashed her face, trying to keep from using too much of the liquid. Water in a war zone was difficult to get—not due to the lack of supply with the Chickamauga Creek close, along with other tributaries, but because of the danger it was in enemy territory. That and if it was too close to the horses or trenches, the filth would be anything but desirable. She shuddered at the thought, though from the looks and lack of stench, this water was clear and still cool. In quick haste, she dressed and pulled her hair up. A box near the inside of the tent flap held a piece of fresh bread, which astounded her in a military camp, with butter and a small jar of jam. Smearing the bread with the butter and jam, she couldn't help but smile. Being an officer's wife did have some advantages. Coffee, though, was not in the box so she'd have to find it and there was no better place than at the hospital, since she had yet to see Doc Peregoy without a cup in his hand.

Stepping outside the tent brought the war back with full clarity. Chaos reigned around her. The mayhem near the tent apparently wasn't the only issue of the day. Around her, horses were geared, with their saddles and reins leathers creaking as they sidestepped with new orders. A short line of soldiers marched side by side down the lane, their faces blank as they followed the sound of their leader, keeping form, which nearly pushed her off the path. Breathless, she gathered her wits and her skirts to walk faster.

Finding the hospital tent, she pushed into the interior and found two men in their shirtsleeves nod at her as they continued breaking down the cots that yesterday held nearly a dozen patients. But these beds were empty now. She frowned, confusion creeping in. Those men, as she recalled, had diarrhea or dysentery, neither illness, as distraught as they were, cleared in a night.

"Ah, Mrs. Duval." The warm sound of Peregoy filtered across the tent, making her relax knowing he was there. "What a pleasant surprise. Good morning."

She returned his smile. "Yes, good mornin' as well. What is going on?"

He chuckled as he turned to one of the stewards and took the cup out of the man's hands, bringing the steaming brew to her. "Apparently, we're moving. Time to pack up shop and prepare for oncoming."

She gulped and almost burned her tongue. "General Rosecrans?"

"Yes ma'am. Shouldn't surprise you. I'd expect that your husband told you."

She squirmed. When would he have time? Pierce had been way too busy enjoying her body to talk. Or had he told her, but she failed to listen. But nothing came to mind about last night outside the feel of him. Managing to give the doctor a look of not knowing, she took another sip as her core began to melt at the memory of Pierce's touch.

Peregoy's gaze narrowed then he shrugged. "We've done this before. Thinkin' its Rosey's way to make sure we're ready or maybe the attack is soon." He snickered and dropped his tone as he leaned closer. "Or, more likely, way to clear my wards. Half those boys have been here before."

Her head snapped back as she frowned. "They make themselves sick?"

"Well, around here, there's plenty to prompt that ailment. Soiled water, under-cooked meats, foul food, poor whiskey and yes, they find ways for that, too, if given a chance." He snorted. "Come down with that gets one out of line and out of a way to possibly be shot." He took the paper an incoming soldier gave him and sent him off. "Those two, folding the beds? They're the end, the last to still be ailed by it. I 'xpect them to be healthy by the end. This type of labor is too beneath them." He nodded toward the two.

She glanced. He was right. The two muttered and their movements were stiff, like men furious to be doing a slave's job. "Well, perhaps this is the best medicine of them all, then."

Peregoy laughed. He had such a warm, welcoming personality, now she knew why she came here for coffee versus trying to find her husband or his aide. She smiled back at the doctor.

Pierce couldn't help but let the water spill over the spout, way too much to drink, part overflowed onto his cheek and down his neck. It was hotter than Hades, he was sure, and the sweat only made his cotton shirt wet and the wool jacket heavier. The only reason he even noticed was because he stopped for water and tried to divert his thoughts back onto the matter at hand and not the woman he had wed.

He'd rolled out of bed, realizing he was probably late, so he'd done his best not to disturb her but grab his clothes and ran. Throwing on his shirt and trousers, he couldn't take his eyes off the beauty in his bed. Thank heavens he'd convinced her to put the chemise back on last night. The air was too hot for a wool blanket over them and he'd be damned if he thought of leaving her in this den of wolves with only a cover on that she'd no doubt kick off due to the heat. Of course, the memory of her naked thigh, visible before he left, had seared his brain and the bolt of lightning plunged to his loins. Damn!

"General, from the General."

He inhaled, adjusting in the saddle, the leather creaking as he adjusted his seat to relieve pressure against his groin. "Thank you, Lieutenant." The name escaped him but he took the scrolled page from him. It was a message from Rosecrans. "Find Minty and report."

Pierce wiped his brow after he pushed the page into the pocket under the frock coat's closure. The general had given him and his bride a wedding night but that nicety came to a screeching halt this morning when Pierce arrived a few minutes late. Rosecrans had not scolded him before the others but the scowl in his look and the assignment he just received made the commander's anger evident. Colonel Robert H.G. Minty and his 973 men of the 4th Michigan combined with the 7th Pennsylvania and 100 battle-ready men of the 4th U.S. Cavalry, had run into a situation that the lieutenant only hinted at the complexity of. Apparently, from what he had gathered, things were dark along the edge of the Army of the Cumberland's line, a mere breath away from Confederate General Braxton Bragg's army. As most men at this point were edgy, Pierce considered Minty more so. He'd met the man prior and his demeanor edged on crazy, supposedly muttering today was going to be a bad day. And from the note, the man must have made his fears come to light.

The long-awaited battle was almost on them. While Pierce tightened in expectation of taking his aggression out on the enemy, a pang of fear and regret battled within. He now had a wife, a woman he was to protect, but instead, he'd brought her to a war....

Over his shoulder, he shot back to Prasse. "Corporal, what was Mrs. Duval up to this morning?"

Prasse instantly came to Pierce's side, his horse stopped short of them being on equal level as the aide knew better than to push his rank. "She woke slowly, sir. Barely had enough time to see her about. She left the tent, heading to the hospital when I was called, sir."

Pierce bristled. The hospital, huh? He knew the medical department was over-demanded with dwindling supplies and support but he wasn't thrilled with her there. And who the hell was this surgeon in charge?

His horse sidestepped, a motion that made Pierce have to rebalance, thus bringing him back to now. He sat a bit straighter and concentrated on the one thing he did make sense out of and that was the enemy over yonder. To stay and contemplate his wife might tempt him to go beyond his rank with the surgeon. No, this was far safer. Gritting his teeth, he pointed his horse toward Minty's command.

With a cup of that black liquid gold down her throat, Cerisa finally felt awake. The chaos outside the medical tent lulled and the quiet inside was peaceful. She leaned against the table the orderlies had left standing and just stood. She was married—again. Yesterday had been a whirlwind of events, blurring everything in her memory except for the sudden wedding, a show for the commander, if she allowed herself to think that way. Granted, she'd allowed herself to be caught in this cyclone of circumstances. Without Abraham's pension, after she lost her job and no one would hire her, whoring was the last resort and that was disastrous. The war made traveling home completely out of the question, regardless if she had the funds or not and she didn't. Only Pierce saved her, but the price of surviving had been iffy, as she discovered here in the Union camp. The world she'd known shriveled to nothing and left her to her own resources.

She should be forever thankful to Pierce for saving her and she was, though was marriage the answer? The last drop of coffee went down the wrong pipe as the answer flashed into her mind of yes, it was the only answer by an honest man. He could've kept her as his mistress but instead, he made her an honorable woman. *Why?*

A chuckle from across the room snagged her attention. She glanced and found the doc staring at her with twinkling eyes.

"You looked so fixated on that cup, I feared you'd lose your footing and fall."

She couldn't help but snort. Something about Peregoy made her slightly giddy. "No, just lost in a thought."

"Well, follow me. We'll get you some more and perhaps, you can help me when the time comes."

As they stepped back into the other adjoining tent, she asked, "When what happens?"

Out of the corner of her eye, she found a few of the ladies at a table. Spread before them were long wooden boxes, lined in deep red velvet and silver medical instruments laying on the tabletop. They sat, rubbing furiously, at the tools. One of the women was Abby Gaines. She looked up and saw Cerisa. The smile on her face was a fake but the venom in her eyes was real.

"What are they doing?" she asked quietly.

"Ah, they're polishing my instruments, preparing me for the day," he answered, filling her cup up with coffee.

"Thank you." She blinked, trying to ignore the woman and focused on the doctor. "How may I help?"

He smiled and she found the warmth from that filled her and that the busy-body over polishing the instruments held no hold on her, despite the pinpoint fire Cerisa felt from that woman's glare. To banish her further, she took the doctor's offered arm. *Abby Gaines could go rot!*

Any thoughts Pierce had about his new wife fled the moment he found Colonel Minty. The man was in complete hell. Little did he know that Rosecrans's order came from the information the general received from Minty, who'd reported the strength and numbers of force he'd encountered. But upon getting closer, Pierce saw the battle and quickly tried to assess the entire situation. He recognized the colors of Confederate General Nathan Bedford Forrest. What should've been a minor incursion had exploded to a fight neither side was ready for. Minty's numbers paled against the Confederates. And it was only noontime.

Pierce pulled back on the reins with the two junior officers, two lieutenants, falling in behind him. He found Minty issuing orders, and two large guns of the Chicago Board of Trade Battery moving into place at the crest of Peavine Ridge. Troops from the 4th Michigan, 7th Pennsylvania and the 4th US Regulars formed a line encircling the ridge top, behind the guns.

Still scanning the countryside, Pierce waited and one of his staff rode up.

"Minty's got about six hundred troops, sir."

Pierce snorted, putting the looking glass down. "We've got General Bushrod Johnson out there, boys. And I see General Forrest's colors. That six hundred won't scratch the dirt off a horse's ass in comparison." He spat at the ground before he gathered his reins. "Looks like we got hell about to explode. Ha!" he urged his stallion into a gallop, his two aides following.

"Colonel Minty." Pierce stopped near the officer. Minty stood firm, his feet planted as he issued orders to the men about him.

"...Sir, I also am in need of Colonel Wilder's aid in this endeavor, for any troops he could send my direction. Bushrod's about to take a stab at our location here, at the Reed's Bridge and we are in need. Very truly, your obedient servant, Colonel Minty," He coughed, the noise rough from exposure to the dust and sulfur that encased the area. "Send that fast."

"Yes sir!" The soldier took off at a harrowing speed.

"Damn rebs!" Minty swore, before he turned and found his visitors. "General Duval, my apologies."

Pierce said nothing. This fight was in part of the territory that was split by the rolling Chickamauga Creek that was broad and anything but shallow. Not easy land to defend by either army. He could see the other side forming for attack right as the courier returned from Wilder.

"Colonel Minty, sir." The soldier panted hard from running. "Colonel Wilder is dispatching two regiments."

"Good," Pierce answered. "That'll help bolster the firepower here as this position is too exposed." The section of land they stood on bulged out into the enemy's side, if the creek ran like a crow flies, but it bent, making them vulnerable on three sides. A rickety bridge across the creek was the only dry crossing. He yanked his hat off his head, the heat of the sun beating down on him made it unbearable. As his fingers combed his hair from the forehead back, he muttered, "Lousy position to get us in."

The soldiers below grew in numbers. He watched as some of the cavalry dismounted and formed a line to fight with the fellow rebel infantry. At this moment, Minty's men were outnumbered and the two field pieces would hardly make a dent if the regiment before them attacked. Frowning, it was clear this defense was ill-timed and he knew Rosecrans would delay in sending any more troops, saving all for the main drive against Bragg, despite the fact the men below were Bragg's as well.

"I didn't choose it, sir. They found me."

Minty's argument fell on deaf ears. Pierce knew the man wouldn't provoke a fight, not with 'old Rosey' in charge.

"And I don't believe it's just here they be after," Minty continued.

That statement Pierce agreed with. But here was a foothold into Federal ground and to take it was an anchor in reclamation of captured territory, something Rosecrans would raise holy hell over and go against the aim of this war.

"Colonel, continue your defense lines. We can't allow

them to push us back. And watch that bridge." Pierce pointed toward the tattered wooden contraption. "If they make it across, with their numbers, we'll have no choice but to retreat and re-form, understand me?"

Minty pulled himself upright, bolstering his own height as Pierce gave him backing to do whatever it took. "Yes, sir."

Pierce nodded and reined his horse to the right, his two lieutenants in tow. The war was about to burst larger than life. He hoped they were ready. And he worried, with Cerisa here. *What the hell was he doing, bringing his Southern wife to the Yankee side of hell?*

CHAPTER TWENTY-FOUR

"We gave more than we caught and swept on in a magnificent charge carrying everything before us till we were halted."

—Pvt. James M Weiser, 54th Virginia Infantry on 2nd day Chickamauga when Weiser's regiment attacked a gap in the Union line, a move that forced the Army of the Cumberland to retreat, September 20, 1863

WHAT HAD STARTED AS another day quickly dissolved into hurried work and tension escalating through the camp. Panic raced on a thread with each double-step of every soldier and blossomed in the civilians filtering into the campgrounds, looking for shelter and assurance all would be well. Cerisa ran into those worried people, women mostly, from the civilian camp as they sneaked past the sentries to the hospital tents, a place they hoped was safe. The last one she saw was no different than the first, begging for help, a service she was at no place to offer. Fact was simple. She had no idea what to tell them because she'd never seen this and the one man who should protect her, for it was part of their vows after all, was nowhere to be found.

So Cerisa turned to the only man she knew who was close—Doc Peregoy. Richard, she corrected. He insisted she call him by his given name, because everyone else just yelled doc, and with all the demands, he'd miss her call. He gave her refuge in the hospital and in return, she did her best to help him and his surgeons prepare for what appeared to be a battle looming ahead. The mere suggestion of guns and war turned her blood to ice, even in the late Southern summertime. Now, a shiver raced through her and she blinked, realizing her hands had gripped the box of medical silk thread tightly, enough so the ridges tore into her flesh. A flash of pain in her right palm instantly made her release her hold and the box fell to the dirt floor but the splinter remained embedded in her hand.

"Shhh. Let me see it."

Gulping the next yip, she nodded as Peregoy took her over to his makeshift desk. Propping her against the side of the table, he opened his surgical box and rummaged through it with a slight chuckle.

"I'm taking it, you've been lucky enough to avoid any exposure to the hell we experience here," he remarked, pulling a pair of tweezers out of the box. Twisting her hand to expose the wound, he started to pluck it out, operating so fast there was no pause for her to breathe, let alone answer. He found the culprit that stabbed her and tugged. It sent a slice of pain in her flesh and she held her breath until he pulled it out, with instant relief flooding her veins.

"There. Got it."

As he picked up a cloth piece and dampened it with alcohol, she finally found her tongue. "Thank you. Ouch!"

Peregoy chuckled. "A little dab of whiskey to clean that spot up." He looked at her, his eyes dancing with light of amusement. "Can't have my little nurse unable to function."

She snarled and yanked her hand back, rubbing the area near the wound. It still stung from his rag. "It's just a poke. Water would've been fine."

The doctor continued to laugh. "Perhaps."

She grabbed a lint roll and unraveled it. She tucked the end in after she wrapped her hand.

Peregoy tilted his head. "You sure you want to stay? I could use the help, but a lot of what we get here can be gruesome, truth be told. Shrapnel, bullets, sword wounds can rip a man to shreds. Broken bones, bleeding holes…they can be numerous as the battle rages."

She remembered the views of people being trampled in the riots last July. Of the murderous gleam in the eyes of the mob and the havoc she saw before being cornered. The hung freedmen, lynched just because they were in the wrong place at the wrong time, ate at her soul. What if that'd been Abraham? It was that thought and how he'd perished at a place like this, all to defend his freedom, that made her nod to his question. "Yes, I'll stay. It's the least I can do." When he looked at her with questioning eyes, she added, "I lost a loved one in this mess. I'd like to think he had proper care but regardless, he died." A lump formed in her throat right as her eyes started to blur. *No!* She'd not break down again.

"All right, then." Peregoy pushed away from his leaning on the table. "I hear men and horses. It's starting. There's no time to move, wounded will come." He motioned her to the main tent and led the way.

She realized this place was wreaking havoc with her soul. The surgeon was good but he needed help so he'd say anything to make sure she'd stay. Pierce offered her his protection through marriage, only last night still plagued her. It was one thing to make love when it was a longing for him and she could just comply and let the beauty of it rock her. But last night was different. Half way through it, it hit her how this was her husband, not a client or a knight protecting her. She'd endured being a whore. It helped her survive it. Was it different now? Pierce followed through, though she did notice he hadn't raced to do so, but pushed by his commander, he did what he promised and she wore his name and all that came with it. So why her heart weep?

Before she could think further, the tent flaps opened to a myriad of wounded, carried on blankets, in the arms of comrades, or half-limping to the hospital. She jumped to see them, directing them to the areas Peregoy had told her certain injuries should go so he could take his stewards and other doctors to set up the surgery without having to leave so many personnel behind for menial tasks. With two others, she began to separate them and found the mass of soldiers before her, after an hour of sorting, hadn't diminished. Instead, the numbers grew.

"Nurse, nurse!"

She turned to the source and found an injured man crawling on the floor, yanking at her skirts. He was dirty, bloody and a total mess of tangled clothes and sweaty hair.

"Please, help me!" He then collapsed.

"Soldier..." she started but stopped. "Steward Michealson! Michaelson, hurry!"

Underneath the prostrate man was a pool of blood. She traced down his form to find the wound, hoping she'd see it without trying to turn his now inert form. It took but a second to see the man's lower leg was askew and the pant leg was soaked with blood. Taking a knife, she ripped up the pant leg and found the leg was nearly severed beneath the knee, the vessels spewing blood among the torn skin and muscle. Bile rose up her throat and it took all she had not to retch. *War was horrible!*

The battle at Reed's Bridge continued all afternoon. Pierce

fought along with Minty and his men, trying hard to keep the rebels from overpowering them, from pushing the Army of the Cumberland back. By late in the afternoon, both Minty, Pierce and Wilder, upstream with his cavalry, were pleased they had held a large Confederate attack back but all would change. The Union's minimal numbers could not stop the Confederates from finding another way across the river. Wilder retreated with his force first. General Bushrod Johnson's rebels pushed again and Minty had no choice but to retreat back across the bridge. Pierce swore. The bridge itself was fragile and narrow, making the army form only two lines to cross, slowing the process down. In a last-minute attempt to stop the enemy, Minty had his men tear the planking off the bridge and toss it into the river, making the bridge no longer useful.

As the day wore on, the attacks intensified and the Union withdrew but by evening, Pierce learned that the Confederates under Forrest had crossed the river, at Alexander's Bridge, roughly a few miles away from camp. He growled, furious they hadn't been stopped.

He rode back to Rosecrans and gave the final report for the night. He was exhausted, hot and sweaty, his cotton shirt stuck to his skin. Nothing sounded better than jumping into the river to cool off but that was impossible. Instead, he settled for a pitcher to douse himself with, food, a drink and his wife.

It had struck him late morning that as much as the gunfire increased, he was distracted by a pretty little Southern belle he'd dragged here in an attempt to escape his father's machinations. He avoided asking what drove her from the South. It must have been something intense to drive her to New York. Her mannerisms, despite being in the lower district of the City and her means to live, indicated she was raised in high society. The man she called husband was a negro and he suspected her slave at one point. Why did she marry him?

His marrying the Irish had been a slight to his father's name. That he'd heard several times, and more than he wanted, in Margaret's presence. It amazed him how a man who was an abolitionist was so anti-Irish. But her death had haunted him. Margaret never stood a chance as he'd brought her into a prejudiced family, one that made sure she was unwelcomed at every turn. Then he left her in the bosom of her enemy so he could fight in the war.

He figured he'd killed her by exposing her to the wrong people—his family. He blamed himself and knew he'd burn in hell for it. Not a day passed without him remembering her…

Until now. In the midst of the battle, as he spun on his mount to grab Minty, his horse stumbled and tilted, slanted so fast, Pierce lost his footing in the stirrups and fell. He landed on the same arm that he'd injured before and the impact sent rivets of pain through him. It was that sharp pain, the type that made him think of what he was doing. He'd run headlong into the attacks, on the lines with the men, not only fighting the enemy but also the enemy within him and that plunge with the fall, made a woman return to his mind, only this time, it wasn't Margaret. It was Cerisa.

That realization nearly got his head blown off. He didn't hear the whizzing of the bullet till almost too late and he tried to turn away but got nicked on his temple by the shot. As blood poured down his face, he yanked a handkerchief from his pocket, pressed it against the wound as it hit him just how mad he must be to bring her here. This was war. Blood and mayhem and death. He cursed.

Cerisa was his wife and he suddenly discovered she was also his heart. But finding her in tears after he'd taken her to the stars and back, or so he thought, shook him dearly. *Damn, damn, damn!*

"General Duval," Rosecrans stated, after he gave his report of the withdrawal but also of the rebel retreat. "Perhaps you should have that wound looked at."

Pierce frowned. He'd forgotten about the bullet nick, especially after he'd pressed the linen against it long enough that the blood had stopped. Only now, at the mention of it, did he feel a slight twinge. He gritted his jaw and answered, "No, sir, it was only a scratch. Let the surgeons deal with the men who truly need it."

Rosecrans frowned for a second but then, he nodded. "Very well then, we strike on the morrow. Sleep is needed. And I believe you need it more than the rest. Go. Until the morrow."

Pierce left, though he caught the flash of anger and envy in Garfield's face. Poor man would have to put up with another all-night rant instead of the rest needed before battle. As to himself, he'd have problems also, because he had a dying need to see his wife, to see that she was real and not a figment of his imagination. Perhaps it was the exhaustion of today, maybe the fear he was wrong and she didn't care a whipstitch about him, though why he questioned that, he wasn't sure. Damn, he was tired.

By the time he reached his tent, he wished he'd bathed first. He knew he was covered in dirt and the grime of battle, sweat, smelled of saltpeter, wool and horse dung but there was no time. It was too late. Until he threw the flap back.

"Cerisa." He looked around the dark tent, shocked and

disappointed she wasn't here. Then it hit him. She'd be with the ladies for supper. He spun on his heel and headed to the ladies' camp. But once there, he found only a small contingent at Abby's tent.

Abby smiled at him until he asked about Cerisa. "Your wife?" she asked, as if that was still a guess. "No, we haven't seen her since this morning at the hospital tent."

"Oh, yes," another one chimed in. "We were there, helping poor Doc Peregoy ready the hospital for upcoming days by polishing his medical instruments. You lovely wife came in but that's all I saw of her." She adverted her eyes and blushed. "We all left as soon as we were through."

"Yes, as is fitting," Abby added firmly. "No proper lady would be in such a place. Simply inappropriate, considering the state in which those wounded arrive."

Instantly, the hairs on the back of his neck bristled. Peregoy. Son of a bitch, Pierce swore. And of course, Abby Gaines couldn't help but make a stab at how his wife was still considered beneath them with her statement. To him, Cerisa was compassionate and helpful, though right now, he'd give anything for her not to be. He gritted his teeth, holding his anger in check for the ladies and managed to paste a smile on his face. "Thank you. Good night, ladies." He bowed and left, heading straight to the hospital.

He stormed down the path, every step fueling the fire inside him. As he turned the corner, he entered the hospital tent and came to a dead cold stop. In the center of the tent, in the midst of the few cots, laden with soldiers wounded from today's fight, stood his wife, her hand inside Peregoy's, her arm bare. She was smiling at the beaming surgeon who said something, what Pierce couldn't hear as blood pounded through his veins, filling his ears with noise blocking his hearing. They both laughed. They were way too close, way too intimate to his taste and his sight turned red by the time he reached them.

"Cerisa, darling, I've been looking everywhere for you," he said, amazed at how cool and soothing he sounded when all he wanted to do was slug the doctor. Quickly, he slid his arm around her middle and pulled her close. He buried his face next to her neck and sniffed the mixture of her mixed with the lavender soap he'd picked up for her, back in Washington and the scent of the two stirred his heart and loins.

"Pierce, please." She wiggled in his embrace but it wasn't to get closer but more to give her some space. He didn't like that and his arm tightened until he heard a slight groan.

"General Duval, if you please, you are battle filthy and in no state to be that close," Peregoy interjected. "Your wife has a slight wound that needs to be handled with care." He reached to finish tucking in the end of the wrapping Pierce now noticed on her exposed arm.

His eyes shot wide open and he frowned. "You're hurt? Here? Who harmed you?" His gaze darted to the surgeon and then scanned the room before he looked down at her naked palm. There, he saw a slightly swollen red flesh with a puncture that was slowly starting to pucker shut. "What the hell happened?" he demanded.

"There's no need for vulgarity, as if I did this on purpose," she replied, pulling her arm out of his reach. "I got a splinter from a box. That is all. Doc Peregoy says its nothing and I will recover." She smiled at the surgeon.

"You take care of yourself, Mrs. Duval, and thank you for all your help today." Peregoy looked at Pierce and added, "Your wife was a great help to the cause, a grand merit of a true champion. None of the other ladies dared to stay, but she did when I needed help the most." He bowed. "My deepest thanks."

Did he just catch his wife blush? He bit his tongue to keep from lashing out at the doctor for being way too close for society's rule. As soon as Peregoy left the room, Pierce glanced at Cerisa, whose face had returned to ivory clean.

"How do you feel?"

She stretched the injured hands fingers and flexed. He noticed a slight hesitation in the one. "It will be fine. Thank you." She looked at him. "No point to act like a bull in a china shop," she added. "I've been helping your army's medical department all day, dealing with the injuries you and your men created." On that note, she walked out of the tent and headed for her own on the edge of the encampment. Pierce followed, his bootheels clicked against the hard ground, kicking up dust.

Once at the tent, he motioned to a junior officer to order food and then he went in. She poured water into the basin and dipped her hands in, patting her cheeks and forehead gingerly with that injured hand. She must have touched the puncture because he saw the wince on her face and the quick withdrawal of the hand to her side. Damn! Last thing he wanted was her hurt! Some protector he was turning into…

With a yank, his frock coat came off, followed by his boots and waistcoat. Then he shucked the suspenders off. "You were the only lady there?"

He found her sitting on the edge of the cot, dragging her brush through her hair. "Mostly. Why?"

"I don't want you to go back there." There. He'd said it.

Her eyebrow arched as she glared at him. "And what is wrong with that?"

"It's not a safe place, nor a proper place for a lady, especially my wife." Abby's reference on propriety hit the subject soundly.

Her gaze hadn't broken but her glare turned to a troubled gaze as she stopped stroking her hair mid-stride. "Why?"

He did notice her accent had returned fully. It sounded delightful, falling from her lips. But it didn't change the circumstance that she was here and open to any man's attention. "You know precisely why." The water he splashed on his face washed some of the sweat away but it wasn't enough to try to cleanse the war off him, nor the anger that hinted at the edge of his thinking.

She had just folded her apron she'd worn at the hospital but instead of putting it to the side, she dropped it on the cot and spun to face him. "No, I can't fathom why, other than you brought me to the warfront and now you've become appalled I'm not cowering in fear with those other lilies."

Pierce had taken a gulp of water and almost spit it out in laughter. She had turned into a spitfire, that was for sure! He walked over to her and tipped her chin up to see her eyes. Her cheeks were flushed, her gaze one of contempt, hopefully at Abby and her kind, and not him. He may not have known her for that long, but one thing he was aware of—life had thrown a cannonball at her, with The Points, the factory work, the prostitution and putting up with him. Shaking in fear did not seem to be in her repertoire of emotions. "Darling, cowering is never a word I would use to describe you."

But she still stood firm, her jaw set, her eyes glaring at him. She was beautiful, all fire and life, willing to take on the whole Union army, he decided. Battling Bragg was difficult but Cerisa made even Lee look like an easy target. His heart swelled when it hit him again just how much his heart filled with love for her. And it was that love that made him afraid. It was war, after all.

"In that tent, there could be a lot of men, men with injuries that are often so grotesque that the sight is unbearable, their pain and suffering hard for even those trained to care for them." He kissed the top of her head and the tremor that went down her spine he could tell by that touch. Hopefully, he was winning the case for her to stay away. "These men are afraid they'll die, and rightfully so. Many are mangled, blood and everything else on full display. I'd do anything to keep you from such horrors." He pulled her fully into his embrace. "Some might even try things that are inappropriate for ladies to see or experience. And the numbers can be quite high. Helping Doc Peregoy now might seem helpful but leave him to his training of dealing with this and you stay far away."

Her glare transformed into a questioning look. "You are serious, aren't you?"

He bit back the extra line of not trusting Peregoy an inch alone with her. That Pennsylvanian quack showed all the signs of a charlatan was what he wanted to say, but he held the remark back.

"I'm just concerned about your welfare."

The moment the words left his mouth, he saw the spark it set off reflected in her eyes.

"*My* welfare? You brought me to this war!"

"Cera, please," he forcibly lowered his tone. "I had little else I could do. I had to return. As a widow, you also discovered you had few choices. You would not and could not stay in Washington and my family was entirely out of the question. I was left with few choices. You haven't even told me where your family is for me to return you to their waiting arms."

He saw the twitch in her jaw when he mentioned her

family. It was a mystery he wanted solved. Surely she still had kin, but where? Her drawl was Louisianan but where he didn't know and she hadn't volunteered. The fight would start up again at daylight, he was sure, and he'd not spend the time bickering with her, not even over Peregoy.

On that thought, he pulled her into his embrace and gave her lips a brief kiss. "I had a fear today of losing you," he murmured, skating a kiss on her neck as he began to pluck pins from her hair.

She stiffened and pulled back. "You argue with me to stay away from the wounded when you are one yourself?" She tilted his head, looking at the nick that his plumed Hardee hat had hidden from view until he'd thrown it on the bed and moved close enough to her that the lamplight glanced off the side of his face.

"It's nothing," he started when she growled and went to grab a flask out of her apron and a square of fabric. "Cera."

"How dare you," she continued. "Think you can now just sweet talk me to ignoring this?" She dabbed the cloth at the tip of the bottle and then touched the wound.

He nearly leaped off the cot she'd forced him to sit on when the fire from that material hit his wound. "What the hell is that?" He wanted to step away but she had his legs locked within the folds of her skirt and the knees beneath.

"A little whiskey, to burn away fever and rid you of dirt."

"Ouch! I said its nothing." He grabbed her hand and yanked it away from his head, the sting of the alcohol still blazing in its wake. *Where the hell had she gotten liquor? From that quack, Peregoy?*

She pulled her hand free but didn't try to clean it again. "Well, it doesn't appear infected nor is it large or deep enough to sew. You got off lucky, sir." She put the cork back into the flask and put it aside. "Trying to make me a widow?"

She looked hurt and even scared, or so he hoped she might fear losing him. It was moving enough he pushed the question about the liquor aside and instead, slowly pulled her back to him and gave her a soft kiss. "Thank you," he murmured at her ear and then skated down her neck in tiny kisses as his fingers returned to her hair and unlodging the pins holding up the mass of curls. "Now, as I was saying, I had fears of losing you today, perhaps that's how I got hurt."

"Whatever were you doing to think that?" Her head tipped back as the last pin didn't want to break free.

"Trying to hold the line," he kissed her earlobe and let the tip of his tongue trail down her neck to the nape, to take a small nip at her flesh. "The rebs were fierce, almost like my lovely wife."

He nipped her again and felt her melt slightly in his arms. She was so soft. The taste of her skin, the feel of softness, nearly drove him over the edge. He'd risked everything for her and today, as the enemy's numbers increased, the guns firing and the assault never faulting, all he could think of was how he'd placed her in such danger, bringing her here. It was that inner fear and building anger at the war itself that made him sweep her up into arms as he kissed her hard and took her to bed.

He loved her too much and it was killing him. All the anxiety of the day, combined with the attack, the battle and the final retreat, along with the sweat and thirst drove him. He needed her. *Damn it all to hell!*

CHAPTER TWENTY-FIVE

"...as I looked at the bleeding remains of my comrades, I felt for the dear ones at home, and can only offer them my sympathy and gratitude of a nation."

—Richmond Enquirer, after the battle at Chickamauga, September 1863

CERISA FOUGHT TO RETAIN her anger at him. Why, escaped her, but she wasn't in the mood to back down. When Pierce kissed her, his lips not only made contact with hers but it seemed like his soul reached inside her, to pull her back to him. The fact that her body responded eagerly to his touch simply made her realize that she couldn't resist him and she truly believed that alone should trigger another bitter chord inside but it didn't. So her body had succumbed to him. What about her herself?

Her question got lost the moment he started to undo her dress while raining kisses on her lips, her jawline and progressing further down the more he peeled off her. His assault on her body gained momentum and she suddenly found her own desire increasing. Trying to stifle a moan, she started on his buttons, halfway swearing at her clumsiness, as the buttons on his shirt were too caked in grime to function right. By the time he got down to her corset, she didn't care about buttons but yanked his shirt. He chuckled but she heard the tension. It wasn't the type that was stressed but veered more toward an urgency, the type that was building inside her. With the last tug at her corset lacings, he pressed the sides at her waist and the busk unhooked.

He pulled her up enough to grab the garment and toss it off the cot, quickly followed by her chemise. A slight breeze of warm air tickled at her bare skin and that sent a shiver down her spine. He hadn't even whispered to her body but the hint he would had made her anticipation skyrocket. Just like the flames in her lower belly, the ones that melted her core, making her lower lips leak with excitement.

"The outfit was stifling, so I wanted to help you rid of it."

This statement was so correct, she giggled. "It was time to change, I suppose."

He grinned at her as he tried to position himself next to her. He had shed his uniform as well, though he hadn't tossed any aside, the role of general had instilled him with propriety. She wasn't sure how she felt about that and opening her mouth to ask, she now saw he had entirely unrobed. Her heart skipped a beat.

Pierce bent over and kissed her. As he trailed a line of kisses down her neck, his hand wandered down her hips and found the apex of her thighs. As his fingertips traced up her inner thighs, her body ignited. When he got closer, she moaned, tilting her back upward, arching closer to his lips. She could feel the warmth of his breath as close as he was and it made her want to beg for more, for him to finally touch her and when he heard her silent pleas, he obliged. She nearly exploded off the cot with excitement. Frantically, she tried to inch lower, to reach down and find his erection but he gave her a low deep chuckle.

"Pierce, please." How could he not just take her? The fire inside her was roaring and only connecting with him would soothe her loins.

"All in good time, my love," he murmured and kissed the inside of her right thigh.

Using small movements, he made love to her with his mouth, tempting her with his lips. Her hips rocked and the frame to the bed creaked with each maneuver. The fire flamed and she knew she was on the edge. All their argumentative words erased from her mind.

His ministrations to her core built the pressure up and she was on the verge of exploding when he suddenly stopped. Her eyes popped wide open while she wiggled closer but then, he kneeled above her. In the dimming evening light, with no lamp lit, she took a minute to see his naked chest, his taunt belly, hard and tight from riding and fighting.

He smiled. "You are gorgeous."

She started to open her mouth to reply when he bent down and slid right inside her. He filled her with all of him, enough that made her tilt her hips up, opening her hips slightly more. Slowly they began to rock, their hips meeting and separating, pleasing and taunting at the same time. The urgency built. Faster and faster they moved. This man, this Yankee, brought her to the brink of sanity and then, as he plunged deep, everything changed and all she could see were a million stars. Vaguely, she could hear him moan, or maybe it was her, as he, too, let himself go.

What seemed like minutes turned into seconds. He lay on top of her, kissed her, devouring her it seemed, then he fell to her side, pulling her into his arms and kissed her earlobe. She sighed. She had just passed through Eden, she swore! Suddenly, she was exhausted. Apparently so was he, as he didn't move but whispered in her ear.

"I love you."

She froze. Her eyes widened, her breathing hitched. Surely he said that out of what they just did and not mean it. But.... She waited for more not never came. Instead, he was breathing steadily on her shoulder, asleep.

Love. Surely, she didn't hear that. Love was something she wasn't sure of. It had meant comfort and pain. This man, her husband, just claimed he loved her. How? Why? Surely, it was just the madness of war that brought him to say that. Did she love him? Could she?

Her mind hurt, her body was sore and she was exhausted. Thanking God for Pierce being with her now, she closed her eyes and tried to sleep. Love would be dealt with tomorrow...

He should've slept like a babe, exhausted, done in and finally physically worn out but he didn't. It didn't take long, after making love to Cerisa, for the sounds of the camp to slowly slip through the tent walls and wake him. At least, that was the way he wanted to believe it. After his declaration last night, he recalled silence. He had fallen fast asleep, so perhaps she had returned the same. Maybe she didn't. He wanted to groan. Why had he disclosed that after all? He knew why—it was war and they were on the precipice of battle. He had fought this day and fell back with the rest of the Union forces in what should've gone the other way. But the enemy had the numbers and the advantage and used it to push them back. Rosecrans had been furious but it was a controlled fury, claiming they'd win tomorrow and they should, being the bigger force in numbers alone but even Pierce had his doubts. And it was those doubts that drove his urgency to find his wife and make sure she knew he loved her.

He glimpsed at the woman lying next to him. His fiery Southern belle was curled into his side, her eyes closed and a slow steady breath indicating she was asleep. Of course, she was curved against his body as the roped traveling cot was sized for one, not two to sleep in. His gaze traced her naked body, slowly going over her shoulders, down to her narrow waist and her flared hips. She was beautiful, dressed or nude.

As much as he didn't want her exposed to the cruelty of war, letting her help in the hospital where war was shown at its worse, he knew he couldn't stop her. And that doc, Peregoy, needed the help, Pierce was sure, but he'd caught the man giving her that side look, the type men gave when they looked beyond the pretty face and noticed the seductive body that accompanied it.

He rolled off the cot, furious at that thought. Rubbing his eyes, he peeked out of the tent. It was still before dawn and most of the camp was asleep with only a few sentries up but he knew Rosecrans was up. Today was pay back for the loss of yesterday. Picking up his drawers, he put them on, followed by his trousers. He went slow and as quietly as he could. Once he was dressed, he went back to the bed, to give her one final look. His angel hadn't moved. And she truly did look angelic. He wished he knew her better. She was alone without him, yet she had family. A family she didn't talk about. Why she married the Colored man remained a mystery. Perhaps she loved him but it still didn't fit with her Southern upbringing.

He cocked his head when she shifted on the cot but she didn't wake so he let go the held breath, unaware he'd held it. No, he was still trying to figure her out. She'd said she had a brother who'd gone to the Point and was still fighting for the Union, only to sign the marriage certificate as surname Walker. The black man's name was Walker. He knew some of the slaves took their owner's surnames, so he bet the man had. With that notion, he figured that was her maiden name, too. But his aide's brief mission to find an officer named Walker had not turned up a soul who could qualify, for many with that name were enlistees or one general, who was old enough to be her grandfather. So the name was not her maiden name. It was aggravating. There was the other name in her signature on their marriage certificate, a name that he couldn't recall, being so fixated on Walker and how what had transpired was real. With stern resolution, he swore he'd pull the paper out to take a look later.

A deep sigh escaped her lips, catching his attention. With a glance at her, curled on the cot and now taking all the room, he smiled. Why did he love her? It was a question that nagged at the back of his head. She was beautiful, seductive, bold and brave, rebel in many ways yet his heart was pulled to her.

Shoving his sword into his scabbard, Pierce grabbed his hat and gave her one last look. No, he was right. He did love her. He just prayed she might grow to love him too.

CHAPTER TWENTY-SIX

"I've got a twenty dollar gold piece in my pocket that I've carried through the war, and a silver watch that my father sent me through the lines. Please take them off when I am dead…to give to my father…"

—Private Robert Stout, 1st and 27th Tennessee, on premonition of his own death. Battle of Chickamauga, September 1863.

September 19, 1863

DAWN BARELY INCHED ABOVE the mountaintop in the distance but its pinkened rays sneaked out, announcing it was another day. Cerisa stretched, rested and sore. She winced as she moved her hips and legs. Apparently, her work at the hospital made her legs ache. With a sigh, she swung her legs over the bed and rose. A quick look about the tent verified he'd left her, again, early and without so much as a good bye. The man was annoying.

Throwing water on her face to refresh herself, in the distance she heard a popping noise, followed by a loud bang. The last startled her and she grabbed the linen, wiping her face before she peeked of the tent. Outside, soldiers hurried by. A band marched quick time past her tent followed by officers on horseback. Orders were shouted and the scurrying increased. The jangle of metal and the stomp of boot heels on hard dirt echoed everywhere.

She pulled back and dressed quickly. Battle must have started and it was just the first lights of sun! She grabbed her hair, whipping it into a braid, twisting it and coiling it up top, shoving a pin in to keep it there. Pierce was out there and she worried, knowing he was one of the leaders and found that thought made her stomach flip. Surely he wouldn't be on the front lines, she prayed.

Pushing the tent flap aside, she was almost run over by a group of mustering soldiers, one of whom apologized as they scurried past. She'd look better before she stepped out next time. It took a moment but she found a space to whiz past the upcoming line of soldiers and she darted through the tents, into the camp, and made a beeline for the hospital.

"Whoa, ma'am, if you please!"

She came to a complete halt, gasping in surprise at the officer that stepped into her path. With a frown, she said, "Sir, please, I must get to—"

"Ma'am, with all due respect, General Rosecrans has requested all civilians to be moved further back." He gave her a short sympathetic smile. "For your safety, of course. He'd not allow any of the fairer type be hurt in the war."

She wanted to laugh. The officers' wives and the soldiers' families that tagged along, even if they were laundresses and cooks, were never going to stay out of the war, considering. But another loud explosion, not as far away, sounded, making the soldier look more determined to escort her out.

"Lieutenant?"

"Yes ma'am. Lieutenant Cooley, of the 4th U.S. Infantry, at your service." He nodded his head in a slight bow. "But we must get you out."

"My husband, General Duval, have you seen him?"

"No, ma'am."

That didn't make her happy but nonetheless, she continued. "I am a nurse at the hospital. I believe Doctor Peregoy has need of me."

Cooley shifted on his heels, his eyes darted both ways, as if looking for support or command. "The wounded are going to be arriving soon, I reckon," he finally mumbled, unhappy to acknowledge she was probably correct. "Please, ma'am, if you find yourself unable or not needed, please retreat to the rear."

"Certainly, Lieutenant." She watched him take off before she turned back on her path.

Turning the final corner, before the lane to the hospital, she ran into another roadblock. Abby Gaines.

"Good morning, Mrs. Duval," she sneered. "I expected to see you with us *ladies* as we move—"

"Mrs. Gaines, I'm going to help in the hospital," she interrupted her. The insult was blatant. The woman didn't think she was a lady. It took every ounce of manners she could draw not to lash back.

"Help?" The woman laughed. "Yes, I see how you've been eyeing Doc Peregoy. He's married, you understand, though she is back home in Pennsylvania, but then you probably know that." She looked down her nose at Cerisa. "But a soiled dove wouldn't worry about sullying with a married man, would she?"

The hair on the back of her neck bristled as anger rolled through her veins. The woman threw her past into her face as she drew a line in the sand between them. She narrowed her gaze. "Mrs. Gaines, I'll ask you again, move out of my way."

The woman refused and instead, gazed down as she inspected her nails in a rather haughty manner. "I suppose such a thing as adultery is common among you Southern *women*."

Cerisa's blood was boiling. She could barely think with the pounding of it in her ears. "Madam, let me state this clearly since your impoliteness seems to have distorted your hearing. I am wife to a general, a man who could make your husband miserable if he heard of this. I am not a slattern, despite your need to ruin me. I am a nurse for the hospital, a hospital that, from the sounds of all around us, will be needing help." Two more explosions accentuated her sentences with popping filling in between and the mayhem of horses and soldiers scurrying to battle all around them. It was like they were figurines in a music box, Cerisa imagined. She did notice Abby's stern look remained though her face paled at her suggestion of the battle and aid. "Perhaps you'd like to volunteer. Doctor Peregoy, who has been nothing but courteous, would appreciate more help."

Another bugle sounded followed by more running feet.

Abby's gaze narrowed, but Cerisa notice one eyelid twitched and she bit back her grin at knowing she was hitting the woman's fears.

"You're a disgrace to a good man! You'll ruin him with your sins! I hope you have your comeuppance and soon," Abby spat and sped away.

It was not a good morning. Rosecrans pushed forward with his battle plans, sending out order after order, ignoring the pleas from incoming missives and changing his plans but overall, it was the same. Defeat Bragg and the Confederates at all costs.

Pierce sat in the saddle, pulling the reins on his worked-up horse, as he assessed the scene in front of him. They were close to the Widow Glenn's house and he breathed a second. His men were exhausted and it was only late morning. They'd been marching and fighting since sunrise, most without breakfast, having left that back in their camps when the sharp shooting rebels opened fire.

Starving himself, he gnawed on hardtack. The hard cracker was anything but appealing, but it worked to stifle the hunger. The occasional popping noise of enemy fire kept him in the saddle and constantly on guard, watching, waiting for reports and trying to ignore the nagging thought of Cerisa in camp.

He'd left her this morning, worrying about why she hadn't said she loved him when in reality, how could he expect that? He'd saved her from a life of prostitution, but he was hardly a saint since it was there he'd paid to be with her. That realization made him shift in the saddle, aggravated. Why would she want to love him? He'd bet two to one, her tears on their wedding night, might be due to the fact it wasn't much of a wedding nor, perhaps, one she truly wanted, but now he could keep her safe with his name. Of course, those tears could've been for the black man who'd held her before him. That was what irritated him. He competed for her affections with a dead man.

"Sir!"

He glanced over at the private who stood off to the side, giving Pierce's prancing horse space. Realizing he held the animal under restraints, he loosened the reins and his mount settled so he could now reach to take the message. More orders. As he looked up and turned towards the troops, Prasse rode up.

"Sir, we've encountered another contingent."

Pierce frowned. "Explain yourself, Corporal."

Prasse halfway grinned but nodded to the right, in the

stand of trees. There, a melee of guns exploded. Pierce pulled out his looking glass. He found men in blue firing at the enemy and in tight quarters. From what he could tell, it was a small contingent but he couldn't see much outside the blue.

"Captain Martin," he called over his shoulder. "I told you to bring the men in tight formation here."

"Aye, sir, I did!" cried the officer to the far left.

Pierce growled, "Who the hell is that, Prasse?"

"Stragglers sir. Colored troops apparently."

"Pardon me? Colored? Whose?" He didn't recall any Colored troops in the southeast.

"Don't know sir."

He groaned. "Probably damn contrabands." Last thing he needed was runaways, the type that 'took up the cause'. "Captain Martin, go send a unit over there and aid those men!"

"Yes sir," the officer replied and then turned to his men, issuing orders.

"Bring those men to me, after they break free," he told Prasse. The aide nodded and turned in his saddle, to ride away.

Colored troops. Black freedmen. *Where the hell did they come from?*

"Here, drink this."

Cerisa frowned and looked up to find one of the stewards shoving a cup into her hand. She took it but stared at its contents, feeling sluggish in every thing she did. Yet a sniff told her more than what her vacant gaze had. Coffee. Pure and black. Nectar of the gods, she reckoned, and one sorely needed at this point. She managed to grin at the man.

"Thank you."

His cheeks flushed red. He looked no older than sixteen,

to her eyes, but for his position, she'd grant him maybe nineteen. Way too young for all the responsibility placed on his shoulders.

"Doc P said you be lookin' like you could use a cup." He nodded and backed off fast.

Young and impressionable, she snorted softly. But the doc was right. She'd raced to the tent at the wee hours before dawn, with only enough time to down a cup, attempted to chew on that dreadful hardcracker the army distributed like it was gold, and munch a couple of strips of crispy pork fat. How these men could eat that was above her way of thinking, but she'd downed them, knowing the work here was mounting and any other fare wasn't available.

The wounded came in spurts. A handful at first, the wounds were minor and nothing she couldn't stomach. Pierce's words haunted her, about the gruesomeness of this place but so far, it wasn't too far beyond farming accidents in the appearance. The group standing at the back of the tent, heads lowered and hands clasped, were the men who could not see 'the elephant' as the soldiers called the war, up close. It was a Godsend in one way, because Peregoy had them clean and remove bedpans and other orderly duties, freeing the medical staff to the vital work. It was also a tragedy, for she had seen the look of utter defeat in the eyes of the slaves who had drudged daily to their jobs without a living spark in them. These men mimicked that and her sympathy deepened.

Of course, Pierce was out there too. She closed her thoughts, because the road this turned down was scary.

I love you.

The words echoed through her memory. It made her smile and cringe at the same time. He didn't know her, didn't know the dark secret that haunted her and drove her to run from home. Love. Everything she'd ever loved was snatched from her in an instant. Her family, her home, the life she'd been raised in and the man she'd grown to love, also gone due to a war she now realized erupted because of slavery.

Now, her head hurt. She took another sip and the warm liquid slid down her throat easily, leaving a touch of calm in its course.

"Your color is returning."

She recognized that voice and she smiled. "Doctor Peregoy, what a pleasant surprise. I thought you had a line of patients."

He chuckled. It was a trait she rather admired, that he was always so jovial, or appeared so. A nice switch from the rest of the brooding Yankees.

"I do, my dear, but at the moment, there is a lull." He sat down next to her, a tin cup full of the same steaming black gold in his hand. "I've learned, over the years, that if you can take even five minutes to sit and breath, you will do much better." He took a sip, gazing at her over the cup.

She laughed and did the same.

"So, the other ladies have moved? Why didn't you?"

She jerked her chin back, surprised he asked. "You don't think I'd up and leave when it's more than obvious you need the help."

"True. But this is not the world for proper ladies."

"And what is? During war, I speculate nothing is." She took another sip and this time, relished in the taste.

He raised his brows and gave her a lop-sided grin. "Yes, I guess you are right." He reached over and took her hand. "If you'll let me," he said, turning it slightly. "How does it feel today?"

She bit her bottom lip. "It is better. Still a bit sore but the pain has subsided."

"Good. I worried, considering wood can splinter upon removal." He rubbed his thumbpad over the injured area.

She cocked her head. "Amazing how that doesn't hurt too much."

He smiled as he wrapped his fingers around her hand. "Not a surprise. Means we got it all." He looked down again, his fingertip still caressing the area ever so slightly. For all the hard work he did and being a man, she would've figured his touch would have been coarse, not smooth and the movement a relaxing one. The slow massage made her hand limp and that feeling, one of no worries, no pain, raced up her arm and spread through the rest of her body without his physical contact moving.

"Doc, we got more coming," an orderly whispered.

Peregoy nodded. "Looks like its time to return to work." He released her, grabbed his cup and began issuing orders.

Cerisa followed, checking on the beds as they walked, looking at a few of the men who'd been treated earlier. They had broken bones, gashes, a few bullet holes, though the bulk were not severe and even the doc had stated no sawing was needed, and that statement alone, even if made in jest, made ice stream down her spine. Worst was, she knew he didn't mean it as a joke.

Again, she found herself one of the few women left to help. It took a moment for it all to sink in as the line of battered and wounded soldiers crested the hillside before the hospital. The howls from the bleeding filled the air, the chaos of demands, entreaties and orders flew as they came closer. The scene reminded her of what the priests depicted hell to be like—men dirty, clothes tattered and blood everywhere. A few were missing parts of their limbs and the bindings the stewards placed to stop the bleeding were tight, making the rest of the limb, whether it was arm or leg, swell. Stench surrounded this crowd, one that was a horrible mixture of sweat, urine, wet wool and vomit. It made her own stomach lurch, especially when the sickly sweet scent of blood swirled among the wretched; an odd smell, of iron yet with a sweetness she couldn't name.

The ghastly scene sickened her, marring her vision with a blackness that threatened to overcome her. Yet deep down, she knew she had to retain her wits. What if Pierce was brought in during this battle? She needed to focus and help in whatever way she could. Just as when she found herself penniless in New York's Five Points and realized all the tatting in the world would not bring her food, making her lower her standards and accept her ladylike ways were not skills for survival, she saw now how her need to help these desperate men grew more important than her frail feminine ways.

Swallowing the bile in her throat, she grabbed a bucket half full of water and a handful of rags to meet the first of the injured. And she prayed to God, she'd never find Pierce among them.

It'd been one helluva morning, Pierce thought as he paced his horse near the rear of Major General George H. Thomas's XIV Corps, close to Alexander's Bridge Road. He watched as Brigadier General John M. Brannan's three brigades pushed to keep the oncoming Confederates back. Confederate General Nathan Forrest's men, filling in as infantry with General Ector's brigade which Forrest had pulled out of General Walker's reserves in an attempt to gain ground against Colonel Van Derveer's men on the northern flanks of the battle field. He could hear the report of gunfire and noticed the staccato held a momentary lull periodically.

He cocked his head to make sure he'd heard correctly.

It was then he saw a commotion where the mounted officers were and a soldier emerging from it, racing back to the XIV's command.

"Sir! Sir!" The soldier yelled above the chorus of gunfire and cannons. "From Colonel Van Derveer!" His arm extended with his hand clutching a note. Walker's man picked it up and gave it to Pierce, who sat closer than Walker.

"Well?" Walker asked.

Pierce opened the paper and scrolled over the hastily written note. "He's running out of ammunition and not sure how long he can hold."

Brannan swore before he turned to his aide for paper and pen. Quickly he scribbled a few words and spoke as he wrote. "Tell them to head to Van Derveer's men and help reinforce."

"Yes, sir!"

Pierce grimaced. "Appears they've found new stock."

Brannan nodded. "Indeed, it does. But I've another thought up my sleeve."

"Then by all means, share." Pierce didn't like it but he couldn't do much else.

From what he saw, to spread into Georgia for the Union wasn't likely. All he could do was pray and try to squelch the fear that was forming a ball in his stomach, a fear he hadn't had before his return home and what was worse, he knew the cause. His thoughts were plagued by a Southern lady, a true rebel, the one he'd dragged with him to the front, the same one he'd married. As another cannon ball erupted up ahead, he couldn't help but grimace. If they didn't win, she could die.

The mere thought sparked a surge of energy, born out of rage. Grabbing the reins in one hand, he pulled his sword from his scabbard, raising the weapon above his head and took off toward the gunfire with a roar.

CHAPTER TWENTY-SEVEN

*"I have fought against the people of the North because I believed
they were seeking to wrest from the South its dearest rights. But I
have never cherished toward them bitter or vindictive feelings, and
have never seen the day when I did not pray for them."*
—Robert E. Lee, General, Confederate States Army

Dusk, September 19ᵗʰ

IT WAS A BATTLE that turned into bedlam. Twilight
slowly descended and Pierce still in the saddle, exhausted,
hot and drenched in sweat. Near Brigadier General Absalom
Baird's men in the northern part of the battlefield, he'd
watched the Confederates surge and be pushed them back
yet the Union barely moved. Bullets flew, cannons exploded
and the wounded multiplied. Colonel Philemon Baldwin's
brigade found itself fired upon by Baird's men and Pierce had
had to swoop in to re-direct the friendly fire back to their
proper targets. And in the midst of all this confusion, Baldwin
started to move against the Confederates, only to be shot and
killed off his horse.

It wasn't the only mishap on the field today. Even now, as
the dark got a foothold on the sky, bringing the fighting to
cease for the night, he found the Union had been decisively
thrown back behind Thomas's new defensive line, not far from
their starting point this morning. As he rode to Rosecrans's

headquarters near the Widow Glenn's house, he grabbed his canteen and splashed water on his dirt-ridden face, knowing he should've saved the liquid but he so badly wanted to wash the stain of defeat off his face. But as he entered the meeting, the hairs on his neck rose.

"Welcome to the latest war council," Garfield greeted, his voice low and barely audible over Rosecrans's volume.

"All are here, finally," the commanding general sneered from across the room.

All heads turned. Pierce inhaled, holding back his own retort. The tension in the air thickened. All the corps and division commanders, those still living, stood around the room with the only furniture in use a table holding maps. Pierce yanked his hat from his head and came closer.

"Gentlemen, our objective still stands. We need to defeat Bragg and head further, not merely play paddy-cake with his troops," Rosecrans barked.

Half the men held their hats in their hands, and Pierce could see many of the brims would be irreparably damaged by the stranglehold they kept on them to refrain from snapping at the general. Others, though, refused to be quiet.

"Sir, those rebels are just like jack-rabbits out there! Multiplying before our very eyes!"

"I see. And what are we? A monastery of monks, praying they won't attack?" Rosecrans shot back.

"Sir, their numbers do increase but I've seen them fall as much as we do." Pierce stepped forward. "And we do have an ally. The Chickamauga lies at their rear. Now, they're trapped."

"Yes! And they'll fight harder!"

Pierce looked at the young officer who broke in. Despite the sunburn on his nose and cheeks, he was as pale as a sheet. He also had his hat in his grip, holding it tight. It took a moment, but he could see he was bleeding through his fingers onto the hat.

"Colonel Smith, you should have that hand looked at," he suggested. The last thing they needed was a weak officer.

"No sir! They'll take my arm if I go!"

Rosecrans walked over and asked to see it. His tone was so soft, even Pierce at four feet away couldn't hear it but he must've as the junior officer released the tight grip of the hand that was crimson at this point. Over his shoulder, he called for another to take the soldier to his personal surgeon.

Pierce walked to the side, where he could fill his own tin cup with water, longing for something a bit stronger, with a bite in it to wake him as exhaustion mixed with heat threatened to overwhelm him.

"Hey," nudged Garfield. "Did you see who else joined us?" He nodded to the front of the tent where Rosecrans had started.

Pierce downed his gulp and looked. Standing there, looking so out of place in his civilian suite, was Assistant Secretary of War, Charles A. Dana. The man's stern expression told Pierce everything.

"So, despite the depletion of supplies and casualties, retreat will be out of the question."

"Exactly," Garfield replied.

Pierce grimaced. More slaughter, more moving the front line back. Defeating Bragg just moved a notch away. He downed his cup and poured more as Rosecrans continued his earlier discussion.

"General Bragg is not a man to stand his ground and win. He retreated at Perryville and Stones River. I predict, on the morrow, with our revived forces, he too shall withdraw here. We must push harder. And I predict, we shall prevail!"

The officers all muttered their agreement, but there was a note of reluctance in part of the assembly, Pierce noticed. Granted, he was indifferent. His bigger concern was for the woman who now wore his name.

"Oh, as you probably realize, they moved the wives back to the Knoxville area. Away from the upheaval here." Garfield coughed.

"Truly?" Pierce's gaze zeroed in on the man. When the general nodded, a small amount of relief washed through him. At least she was back, away from this mess. All the anxiety poured out of him, like water sluicing off his skin in a waterfall. He could breath and his lips struggled to curve into a smile.

"General Duval, if you have a moment, please."

Startled to be called, Pierce glanced toward the crowd and found Dana heading beeline toward him, with Rosecrans in tow.

"General, we have the pleasure," Rosecrans began with a slight twinge in the word pleasure, as he, like most of the military, objected to civilians, especially politicians and diplomats, coming to camp. "Of having Assistant Secretary of War, Mr. Charles Dana, join us in our smashing the Army of the Tennessee."

"Mr. Dana, what a surprise to have you with us in this spectacle down in the plains of hell," he greeted with a smile. "It's been ages." He was never a fan of Dana, having met the man through his father. Fact was, Pierce knew more politicians than military leaders, thanks to his patriarch, and he had yet to meet any he truly cared about. And that included his father.

"Indeed it has. I heard of your advance, General, and offer my congratulations." He smiled and offered Pierce his hand.

Now he was stuck. He had to accept the shake, despite his sudden desire to flee the tent for fear of retching. It was an awful affliction, he supposed. Any politician made him want to gag and the mere presence skyrocketed his heartbeat, making breathing difficult.

"Thank you, sir." He pulled his hand back fast, as if it might be bitten by a copperhead.

"It was brought to my attention, General, that you encountered a loose group of freedmen, fighting the rebels," Rosecrans began. Pierce's stomach lurched as premonition slammed into him. "From what I heard these men wore rags the color of the Federal army."

He gulped. "Yes, sir, definitely the hue of our enlisted men."

"I understand it was a fairly decent sized lot. And they seemed to hold their own."

Pierce's gaze narrowed. "Yes, sir. Had my aide, Corporal Prasse, go appraise the situation."

"And where are these men, General?" Dana asked.

The rolling of his stomach flipped again. "I believe they've set up a camp, just to the north of Thomas's division."

"Good," Rosecrans said, bending over the desk and with a fresh leaf of paper, scribbled furiously. "I will have them under your command. Make use of them well. If we're to free their type, they might as well join us in the fight, don't you agree?"

"Yes, sir." His turmoil turned sour and fast. Commanding a Colored troop—his father's wish come true.

Rosecrans signed the form and smiled. Pierce forced a nod and spun on his heel to leave. *Damn!*

"Private, no, not that way."

The young soldier glanced up at her from the bedside. He

looked very young, more like fourteen at most. Skin ashen white and eyes wide with fear, he was at the cot of a wounded man whose arm had been ripped wide open with shrapnel and the flesh was raw, red and black from gunpowder and dirt. The first of these she had seen, Cerisa had to cover her mouth to keep from retching and averted her eyes, only to see more of the incoming wounded. War was terrible and hell seemed to erupt about her but that wouldn't help those on the cots or on the floor, who cried and whined and screamed to the heavens for death. She pulled from inside a strength she didn't know she possessed, downed the bile in her throat and dug in to help.

Some of the soldiers, who were called 'yella cowards' or 'shirkers' because they avoided the front, and any chance to be shot, were thrown in with the hospital staff, either to carry the wounded off the fields or help care for them. Peregoy shrugged when Cerisa pointed out they weren't going to listen to her, stating simple they needed the help and these men could assist with patients and beds so buckets of water and soiled bedding was nothing and it had to be done. So she goaded them to work but this boy, he was shaking at the mere thought of trying to take the filthy jacket and pants off the man, who was unconscious.

Pasting a smile on, she wadded the sheets and soiled wool blanket and shoved it into his arms. "Private Evans? Please take these to the laundry."

With the fastest nod she'd ever seen, he bolted out of the tent, leaving her with the wounded man. With a heavy sigh, she picked up the wash basin and rag and sat to tend the soldier but saw the linen scrap was already browned from overuse in wiping dirty, bleeding men and the water was a shade far from clear. She closed her eyes. No matter what the doctor said, she refused to reuse the same on every single patient. Taking the bowl, she dumped it outside the tent and went in search of fresh water.

"You do that ever time, we won't have any left."

She blinked and turned to find who said that. It was that nurse, or so she said she was. Miss Henderson, sent by Miss Dix who managed the new women nurses for the Union Army. Henderson was average in every respect of height, weight, her black hair pulled straight back, no jewelry and wore a simple, hoopless navy wool work dress with a white pinner apron. It was as dull as the woman's bland face. She chided Cerisa on her outfit and informed her that she was to appear as plain as her. The intention was to look uninteresting to the men, so as to not get them excited to see her, fumbling to look their best and possibly opening their wounds, thus hindering their recovery. Well, Cerisa thought, the woman won the award for dullness. She doubted if the men ever saw her. After the third lecture on appearance, Cerisa shut her out and tried to ignore her, which was usually successful, as she worked this tent and Henderson the next. But they did cross paths.

"Good afternoon, Miss Henderson," she started, way too tired to start off telling the woman to mind her own business or maybe learn something new.

"Yes, Mrs. Duval," she spat, angry at being reminded of manners. "But you keep changing that water when the standard protocol is to use the same through your ward."

Having found a fresh ewer of water, Cerisa bit her bottom lip to keep from lashing out. It took two hands to pour the heavy container but she succeeded. But the woman stood, fists on her hips, this time ready to go at it.

"Miss Henderson, you seem quite ready to battle this out,

but let me inform you. I will do my upmost to keep my men washed with clear water, not dirty soup as it often turns into from all the debris sponged off the others. It was how Aunt Jenny taught me and as I recall, our help recovered quite well from that method." The woman could go strangle herself, Cerisa inwardly cursed. Miss Jenny claimed to be taught medicine from her mama's people and considering the wellness maintained at Bellefountaine, the woman was a saint.

Henderson's face mottled with anger. "You keep your sinful slave-owning stories to yourself. Your people are what caused all this!" her arms made a wide gesture about the wounded lying before her. "All these men were wounded and could die for you to go learn from your *Jenny* how go get fresh water when it ain't necessary!"

Cerisa's blood started to boil. This nurse wasn't any better than those New Yorkers who wanted to lynch her for being a Southerner. Every nerve inside her wanted to throw that bowl of clear water at the woman and she shook so bad, she almost did.

"Ladies, do we have a problem?" Doc Peregoy asked. Cerisa hadn't seen him enter the tent. He looked tired his hands shoved in his white coat pockets. The stains down the coat demonstrated her point on how awful it was in there, but the doctor was a wonderful sight to see.

"No, sir." Henderson stood her ground but had lowered her fisted hands.

Cerisa inhaled, raising her chin a bit. "No, just discussing the use of water."

Henderson's eyes still flared but she gave a terse chirp, throwing her head up and spun to leave.

Cerisa breathed, giving Peregoy a nod of thanks and

walked back to her patient. She sat and realized she had no linen strips, so she reached under her dress and ripped off a strip from her under petticoat, way too tired to get back up and get any rags. As she tore the strip in fours and threw the first piece in the bowl, she pulled it and squeezed the excess out before she started.

The doctor walked up. "Cera, you are an excellent nurse. The men have done remarkably under your administration."

She smiled, relishing the compliment. "I'm sure they are doing well under Nurse Henderson, too."

He raised his brows and shrugged then crinkled his nose. "I think they enjoy your manners better. She can be a bit abrupt."

"Just a northern way," she blurted than stopped. "Apologies. I mean, I'd bet it's the way Miss Dix trains them."

On that he openly laughed. "I think you're right." He sighed. "I must get back to the surgery table." He glanced down at her patient. "He's going to lose that arm."

She closed her eyes. The wound was way too deep and the orderly had tied the arm off, to stop the bleeding, but the shredded flesh left little doubt the arm would never be of use.

Peregoy put his hand on her shoulder and squeezed it. A look at her passed out patient made her want to cry. He was too young to lose an arm. Too young to fight! Biting her lower lip, she continued to clean the man and get him ready. The horrors of war never ceased.

So far, God had heard her prayer. Pierce was not on any of the incoming wounded. But as the sounds of artillery still roared in the distance, she wondered how long till this nightmare ended? Her fears for her new husband never stopped and what was worse, she realized her fears were well grounded because despite all her attempts not to love a soldier, she was falling for him.

"Prasse!" Pierce dropped his reins and slid off his horse. It was pitch dark, which didn't help his attitude. His father had won and he was now in charge of a Colored unit. God, he hoped they were freed and not contraband. Last thing he needed was some outraged owner demanding his chattel returned, something that wouldn't happen under his command. *Damn!* He figured he should find these men and tell them of their new status but in the dark, how the hell was he to find them?

The corporal came running. "Yes, sir!"

"Where is that group of Colored soldiers you saw fightin' earlier today?"

Prasse frowned, rubbing his eyes. Good grief, he'd woken the boy. "Thinkin' they're over there, sir," he answered, pointing to a pile of sky-blue wool, near the next small fire.

Pierce groaned. What little sliver of light the stars gave the night, along with the handful of small fires allowed, showed him that sky-blue matched the Union infantry's pants. Shoving his hat on, which seemed ridiculous, considering at this pitch black, who'd know if he had it on or not, Pierce started across the field. It took him a couple steps to recall the possibility Confederate sharpshooters could be on watch and an officer was a prime target, especially when he was so easy to see, with him sprouting a plumed hat. He yanked it off his head.

The Union Army slept on its arms that night, some almost literally, Pierce noticed as he went through the makeshift camps. During an onslaught like this, commanders often had their men sleep on the ground where the fight had ended, positions placed so in the morning, the men could rise, pick up their weapons and the battle could resume where it left off. It was not by any means a comfortable night, though many would not put their guns aside when the fighting was this intense—fear of a silent attack plagued all. The officers' version of that was the compound Rosecrans set up, camping near the Widow Glenn's house but after tonight's turn of events, Pierce took a ride to check the cliffs, still in Union control, before he returned to his troops on the field and a reality that was easier to swallow versus the tight control of the leaders.

He heard a scuffle behind him and knew Prasse was racing to catch up. The boy was a good aide, eager to please though a bit young for this type of living, Pierce decided. "Corporal, why did you sign up for this fight?"

"Pardon me, sir?"

He turned and faced the kid, though he was hardly a child in height or age, according to the army. "Why join the Union blue?"

Prasse coughed, though it could've been a hidden laugh. He halfway grinned, his youthful face turning red. He reminded Pierce of one of the reasons he was there, to keep this country free for the next generation to grow.

"Sir, I signed up with the rest of my brothers and friends. Made a celebration out of the signing, we did. Girls pinned Union cockades to our jackets. Still got mine." He snorted. "But we all signed up to fight those rebs. Gotta set those darkies free."

Pierce inwardly groaned. "Have you ever seen a slave, corporal?"

"No, sir. We ain't got 'em in Pennsylvania. 'Sides, we got nothin' but farmland around us. But I read the papers and sat through a reading of Uncle Tom. People of the South gotta know, slavery is wrong."

The abolitionist papers blasted headlines of the sins of slavery. Heavens knew, his father subscribed to the bulk of them. And Harriet Beecher Stowe's novel *Uncle Tom's Cabin* had lit a fire in the movement to free the slaves. But not everyone in the north wanted them freed and able to come up to their state. They all believed, and Pierce feared more true than not, that many of the workers in the factories and on the docks would lose their job to the cheaper workforce of freedmen. Visions of Cerisa being cornered by the mob, just because of her husband being of a dark skin color, echoed in his mind.

"And if we win and the slaves are set free, do you want them taking your job, settling next door?"

The boy stopped and glared. "My daddy is a farmer, and I plan to be one also, so I ain't worried about a job outside that. And our neighbors have lived there all my life and more, my daddy said, so I don't think them taking land nearby will happen. But I 'pose if they do, they can." He paused. "Sir, isn't your father a senator for freeing the slaves? I mean, ain't that why you're here?"

Pierce breathed deep. How could he explain, he'd joined for many reasons, one of which was to escape his father? While he never believed slavery worked and was a terrible practice, freeing all and the results could easily have the impact Margaret's people feared. He was torn in several directions.

"I'm here to support our government and the debt we owe to the founders of this nation, who sacrificed all they had to be free of England's chains." That sentiment was true.

"Yes, sir." Prasse said and then pointed before them. "Up ahead, sir, are those darkies."

Pierce breathed a sigh, glad they could move on. He knew

he'd started the conversation, but he never meant to let it go this long. He knew the young corporal wanted him to be fighting for the same cause. They were, Pierce believed, but he was in it for so much more.

"Gentlemen," he started, as they approached the set of reclining solders.

The few awake, nudged to get up for a senior officer by the one standing soldier, but he put his hand up to stop them.

"I am General Duval of the IX Corps. Whom do I have the honor of addressing?"

The men looked at each other, as if deciding who might be the one to speak. Finally, the one who'd prompted the others up stepped forward.

"Sergeant Walker, sir."

Pierce's gaze narrowed. The man standing before him was tall, though he often noticed the freedman and his slave brother were often times slightly taller than many white men he knew. The man was broad-shouldered, his shoulders and upper arms barely fitting into the navy jacket he wore. His dark gaze held a determined look, one that he'd seen on many commanders' and soldiers' faces and perhaps one of the main reasons for the fighting to be so fierce, driven by men who refused to give up. Yet there was something else about Walker, but what, he wasn't sure.

"Sergeant, explain yourselves. How is it we ran across a group of negro soldiers so deep in the South? What division are you part of?"

Walker gave him a hint of a smile. "We be from Massachusetts, sir. Only survivors from Fort Wagner, or those not killed outright."

Pierce sat and waited. Walker inhaled.

"So, the Confederates took you as prisoners?"

"Did more than that, sir. Did as they said they would and sold us back into slavery. Kept us with 'em, to clear roads and tend to their horses but we few of the 54th, we waited, knowin' they'd slip and we could fight our way free again."

The man's cheek glared in the starlight and it took a moment for Pierce to realize it was a scar. He wondered for a moment if that was from the war or punishment for some offense but he refrained from asking.

"They held you this close to the line?" He still had a hard time believing this.

"It's true, General. But thinkin' they had us beat back as slaves, and without weapons, we'd stay back." He guffawed with a couple of the others joining. "But they left us to take care of the horses and livery." He shrugged with a smile. "Meant they gave us transportation out of that hellhole."

The group chuckled and even Pierce snorted. "When the fighting started, why didn't you head north?"

"No, sir, we're freedmen and Union soldiers. We couldn't leave without *helping* out our side, sir." His grin grew large.

"Well, sergeant, I commend your loyalty to the Union. Welcome back, all of you, to the U.S. Army."

The sergeant turned to say something to his fellow soldiers and they all laughed, apparently pleased at his statement but Pierce didn't pay much attention. No, something else grabbed his eye. It was the way Walker turned to face his fellow soldiers that rang a chord in Pierce's memory. His brows furrowed. He didn't recall ever meeting any of the recruits for the Colored troops, so fast had he fled Washington before his father could force the issue of leading a unit. But there was something about Walker that bothered him. In fact, it struck a pain in his temple, like a headache, something he rarely had. Perhaps all the day in the heat and sulfur set it off, or the lack of water and food. Whatever it was, he bid them good night, leaving Prasse to tell them where to report at daybreak. He took his horse's reins and walked away, back to the makeshift camp.

Something wasn't right. He couldn't figure it out now but he swore he would if it didn't kill him first.

Cerisa finally sat on a low crate near one of the hospital cots, gently touching the forehead of one of the patients and letting a sigh go. The man was still warm, though not as hot as earlier and she thanked God for that.

It'd been a trying day. After late morning, the incoming didn't seem to stop. Her job was simple enough—keep the wounded as comfortable as she could before the steward or surgeon arrived for inspection; keep the ward clean, the patients tended and the orderlies to their jobs. Easy but overwhelming considering the constant flow of incoming, and her domain was only this wall tent but she soon discovered this canvas could cover over twenty patients with little room to move. She spent the day running from one end to the other, trying to do it all, so when it was finally dark, she virtually fell to the crate, her eyelids getting heavy, but this patient needed to be looked at one more time…

"Whoa!" Arms encircled her waist, one hand on her upper arm while the bowl slipped to the dirt floor. Startled, her eyes flew open and she struggled to break free of the grips of sleep.

"Oh, my!" She gasped, her feet trying to find footing on the floor as she struggled to break free. The grip moved to just supporting her elbow as she gained her senses.

"Are you all right?" It was Peregoy. All tension evaporated. She was safe.

"Yes, yes, I believe so." She touched her hair in an abstract way before she bent to pick up the empty basin. "Oh, dear, I must have fallen asleep." Her cheeks turned warm, embarrassed to her ears to have done so.

"You've pushed yourself too hard today," he scolded, but his tone was warm and he sounded concerned. "Taking care of the carnage here is not proper for a true Southern belle."

There was a comfort in those words, but if he only knew the truth about her, he might reconsider that statement. Her vision blurred and it made her want to scream, refusing to blink because she didn't want the tears to fall.

"Oh, Cerisa, don't cry," he soothed, yanking a handkerchief from his waistcoat pocket to dab at her damp cheeks.

She realized his sympathy touched her. The surgeon was a nice gentleman, even if he was a Yankee. Surprised that she actually, mentally, made that distinction, especially considering her situation, she sniffed, then pulled herself upright, stopping his wiping her tears. "Thank you," she inhaled deep, vowing to stop crying. "It's not right for any lady, North or South, but it needs to be done." She managed to smile. "I'm just a bit tired. And I'm sure you feel the same way."

Shoving the kerchief in her hand, he raised his brows as he stood and pulled her up. "Of course, but that is my job, to care for these lads and run this hospital. I also am to take care of my staff, which, Mrs. Duval, I consider you a member of, considering all your hard labor. Even Miss. Henderson commemorated on your efforts, if you want to place value in that old battle-ax woman."

That made her giggle. She looked at his boyish expression and laughed again. "Doctor, I think you are terrible."

He laughed as he spun her around the corner to a flap near the rear. "Actually, that is part of the medical training, my dear."

She threw her head back and closed her eyes, laughing and it felt good. But when she opened her eyes, she saw they were walking outside the tent. "And where are we headed, Doc?"

"I'm escorting you to your tent. I want you to finally rest." At that, he stopped—right in front of her tent. "And here you are."

He released her arm. Silence engulfed them. The buzz of insects and the low vibrations of others talking filtered in but she couldn't move. Peregoy was standing close, perhaps too close she decided, but before she could slip away, he reached out and tucked an errant strand off her cheek to behind her ear. For a man, the movement was light, barely noticeable, like a butterfly fluttering about, but it branded her, as if she was still a whore or worse. His expression was intense or perhaps she read too much into his stare but his gaze was locked on her. With a gentle ease, he grabbed her hand and brought it to his lips to kiss.

"Sleep well and know you have my many thanks."

Stunned at the intimacy of his touch, she stared, her tongue momentarily numb.

"Good night," she mumbled and stumbled back into her tent. Her heart was racing and it made breathing difficult. Oh, why did he do that? She wiped the stain from her hand in a nervous motion, her skin tingling. She needed Pierce here, to tell her she was all right. Frantically, she looked but found him nowhere. With total frustration, she fell to her bed and sobbed.

CHAPTER TWENTY-EIGHT

"All night we could hear the wounded between ours and the Federal lines calling some of their comrades by name and begging for water…"

—Lieutenant R.M. Collins, Fifteenth Texas Dismounted Cavalry, Battle of Chickamauga 1863

Morning, September 20th, 1863

FEELING LIKE SHE WAS swimming under water, Cerisa fought the cover, wanting to remain asleep after an exhausting day that had left her too tired to sleep at first. Finally succumbing to the realms of sleep, she'd been plagued by nightmares, dreams of people no longer of this world nor, for those remaining, being anywhere near her. Visions of her brothers, her parents, Abraham and days of old, played at the edges of her sanity, jabbed with scenes from the hospital, of men mangled and holding on for dear life. She curled into a ball, praying it would go away but the sounds coming through the tent flaps slapped reality up close.

With a sluggish effort to remain unconscious, she lay still and let the day eke in. The sounds of horses, their hooves pounding on the hard dirt roads that paved the camp, along with a few nickers and neighs. The added beat of boots on the same paths, the rhythm of men talking, the crackle of burning firewood and the scent of fried pork fat and coffee slowly pulled her out of the arms of sleep and into the throes of the day.

Irritated with no reason, she threw the cover off and stood, stretching as she assessed her upcoming day. No sign of her new husband, though she strongly doubted he'd return to her tent with the fight still going on. It had been a parting laugh on Abby Gaines' tongue as she left, of how no true lady would remain here, especially since her husband had soldiers to lead. At the time, she didn't pay that woman much nevermind. All she wanted was for that sour-mouth cur to leave, but now, her words haunted Cerisa. What if he fell in battle? Or was captured? Would they think to tell her? Or would she have to wait to see the gurney men retrieve him and bring him back? Fury rose inside her, angry at Abby and the dire thoughts she'd stirred. He was fine. She had to believe it, she vowed, shrugging the old wool dress back over her head. She pulled her hair back to pin it and splashed water across her face to revive her, then left for the hospital.

The crowded camp outside her tent as she made her way made her stay to the edge, trying to blend in with the tents to keep from being run over. None of the soldiers seemed to notice her, except for a few who tipped their hats, but most appeared in a hurry. Her first sight at the hospital tent made her stop.

Guarding the entrance, Nurse Henderson stood and looked past the man before her and found Cerisa.

Not her favorite person but they weren't here to be friends, Cerisa reminded herself, just to help the patients. Swallowing her pride, she continued.

"Good morning, Nurse Henderson."

The woman gave her a half glare. Or maybe it wasn't one at all. Maybe it was just how she looked in this extremely dull appearance of hers. The woman ranted how Dorothea Dix wanted them plain looking but this was beyond plain.

"Mrs. Duval," she gave a slight nod.

Cerisa was through with her and started to walk past when Henderson continued.

"Despite what I still believe is an over use in water, the men in your ward are still among the living and those with wounds look admirably good, not as red and swollen as is expected."

Cerisa nearly stumbled. Had that woman just given her a compliment? It took her a minute before she finally mumbled, "Thank you. Simply following orders." She turned to push forward when the woman interjected.

"Not under Major Peregoy's orders, nor any other surgeon's."

Instantly, her temper flared and it took every ounce of energy to bottle it. "Perhaps not, though it may become such. Aunt Jenny preached this and upon doing so, we saved many lives—"

"Ah, yes, your beloved house slave. Yes, I heard your accent, all over through the canvas."

"Nurse Henderson, I believe Dr. Dreyer is in need of your skills," Peregoy interrupted loudly. "He's in surgery as we speak."

"Yes, sir!" She grabbed her bucket in one hand, skirts in the other and left. But not without a sneer at Cerisa, whose blood boiled to lash out but she refrained, with Surgeon Peregoy there.

The surgeon stood, cup of steaming coffee in his hand but his blood-stained jacket and a mar of red on his hands told her he had been up for a while. She gave him a nod as she took a step closer.

"Thank you, sir."

He offered her the cup. "You're welcome. It'd be better for us all if you two would not bicker so. Looked like it was about to get ugly." When she hesitated on the cup, he added. "No, take it. Haven't had a sip and there's plenty more cups in the back. You'll need it for today."

She bit her tongue from wanting to argue they weren't bickering but the desire for the black liquid won so she said nothing and took a sip as carefully as she could, the tin radiated the heat of the contents but she relished in the taste. It took a bite out of the fog that still threatened to cloud her brain, despite the ill-mannered nurse. "Looks like you've been busy." She nudged toward his jacket and hands.

He snorted. "A few soldiers dragged in last night, found straggling on the fields, in need of medical help." He glanced down at his coat and shrugged. "Not as bad as it looks."

Cerisa couldn't help but cringe.

"I must say," the doctor continued. "I like a woman who won't allow another to trample her or her home. You are quite a woman, Mrs. Duval, a Southerner that'll take the entire Union Army to conquer." He gave her a warm smile. "We shall be at war forever against your type."

"She had no right to judge me," she blurted before thinking. "And thank you. I think."

He laughed. When he did, he didn't look as tired or as stressed but more at ease, even jovial. Yet it was his gaze that worried her a bit. His brown eyes looked darker than she recalled and very warm, enlightening even, yet they also gave her a gaze similar to what lions gave their lionesses, or prey, before they devoured them. It made her breath skip a beat. Did he know of her past? Was that a look of desire, for there was a hint that could easily be categorized that way. It made her want to melt and she worried.

At a loss for words, she swallowed the coffee and frantically looked for a way to divert any such wayward thoughts. When a cannon shot rung through the air, she startled. But it made Peregoy snort and shake his head.

"Drink your coffee, my dear. I expect casualties will be arriving soon."

Morning broke and the soldiers were long awake, trying to make a breakfast that held a high chance of never being eaten. The war had gone on too long for any of them to think today was any different, for any night sleeping 'campaign' style, as the tentless set was, usually equated to fast action on the battlefield and little time for food.

Pierce did make it to Rosecrans's camp, long enough to down a cup of coffee before riding with the commander to inspect his troops. As Rosecrans rode further north, Pierce's aide found him. It always amazed him how fast and silently that boy could move.

"So are they still here?" he asked, pulling out his looking glass at a momentary stop.

"The Coloreds? Yes sir. Right over there." Prasse pointed to the north a bit, on the edge of the northern frank of the Thomas's XIV Corps position.

"This line isn't solid," Rosecrans decided. "Send Negley's men left of Thomas's line as soon as possible."

"Yes sir!" The soldier took off.

"Good, good," he murmured, assessing the field. As they rode, Rosecrans made several more rearranging of troops. "Our foe," he started, looking at his aides and officers. "Appears to prefer slumber over battle."

The men laughed, but their edginess was as sharp as glass.

After yesterday's resounding defeat, Pierce thought the rebels would be up early to conquer them but no one was stirring and that was unnerving.

The morning continued to drag, with a few gunshots being heard. But after the second round, he looked across the field toward the enemy. What had been a quiet start, there was now rumbling and then all hell broke loose.

He'd barely made it down the first row of soldiers in Thomas's line when the Confederates opened fire. "Here we go, boys! By rank, fire!"

The soldiers loaded and fired their weapons, going row by row back. The moment they fired they fell to their knees to clear the space for the next row to fire while they did the designated nine steps to reload their weapons. Bullets whizzed through the fields and trees, buzzing as they slipped through the air toward their targets. In a rain of gunfire, troops started to move into a more limited space to work.

Pierce rode close to the end, where the Coloreds were. There was still something eating at him over the one man and he hoped in the light of day, he'd recognize it, otherwise, they still held the ground despite the Confederate push. Walker led the men, all Coloreds but two, who were privates. He stood his ground as the bullets whizzed by, issuing commands that kept his small group continuously firing. Confident they'd stay, Pierce turned in the saddle and found McCook, who was seething.

"He's moved men here, leaving a wide gap below. Tell me how to tell him that!" the general yelled, his face red and smoke, Pierce swore, poured from his ears.

"Spies claim the gap is up here."

"Where? Where? I see one maybe forming, behind those areas vacated to joining up here. We don't have a gap! That's what I've been sayin'!"

"Look, you keep your end up and I'll see," Pierce stated and turned in his saddle. He stood on a ridge, assessing the situation. The Confederates seemed to be increasing, the numbers escalating like ferrets over the field and then thinning as the morning continued. The fields were laden with bodies of the injured and dead but that wasn't what pulled the enemy numbers down. Puzzled, Pierce turned only to hear Prasse's call. He looked and found the aide pointing north, toward the Colored's section. He zeroed his gaze north and what he saw froze him in the saddle.

The Black unit was fighting along with their fellow soldiers tooth and nail to drive back the Confederates but they were slipping. He saw two of them fall to the ground. Their leader moved and his face was turned south, where it shined in the sunlight. It was there, Pierce recognized the man. It was Cerisa's freedman! He couldn't move, shocked beyond belief. All reports showed the entire 54th was mowed down by the Confederates, so how the hell did he live?

Then last night's tale came back to him, of how the few that lived were enslaved, just as the Confederates had warned would happen. He gulped. He'd married another man's wife! Or had he? The man was listed as dead.

Halfway across the small battlefield section, a barrage of firepower hit Scribner, King and Starkweather's men, causing several to fall to the ground. He heeled his steed and bent low as he heard the buzz around him, the air seemed to whiz under his nose and near his ear as bullets flew. He was close to getting hit. But he had troops to lead and a chance to get into the fight, a battle he had to concentrate on.

A jolt of emotions raced through him—anger, fear, jealousy and confusion. Anger that that man went to war, leaving

Cerisa in poverty with no recourse; fear that she loved him more than any emotions she might have for Pierce; jealousy for that darky having her first, though he'd be mad at any man who was with her, and that number grew exponentially in his mind; and confusion as to how this man still lived. What was Pierce to do now? She was married to him. Army records made her a widow, yet how could he deny her if she loved this freedman? While he expressed his love for her in the heat of the moment, and it was true, he didn't know if she even cared for him or not. Heavens, his head hurt! And why the hell was he worried about this now, when a battle raged? He growled and yanked his officer's saber from the scabbard. Raising the blade high above his head, he roared.

Guns exploded around him with men yelling from both directions. The faster he rode, the more his blood raced and he felt strangely free, the sound of the pounding hooves barely audible but he couldn't help but imagine that man beneath them as he snuffed him out of her life. So caught up in his expunging the threat to his marriage, he only vaguely heard a thud nearby followed by a heavy but short push against his shoulder. His body tensed as he rode faster. Off to his right, he watched the Colored troops at battle, and he couldn't ignore how they handled it well, very well in fact, aiming their rifles, firing on command and reloading again. The intensity of the fight escalated as they zeroed in on the other side. Pierce rode, slashing at a few who tried venturing towards his men but for the most part, he stayed with his command, encouraging them, urging them to lay down more firepower. The air turned hotter and smoke rose, making sight more and more difficult.

Pierce pulled on the right reins, adjusting to turn right and as he did, the smoke cleared enough to expose an enemy cannon stood right in his path, the opposing artillerymen readying to pull the lanyard and set the piece off. Pierce jerked his horse to the right to round a fallen tree, but his movements were too rapid, putting them in the firing range. Another tune sounded in the air as the horse spun and reared, striking out at all with both front hooves, throwing Pierce off the saddle. When the horse came down, it shook its head, snorting and blowing before it took off running in the fields.

His hearing rang loudly, to where he couldn't hear even a musket firing but the ground beneath him rumbled like mad. The sky exploded in a haze of fire and smoke, raining ashes and burning drops. His thinking muddled and all he could concentrate on was how his heart felt on fire, for he had fallen in love with her. He'd cherish every moment he had with her and would never leave her alone, bereft and broke. Even now, he had a copy of his will in his pocket, along with a note of who he was, in case he fell in battle, a practice many of the soldiers had started after the carnage left many un-recognizable after the battle.

His thinking, like his vision, blurred as the stabbing pain in his side grew from the low throbbing annoyance to a volcano. It came from his left side and tentatively, he reached to check it out. The moment his fingertips touched it, a shot of extreme pain stabbed him and he flinched, yanking his hand back. His vision darkened and he caught a glimpse of the blood that dripped from his hand.

Oh, my God… He collapsed as his world turned black.

CHAPTER TWENTY-NINE

"As I knelt by the boy and searched his pockets …. [I] found… pictures of the wife and the chubby children, and the locks of hair and soiled and worn letters from home, I felt like a murderer."
—Lt. Wilson Vance, 21ˢᵗ Ohio, Battle of Chickamauga

WAR WAS NOTHING SHORT of hell. Every man on the field that day knew it. So had anyone who had been part of it over the last two years.

Abraham Walker pulled at his collar again, fighting the restraint around his throat that reminded him of his days as a slave. Oh, he'd never been collared, like a few slaves he knew of, but the Fontaines didn't use that tactic. Ideally, all went smoothly there, as long as they followed the rules but it was some of those rules that grated at a man's soul. So when a chance came to run, he took it without ever looking back until the last month…

"Sarge, you okay?"

Was he okay? Valid question, he thought. The last four months, from the time he'd joined the army, had flown by and so much in his life had changed. He'd wanted to write to Cerisa repeatedly but his skills were not good so he sent a couple of short messages, got a couple from her, but after Fort Wagner, when he was injured and captured, things were different. His wound came from being hit in his leg by an explosion that left him unconscious. When he woke, he was chained and in a Confederate cell, lost and mentally confused. Even now, his temple throbbed at the memory. Everything he'd fought for, survived from, meant nothing for here he was, again enslaved to the whites.

That was two months ago. Two. It'd taken over a month for his memory to return before he could start to feel comfortable with himself, rediscovering who he was. Now, he knew, the final straw landing into place when their new commander arrived—the man who'd saved him and Cera in New York, *General* Duval. Instantly, he wondered if the general knew how his wife was doing. Was she still in New York or elsewhere? Had she re-married—a thought that disturbed him but made sense, for no doubt with him missing, he might be called dead. He wanted to ask but had lost his nerve.

The whizzing noise of incoming fire broke his melancholy and he shot the private next to him a glance and smiled. "Yessum. Now, get your rifle ready!"

"Yes, sir!" bellowed the line of Colored soldiers in front of him.

The men across the field, the grey and butternut soldiers of the Confederacy, stirred early this morning and to a man like Abraham, that movement meant only one thing—another chance those bastards would throw them back under the whip. Well, he'd refuse again and again and again…it was the shock they'd enslaved them and the bigger realization that they had to dig the roads and clear the fields for the Southerners to fight the Yankees that set the plan into motion to resist. And the closer to the fight they came, that momentum exploded. Abraham knew the Lord was on their side, so when the Lincoln-boys arrived, their Southern masters were no longer in charge.

"Fire at will, boys! Fire. At. Will!" He bellowed the command as he grabbed his own rifle and began the nine paces at a quick speed then raised, aimed and fired at the oncoming rebels.

But despite the number he took out of play, double appeared to take up their position.

"Sarge, that number out there, it growin' sir!"

Eli, his number two man, stood next to him, his lips half black from gunpowder and his sooty face soaked in sweat. He was no doubt a reflection of him, Abraham thought, but he did agree. It was then he heard the command to fall back. A bugle issued the retreat right as the Confederates charged.

They grabbed their weapons and supplies, a couple firing at the enemy as they fled back. The firing went back and forth, the Union losing ground. Abraham pushed his men until the tide rolled them back. All he could see were the demons of hell sent to destroy them and he roared as he aimed, determined to blow them into kingdom come....

"Nurse! I need a nurse!"

Cerisa spun in heed of the cry. It was one yelled so many times, she began to think she was hearing things. Unfortunately, she was wrong and another hospital steward was in a situation needing help. With the number of wounded piling up outside, the surgeons were too busy to help and that left the orderlies, who were anything but helpful, and her. She discovered she was only nurse in this tent. At the rate they needed her, she'd bet her bottom silver dollar that Miss Henderson was swamped as well. The very thought of that sour hag being busier than a queen in a beehive somehow made Cerisa smile as she hurried over to the steward but she stopped, shocked at the scene and the instant nausea that inched up her throat.

Hospital Steward Diego Solar, a young man from Texas, struggled against a patient who was thrashing about his bed, yelling obscenities at the top of his lungs.

"Nurse, I need your help." His expression was bland except for the eyes, which told her the depth of his situation. The soldier before him had a grievous wound, one she'd seen too many times when she'd ventured to look outside her ward-tent at the line of wounded filing off the battlefield. His hand had been scored by the enemies' bullet, and the lead conical-shaped projectile had entered the man's hand and traveled a couple of inches inside his wrist to his lower arm. It was a ghastly sight, all the skin peeled back like a ripe peach's skin, exposing the flesh and blood beneath. It was ugly and bled like a head-wound, she decided. Tourniquet applied, he'd been shuffled to the surgeon's line, knocked out by some concoction she'd heard about but never seen, and the arm up to the elbow was amputated in a whopping fifteen-minute procedure, only to be shoved out the surgeon tent while the practitioner called *Next!*

These patients were brought to her tent and left to recover. It'd been a busy morning and outside the cup of coffee, she'd no time for anything else as she went on her mission to care for her wards. And several had acted up but none this harsh and with the stewards around, she'd been left to carry on but now, this man would have nothing with lying still to recover.

"Damn you all! The enemy is there! There! They'll kill us all!" the man shrieked and at first, her nerves did jump but she held back from looking, knowing they were hundreds of yards from the battlefield and no gunfire nor rebels were outside. A closer look at the man showed signs of high fever—pale features, a sheen of high body heat and haunted and dilated eyes told her all. But what was worse was he'd struggled to rise, using his stump as if the arm still existed and now the linen wraps were soaked in blood as they started to unravel.

Steward Solar begged her to draw closer. "He's been fighting the bindings. He won't stop fighting me to let me see if he's done any damage."

Swallowing the sour bile in the back of her throat, she sat on the other side of the bed and took the man's shoulders in her hands, feeling him buck against her grip and hoping she could calm him fast as Solar pulled his own hold off to inspect the wound.

"Sergeant?" she asked, trying to find a way to address him. She'd bet from his vile swearing he was not an officer, though she realized she had no basis for that assumption outside his injury infuriating him. "Sir, please, who are you?" She dropped her tone, letting her Louisiana accent lull a tune for him with its cadence.

He stopped thrashing and cocked his head. "Sergeant Vickers."

She smiled, though it took every ounce of energy she had, once she made the mistake of checking how Solar did at the man's wound. He'd unwound the bindings a bit, exposing the black threaded stitches that had broken—three of them to be exact—and the raw flesh with severed blood vessels now reopened poured bright red blood.

"Sergeant Vickers," she tried not to stumble but it was hard. This was a violent wound, even in after care. She thought of Surgeon Peregoy and the heat on him to fix these men…she swallowed again and pasted a smile on her face, like the ones her mama had taught her. *Be respectful and polite. Show how he's important*…Good grief, she could hear dear Mrs. Fontaine chatter on about niceties. She doubted her mother would ever consider her lessons on manners would be used this way!

"Sir, please," she continued, ignoring the laughing voice in the back of her head, thinking of her mère so... "You've been hurt. The doc has done his best to keep you with us. Let us try not to undo his and God's holy work." She prayed the sergeant was a Christian and not one of those type who didn't believe. After all this bloodshed, though, she might see why they'd think that.

"I ain't whole!" He fought back. "I got a damn fire under my skin but it burns here!" he raised the stump, looking at it at the same time. In that split second, she saw the pain, anger and regret flash across his fevered eyes. "Damn, they done took my hand!"

He flipped in the bed, in anger, pain and fear driving him. Her strength wasn't enough to hold him from making it worse but she tried harder. Solar, who had seemed to disappear, suddenly was at her side, a tin cup in his hands that he forced to the sergeant's lips. The man had no chance but to down half the liquor and he did in spurts, sounding more like he was drowning versus swallowing. Solar, when through pouring the contents down Vickers, tossed the cup and took hold of the man, nodding to Cerisa he'd hold him.

She watched in amazed horror as the patient looked right at her, all the war playing in his gaze, a mix of sheer horror and hatred blazed, then he rolled his eyes back in their sockets and fell on the bed, limp as a ragdoll. With a narrow gaze, she stared at him and then at Solar.

"Morphine," the steward mouthed. "To knock him out." He stood and moved to the next bed, taking his box marked with the medical seal with him. Later, she learned it held the drugs they used and she cringed.

Opium. Morphine. The makings of concoctions like laudanum…. that painkiller had opium and whiskey. She knew of people who used it as a basic painkiller. Some users overly relied on it to make it through the day. With a look of horror, she looked back down at the sergeant, who had collapsed on the bed. The man had complained the hand that didn't exist hurt. And if that caused that outbreak, how much morphine would it take to let him live? Or would it kill him? She shuddered.

A quick look about the room made her sigh in despair. More patients, few actually sleeping, with more mouths to feed, more sheets to clean and an overwhelming number of wounds to tend to. The screaming outside the tent won the battle over which patient was louder, but she figured these men here took the quiet award simply because they were too tired and in too much pain to care.

One of the aides popped his head inside the tent. "More casualties comin'!"

Her nerves skipped a beat. Whipping her palm over her hair in a nervous attempt to 'freshen up', she grabbed a rag and a bucket of water, fearing who she might see in the incoming batch…it was a thought she had to squash, for it did her no good.

Men poured over the hillside before her, including more than just the wounded. It made her curious. She hadn't heard much about the progress out there. Most of the wounded were centered on their pain and the docs here on mending them, not in how they were doing. She'd heard rumors, hidden by covered lips, as if she, as a woman, wouldn't understand nor did they include her. It stung at first, but her work quickly made her get over any possible insult.

Three stewards were out, quickly assessing the injured as they arrived. She found Solar and went to him as he worked on a soldier. By the time she got to him, he was putting his hand on the man's forehead and told the transport to carry the man, who looked so forlorn and she cocked her head, wondering why Solar was sending him away until she saw the belly wound with all the blood. She bit her bottom lip to stop the gasp that wanted to escape. Abdomen wounds were death, one deemed eminent so they had them deposited under the shade of a tree, referred to the dying tree, while the doctors tackled another whose wounds could be repaired. Silently, she crossed herself and said a brief prayer for the man.

The next patient held his other arm, screaming at the top of his lungs. "Don't take my arm! Please!"

Solar peeled the hand away to see the wound. Cerisa hummed to the patient, trying to get him to lower his voice. She wasn't sure what she said that got him to be quiet but suddenly, he was. Then she made the big mistake of looking at what the steward had found. The man's arm was ripped open, tendons and bone exposed, flesh black and red, drenched in blood and the limb was twisted wrong.

"See how he held it? He squeezed it to stop the pain, I'd reckon, but it also tore it worse, from what I'm thinkin'," Solar assessed. He dropped to a low whisper, "It made the broken bone drive into the veins." Slipping a tourniquet on, he pulled the strap and motioned the patient into the growing line for the surgeons.

"He'll lose it," Solar stated as soon as the man was out of hearing range.

Cerisa's eyes widened, the whole scene too grotesque to imagine. Her blood raced and her ears began to hum to the point that when the steward said something, she couldn't hear him. What if that'd been Pierce? Where was he? She'd scanned the group and didn't see him but her fears grew with every patient she saw. Ice cold slid down her spine and her vision started to blur. She lost the grip on her bucket of water and as it crashed to the ground, with her not far behind.

First thing he noticed was the buzzing sound. Annoying noise that brought him out of a deep slumber and at first, he tried to fight it, because the darkness was soothing and gave him a blanket of safety, something he hadn't had in ages, so he refused to give it up easily. Yet once he heard it, he couldn't fight it no matter how hard he tried. It was soon followed by voices instead of simple buzzing, though there was that too. Insects.

He realized he was lying down on a bed, though he had no memory of going to sleep. It was dark now and hot, extremely hot. And he was thirsty, his mouth and throat so dry, he imagined he must have swallowed cotton! Inwardly, he croaked a guttural laugh, though it might have been out loud, but when was the last time he saw any cotton plants? Last he recalled, he was in the South, but his mission here actually destroyed cotton plantations, not inhaled them.

But the buzz now was at his face and he felt a flicker at his lips. It really was a bug and he went to swipe at it. The moment he raised his hand and moved, a sharp pain stabbed at his side, like a blade ripping into his flesh. He moaned, trying to bend but that didn't help and the fire spread throughout his body, burning everything. His eyes shot open and the discovery of where he was made him go still, with his hand lowered.

He was inside a tent, on an army cot. The other noise he

heard was men talking and he got a look at them, though every movement he made hurt. One thing he did notice, though, was this hospital tent had doctors from the look of the dirty, blood stained coats they wore and grey trousers. Their aides and others were dressed in grey. He blinked as the realization hit home. He was in a Confederate hospital, not Union. *What the hell?*

"Looks like that Yankee is up."

Pierce swallowed and stared at the man standing next to his bed.

"Colonel, how are you feeling?" asked a young doctor. He reached to touch Pierce's forehead. "You're still hot. That fever is hard to manage."

Pierce frowned. Fever? And colonel? It dawned on him, the frock he had on still had the side boards of a colonel as he waited for the general boards to be delivered. "Its General Duval, if you please."

The young surgeon gave him a wide-eye stare but laughed. "Certainly, sir. Please forgive me. Bet you're wondering how you came under my good graces."

Of course, he was, he wanted to blurt, but that dry mouth ached after his last sentence. "Water, please."

"Of course, apologies, how thoughtless." The doctor grabbed a pitcher and poured into a tin cup. "Have no fears, sir. It is your cup, found in the bag of that poor animal you were found close too. Had all the stampings of an officer's animal, so figured it was yours."

"My horse?"

"Yes sir. One of the many casualties of war. Pity. You were found unconscious, a horde of canister shot and men all over ya. You'll have a nasty wound on your side. Canister is terrible stuff." He stifled a shudder as he helped Pierce rise off the pillow and pressed the cup against his lips.

Pierce took a swallow, the water was like the nectar of the gods, threading down his throat with ease. He wanted to down the entire contents but the surgeon stopped him.

"Na, na, now. Can't have you retching by drinking too much."

Fury raced him. *They'd let him die from thirst?*

"Sir, believe me when I tell you, as long as you've been out and with your fever, too much water at one settin' will cause a most adverse reaction." He cocked his head. "You a new general, seein' as what rank that shredded jacket of yours said?"

"Brevet General Pierce Duval, of the IX Corps," he managed to choke out. Damn, he wanted more water! He tried to move to a more raised position but that pain in his side promptly stopped him.

"General Duval, please try to stay still." The surgeon lowered the blanket and moved the wrappings.

The warm air felt like a cool breeze against Pierce's skin once the woolen piece was moved. He realized he was in his shirtsleeves and still had on his trousers, which he was thankful for but his side hurt like a torch had pressed against it. The doctor touched the flesh near the pain and Pierce thought he'd launch toward the ceiling as the tender wound demanded no one get close.

"I'm hoping for the best, sir. This wound is deep. You got a bullet lodged into you, taking part of that fancy coat and shirt with it. Done the best I can but to be quite honest, its only 'cause you're an officer I could do that much to the enemy at this moment."

Pierce frowned.

"Sorry, apparently my manners went out with my joining

the Cause. I'm Dr. Hollingsworth, from Athens, now part of General Bragg's staff, though I'd prefer not to be." He sighed and pinched the bridge between his eyes, exhaustion plastered across his face.

Pierce strained to hear if there were cannons or gunfire in range but heard nothing other than insects and men. "How did I get under your care?"

"Oh, you were brought in with several other Yankees," the doc stated in a stoic tone. "Apparently, the tide has turned and your men are retreating."

That statement made Pierce's heart skip a beat. From memory, he recalled the Union numbers were bigger than Bragg's, plus they had better supplies and the better position against a worn out general, who was retreating. Or at least that was what Rosecrans had stated that long night. What the hell had happened?

Another thought made his stomach flip. *Cerisa!*

CHAPTER THIRTY

"A few are holding out upon the ridge up yonder…"
—General James Longstreet reported on battle status
Battle of Chickamauga, September 20th, 1863

A ROAR SWEPT OVER THE camp as more wounded were brought in. Every time she stepped out of the tent, Cerisa's anxiety grew to the point that she dropped a pitcher of water in the tent, losing all its contents. Doc Peregoy, who had taken a moment to step back from the carnage he dealt with, happened to be in the area, walking, when he saw her accident. He put his coffee down and raced to her.

She was sopping up the water with the end of her pinner apron. He stopped her, whipping off his dirty white jacket.

"There, now, use this," he handed her the coat and she could barely see, her eyes so filled with tears, her sight was blurred. "Oh, darlin', there's no reason to cry over spilled water." He gave her a small smile.

She blinked, one tear flowing down her cheek, which his fingers stopped as he caressed her jawline. "I'm sorry. I'm just worried—" She couldn't finish. What if she voiced her fear and it came true? She'd never forgive herself.

"Shhhh," Peregoy soothed. "It will be all right. He's an officer."

She sniffled, fighting more tears. "You said you are

married, Doc?"

Peregoy snorted, a corner of his lips curled. "Yes."

"Do you miss her?" She so hoped she wasn't as pathetic sounding as she felt. At the moment, she was confused, exhausted and frankly, overwhelmed, though she'd never admit that.

He was calm for a moment. "She and I had a heated discussion before I left. She didn't want me to go. I had to." He gave a chuckle. "That woman has a temper but she is my best friend, so—"

She pulled his hand from her cheek. "Thank you. I'm sorry. I lost my first husband due to this war. To lose Pierce, well—"

Peregoy reached over and kissed her forehead then whispered, "It'll be fine." Then he was gone, back into the surgical tent.

She took a deep breath and turned. A few more wounded were carried forward and she found Solar to help when a something caught her attention. Black soldiers, carrying two and supporting two more limping, came over the ridge. Her breath caught. A huge debate raged in her head, to run to them and see if they knew of Abraham but her mind screamed the army claimed he died. Clenching her fists buried in her skirt folds, she closed her eyes, forcing herself to think of now and, perhaps, find them later. But when she opened her eyes, everything stopped. Before her, in ragged uniform, supporting another soldier was a man who resembled Abraham. She blinked and re-focused. It couldn't be…. but, on closer inspection, she discovered it was.

"Abraham!" Without a second thought, she grabbed her skirts and ran to him.

Love was the only thing that kept him going. Pierce's fever

rose and so did the pain. He was in a bath of molten lava, speared by the demons of hell, he was sure. Perhaps it was Margaret's revenge for leaving her with his prejudiced family. Or perhaps her revenge for him heading to a brothel for a Southern whore and then marrying that rebel. Then his mind argued it was Cerisa for him forcing the marriage down her throat. Despite the fact he had saved her from being abused as a whore, she fought respectability and protection of marriage. His thoughts blurred and became more and more distorted, with periodic episodes by the stabbing pain.

Vacantly, he caught what looked like the Confederate surgeon, Hollingsworth, shaking his head and muttering, "His fever is rising."

The man before the surgeon scowled. "He's a prisoner of war!"

"And I'm not going to let him die because he's a Yankee!" Hollingsworth ran his hand through his hair. Pierce blinked, thinking the man's head went bald but when his eyes opened again, he realized it was the fever talking. It was too hot to be prostrate like this but when he tried to get up, the pain in his side flared unmercifully.

"We still have wounded being pulled off the field as we speak. We may have won the day but the battle ahead for the wounded will be much harder to conquer," the other officer said. "Do what you can for them and I'll see if there isn't a way to rid ourselves of the Yankee guests, since our own resources are so low. I'll need to transport all to Stout's hospitals way back and that'll take some manipulation as it is." The surgeon spun on his heel and left.

Hollingsworth's expression was unreadable.

"Thank you, sir," Pierce croaked at the doctor.

Hollingsworth snorted and bent to let him sip out of the

water cup. "Our surgeon, Doc Flewellen is a good man. He'll not allow a life to pass on his watch, nor will I. Just, thanks to your side's blockade of our ports, our supplies are dwindling, considering the numbers of wounded."

The water was cool and inviting. It slid down his parched throat and as it passed, so did his unrest. Made him wonder if the man poisoned it as a way to eliminate a problem, like his father's servants did the rats. When Hollingsworth laughed, he gave him a puzzled look.

"It's not poison, sir." The surgeon pulled the ragged sheet up again. "Has a bit of willow bark in it. Will help on the fever," he said. "Your rank may save you, sir. Higher officers often given care first."

Swallowing the last drop, Pierce frowned. "So we lost the battle?"

"Yes sir, from what I hear. Now get some rest."

He heard the man's boots on the hard dirt floor as he walked away, letting the impact of the words sink in. As it hit, his heart pounded furiously. If Rosecrans retreated, he was lost...

"I was told you died," Cerisa moaned, burying her face in Abraham's neck, letting the familiar warmth of being in his arms encompass her. He squeezed one last time then put her down.

"I thought I was dead," he confided but he gave her a lazy smile. "But God wasn't ready for me yet, so here I am."

Her heart sang. Yes, God had heard her prayers and he lived! She wanted to sing when suddenly, the present slammed into her when the curious, and some angry, glances bore down on her. The wounded surrounded her, bringing everything to now. The War. Pierce.

"Why did you let me believe you were dead? Why?"

He shook his head. "That battle was hard, Cera. Those rebels had the high ground and could pick us off like pigs in mud. I was part of the initial run up to the fort when they fired a cannon. That explosion sent me flying backward and I struck the ground hard. Woke up in some field hospital with my head hurting something awful and no memory of who I was. Hard to write you when I had no idea who I was, you or anything else."

She stared at him hard, totally not understanding though she'd seen enough wounded in the last day and a half to bear credence to his story. "But you're here and now and know who you are."

"Yessum." He nodded his brows furrowed. "They said they'd send us back to slavery if caught and they did, making me work for them to win in this war. As much as I understood that's not who I was, I remembered being enslaved and answering to their kind. It took seeing that general, that man we met in New York, to make my memory grab onto who I was. You remember that man, right?"

Cerisa swallowed, nodding her head, fighting the tears that threatened. That *man* was Pierce and her husband now. *How could she tell Abraham that?*

"I owe him a ton of thanks for making me remember right," Abraham continued. "Shame that bullet kilt him."

Cerisa's heart stopped. "You saw him?"

"Yessum. We's be under his command. Saw him out on the field. Brave soul, raising his sword and yelling holy hell to them rebels just beyond the clearing." He shook his head. "Made him a prime target, running like that and all."

Cerisa could barely hear him by the end, her ears were ringing and her heart sinking. *Pierce was dead? Why? God, please, why?* She pleaded and pleaded with no response. Tears began to pour out of her eyes as her heart began to crumble.

Abraham had her hands and held them tight. "I'm sorry, Cera. I had no idea." She realized he was staring at her hand. She knew he saw the yellow gold band, just a wisp of gold, resting on her left-hand ring finger. He gave her a sad, half-smile. "You married him?"

The tears fell down her cheeks. "I was told you were dead."

He lifted his chin and nodded. "I'm not mad," he said softly. "I thought I was dead. And believed you'd moved on—" After a moment, he added, "I'm sorry. For everything."

She frowned, trying to regain her footing again. She was lost, here in a Yankee camp, waiting for a husband that wouldn't be, finding her deceased former husband alive. Her temple throbbed, trying to comprehend everything. But her time to grieve came to an abrupt end as Peregoy emerged from the tent and called for her.

"Cerisa, we have to get the patients ready to move. We lost the battle." The words spilled so fast, he didn't see her state and he stopped, a questioning look forming on his face. "What happened?"

"General Duval, sir," Abraham chimed in. "Last I saw, he fell, gunshot wound it seemed."

The doctor frowned. "I'm sure we'll see him soon. Cerisa," he called to her again. "I need your help. Please."

Moving patients. The Union had lost this battle and had to flee. It'd be busy work and she wanted to stay with the hospital. If Pierce arrived wounded and not dead, well, either case, she'd see him here. With a nod, she agreed and Peregoy looked relieved, issuing orders as he left her on packing up.

Abraham disappeared. She'd wondered where to, but she moved, starting to get all packed when a hand snagged her wrist. Startled, she looked down at the man on the bed. It was that soldier that recognized her from Madame Nikki's and her heart thudded.

"So, I see you like to spread yourself everywhere," he sneered. "Married, white or black. Tell me, is that buck's dick as big as they say they are?"

Her mouth fell open. She'd never been so insulted. "How dare you!"

Lt. Smitherton chuckled. "Maybe, when I'm healed, I can get you to sit on my lap."

Smack!

"You will mind your manners, sir!" she snarled and stormed off. She feared her slap of his cheek wouldn't escaped anyone's notice, because even if they didn't hear the flesh beating flesh, the mark on his cheek was brilliant red. If it weren't for the well-being of the other men who couldn't leave if they tried, she focused on her work and steered clear of that man.

The wounded from Chickamauga seemed to grow, like jack rabbits, as the afternoon passed. Peregoy checked the next patient and sent him to the ambulance to head toward Chattanooga's hospitals.

"I've sent those who could walk to the field hospital in Stevenson," he reported to chief surgeon Perin, who hovered nearby.

"Send the critical to Chattanooga, to Surgeon Moses." The doctor looked at him. "I've inquired with the great Rosey," he started, emphasizing Rosey with disdain, "in regards to retrieving the wounded they've collected. So far, I've received no word he's even come to grips with this loss, let alone dealing with the outcome."

Peregoy examined the next patient. "This one to

Chattanooga."

Perin grumbled, "Too many damn buildings to man there and not enough surgeons. We're too thin as it is. My main concern is if Bragg sends an attack, we'll never get anyone out. Can't compete with the front line if they retreat. There's only the one pontoon bridge to cross the Tennessee."

Cerisa sat next to a boy on the far side of the tent, trying to console him for losing his hand during the madness. He cried for his mother and it made her sad, for he was too young, as far as she was concerned, to be at war. His fever climbed and the amputation area was red and swollen. She'd finally gotten him to sleep so the words of the doctors were clear. Rosecrans?

"Pardon me, sir," she couldn't keep quiet. "General Rosecrans?"

Perin gave her an odd look. "And to whom am I speaking?"

"This is General Duval's wife," Peregoy intervened.

"What in the name of heaven above is a lady doing here?" He gave her another inspection. It made her cringe a little. The factory dress she continued to wear had turned rancid even in her view at this point, the skirt's hem was stained and torn, the apron barely resembled white, but they had little to compare with their white jackets carrying the marks of the wounded blood and filth. "You look way too pretty to be one of Dix's staff."

"My husband," she continued, ignoring his stiff remark. "Is among the wounded who are missing." She refused at this point to reconcile him as dead. "We need to get him."

"Next, I expect you'll tell me you have an acquaintance with the general that could get him to write the note to retrieve this husband and others?"

She did not like his attitude towards her. "I think my

request might push him further, yes."

Peregoy jumped in, "Sir, she and the general are close. Since she has volunteered, and I think it'll do her a world of good to take a step away from the hellhole we pass off as a hospital here."

Perin drummed his fingers against his chin. "Fine, then by all means, see if you can't get the man to move, before General Bragg realizes he has the advantage here."

Outside the hospital tent, the rush of fresh air revived Cerisa and gave her the jolt of energy she needed to see the commanding general. She pinched her cheeks for a dash of color, for she'd no doubt she was as white as a ghost. Little sleep and not much to eat had left her exhausted and done in. Her stomach growled and she gnawed on a piece of hardtack Peregoy had slipped her but the piece was so hard, she barely made a dent in it, leaving her still empty.

Twilight had fallen across the camp and the remains of what was a bulging Federal army was reduced as the soldiers took everything down for the retreat. She didn't understand how the military worked, but she did notice that Smitherton was gone and for that, she was grateful. He was a man who could do serious damage to her reputation and without her knight, Pierce, she'd be doomed.

"Cerisa."

She stopped and looked around. That voice she'd recognize anywhere. Scanning around her, she couldn't see him until he moved out of the shadows. It was Abraham. She couldn't help but smile.

"Good evening."

"Good evening." She waited but he said nothing else. "Abe, perhaps we should talk."

He cocked his head and gave her that warm smile that had gotten her through the rough days in New York City, when they first arrived. That was before the war, when life seemed easier. Memories of those times stopped the moment he took her left hand.

"You married the general," he stated, his finger rubbing the wedding band. "That's the way it should be. He's a good man, from a respectable family, I'm sure."

"Abraham—," she started but he shook his head.

"I was wrong to leave you like that. I heard the money wasn't easy for you to get. Figured since I was 'dead', mayhap you got my pension."

She bit her bottom lip. "The Army didn't believe we were married. It," she stopped. He couldn't change the past or what she had to go through, nor was she going to blame him. "I never stopped loving you."

He smiled broadly, though it was tinged in sadness. "Nor I you. But this is for the better, don't you see? You'll be respected again. Won't have to work, no factory or anything."

Tears began to form and her tongue got stuck. "I'm so sorry," she managed to whisper.

"Shhhh, it will all be good. Dear Lord says it so." He kissed the top of her head and slipped his hand from hers, vanishing into the darkness.

She closed her eyes and her hands formed fists. How could she love two men at the same time? And to whom was she married? The urge to scream built inside her but she tampered it down and forced herself to breathe.

If she couldn't convince the general to get the wounded from the other side, she might have her answer, for Pierce could die, prisoner of her inherited country. Her anger at it all returned with a vengeance.

CHAPTER THIRTY-ONE

"My Dear General, I am afraid you are thoroughly outdone."
—Bishop Charles Quintard, chaplain of the Army of Tennessee to General Braxton Bragg, July, 1863

September 29ᵗʰ
Chattanooga, TN

IT WAS A CIRCUS. She had waited almost ten days for Rosecrans to write Bragg for a truce of sorts in order to retrieve the Union wounded held in the Confederate hospitals in Chickamauga Valley. It was an orderly affair with ambulances crossing the boundary, surgeons and stewards onboard to examine the patients to see who could survive the six-hour trip to Chattanooga. The physicians distributed crackers and coffee to the other side as they examined the Federal wounded. Those ordained strong enough to make it were loaded and the ambulances left, their drivers changed at the picket lines back to Federal men and the long trip began.

The worst part was she could not go. Despite all her arguing how it made sense for a Southern woman to go, Rosecrans would not back down, claiming she was his responsibility until her husband returned. Frustrated and anxious, she paced, looking out the window, down to Hospital No. 2, based at the foot of the hill, to receive the incoming. She was with Doc Peregoy at the Officer's Hospital, Hospital No. 8, which was a large private mansion converted for the wounded. He assured her he'd have him brought there, if he was that bad off. No one knew and Abraham's story of seeing him hit and falling wasn't much in detail for her to know, which made the waiting just that much worse.

She stopped pacing on that thought. Her heart and mind were torn. She was thrilled Abraham was alive, not understanding just how badly she'd missed him, and how that void in her life had led her on a crazy trail that placed her just where she needed to be to see him. But the price tag? Being married to another man. She gulped. This was a situation her mother had never prepared her for. Did her marriage to Pierce make her guilty of adultery? What would Pierce say? She couldn't believe Abraham would divorce her so she could marry a white man, thus 'restoring' her reputation, which she hadn't felt was in shambles…until, of course, she became a prostitute.

All this fear and insecurity was such an unpleasant feeling, but how else could she tend to this? Her mind constantly argued the point of Abraham and now. Of course, if Pierce was dead, then nothing was wrong. Her stomach flipped.

"Ambulances comin'!"

She spun, swallowing the bile that had climbed up her throat, thanks to her thoughts. She took a peek out of the upstairs window and saw the long line of Army ambulances lumbering toward them from the South. *Dear Lord, please let Pierce be on one!*

Pierce's jumbled thinking resembled his body, jumping from one place to another on the long journey. His dreams were divided between nightmares of the battle, of bullets whizzing by and how his beautiful Cerisa appeared, like an angel, walking amongst the carnage. His visions of her made her as precious as a rose thrown into the throes of hell, on the brink of disaster and when he saw the cannon ball barreling for her, he leapt in between, to shield her from disaster, only for him to be hit in the side, an excruciating pain that sucked the air from his lungs as he collapsed.

He laid quietly, trying to relax, which was hard on the rocking wagon. Vague memories of the last few days, or was it hours, flashed in his head. The visions of the Confederate surgeons, Hollingsworth and Flewellen, arguing over whether Pierce should go or not, though he didn't know where they meant. Then, after what seemed like an eternity, there was a lot of commotion in the tent and he caught a glimpse of navy-blue colored uniforms and that caught his attention. The group mingled about the patients and it suddenly registered in his fever-soaked brain he wasn't the only patient there.

The hospital steward of the US Army approached him, giving him a look over.

"General Duval, I'm Lt. Diego Solar, US Medical Corps. We're here to retrieve all the Federal wounded and take you back with us. Tell me," he said, turning Pierce's head to the left and right. "How do you feel?"

"Miserable," was all he was able to croak out. Again, cotton lined his mouth and he was lethargic, his body racked with fever he was sure, since he was hotter than a fire poker, only to freeze like ice the next. The stern look on the steward's face concurred with his own self-diagnosis.

Solar found the packing on his side and the moment he touched it, Pierce nearly leaped out of the bed at the pain.

"Did you find the cause, Major Flewellen, for the general's wound, or just allow it to fester?"

"How dare you!" the major snapped.

Hollingsworth stepped forward. "Sir, as you may know, our supplies are limited. We do what we can for your brothers in arms, but our men come first. Surely, you understand that."

With a deep sigh, Solar stood and looked at the two Confederate medical staff. "War is an evil creature, making monsters. Rest assured, we brought what we could to add to your supplies, along with crackers and coffee. And we will take them all, the ones that'd survive the journey."

Flewellen's voice dropped but Pierce thought he heard the man argue he wasn't sure Pierce would survive and those words, with the thought he'd never see Cerisa again, made what was left of his determination grab hold of his energy as he spit out the words.

"Get me the hell out of here!"

Cerisa raced down the staircase of the mansion to the front door. The grand old house, built for the wealthy, stood wide open now to the wounded and dying and at first, it had made her sad that the Union Army had 'occupied' this home, though she put it more like they stole it, for the use of the medical department. Despite the opulence of its grand staircase, it's open rooms and ballroom on the third floor and expansive balcony that encircled the house as many old-time southern homes did, to block the glaring sun's heat, it was exactly for this design that the surgeons used it. The house could hold up to a hundred patients with room for the staff.

Right now, all she cared about were the patients about to be brought in. As the long train she had seen in the distance now dispersed to the various hospitals through the city, she was only curious of the two that headed her way. She found her breathing was getting hard, her heart raced and she felt like she might retch, her anxiety rising in hopes Pierce was there. Then she noticed the driver of the front ambulance. It was Abraham and she prayed he'd drop her a hint. It was as if God had heard her prayer, for the freedman found her and gave a slight, barely noticeable nod from his perch in the driver's seat. She nearly squealed in excitement.

A man chuckled next to her. Doc Peregoy said, "It appears we have new patients, Mrs. Duval. Mind you, all are to be treated with equal care."

She whipped her head around and found the doctor giving her one of his warm smiles, the type that let her know he understood her enthusiasm. "Of course, sir," she drawled daintily.

As the wagons stopped, they both went to them. The soldiers assigned to help the medical corps began to pull the wounded out and that's when Solar joined them.

"Mrs. Duval, I believe who you are seeking is in this one." He pointed to the wagon he had ridden in.

She stood, tense, as the first patient was removed, a man she didn't recognize. Peregoy gave him a quick look over and ordered him taken to one of the rooms. But the second man was the one she'd been praying to see – Pierce.

Two soldiers held the ends of the taunt stretcher as she ran over.

"Pierce, darling," she greeted, all smiles but his condition instantly made her cheery mood vanish. His face held the infamous fever sheen over the pale pallor, his lips drained of color and she feared he'd died on the way in. She put her hand on his cheek and the skin was red hot, like the way coffee made her tin cup hard to hold. But what scared her more was the seeping wound at his side.

"Doc Peregoy!"

But the doctor was there, his hand pulling a thin silver rod from his pockets as she picked up what Solar was reporting.

"That wound should be better by now," he stated. "But Surgeon Hollingsworth informed me that his men came first, which I understand if only a few of ours were there, but sir, there are hundreds. We only got out about two hundred and fifty souls, but there are well over a thousand there." He shook his head in despair.

Peregoy frowned. "He's burning with fever."

"Yes sir. They informed us they did what they could but supplies are low."

"Best reason I can think of to stop this madness," the surgeon snarled as he took a small blade to cut the bindings off. When he yanked the padding off, as it had stuck to the wound, they all leaned back at the stench. "Dammit, not only is he wounded, but they allowed it to fester."

"Sir, he wasn't this bad when we left. If he had been, it would've been safer to leave him."

"I'm not blaming you, Lieutenant, just stating a fact." He touched the flesh around the puncture and Pierce winced. He then pulled the long metal rod out of his pocket again. Cerisa's worrying skyrocketed.

"You must save him!"

Slowly, Peregoy peeled her fingers off his wrist. "I will, ma'am." He took up his instrument and went to the wounded side.

"What are you doing?" She nearly shrieked when she saw him bring the porcelain tipped end to the injury. She simply could see no reason to poke him.

Peregoy inhaled and gave her a quick look. "Cera, the man has a high fever and a punctured wound. By all sound reason," he bent over and with his free hand, slightly pressed against the edges of the slit. "He probably has a bullet or shrapnel or even dirt in there, causing his body discomfort. He's fighting it the only way he can but his body is on fire. I can find it with this." And on that, he inserted the piece.

Pierce moaned, and he started to squirm, but was limited where he could move. Cerisa paled but she went to him, stroking his sweat-soaked hair. "Darling, please try not to move. Doc is trying to help."

Peregoy moved the wand inside the opening, and Pierce flinched, trying to move away when the surgeon suddenly stopped and withdrew the bloody instrument. "Found it!" He looked at the tip. "See? The porcelain is black. He's got a bullet or metal in there. I have to operate." He turned to the two carriers. "Take him into the dining room."

As Pierce was taken into the house, the surgeon wiped the blood off the wand and put it back inside his coat pocket before he spoke. "My dear, I will take care of him. Have no worries."

She watched the doctor walk away and close the door to the surgery room behind him. It took her a moment to recover. She trembled, her body so tense for so long, she didn't know how to act. He was here. He was alive. But that wound looked horrid. How long had he suffered? And what type of torture had the Confederates put him through? Part of her screamed it was reported they lacked medicines but she was angry, upset, scared, and worse, for now, her heart wept. All uncertainty fled the room—she was in love with him. She shook her head. What was she to do? That scared her to think of the whole problem. For now, she had to be content he was in surgery, with a qualified doctor who had the supplies, yet... Oh, dear Lord, what if she lost him now?

The rag she'd had in her waist tie was in her hands and she twisted the piece, terror now starting to seep in. Out of the corner of her eye, she saw Abraham, half dusty and dirty from the drive. She swallowed hard, but the lump in her throat didn't pass, nor did the tears that formed go away. The pain and worry inside her was making her heart beat wildly. Her stomach knotted. Unable to speak, she began to shake, which soon turned uncontrollable. Her vision blurred. And in that instant, Abraham was there, taking her into his arms as her legs buckled.

CHAPTER THIRTY-TWO

"Boys, we're glad to see you, but there is more fighting Yankees right up there than a little."
—A soldier from Govan's brigade, Winfrey Field, Battle of Chickamauga, September 19th, 1863

October 1st

TWO DAYS. TWO. HE'D been unconscious too long in Cerisa's way of thinking. She pulled the linen scrap out of the water, squeezing the excess out and replaced the one on Pierce's head, in an attempt to lower the fever he had. It wasn't as hot as before, and he seemed to fair better than some of the other patients, but it still bothered her.

"So, Nurse Cerisa, how is our patient this morning?"

Despite how exhausted she was from sitting with Pierce all night, worrying about him, she still managed to give a wane smile to the surgeon.

"He's not as hot but still too warm to be out of it."

"No sweats yet?" Peregoy strode over and moved the cover. She shook her head.

The surgeon sighed with a frown, staring at the wound.

"What is it?" she hadn't checked it for a bit, heavens, she couldn't remember when. There was a slight buzzing in her ears, and as she turned to face the doctor, she realized she was lightheaded.

"Whoa!" Peregoy came to her, catching her before she fell. "You don't look very good, either, my dear." He led her to another cot, one that had been cleared yesterday. He touched her forehead. "At least you are not warm." He raised an eyebrow. "When did you sleep last?"

When she opened her mouth to say but couldn't recall, he snorted in disgust.

"And your last meal was when?"

She bit her bottom lip. "I had one of those hard biscuits sometime…"

He brought her a cup of water. "Drink this. You rest for a bit and I'll get you something to eat."

That brought her upright. "I'll be fine, truly. I just couldn't bring myself to leave him. He was having fits and I didn't want him to wake alone or toss and turn so much, he'd split the wound open."

Peregoy growled. "I'm still going to find something more for you to eat. And I do insist you rest! That's the doctor's order, you hear me?" He caressed her cheek, an odd look in his eyes.

A shiver raced down her spine. There was a mystery about him she didn't get and figured she shouldn't. That caress was too long, way too intimate for a doctor and nurse or patient. It was an awkward silence, one she couldn't allow to continue as Pierce's life was held in the balance.

"How did the injury look?"

Peregoy blinked and his gaze returned to the warm, jovial look she was used to. "It is healing. That shrapnel wasn't easy to find, buried pretty good. Nasty pieces to get. They can cut right through an artery with just a sliver of a piece. But I think I plucked them all out. It'll take him time to heal, especially since it'd been in there that long and I had to go deep. But I see its beginning to pus, so—"

"Pus?" she flew off the cot and to Pierce's side. With a slight tug, she exposed the wound and looked at it and the bandage. She could see the yellowish stains on the cloth and the glistening of the puckered incision, which was still swollen and pinkish, though not the bright red it had been. She touched the area with her forefinger. Pierce barely moved. The liquid on her appendage was slightly sticky.

"Whyever would you think pus would be good?" she snapped, racing to the fireplace and stirring the embers of a flame that had virtually died.

"The flesh isn't as hot, nor as swollen. Simply the body removing the filth."

She got the flames revived and heating the pot of water that hung over it. Grabbing more linens, she glared at him. "Ever seen what happens on a farm, doctor? When the men get hurt from the lance or the plow? Wounds those make are similar to this and pus is anything but good, because if you move the area in cleaning, you'll see how it is an infection the body is trying to get rid of, through fever." She rinsed the wound in the hot water and Pierce withered under it, but she got the area clean and pushed the sides a little wider, finally cutting the stiches. There, even Peregoy could catch a whiff of it.

"Well, I'll be," he stated. He maneuvered the cut a bit and took the hot water to wash the pus away. Then he pulled a vile from his medical bag he brought with him and popped the cork, to sprinkle the white powder on it. "A little bit of sulfur to clean it." After a layer, he corked it and put it aside.

"I think I'm going to have him moved to Nashville's facilities. I simply don't have all I need here, particularly since I've got patients scattered over the place. If Bragg turns and attacks north, we're right in his path. Can't have all these wounded like this." He frowned and looked at her. "It'll take a bit to get this arranged. I'm betting I can't find an excuse good enough to keep you here," he started, softly. "With me? To help, of course. Your skills are invaluable to me, I mean, the Union."

Cerisa stood, shocked. The surgeon appeared honest in that statement. Outside of that Dix's nurse, there were no other women to nurse here and the recovered men were returned to the front, but it was the look he gave her and the touching that had made her wonder. But he was married, she'd argued to herself. Yet she worried the look in his eyes covered more than just viewing her as a nurse in a professional manner. She swallowed hard, feeling sick to her stomach. Wasn't she ever going to get past that moment in her life when she had had to sink that low? Was it on her forehead, a sign that all the men saw? Once, she knew she was beautiful and the catch of any man's eye but that was years ago and before the world turned in her youthful eyes. No, now she was seen as a catch—one for a carnal need. Distantly, she wondered if that's all Pierce saw her as too? Her heart sank.

"No, sir. I appreciate that, but I must stay with my husband," she stated firmly and prayed she was right.

Pierce was exhausted. Exhausted and thirsty. He'd even throw in being hungry but he had no energy to do anything more than halfway open his eyes. His side hurt, like pins and needles were lodged into his flesh and any movement sent waves of pain through him. Every muscle ached and he wondered if his horse had run over him, or perhaps he'd been run over by the whole Union Army, the torture to move so bad he didn't. So he simply cracked his eyelids opened and immediately saw something he hoped and prayed wasn't real, but another nightmare of the fever for before him, he saw Dr. Peregoy touch his wife and she did nothing to stop him. Deep inside him, he wanted to yell at the man to stay clear of her. And then, again, he poised that he might be dreaming this. No, if that was true, it was a nightmare.

Then, they turned in his direction. He was way too weak, it was like he was chained to the bed as every inch of him hurt if he moved. Hurt even if he didn't. And even as he fought it, exhaustion won and he was out.

In the world of the near-death, his thoughts returned him to the sight of her and Peregoy, only this time, they were kissing…

His blood started to boil. When he got to where he could stand, he'd kill that surgeon and send him home in a pine box! But the sudden spurt that drove him to swear what he'd do also drained him completely and he sank into darkness.

Nashville, Tennessee
October 5th

ABBY GAINES STRODE DOWN the occupied city's streets, enjoying the sunlight and the spectacle around her. She and the other ladies who remained in the South, close to their husbands, had retreated to Nashville on Rosecran's orders. Dear old Rosey had believed Chattanooga wasn't safe enough for them because it was "too close to the enemy" and if General Bragg attacked, Chattanooga with her railroad heads, was a prime target to scoop back. So with reluctance borne of having to be shipped that much further away, Abby and the others packed.

Of course, that whorish Southern slattern remained, and from what Abby heard, the woman had found refuge in the medical tent, aiding all who came. Yes, she'd no doubt that woman helped. Hardly helping the poor staff at all, she decided, so she penned a note to her contact at camp. His response was just returned via that Colored soldier, who arrived half way out of breath to see the surgeon in charge. She didn't stay to find out what that man said but took the letter and called for her lady friends to meet.

"Hey, Yankee, we want you to leave!" A young boy yelled at her from across the street.

Startled, she turned and found a youth, boy just too young to fight, spitting at her from across the street. Pity, she thought. He'd be great fodder for the army, the Confederate Army, to eat up in their current situation. Everyone heard the rumors how they were running short on more than just supplies and were now recruiting men both too young and too old to join the fight. If nothing else, she was surprised the lad was still here.

The boy wanted a fight, wanted her gone. She bit back the laughter that threatened to spill. He wanted her to leave his Southern town when it was no longer his to give. It was occupied by the Union Army! Her smile, though, she didn't try to hide.

"Laughing at me?"

"Son, go home and see your mama, while you still can. We're not leaving anytime soon."

At that instant, one of the Union soldiers heard the Southerner curse and raced to correct his behavior. Abby noticed he was one of the Colored Union boys. Good, she thought, very fitting that a member of the race they'd enslaved should correct him. She picked up her skirt hems and turned, trying to keep the bottom from dirt on the road.

Crumpling the letter in her pocket, she went to the tall blue house where Clara Francis was with her other friend. The ladies were so excited to see her, they didn't even let her knock nor let their hired hand butler open the door.

"Clara, Mary, do I have a treat for you!"

They took a seat at the parlor table and as Clara's maid filled their cups with tea, Abby pulled out the letter.

"I received this letter yesterday from my fine friend still with General Rosecrans," she started.

"Yes, yes, we know that. You put that in your note for our tea today." Clara took a sip out of her cup, looking slightly annoyed she had to wait. Abby wanted to laugh. They had been waiting a long time for anything other than war for her to be this short about it.

"I think you'll find this worth it. Now, as I was saying, I received this from one of the soldiers there, a Lt. Smitherton. You might recall him."

"Oh, yes," Mary swooned, fanning herself. "He is very dapper indeed."

Abby's brows rose. She had no idea they might find him intriguing. "Yes, well, he sent me a missive about that Southern woman, who stole dear, sweet General Duval right from under our noses!"

"That woman is no better than the ones we find here. Southern trash!" Clara declared.

Abby nodded. "True, but it gets better."

The women looked aghast and leaned forward.

"Apparently, she was helping at the army hospital, but thinking she was doing more than sanitary issues, you might say." Abby smiled as their mouths dropped open. "There seems to be some liaison between her and Major Peregoy."

"Surgeon Peregoy? He's married." Clara added.

"Yes, but you might remember he had been attached to Libby Woodell for a while, as well, in the spring. He apparently enjoys the ladies." Abby sat back in her chair, pleased with her windfall of news. "And, she is married to our darling Pierce. Quite the scandal, wouldn't you agree?"

They nodded, somewhat shaking their heads at the tragedy forming for Pierce.

"Oh, and there is more," she said, quite pleased with the reception she was getting. "There is also an intimate moment with a Colored soldier."

"Colored?" Clara's mouth dropped open.

"Oh, my, no!" Mary began fanning herself furiously.

"I am afraid so." Abby closed the note. "I believe we must take drastic measures. After all, if she's this risqué, how do we know she really isn't a spy? Or worse."

"You are right, we must do something," Clara remarked, clutching her lace handkerchief tightly. "But what can we do? She appears to get along well with General Rosecrans."

Mary snorted and added with disgust, "They are papists, after all."

Abby gave a tight smile, working hard to hold back her enthusiasm, because that wouldn't seem right. Flipping her fan wide, she slowly smiled. "I think I know just who'd like to hear this. I will write them currently."

The other two agreed and then, the subjects went back to the menial chores they had in a town that wasn't theirs and with a populace who appeared to despise them. But not Abby. Put her in her place, was it? Abby snorted. These women demonstrated how proper should be and how those from the lower orders needed to stay in their place!

Oh, only to have Pierce here and she'd show him what a bad choice he had made!

CHAPTER THIRTY-THREE

"There they are, boys, give them hell!....May God forgive me for that."

—Major John Stackhouse, 8th South Carolina, Battle of Chickamauga, 1863

Cumberland Hospital, Nashville, Tennessee
October 8th

THE TRIP UP TO Nashville took much longer than Cerisa wanted. She watched Pierce, holding his hand as they rode over the ruts and pocked marked roads to the city from Chattanooga. Peregoy was right. The Major Surgeon had been worried if Bragg attacked, it'd be in the hospital's direction and the way it was looking, he'd be right. It may not have pushed Pierce's departure that much faster but it seemed to her it did.

She glanced down and found Pierce's glassy glaze on her. She smiled. "And how are you?"

"Still feeling like this buggy has rolled over me several times and that this is hell, reliving that feeling," he mumbled.

Cerisa laughed. "The journey was rough, but this is easy. Sorry, though, the lazy Southern way doesn't exist in the Union Army."

Pierce looked at her. He choked out a laugh and then abruptly stopped, his eyes reflecting the pain he must've had when he laughed and how it pulled at his injury.

"I'm sorry. I didn't mean to make you hurt."

She was trying to fluff up the stale flat pillow he had. On the hammock styled floating bed, how could he be more propped up? "I'm fine, Cera. Absolutely fine. It's getting better. It didn't hurt as much this time."

She inwardly cringed and mouthed *I'm sorry*. He needed to recover, she prayed every second, because this was killing her. Sleep eluded her and she couldn't eat, worried to death even her little bit of medical knowledge, added to the doctors, couldn't save him.

His grip on her hand squeezed hard. "Stop that," he ordered. "You carry the look as if I'm one foot in the grave."

She gave him a timid smile. "I know you won't be with fortitude like that!"

"Yes, but I'm more concerned about you, my wife."

Wife. A title, she thought, but one she proudly wore. Though the problem still remained about Abraham. She needed to discuss it but now wasn't the time, she reassured herself. He needed to be able to think straight and as he still was in recovery, it wouldn't be soon.

"There is no need to worry. The doctors say I'm fine, just need to rest and that I will do once we get you settled." She patted his arm and hoped he'd drop the subject.

Instead, he glared at the ceiling. "I cannot stand staying in bed like this. I have a job to do, not shirk my duty in a hospital bed."

The mere thought of him returning to the war made her heart skip a beat, but she understood he was right. Trying hard to steady her voice, she pasted a smile on her face. "I'm sure you'll be back on your feet before you know it."

The ambulance hit a rut and the wagon bounced. He

groaned. She fought the cringe that came over her and swallowed the bile that rose up her throat.

Abraham had had enough of Nashville. Occupation patrol was dull or worse. Most of the rebs stayed away from him and his men, not wanting to 'lower themselves to speak to a nigra.' Well, he really didn't want to talk to this white trash either, but when he found the one yelling demands at a white woman, didn't matter where she was from, his upbringing demanded he step in. Just staring down at the boy, who he'd bet was maybe twelve, put the boy right, left him speechless in fact. He took off running, perhaps like Mrs. Gaines had pressed him to do.

He had driven the ambulance that carried General Duval here and he remained, commands to him and the remains of his patrol who had tagged along, had yet to reach him. But after this afternoon's spectacle, the boy's rude comment and the dying urge to extract a more proper punishment made him realize he needed to return to the war.

Of course, Cerisa was another matter. He tugged at his collar, trying to breath. When the general was asleep, she'd tried to talk to him but he had left her alone. He had a decision to make, and he knew the answer but hadn't found the words. Now, after this incident, it didn't matter. He had to go. His chest tightened. *Damn, but he loved that woman so!*

Walking up to the building the Union had commandeered and turned into a hospital, he went to find her. He found her asleep on the settee in what was left of the front parlor. She was the only one there and it was so quiet, he was afraid to take a step for waking her. Sleep was something she needed badly. He'd noticed her frail movements, her gaunt face and the dark circles under her eyes, though she was still beautiful.

Beautiful and graceful, raised in a house of no wants. She ran from it and took him with her and that was the best day of his life, for he'd been in love with her for years, since they were children. But back at the Big House, he'd never gotten close to her again after they'd grown up together. He was sent to the fields, then pulled back to tend to the horses, a move he always thought she had begged for, because she loved to ride and no Southern belle ever rode unescorted.

He gave her a faint smile, deciding to just leave his letter instead. As much as he wanted a goodbye kiss, he wouldn't wake her for his own desires. Plus, he knew she'd try to stop him. He loved her too much to prevent that. So he slid the folded note under her hand and gave her forehead a light kiss.

"Good bye, my lovely Cera."

And he was gone.

"Cerisa!"

The sound of Pierce's yell woke her up in a flash, though she was sluggish in her movements. The instant jump to get up made her world turn and her stomach roll so she sat for a moment, inhaling deeply. It was then she heard the crinkle of paper under her hand and she picked up the folded note, labeled *Cerisa* on the outside. She cocked her head. That looked like Abraham's writing...

"Cerisa!"

She shook her head, re-focusing and shoved the note in her skirt. "Yes, darling, I'm on my way." By the time she made it up the stairs, to his room that overlooked the back of the estate, her mind was on Abraham when she made it to the doorway and came to an abrupt stop. Pierce was standing, the first time out of bed in two weeks. He even had his trousers on, a grin, pained but still there, on his face. She was speechless.

"So what do you think? Not bad, huh?" He had his hand on the back of the chair, steadying himself.

Still amazed, she stepped closer. "I am pleasantly surprised," she admitted. "You must be feeling better."

He nodded, gripping the back of the chair tightly. His legs didn't look sturdy, and he was a bit pale to be up so soon.

"Yes, finally. Though," he turned every so slowly. "I think I must take a seat." He sat in the chair, slightly out of breath.

She came straight over and placed her palm on his forehead. "Slightly warm. But nowhere near as bad." She looked down at him. "You do realize you had an infection in your blood from that bullet lodged so. Therefore, its amazing you're up."

"Damn war," he muttered.

"Not the thing for a general to say," she started. "But I'm glad to see you looking better. I almost lost my husband." *Lost her husband again*. No, she wouldn't add that.

He glanced away with an irritated expression on his face. She couldn't figure out why he'd be that way. After all, she just told him she'd been afraid of losing him.

"Well, if that was true, your other one will step right in," he growled.

She frowned. To her, his words dripped with anger. "I take it you mean Abraham." It was her turn to glare. "I fail to see why you are so upset by him. After all, you somehow managed not to tell me you found him and his men and took them under your wing."

Pierce stood, somewhat shakily but he stepped toward the open window. "I found them fighting rebels during the battle on the first day. What truly caught my attention, besides the fact that Black men were fighting rebels, was their tattered Union blues. Didn't know if they were Colored troops or contraband."

"Contraband?"

"Yes," he ran his hand through his hair with his eyes closed. "Project started by General Butler during his occupation of New Orleans. Confiscate the slaves as contraband and then dress them in army blues and use them for slave labor, basically."

The general's name hit a cord inside her. She'd heard of the 'Beast' Butler in New Orleans. She gritted her teeth. While she understood the war enough to want it to end, this conversation was making her despise Yankees. She wiped that thought from her mind, as she sat in a Union hospital, in a Union occupied city and talking to her Yankee husband.

"Why didn't you tell me Abraham was alive?"

Why hadn't he? The scene he swore he saw in the infirmary in Chattanooga came to mind, of her and the surgeon. Why would he tell her he'd found her first and true husband after seeing that? Basically, because he was in love with her and the thought of giving her up, even if he had to, rubbed him wrong. And he feared he was losing her as it was.

"What if I had? What would you have done? I could hear the scandal now. It would label us both with adultery. And you felt the anger in New York of people not liking mixed marriages, how do you think the Army would treat it? Your reputation would be destroyed."

"So you said nothing to protect my reputation?" she snarled. "By Society's standards, both North and South, my reputation has been destroyed for a while, so—"

He toyed with different responses though he was just sidetracking the marriage factor. "Cera, when did I have time to tell you? I slept on the battlefield with the rest of the men after the first day's battle. I was injured the second and not fully able to think till the last couple of days, and I was in a Confederate hospital." He ran his hand through his hair, frustrated. "So what did you want me to do? Send you a note? Honey, I found your first husband and he didn't die at Fort Wagner after all?"

She got up and began to pace. He wasn't sure he liked that. Perhaps he was wrong at snapping about her question, but he had answered truthfully—considering the circumstances, when could he tell her? There was a torn look on her beautiful face. A face that was way too thin and pale, more than he remembered. It was the haunted reflection in her eyes that made him want to ask her who she felt she was married to yet he couldn't form the words.

The tears formed in her eyes and he saw one escape down her cheek. *Damn!* "Cerisa—"

"No, you're right. It is a problem. He has told me I'd be better with you for the same reasons you're implying." She faced him, anger and sorrow clearly on her face. "What am I to do?"

She shouldn't be too surprised at his accusation. The army had informed her that Abraham was among the dead at Fort Wagner, thereby making her a widow. A Southern widow in a Northern city, jobless and homeless, in one of the worst places for her to be—the Five Points, where the Irish lived. These immigrants despised the South and the Blacks, freedman and slaves, who'd steal the few jobs the Irish were able to get. Only able to work as a lady of the night, she'd sunk low but her determination to survive drove her.

This man before her had rescued her, saved her from a life of ruin and promised her a chance to live again. Perhaps she'd pushed the marriage since he hadn't followed through and the men in camp made her leery. Of course, those Yankee women hadn't helped, making her feel like she was a leper in their midst.

In the long run, Abraham had been her friend since childhood, her protector in her mad-dash run from home, and how he'd refused to leave her when they made it North. But he knew the secret, so she was safe.

Pierce, though, was another matter. He was everything she would have wanted when it was time to look for a husband. He was a man who could take care of a woman and, from what she saw, he came from wealth and status. He said he loved her, a declaration that took her breath and even now, made her wonder if it was true because he said it after they'd made love, those words came right as she was almost asleep. Afterward, she didn't really see him nor had he asked if she returned the feelings. Did she love him? All the thoughts and emotions of the last two weeks whizzed by her head yet deep down, she knew the answer—she did.

And that was the problem. She loved them both.

"I can't tell you," he answered her question. "I do not want a wife who loves another man. So I won't make you stay." The pain of his words reflected clearly evident in his eyes.

She sniffled, her eyes blurred. Confusion mixed with the growing pressure and discomfort of being in the midst of Yankees. It did hit her that he was tiring, standing for so long. The need to make sure he didn't ruin his progress by over exertion forced her to move.

"Come," she started, wiping her cheeks with her handkerchief. She offered him her hand. "You need to lay down. I won't have you wear yourself out."

He frowned but his mouth thinned. Placing his hand in

hers, he pulled up using the chair arm as leverage. She knew his honor pushed him to be strong, to be the able man he'd been before this, so this was eating at him as it did her. On his feet, he looked at her. His eyes were dark and she was unsure how to interpret that therefore, she turned to take him to the bed when he pulled her back to him, slamming her against his chest and he bent down, locking his lips to hers. Her gasp got swallowed by him.

His kiss was hard and fierce. It was demanding, as if he was branding her as his. She could barely breath, but she returned his fervor ten times over. Wrapping her arms around his neck, she automatically pressed her body against his, discovering that even though he'd been bedridden since the fight, his chest still was hard, his stomach lean and taunt, not hollow with bedridden injury. Her skirts were a thin barrier to the bulge in his trousers. Amazed and pleased that after all this, he still wanted her, she instinctually inched closer until realization rang in her head that he'd been ill, dreadfully ill, and to ache for him was natural yet to act on it in his depleted state wasn't good. Fighting the drive within her, she leaned back, trying to gently unlock her lips.

As they separated, she saw he was panting as much as she was. He gave her a sly smile and she laughed. "You, sir, are too sly, sneaking in like that."

"I want you," he whispered longingly.

That made her heart sing, though they had to get through a few issues, one of which was Abraham. But for now, she'd let herself enjoy the moment. "Yes, I gathered that but I must insist you go back to bed—"

"That's exactly where we were headed."

"—to rest. I'll not have your progress halted by..." she searched for it. "Passion." She tucked him in. "Now, rest. I'll be back later." Then she kissed the top of his head.

But as she walked out of the room, she felt it coming and raced to the end of the hall, reaching for the edge of the potted plant just in time to retch.

Dr. McElroy peered at his patient over the rim of his spectacles. "Thought I told you to eat more and sleep proper, missy. Not spend every second of your day on that man. He needs his rest too. What I don't need is for his fever to flair back up and you," his gaze narrowed, "To over exert yourself. You are not in any condition for this."

Cerisa sat on the side of the bed, biting her lower lip. "Dr. McElroy, I was just as surprised as you were that he was *standing* on his own today. Do you not think that is a miracle on its own, considering how sick he was?"

The doctor hummed, tipping her head up then motioned for her to lay down. "Miracle? Yes. But he's not well enough yet for me to release him. One ride on a horse now could be his undoing. That wound is barely sealed right. From what Surgeon Peregoy wrote, that projectile ripped into him and buried itself deep. The failure of those rebels to remove it only made it worse."

She wanted to lash out in defense of the 'enemy', which were her people. Taking every ounce of energy she had, she tempered her rage and simply added, "The Union has blockaded the South, so they don't have supplies. He would have been covered better if they had more to use."

The doctor gave her a slight nod. "Miss, I know you are Southern and no doubt feel akin to those people but I'm only concerned about my patients, and I won't let any suffer any longer than needed because of the uniform they wear." He checked her pulse and waved his hand that she could rise.

"You're not bleeding, which is a good sign. I'm ordering you to go eat and then get some rest."

Slowly she stood, flattening her skirts. With a nod, she headed to the door, all intent on heading back upstairs to Pierce.

"Missy, did you hear me? Food and rest first."

Thwarted, she stopped but didn't turn around. "Yes, sir." She spun and headed towards the kitchens.

"And Mrs. Duval, do tell him soon."

CHAPTER THIRTY-FOUR

"Surrender, boys, we've got you."
—From report of Pvt. James M. Weiser, 54th Virginia
Infantry, 20th September, Chickamauga

CERISA DID HER BEST to follow the doctor's orders and grabbed a bowl of stew from the hospital cook, whose pot for the staff always seemed full. He smiled handing her a bowl, stating he had to keep the staff full, because after a while, fever soups and other bland foods on the patients' diets would drive him to drink, though she suspected the man no doubt had a bottle nearby for his use. The stew was delicious and she devoured it all, along with a piece of real bread. It'd been ages since she'd had that and it went so much better than that hard crackers she'd chewed on during the battle itself, when the cooks packed instead of created.

Finished, and still desiring more, she found herself too tired to ask for it. Instead, she grabbed another piece of the bread and went to find a bed before she curled up in the corner. She fell into a deep sleep only to be rudely awakened by a train horn filtering through the open window. A bit of remorse swept over her because, for once, in her dreams, she was home, long before all this current unpleasantness, when life was good or so she thought. Home with her family and Abraham nearby, though as a slave. She blinked, trying to get past that memory. To her recollection, she never thought the Fontaine slaves were abused—until that night, when all blissful ideas went flying out the door. The train whistle brought the current world slamming back into place and she groaned. It'd been two years of war. And longer than four since she'd been home. A single question loomed in her head, wondering how her family was, but it was one triggered by the past that also put a stop to those thoughts.

Inhaling deeply, she got up, straightened her dress and ran her palms over her hair in an attempt to tame any loose ends. The nap, regardless of how long or short it'd been, had refreshed her energy and had her feeling more like herself. Now, she pinned her apron into place and took off toward the nurses' room for supplies.

At the back of her mind, McElroy's suggestion echoed through her thoughts. *Mrs. Duval, do tell him soon.* News of a child should bring joy, she thought, but their marriage was based on necessity and fraught with issues like unintended bigotry and distrust. She glanced at the mirror in the room, shoved to the side for space. Her stomach showed no signs and as long as it did, she'd keep her condition to herself. No point to discuss this until everything settled.

Deep in thought, as she walked down the hallway to the back parlor of the house used for this part of the hospital, she turned the corner and walked straight into another man.

"I'm so sorry," she said, stepping back, her hand at her middle as she gulped for air, startled.

The older man gave her a slight bow. "Pardon me, my lady. I did not look where I was going."

She smiled at his politeness. "Apologies. I'm not accustomed to running into anyone back here."

"Good to see someone, for I think I am lost." He laughed

as he pulled himself up straight. "Let me introduce myself. I'm Senator Duval, Colonel Duval's father."

Her heart skipped a beat.

Abby Gaines had heard how the wounded ended up in Nashville and a certain bird let her know that darling Pierce Duval was among them. They'd also informed her how he had a serious injury and wasn't sure if he'd make it, which made her heart sink. It was one thing about this war that so infuriated her, that it'd take life indiscriminately. To her, all the Southerners who caused this needed to pay for it, but not at the life of her Thomas, of course, or such charming, handsome ones like Duval. So, since her husband was still 'at the war', she'd go and visit the hospital, to cheer the wounded. And if she ran into the handsome Duval, even better. Putting her bonnet on and adjusting the flower on it so it was adorable, making her more so, she grabbed her gloves and parasol.

The mansion the army had confiscated for recovery wards for officers like General Duval sat on a hill, next to the main facility. She stared at its beauty and thought, while a shame to ruin such a home with disease and blood and whatnot, it was fitting that it was Union blood that inhabited it. She breezed into the doorway and quickly found a nurse, a *proper* nurse, not a rebel whore acting righteous, and found out where Duval was. Gathering her skirts, she went up the stairs to his floor. Eyeing no one in the hallway, she looked at the looking glass at the end, which she considered an odd place to put one but pleased it was there so she could review her looks, pinched her cheeks for a touch of color and then, smiled. His doorway was the third to the left. Her smile became genuine and she knocked.

Pierce was beyond tired of being bedbound. Roughly two weeks in one made a man grouchy and he was that. But his side still smarted fiercely at times and that slowed his step, so he calculated in his own diagnosis that he'd allow them two more days of keeping him here then he was going back to the war.

Yet his conversation with Cerisa bothered him. Frankly, he'd hoped, as ridiculous as that sounded, that she'd never discover her first husband was at Chickamauga. And he wanted to hate the man, after all, he had deserted her and left her in dire straits, but after what he saw on the battlefield, he couldn't. The man was a fighter, more so than some of the other men he'd commanded. But with him back, that put all three of them in a particular situation.

She'd left in a hurry. His behavior probably the cause. Though she seemed to enjoy the kiss, perhaps as moved as he was, but he had no way to know as she skedaddled out fast. In fact, she left so quickly that it wasn't until he couldn't rest any more that he saw the folded note to her on the floor. He let his curiosity take the better of him and he picked it up, enraged that that doctor or some other man, was chasing her and now she was receiving love letters, when she was a married woman!

Angered by the whole idea, he tore the note open.

Dear Cerisa,

You know I love you but as I said, you are better off with him. I am sorry for all the pain and suffering you had to go through for being tied to a freedman. I have seen the looks from others and how they think of you less than a lady and I know I am the cause. We have had our share of hard luck, with you having to work since no one would hire a black man, how the father did not want to marry us, how the army refused me putting you as wife and the hardship that put on you. I am sorry that because I am a black, you lost all you had at home. It came to my attention that because I was not kilt at Fort Wagner, you did not get a pension, even they, at first, had me on the dead list and I heard what you had to do to live.

When I saw you again, I praised the Lord for our reunion but you had moved on and married the general. It was a good decision. Stay with him and let him do what I caint. I know you be as stubborn as a mule when needs not to be, but I know you won't if I stay so I am returning to the war. I got me some fight left and need to use it, for all my brothers still chained. Not sure if that father ever registered our vows but you need to get that gone and stay with the general. He can protect you and give you anything you need. Just remember I do love you and will see you in heaven.

Yours forever,

A

Pierce closed his eyes. The man knew her well. Even Pierce knew she'd fight like hell over this. No doubt, she'd blame him. He released a heavy sigh, pulling the letter he'd received today that he'd failed to open. Yanking the flap open, he read it. It was from his friend in New York, Edward Brooks, who was a lawyer. His response was what he feared. Brooks told him the marriage was indeed registered, though to a Cerisa Fontaine, not Cerisa Walker, and to Abe Walker. While the page was there, it was never fully registered, so it could easily go missing...He ran his fingers through his hair. He could tell Edward to make it so, but that'd make her sullied by the man who so cared for her. *Damn it all to hell!*

"Knock, knock."

He looked up and found Abby Gaines at his doorway.

Inwardly, he groaned. She was the last person he wanted to see.

"How is my favorite general doing? When I heard how grievously you were injured and that you were here, I just had to pop over," she said, walking straight into the room without him saying a word.

He closed up Edward's letter and put his hand over both, sliding them under the covers. "How nice of you to stop in," he replied, pulling himself into a more covered, seated position. "So nice of you to come see us Union men," he stated, implying her presence shouldn't be for just him.

That caught her off guard as her step hesitated a second. "But of course I'm here to see everyone and wish them a speedy recovery." Her smile never waivered. "Has Mrs. Duval arrived also? Or was she able to find a way home?"

Her question made him think that when she referred to Cerisa and her 'home', she meant did she return south. The hair on the back of his neck bristled. "No, my darling wife is here, with me."

Abby walked to the window, after she raised a brow with his reply. He never doubted for a second she hoped he was alone. So now, she stared out the window.

"Pity such a fine house is filled with wounded." She turned to him. "Not that it wasn't needed, of course, and it was a Southern home so appropriate to have Union blood and whatever else here. Though for the officers, only." She nodded, trying to put on that naïve grin. He was beginning to think she had never been innocent.

"You here with the major, madam?"

"Oh, heavens, no," she said with a whimsical note to her words. "He's still with General Cook, though rumors abound that General Rosey has been sent west."

He frowned. Nothing like a scapegoat to blame the loss on. But her answer still seemed too happy. "Yes, well, if you'll excuse me. I'm having dinner with my wife."

The quick look of disappointment fluttered across her eyes before she smiled, trying to look her sunniest. "Of course, of course, though I did come to let you know what has happened."

The hairs now pulled at his skin. "Whatever do you mean?"

"I just thought you'd might like to know how your new wife has taken quite a fancy to Doctor Peregoy and he to her while you were fighting. They were overly close, in fact," she took a step closer. "After the first night of battle, they were seen having coffee but then, they never parted."

He frowned, anger rising, along with a twinge in his neck. "Whatever do you mean? Please explain."

"Well, according to several accounts, she stayed the night with him," she stated nonchalantly, like she was talking about the wallpaper.

Suddenly, visions of the two popped up in his mind. He remembered, but thought it was delusional of the surgeon hugging his wife. At the time, there was a moment he thought they'd kissed. Inside, his heart exploded with anger and sadness. Peregoy he understood. The man was a scoundrel in the worst way with women. The fact he thought he could steal Pierce's wife, though, could mean pistols. But with Pierce down, would she sleep with him? He shook his head to clear the image and when he looked at her again, he saw Abby looking at him, a twinkle in her eyes and slant to her chin. His own gaze narrowed.

"Mrs. Gaines, just what are you doing?"

She raised her brows in surprise. "I believe you should know how you have attached yourself to a white trash

Southern slattern who only married you to save her hide and have access to the riches your family possesses." She sat down daintily, her gloved hands crossed with a look on her face like she had taken his queen in chess.

It hit him in the chest like a cannonball. Peregoy wasn't the only vermin. "Mrs. Gaines, I do believe your visit here has ended."

"Oh, you wouldn't want me to leave when we have all this time to ourselves," she started, taking her gloves off.

He did a double blink. "My wife is here!"

She gave him a knowing look. "You deserve so much better, my darling Pierce…"

His brows furrowed and he scurried to get out of the bed before she got any closer. The shocked look of disappointment flashed across her face. Obviously, she hoped he was in his drawers or nothing, but he'd collapsed in his pants. The quick jump off the bed tugged at his wound, like a sharp knife in his side, so he forced the pain to go away so he could step further away.

The door opened wide again. "General Duval…"

His aide, Corporal Prasse stood, trying hard to conceal the scene he walked in on. At least, Pierce thought, he was out of her reach, because he knew she'd want to be seen in his arms, which was insane to his line of thinking.

"Yes, Corporal, do come in." He looked at Abby. "There is a war. If you please," and he motioned to the door.

Grabbing her gloves and shawl, she stormed out of the room.

Cerisa's mouth went dry. Pierce's father, the abolitionist senator, the one she'd read about in the papers when she went looking for news about Abraham after he enlisted.

She vaguely recalled Pierce not mentioning much about his family, but then again, she hadn't discussed hers either.

The senator was a tall man, she guessed Pierce's height. He wore a suit, the frock coat finely tailored, the shirt snowy white and the necktie shined like good silk. Dark hair, brown eyes, his nose raised so he looked down on her, as if she was no better than the help. Granted, she wore one of her dark worn wool dresses with a corded petticoat with a white pinner apron that was far from pure white due to use. Frankly, she looked no better than house slaves did.

"I'm sorry, Senator, it's been a while since I've seen company and my manners have fled the room. Mrs. Duval, so nice to meet you," she curtsied, wondering if he caught the pause as she told him who she was. Perhaps, she should have reserved that.

Duval gave her a look then he smiled. "I had heard he had married but I failed to believe his new wife was so attractive. Good afternoon, madam," he bowed.

He still made her nervous.

"I understand Pierce is here, recovering from a battle injury?"

She nodded. "Yes, sir. He took a terrible wound during battle, leading a charge. He is in room three." His eyes seemed to burn holes into hers, as if he was drilling for knowledge yet he wasn't asking much.

He nodded. "You know, Pierce is my heir as my last remaining son. He has a bit of a wild streak. Married first to an Irish lass, no older than you I'd reckon. Woman was the worse type for an up and rising young man headed for the capital."

Now, she could see why Pierce ran to the front. The senator was domineering in speech and actions, particularly if he came to Tennessee to see his heir. He made her uncomfortable and her stomach threatened to lurch sideways. *Oh, no! not here!* She gritted her teeth to keep from retching.

"Sir, if you'll please excuse me. I do need to go," she started but he stopped her.

"That voice sounds particularly Secesh to me," he claimed, though still with a slight grin to his lips. "Sounds like we have a traitor in camp."

"I beg your pardon?" she was shocked. Who was this man?

Any jovial look vanished from his face as he stepped toward her, making her feel like he was locking her into a corner.

"My dear," he started. "Pierce married wrong the first time and I'll be damned if I let that happen again. He is engaged, to a fine young woman, of proper standing and of a good family. She's waiting for him right now, in New York City." He paused, watching her. Inside, her heart fell and she couldn't breathe. He gave a tight grin, as if he knew he'd broken her.

"You see, I know about you," his tone now menacing. "Some Southern piece of trash, married to a nigra, just like those Irish whores. When he gets the notion to leave ya, he does and you, fired from a factory, showing you can't even do the simplest jobs, ends up doing the only thing a woman like you can—lying on your backside, thighs wide open. Oh, don't be lookin' so shocked. I saw you there at Madame Nikki's and when I decided I'd love a little Southern belle, you're gone, 'saved' by an officer. Little did I know it was Pierce."

Her stomach fluttered as anger and fear whirled inside her. She wanted to scream, slap him across the face and run. He was painting a scene that'd make her world fall apart.

"I also know your nigger-husband is back, so any marriage

to Pierce is now null and void, so outside of a few court filings, he can now marry his fiancée."

Tears welled in her eyes. It was like having her life read to her but in the worst way possible. "You don't understand," she managed to spit out. Her stomach rolled and the bile inched up her throat.

"Oh, that's where you are wrong. I do. You convinced him to marry you so you'd have the money you've always wanted, plus a little fun on the side while he will aspire to help lead this nation!"

She was going to be sick or cry or scream while fury raced through her veins. But she was a lady, she had to remind herself as her call to action would eliminate that, and ladies do not lower themselves to the level of the malcontents, even if they were rich, well-connected politicians. Unable to stop the tears of anger and fear, she did the only thing she could think of. She ran

CHAPTER THIRTY-FIVE

"I am sick, tired and disgusted. There is an immobility here that exceeds all that any man can conceive of. It requires the lever of Archimedes to move this inert mass."
—General Henry Halleck

THAT EVENING, PIERCE DRESSED, determined to look fit for his wife's visit. He refused to believe everything Abby Gaines claimed. It had been hinted to him over the last weeks of how the woman was always prying into things that weren't hers to start. He knew of her advance on him, at first mildly appreciated but when she caused Cerisa problems, he wasn't happy. But part of what she said didn't go away and that was the implication with Peregoy. What was he to do about that? It angered him, so much his main thought was to beat the man but he was also angry and hurt by her. Had she done that? It was that question that drove him to get up, fully change and wait.

The dark shadows of fall's early twilight started to darken the skies. The fire in the fireplace roared and the roast and side dishes he had Prasse get made for him had the room smell ten times better than any gruel they'd had him on for a long time.

There was a slight scratch at the door and it nudged open. Cerisa. His heart skipped over the thoughts of her possible indiscretion as he admired her now. Still dressed in the nurses' clothes, she was a beauty. She gave him a slight grin and came in.

"My, aren't you quite dapper."

As her gaze looked him over, he tightened.

"You must be feeling better."

"Yes, I do. Please," he motioned her to a seat. He noticed her slightly puffed eyes and her pale color. He frowned. He must have upset her over the freedman more than he thought. "I had Corporal Prasse rustle us a better fare than what's served here."

She laughed. "Tired of burnt toast and gruel? But they are the best for the ailing."

He snorted. "Think I'm past that." He handed her a glass of wine and enjoyed her surprise. "A little too much for a nurse?"

"I'd like to give up my nursing position if you please." She took a sip.

"But you're good at it. I have no complaints on your skills or manners."

She smiled. "Charming to hear, since you had no choice in the matter. You weren't aware enough to care if you'll remember."

"Well, I'd recall if it was a soldier stuck doing bed pans over a lovely lady—"

"That Union nursing lead, Miss Dix, doesn't want a 'lovely lady' but a working woman with nothing attractive about her, to keep you men from getting too excited, thus moving in a way that opens wounds and so forth," she countered.

He took a bite. The taste of real food was heavenly.

"Tastes wonderful," she sighed.

He swallowed another before he couldn't stop himself, because it was eating at his heart. "I'm sure Surgeon Peregoy enjoyed your work."

Her brows raised but she nodded.

"Did he want you to stay? After all, good workers with your skills can be hard to find."

She swallowed hard. "Yes, in fact, he begged me to stay but I couldn't. He understood, or so he said." She snorted. "Even that Dix nurse appreciated my help in the end."

"Begged you?" His blood started to boil. "You know, when you're in a hospital, all sorts of things come to life when you have the time. In fact, I have a vague memory, that a visitor assured me was true, of you two hugging and a kiss."

Her eyes widened as she dropped her piece of bread. It appeared her skin paled further and he suddenly wanted to take the words back, though his main thoughts refused.

"How could you?" He whispered in response to silence.

He could see the puddle of tears in her eyes and the sob in her throat. She shook her head and got up from the table.

"Cerisa," he called, trying to rise as in her hurry to get up, she knocked over her chair. She appeared not to notice.

"No," she said through a sob. "No." And she spun, slipping through the door.

His mind was a jumble as he heard her heels running down the hall from his room. He was sure of what he saw, only adding to Abby's accusation, though that woman's entire visit was to drive him and Cera apart. Well, that fear of his was bolstered by Abby and now, when confronted with it, his wife ran. Intense pain hit him and hard, right in his heart. His blood began to race and all he could think was she had betrayed him.

Leaning against the doorframe, he slid to the floor, his side burning, feeling as if she'd knifed him but knew that wasn't it. He pushed the pain aside, his whole being shaking. He

couldn't think except how, that despite her denial, she ran.
His own tears fell.

Cerisa ran to the top floor of the house. It held a ballroom,
so typical of the houses of this size and grandeur, she knew it
had to be here. Oddly, she thought how the surgeons would
have appreciated the room to work or house patients, but
this high up and with little window space to help 'air out' the
ward, it wasn't used. Here, she could be alone and she fell to
the floor like a crumpled rag doll and let the tears flow.

Pierce was engaged? Why hadn't he said so? It was possible
his father fibbed on that, as part of his method to drive her
away. But then, why would he tell her? Their marriage was to
be in name only, just a ruse to get past anyone who questioned
his escorting her, since a single man housing with a widow
in polite society was frowned on. Of course, her widowhood
had proven untrue and somehow, she was the last to know
her husband was alive. Why hadn't he told her? Come to her?
She heard him when he stated she'd be better off with Pierce
and perhaps, at the moment he said it, it was true, if she were
the type to worry about all the rules polite society followed
yet the moment she ran away with him ruined her when it
wasn't sanctioned by the family.

She sobbed. She was in occupied Tennessee, with the
wrong side, as it was so often painfully implied to her by
Abby Gaines, the men in camp and, she guessed, Abraham.
She was a whore, married to the wrong color, an adulterer,
practicing bigotry and accused of being white trash. And, to
top it off, she carried a child who, if the senator got his way,
would never know its father. As to Pierce's behavior, she'd
gone to have dinner with him and planned to find out if
what his father said was true so she had pasted a smile on,

put on her best front and found her courage to find the truth when he accused her, very wrongly, of sleeping with the surgeon back at the battlefield. With a big gulp, she realized Peregoy's advance on her must have been seen but by who? Outside the patients there, who she had not seen here in Nashville, especially not at this hospital, besides, most of them who had witnessed a scene that never went further than a slight embrace started by the doctor himself, were asleep from their injuries.

It didn't take long in sobbing for her to feel totally alone and abandoned here. Even Abraham seemed to have left to return to the war, since no one knew where he was, thus leaving her with 'the general.' She shuddered. Her emotions were too strung up. The courage she had that got her out of Louisiana and up to New York and had helped her to survive the hard times vanished. Here, she had nothing apparently, except she was in the family way and a strong urge to protect that unborn child blossomed inside her. Drumming her strength, she inhaled the last sob, found a somewhat dry corner of her handkerchief to dab at her eyes and pulled herself up. Flattening her skirts and straightening her shoulders, she felt a slight nudge at her corset. The babe letting her know he was there, though she still had no bulge nor was she far enough to feel too thick in the waist yet. She bit her bottom lip, realizing she had to leave and go the only place she could find safety, even if it cost her her dignity.

She had to go home. *Heaven help her.*

It was a long night. Not that he hadn't slept alone for a while but it'd never been the result from him sending his wife running away. He slammed the pillow again. *What the hell happened?* He twisted again which was a mistake. The pain in his side flared and he buckled up in response until the flash passed. Slowly he undid himself and just didn't move.

So she claimed she was innocent. And his source had been an overly flirtatious married woman who talked of a man whose morals were loose as well. Even in the dark, on his back, he put his hand to his forehead and grimaced. Of course, biting back when she accused him of not telling her Abraham was alive was also wrong for him to do. The man had been her husband before him. Besides, wasn't this marriage a lie to begin with, between her and him? He wanted to protect her, to save her from men doing evil things to her and yet, had he done the opposite? Women attacked her, men molested her and he kept the man she had married at a distance. So he expected her to jump into his arms and kiss him? *Damn, he was such an ass!*

He rolled out of bed and gingerly stepped to the washbasin, letting his body get used to being up. It'd been a long time since he'd managed much on his own and it was time to return to that. Splashing his face with the tepid water was similar to Cerisa slapping him. He chuckled at that memory from before their marriage and decided to tell her that when he saw her later today.

Dawn was starting to stream into the room. It was going to be a sunny day. A day he would use to its perfection to make Cerisa realize how much he did love her. With that decision made, his mood lightened and he bent, slowly pulling up his pants when there was a knock at the door. He gave a half smile, pleased she was here so early and answered, "Come in."

But it wasn't Cerisa, but another nurse. He tilted his head. "Where is Mrs. Duval?"

The very prim woman, dressed in a dull navy dress, white pinner apron, her hair pulled back and neat and wearing no adornments startled and stopped in her tracks, the items in her metal bowl rattling. "General, I do not know."

"Who are you?" The question came out as a sneer, but he couldn't help it. A hollow feeling ate at his insides as each moment passed.

"I'm Nurse Henderson, sir."

Ah, the Dix nurse Cerisa had moaned about. He shook his head. "I'd like to know where she is."

Henderson put her goods down and approached him calmly. "General, I do not know where she is. I was asked to take a look at your wound."

Pierce growled, wanting nothing to do with this woman or to have his injury inspected. He opened his mouth to protest when another knock came and his staff corporal poked his head in.

"General, you have a visitor," Prasse announced.

Pierce's gaze narrowed. His irritation, though, hadn't deterred the nurse. She was at his side, totally ignoring his expression, captivated by his self-bandage techniques or lack thereof, and the wound beneath. She striped him of the binding and looked at the gash.

"How is the pain?"

"Tolerable," he snapped. He just wanted her gone! When she touched the skin, he jumped back. "That'll be enough."

"Sir, Doctor McElroy said—"

"Madam, I don't care if the US President said it, that's enough. The pain is tolerable and it's not bleeding." Or so he hoped.

Henderson rolled back on her heels, a stern expression set on her face. One thing was for sure. She wasn't pretty enough to make a man jump, though a wounded soldier in the battlefield would take anything.

"You skin is warm, the bulge slightly temperature related and its not bleeding but weeping poison some, which would be considered good, but I recommend bedrest—"

"Go tell your doctor," he started, taking her hands away from his skin. "I am breathing and walking. And that I intend to be leaving. Now," he turned her toward the door. "You may leave."

Stunned, she started to talk but he shooed her away and spun toward his aid. "Mrs. Duval has taken herself someplace to rest. I need help finding her."

CHAPTER THIRTY-SIX

"...a bullet hit me on the left shoulder and knocked me down as quick as if I had been hit with a sledge hammer..."
—Sgt. James Sullivan, 6th Wisconsin Infantry, July 1, 1863, Gettysburg

NOW, HE HAD A plan. Leaving here was the first agenda. As he fought with his shirt and arranging it so it hopefully would not touch his side, he didn't notice the door swing open and close until he heard the latch grasp. When he glanced at the intruder and recognized it was his father, he virtually foamed at the lip. That man was the last person he wanted to see.

"Brevet General," Senator Duval announced. "What a noble honor. Congratulations." He tipped his hat before he put it down on the bedside.

"Hello, Father," he stated, a bit of irony to the title. "Did you have anything to do with this?"

"Well, it is an award given to those whose loyalty is true and who's courage on the field ordain him award-worthy." The man grinned. "Word is you were placed in charge of a contingent of Colored troops. I'm so proud of you."

Pierce continued to dress, his movements slowed. Colored troops. Of course. He'd done the one thing he'd sworn he wouldn't do and that was command Colored troops. It was never that he was opposed to having Colored men in arms.

He just wasn't in the mood to command them. While his adopted unit in this battle was foisted on him, he did find these men were valuable on the battlefield. But it didn't change his plans now. "Yes, well, thank you is in order." He winced as he tucked the shirttails in his trousers, but he bit back the groan that wanted to escape.

"You seem in a hurry, son."

Son. Not much of a loving title from this man, he mused. "I do have duties to perform."

He caught the man's gaze flicker and a quick burying of his feelings for being accused of barging into his room.

"Are you sure you're up for this?" The man looked genuinely concerned for once, but that didn't make him leave, either.

Is he up for this? What the hell! He spun toward the man as he buttoned the shirt.

"Father, I find it interesting how you appear at my door, in the middle of an occupied Southern city, away from your safety of the Senate. No doubt you have heard of my wife and raced here to confront me over her."

Senator Timothy Duval pulled himself upright, his friendly expression gone to that of a reprimanding father. "I am a representative of the people of New York and they want to know how their men fare in this conflict. When I arrive, I discover my living son and heir has been gravely wounded. Of course, I would endeavor to find out more and see you. Low and behold, I also hear that you've taken another to wife, forsaking dear Charlotte for another questionable mate."

"Questionable?" he hurled back, his fury mounting. "Let me get this across as clearly as I can. Charlotte was *your* choice for me, a man still in mourning for his deceased wife. I told you then and again now, I would not marry a set marriage arranged by you and your bid for the next election."

"That is not the tone to use with me," Duval argued. "Charlotte was who you should've married in the first place. She is of good breeding from a respectable family."

"Good breeding? You make her sound like she is a mare!"

"That is better than tying yourself to some Southern trash, one who would spread her thighs for the bucks who threaten to invade our city!"

Did he just hear him correctly? He laughed. "You fight for the Blacks to be free of their chains but not the freedom to live where they want? And you present yourself as protector of our rights to liberty?"

"Yes. And they need to be free! It is sin to enslave them!"

Pierce's vision turned red. "You will take that insult on your daughter-in-law back. I love her. And that is all that matters to me on my marriage!"

"I will have the priest dissolve your marriage. After all, she is married to a field hand who lives."

"Father, you do not have the right to interfere in my life! I am an officer in the US Army…"

"Yes, a general. Brevet, no less. And who do you think pushed for that advance? Certainly wasn't you, as it was yours if you lead a regiment of Colored troops."

Pierce snorted. "You'd have me lead a team of Colored, even see to my promotion, just to push your office? Dear Lord…"

"Someone must defend this family, and it appears, that is only me!" His father snarled.

Defend? Where was he when the bullets raged and cannons roared? In some damn office, pushing a pen and making connections. Pierce became enraged. It was the pen pushers who made this carnage breathe fire and he'd be damned if he'd continue that legacy.

"Get the hell away from me." His voice was level, low and very dangerous even to his own ears.

Timothy Duval's dark brown eyes met his son's, each set spitting fire in their stance. The senator's jaw tightened as he grabbed his hat and gloves. "We will speak on this further when you have recovered your senses." He spun on his heel and stormed from the room, the heavy click of his shoe heels fading as he left.

Pierce was left, his breathing hard and fast from the anger that soared through his blood. His father was a powerful man and most of his life, Pierce had tried to avoid him for fear of being controlled by him. Now was not the time to hide but to finally stand on his own and sever the ties. The moment he heard the door to the building slam, he roared, "Prasse!"

The corporal slipped into the room so quickly, it made Pierce wonder if he'd just been in the hallway, listening to the exchange. Didn't matter. He had another issue that demanded more.

"Corporal, where the hell is my wife?"

Cerisa was amazed on how easy it was for her to leave. After the debacle with Pierce's father, and the moment she allowed herself to let the anger and pain roll through her, she straightened her shoulders and back, packed her belongings into her satchel and counted her money one more time before she walked out the door. She had fifty US dollars, money she'd made at the factory and her 'sin' money, but at this point, it was her ticket home, because the one leverage she had was U.S. money, which many in the Confederate lines would grab over the valueless Southern cash, a currency backed by nothing other than a promise. US currency was backed by gold and that Southerners understood.

In addition, she grabbed a hard cracker from the cook's pantry on her way out because pregnancy didn't care what was going on in the world, she now found herself constantly hungry and nauseous. That hard cracker, made mostly of flour with just enough water to hold it together, had no flavor nor anything else redeeming other than filling a hungry body up and strangely calming her stomach.

She left the hospital on a wagon heading down the hilltop toward town. It was early in Nashville, not much moving outside the troops that occupied it and their operations. There appeared to be some civilians, though if they were those with the troops or city inhabitants, she wasn't sure. With a thanks to the wagon driver, she stood not far from the army's stables, trying to form her next move. Clutching her satchel handles tight, she realized she hadn't thought this through, just like those years ago when she ran from home. But then, she knew of her parents' summer home in New York and had headed that way. She also had Abraham with her and his presence gave her strength but this time, she was alone.

"Whoa!" A horse suddenly whinnied as the driver yelled, followed by a stomping noise of hooves on hard dirt, leather slapping and metal grinding. She looked up and found a horse and wagon trying to halt before they ran over her and she jumped back, her heart in her throat as her blood raced madly. She dropped her bag in the street and watched as the equine stomped, trying to bypass it as if it had claws and fangs. Horrified, she clamped her hand over her mouth, knowing better than to jump out and try to retrieve it but also feared if the animal trampled it, what little she had would be destroyed.

The driver maneuvered the reins and moved the horse

over to the other side of the road, a cloud of dust off the dirt road flying. Cerisa found she could barely breath and had to wave the air before her with her tattered fan in an attempt to clear it as the driver jumped from the wagon and raced over to her, picking up her bag as he came.

"I be so sorry missy," he sputtered, the dust choking him as well. "Ole Sparty, well, he's used to seeing pretty ladies, though not so close in front of him. Think boy ain't awake and you scared him." He yanked his dirty tan hat off his head and gave her a nod. "You be all right?"

On top of fighting for breath, she stood stunned to see a young man before her, being ever so polite and worried about her that she didn't know what to say. Perhaps it'd been too long since good manners were practiced or she'd been in the low areas of New York too long, where manners didn't seem to exist. But here this one stood, his tattered clothes that of a poor farmer or worker of some type, and she realized she'd left him with no response.

She blinked and put a smile on. "I'm fine. And thank you for having such excellent skills. I feared I was about to be run into the ground, like a pebble."

He laughed. "Pebble? I'm thinking more like a diamond, my lady."

Since that the accident didn't happen, she darted a look around. Last thing she needed right now was to be noticed. She figured Pierce would wonder where she was but he probably wasn't awake till now, so she had a few more minutes.

"Somethin' wrong, missy? You still lookin' bit frighten. Sparty be all calm right."

She turned back to the driver and her thoughts pooled. He was a farmer, she reckoned, but being here in Tennessee, perhaps… "Who are you?"

He chuckled. "Guess I ain't got this manner thing down right yet. My name is Horace Williams, ma'am. Just drove up from Corinth, couple days ago. 's'cuse me for my appearance. I ain't dressed to be meetin' a lady."

She slanted her head and gave him a tight smile, pushing further. "You're from Mississippi, Mr. Williams?"

"Yes ma'am, right about Rienzi, just southeast of Corinth."

Her mind had all sorts of ideas. A poor farmer during a war with probably both sides taking goods and paying for them with hollow promises, if what she read in the papers held any truth. Even if not, he still might be tempted. With a smile, she offered her gloved hand to him in greeting.

"Nice to meet you. I'm Miss Cerisa Fontaine from Louisiana."

The man took her hand lightly and she could tell he knew better than to soil it with his dirty hand and chapped lips, though he went through the motions, like any Southern gentleman would. He eyed her speculatively. "Secretary Pierre Fontaine's kin?"

She blinked, but kept her lips curved upwards. Shouldn't surprise her that her father found his way into the Confederate governmental cabinet. "Why yes sir, that is my papa."

"Oh, please excuse my ill-mannered pony and me. We had no idea we were goin' meet royalty," he sputtered. "But missy, you be lookin' like you're lost."

Perfect. "Why, yes, Horace, you have no idea. By any chance, could I convince you to help a Southern belle in need?"

He attempted a bow. "I be at your service, Miss Fontaine."

"I'm so grateful! I'm in need of transportation." She lowered her voice. "A way back home to Louisiana. And I'd be more than happy to pay you for the inconvenience and silence on this matter."

His gaze narrowed as he thought. "I can keep a secret but, I donna be wantin' any reb dollars. Gotta 'scuse me, but it ain't worth goin' through all this for paper that caint buy nothin'. I mean, you be a lady and all, but I've been selling to the army and makin' cash, US cash by the way, so why would I give up a couple days work for ya?"

She wanted to laugh. "I'd pay you a silver dollar, US made." That'd take a good portion but not all. She pulled the coin out for him to see. He took it and bit the edge. Many of the cheap Yankees she'd seen in recent weeks coming to the South, offered cash for services but many were hollow wooden coins painted to look real, so his bite only made her think he was considering it. It was a gamble on her part but the quicker she got out, the better.

"Ha!" He spat to the dirt road. "Ain't holler!" He smiled. "Where we be headin?"

Pierce worry about Cerisa increased ten-fold every second. He'd bet his father and Abby Gaines had a part in this since they both appeared out of the blue and both made accusations about his wife. The whole conclusion that they drove her away angered him, especially since they tried to convince him she'd betrayed him, and that growing animosity ate at his core. They'd pay if anything happened to her!

He grabbed his hat and shoved it on, adjusted his frock coat, moving the fabric seam on the side slightly off his injury, and picked up his gloves. He'd told Prasse to report to him at the stables within an hour and last he checked, that time was quickly approaching. He stormed out of his room and headed to the stairs, finding he had to take his time on his right step since it tugged at his side but he did make it without falling. Pleased, he headed to the door when he heard his name.

"General Duval, what a pleasure to see you up! Do come here and let us take a look at you." Dr. McElroy called from the hallway and next to him was a man who set Pierce's blood to boil. Peregoy.

Slowly, he walked over, knowing full well he could just head out the door but then, he wasn't cleared so it wouldn't look good. In this war, in the game of politics on the warfront, he couldn't let that happen, not if he was to keep his status and hence, his own orders to himself to go find his lady. He carefully managed his steps, striving to look natural yet keeping from any hitch if he could help it.

"You seem in a hurry today, sir," McElroy stated, as they walked into the makeshift office.

"I do have a job to do," he answered but offered nothing more. Every second he waited, the further the distance could be if she had bolted or was taken, so he tried to remain quiet, hoping this went quickly.

Peregoy added, "Good morning, General. Brought the last of wounded here, barely able to get out of Chattanooga in time. You look much better, having been under McElroy's care."

The other surgeon snorted. "Thankfully, you got that bullet out. Fever finally left yesterday, right, General?"

He didn't give a damn but nodded. He peered at Peregoy. "Chattanooga attacked?"

"No, sir. From what I gather, it is under siege."

Siege? Considering Bragg's win at Chickamauga and if Rosecrans didn't plan right, if Bragg pushed further, his men could surround the town from on high and cut if off, meaning to starve them out. Which would result in Peregoy with the heavily wounded here instead.

Another thought etched into the corners of his mind, while the two doctors talked about his condition. What if she had run to Peregoy? His blood pounded through his veins, making enough noise he could barely hear them talk.

"General Duval, being up and about is marvelous, but way too early to return to the war. If your condition remains the same, I'd set your release in three, maybe four days," McElroy decided.

No!

"Sir." They all turned to see Prasse at the doorway. Pierce gave a brief shake of his head, thinking the corporal had come to him since he was waylaid but he held a note in his hand, addressed to Pierce.

Opening the letter, he frowned, frustration now added to his anger. "Gentlemen, it appears the Union Army is overriding your decision." He folded it up and shoved it into his jacket, fighting the intense agony this order sent. "I have to return to command and try to find a way to end that siege you," he nodded to Peregoy, "speak of. And if I could get a moment of your time, sir, I'd be most grateful."

Peregoy answered, "Of course, General."

Motioning him aside, he decided not to waste any time. "You, sir, are to leave my wife alone!"

The doctor took a moment, a myriad of emotions flittering through his brown eyes. "I have no idea what you speak of—"

"Of course, you do," he snarled. "Is she with you now, you snake charmer?"

Peregoy looked surprised. "Cerisa? No, I have yet to see her."

"Liar!" he hissed. "Stay away from her. You have your own

wife, if she can stand you long enough, stay with her because if you come close to Cerisa again, I will blow your brains out!"

CHAPTER THIRTY-SEVEN

"[t]he patriotism of the people has proved equal to every sacrifice demanded by their country's need."
—Jefferson Davis, 1863

October 15, 1863

PIERCE ARRIVED ON THE outskirts of Chattanooga, along the ridgeline of the Confederate soldiers, solidly in place to starve off the city. He snaked his way into the town by downdressing himself and his horse. Alone, he had the better chance of pulling this ruse off than if he had brought his aide with him. He'd left Prasse to find the whereabouts of Cerisa and to leave no stone unturned. His written orders were vague, about possible spies within the ranks, allowing the boy to cover ground without too many problems.

But he wasn't ready for what he found in Rosecrans's command. The troops morale was low, defeated at this point, and their commander was far worse.

"Sir, reporting as commanded," he stated, saluting the major general.

Rosecrans looked up and gave a nod but never rose, nor said a word. "We are done," was his only comment.

What had happened to the man who had pounded his chest with enthusiasm prior to the attack at Chickamauga?

"Sir, the enemy has the high ground. The city is secure but…"

"Yes, the supply lines. I know, sir." He put his head in his hands.

The junior officer there handed Pierce a telegraph from Lincoln with pieces behind it telling of reinforcements coming. The last one was of Major General Ulysses S. Grant sending 20,000 men from Vicksburg, with the more damning twist—it listed Grant to take over command of the newly made Military Division of the Mississippi and head to Chattanooga.

Pierce inhaled. He knew little of the western general, outside that victory seemed to follow him. An underdog, or so his father stated, Grant also had a tendency to throw all his men into the fray and in the end, he had won Vicksburg, putting the entire Mississippi River under Union control. With that achievement and moving east, the idea bubbling along the government lines was that the war might change and the North become victorious.

But apparently, Rosecrans had been defeated and by the looks of it, soundly in the general's eyes.

"Sir, we have to plan some way to get supplies. The men will not make it."

Rosecrans looked at him, as if seeing him for the first time. A flicker of light in his gaze told Pierce he'd hit some chord inside him. The general called for "Baldy" and the room lit on fire with response.

Running his fingers through his hair, Pierce groaned. He was not here to be the man's babysitter nor morale booster. He had his own situation of a Southern wife scared from him by two people in his life who'd claimed they'd done nothing. What if he lost her? He needed Prasse to find something, anything at this point. Meanwhile, he listened to Rosecrans, hearing a skip in the man's previously solid command...

What the hell was he going to do to get the out of here? Cerisa!

The long winding road to Bellefontaine Plantation still looked as pristine and full of Southern elegance as it did during her childhood. The arched trees with Spanish moss draping down like subtle sheers in a window casing, giving the arriving guests a hint of the magnitude that lay before them. Magnolia trees stood like guards along the drive and around the house, no flowers at this point in October, though the smell of other flowers and the river wafted around her. She was home. Roughly four years, she imagined, but it seemed like longer. She'd left when the South reigned as king in power. Now, torn by war and death, it clung to life but not here. No, at the Fontaine properties, life prospered.

Prospered, but would it survive? Did that practice still prevail? And why did she return? The reality hit her hard, like a kick in her ribs—because she had no where else to turn to...

Williams pulled his worn but sturdy wagon up to the front of the house. She turned to thank him when the front door swung wide open and her brother, Jack, stood there, his hand on a revolver that lowered to his side when he saw her.

"Cerisa?"

Her vision blurred. All she could do was nod, totally inarticulate at the moment. It didn't matter. He raced to the wagon and lifted her off, pulling her into his arms.

"Oh, my God, Cera! Where have you been?"

She pulled away and sniffled, pulling her handkerchief out. Her stomach rolled, the baby's presence only a flutter but one she keenly felt. "Oh, Jack, I've missed you!"

The house was buzzing with her home. Jack, dressed in his Union blues, drilled her with questions but the reality was the same for both of them. The family's dirty secret. In the few moments they had before the rest descended on them, he pulled her into the library, where he had made his office and poured them both a glass of whiskey.

Handing her one, he raised his high. "Welcome home, sister."

"Thank you, brother." They clanked the glasses. While he downed his, she sipped a tiny sip and again, the flutter started as well as the stomach tightening.

"Where the hell have you been?" He sat her on the settee to the side of the room and took the seat next to her. "No, wait. *What* made you run?"

She crumpled her nose. "The same reason you escaped."

His jawline tightened and he poured himself another shot. "I left because I was subjected to that 'ritual' they all participated in." He downed it then put the glass rim-side down. "Ladies don't play that game."

"No, they don't. But it didn't stop a curious young girl from wanting to find out what all the hoopla was about. So I hid and peeked." She shuddered.

He exhaled, shaking his head. "Well, you'll be pleased to know, that no longer happens here."

"You stopped it?"

"Yes, ma'am."

"Oh, thank God," she squeezed his hands. The navy wool scratched her flesh and she frowned. "You are still with the Union?" At his nod, she squinted. "Why are you here, then? This is rebel land."

He snorted. "I got my reasons."

Almost on cue, his name rang through the halls. It was a woman who called for him. Cerisa waited, curious.

"My wife, Emma. Come, let me introduce you." He stood and offered his hand. Cerisa got up but suddenly, the world tilted and she squeezed his arm where her hand rested, trying to right herself. He took it more like a motion of trust and love, she guessed, because he grinned and asked nothing else.

They walked out into the hallway, headed to the front parlor, near the grand staircase when before them stood a beautiful woman, with luxurious auburn hair and wearing a stunning sheer morning dress in spun yellow with embroidered white and purple flowers scattered across it. Cerisa was in awe of her and especially of the elegance she presented with her bulging tummy.

"Emma, my darling," he called. "Look who finally came home! My sister, Cerisa."

Emma floated down the stairs and made Cerisa envious. She hoped she'd look half that good in the following months. The flutter in her own lower abdomen, with her slight bump that folds of her dress still hid, reminded her of the child and how hungry she was.

"Cerisa, yes, I remember you from Jack's West Point graduation!" Emma smiled and reached to kiss her sister-in-law's cheek. "Truly a happy moment here at the Fontaine house."

"Cera?"

She whipped her gaze to her left. "Francois!" She ran to her oldest brother's arms and he hugged her tightly.

"I'm so pleased you're home," he whispered in her ear. "Wherever you've been, you look good. Perhaps a bit too good, huh?" His eyes roved down her and back up.

"Maybe." Did she look pregnant?

"Let me see my baby-girl!"

She smiled. "Mama!" she raced to her mother and hugged her tight.

Marie Fontaine took her daughter's cheeks in her hands and eyed her closely. "Very ill-mannered, young lady, disappearing in the night, without so much as a word to your dear, sweet mother?"

Cerisa cringed. "Apologies, mama. I just didn't think. I saw—"

"Shhh, shhhh, your sweet brother, Jack, made things right." Her mother kissed her cheeks again and she caught in a glance to her brothers Jack beaming and Francois's jawline tightening. "Now," Marie continued. "Where is Abraham?" Her mother looked about for the slave she ran with. Did she tell her she'd married him?

She gulped. "He's fighting in the war, Mama. He's one of the Colored soldiers."

Francois spit. Jack's eyes widened. "He is? Good for him. Always a good boy, worked really hard, if my memory is correct."

Emma's face looked like it was pinched as she looked at her sister-in-law. "So, is it his baby you be carrying?"

Silence fell over them like night. All Fontaines turned and faced Cerisa. She gulped.

Pierce watched in utter amazement the moment "Unconditional Surrender" Grant arrived. The animosity between him and Rosecrans was thick enough a knife could cut through it.

Grant arrived in Chattanooga on the 23rd. Two days prior, he had selected Major General George H. Thomas, the 'Rock of Chickamauga' as he was nicknamed, for holding ground despite the bulk of the Union army retreating to Chattanooga, to take over command of the Army of the Cumberland. Grant had no choice, he muttered to Pierce and Thomas.

"I interviewed Rosecrans two days ago. The general filled me in quite adequately on the situation here and even made some excellent suggestions as to what should be done. My only wonder was that he had not carried them out." Grant shook his head but moved on with completing the plan that had been designed by Rosecrans and Brigadier General William F. "Baldy" Smith to re-open the 'Cracker Line' to resupply the army Bragg was attempting to starve.

Pierce remained with Wood's Division and the remains of his Colored regiment was there. But Abraham was not. His responsibilities made it hard for him to take the time to go to those men that were still there and see if he could find the man. He was on the verge of making a beeline there despite his duties when suddenly Corporal Prasse appeared.

"General," he said, almost out of breath and red-faced. Pierce looked past him and saw his sorrel pony was sweaty and prancing from a hard run.

He pulled the corporal aside, praying for news. He'd been back here for almost two weeks, separated from his love by virtually a month. Only the war had distracted him enough to keep from just breaking rank and running, but as a good soldier, he couldn't do that. So he ground his teeth and helped plan strategies, even if they did die as long as Rosecrans continued his spiral into depression. But with Grant, that would change, Pierce was sure.

First, Prasse handed him a list while he fought to regain a breath. Pierce opened the scroll. It was a list of the deceased and his heart jumped, fearing her name among them but then realized it was of soldiers fighting for the Union. As he scrolled down, he found the answer to one question. Listed as killed in Tennessee, after the Union victory at the Battle of Blue Springs three weeks ago, was one Abraham Walker, a Colored man who died due to injuries from the battle. Pierce closed his eyes as he wanted to crumple the report but decided not to. As he rolled the page back up, he remembered he still had the man's letter to Cerisa because he'd never gotten a chance to return it to her. Now, he'd claim it came with the report and other items from the soldiers so it must have split off the seal then, thus hiding the truth that he'd opened it.

"Is that all?"

Prasse took a sip of water, finally able to breath. "Found a farmer, one who's been supplying the Union in Nashville. He claims, for a few dollars, he did take a Southern belle out of town about the time you left. Claims she called herself Cerisa Fontaine, sir, and he took her home to St. Francisville, Louisiana."

"Fontaine?" He rolled the name in his head. He'd heard it before, from his friend in New York. So she left not using his name. He frowned.

"Sir, there's a major down in that area, assigned to the Vicksburg area, called Fontaine."

Pierce paused. He'd heard there was a member of Jeff Davis' cabinet by the same surname, confusion took over. "Wait, is Fontaine a Unionist or Confederate?"

"Appears both, sir."

He sighed. Now, he had to find a way to get transferred to Mississippi…

She retched again, hoping this was the last of it. She fell back on the settee, her hand on her stomach and closed her eyes. If the next six months meant bending over a chamber pot every day, this'd be the only baby she'd have. Both her mama and Emma said it didn't last, but that was three days ago and it still continued. Her breath had to be horrible at this point so she reached for the peppermint leaf and chewed as she stood and walked out onto the veranda. She stood at the railing, overlooking the gardens. Still working in them were the slaves, just like days of old. Jack assured her, he'd freed them all and then hired those who stayed, yet she did wonder the truth of that, because they looked just like they did as slaves.

"Cerisa."

She turned. "Franscois." She held out her hands for him to take. He lifted one then the other to his lips and gave them a light kiss. "I'm surprised to see you here, all dressed fancy-like, as if it were Sunday or a weddin'." She smiled.

But he didn't give her one in return. Instead, he gave her a tight one. "I'm coming to say farewell, ma chère."

"I don't understand. Where do you think to head? There is a war."

"That's exactly where I'm going."

She grasped his hands tight. "No! I've seen it. I won't lose you to that hell!"

"Oh, ma chère, to stay is hell."

She stood, glaring at him, demanding to know why in a look when it hit her hard. She'd seen the glimpses here and there, a hint of a loving gesture denied. He was in love with Emma, but she loved her husband. "Oh, Francois…"

"Non, non, ma chère, it is good. But I can't take it any more. I must go." He kissed the top of her head and hugged her tight. "If you love someone, don't let them go. Emma was in love with Jacques before she met moi, so it was not meant to be. But you? You pine for the father of that child you carry. Do not let life keep you from him. It is too short to forsake love because of something like hearsay, tu comprends?"

She understood. She squeezed her eyes shut, the tears forming. "Je t'aime."

"Je t'aime." Another kiss then nothing but a breeze as he was gone.

She stood for a moment, her heart torn. Her brother must love Emma so much, that to see her with Jack was too much for him. She understood that. But she feared for him. This war, this awful war!

Jack barreled his horse down the lane toward the big house, the wind whipping past him and the stallion's mane lashing his cheeks as they edged closer. Leaning back in the saddle, he pulled the reins back, signaling halt. The grey thoroughbred beneath him was sweating and snorting. Jack laughed, finally a bit unwound. He had had to get away. Way too much war, tension and the nagging fear of Emma's delivery, a moment that made him remember his first wife and how she hadn't lived through the childbirth. The mere whisper of that memory made him take to the saddle and ride hard, to feel the wind on his face and the freedom of his rancid thoughts. He'd be no good for her condition fretting so.

Stopping in front of the house, he felt refreshed and in control of his fears. He prayed fervently for a peaceful birth.

Little Robbie, the young lad who loved the animals, despite the fact that he was short and young enough that the horses still towered over him, raced out to get the horse. Jack grinned. The boy looked at him, his gaze reminding Jack of the sins of this family, but he'd never let him know those blue eyes were his fault.

"Jacques."

Jack looked up and found his brother on the porch. "Francois," he started, tossing the boy his reins as he slid out off the saddle. "Something wrong with the ladies?" It took him a moment to realize his brother was fully dressed to travel, a carpetbag in his hand and his other hand held his hat. Jack frowned. "Where are you going?"

Francois's expression was a mix of sadness and determination in his blue-gray eyes and his lips formed a tight line. "I need to go. You know why."

Jack shook his head as his heart sank. "I wish you wouldn't. Where you're heading is…well, war is hell, Francois."

His brother shrugged. "She loves you, more than me. I can't stay and watch."

"I know." Jack stopped in front of him and stared. The silence grew. On the return of his long lost sister and the coming arrival of his child, he'd lose his brother now, all because they loved the same woman. Having faced the elephant himself, Jack knew the odds were not good, especially the route Francois would take. It was a moment, the weight of the world descended on his shoulders, but he understood, for he would have done the same if she'd picked Francois over him. And it had been close… He hugged his older brother and Francois returned it full fold.

"Good bye, mon frère," Francois said as he pulled back and picked up his bag. "Take care of you, Cera and my darling Emma."

"I will." He laughed. "Thought it'd be you to run this place, being the older brother." With a grave look, he added, "Take care of you."

Francois tipped his hat right as the stable boy directed the bay stallion over to him. Tying the bag, he mounted the animal and gave Jack, and the house, a look. Jack was sure he was hoping to see Emma. Then, Francois gave him one last smile and spurred the horse down the entrance path.

Jack shook his head and heaved a sigh. His world erupted when he heard Emma scream.

An hour earlier, Cerisa sat on the porch, glass of lemonade in her hand. It was a lazy, hot day in Louisiana, the bugs buzzed happily about the porch but the mulatto girl kept the big fan blade swinging up and down, as if she was still a slave. Jack claimed they were free yet to Cerisa, they continued to act like slaves doing chores, paid or not. Despite Jenny telling her to *shhh* and how they didn't see it that way, she still found it hard to watch, particularly since the child had such pale blue eyes. A shiver ran down Cerisa's spine as ghosts of the past echoed in her mind, so she closed her eyes to chase the images away.

"How do you feel?"

She glanced up and found Emma waddling out on the porch. Her long flowing morning gown made her look more angelic as it was another sheer one and in the slight breeze, it moved easily so the waddling didn't look so succinct but her bare toes poked out underneath. Emma must have seen Cerisa see her toes and she laughed. "I know. Barefoot and in the family way. I'm not receiving anyone so it's fine. Besides, they're too swollen to wear shoes." With as much grace as she could muster at her size, she lowered onto the settee.

"When are you due?"

"Anytime now, Miss Jenny tells me. Your mother agrees."

"Shouldn't you be in bed?" It was the course of action, she had heard. Last three months or so in bed. Emma chuckled.

"Perhaps but they tell me to keep walking. Make that baby

come, is what Jenny says. Besides, I can't be in bed." She looked at Cerisa. "You worry, don't you?"

Cerisa bit her bottom lip, tears threatening again. That irritated her. Or the absence of the men in her life did. Or perhaps, the memory of what Pierce's father accused her of.

"Don't be mad because you want to cry or scream or laugh, all at the same time," Emma cautioned. "Its normal, considering your condition."

Cerisa didn't realize she was so readable. Trying to mask her emotions, she turned the conversation.

"So, how did you end up with my brother? He is a Yankee, after all."

Emma smiled. "He chased me. We met through my brother. You'll meet Charles and Sarah tonight. My brother and yours went to West Point. Remember, that's where I met you? Well, after that, he had a hankerin' for me and so, after much, we ended up here, married and expecting our first." Her hand rested on her large belly.

"Mama, Mama!" A little boy ran up to Emma, his eyes a sparkling green, just like Jack's, Cerisa thought.

"Mr. Nathan, you leave your mama be."

She turned and found Aunt Jenny grabbing the boy's hand.

"Come now, Mr. Nathan, you be needing a nap," she smiled as she directed the boy away.

Cerisa's brows rose, questioning that encounter.

"Yes, Nathan is Jack's through an earlier marriage. And Francois was a life saver to me when I got here, alone and carrying Jack's child, believing Jack was dead." She frowned. "I don't think he's happy. He had proposed to me when Jack, who defied death, arrived to claim me back."

Cerisa's thoughts were racing, trying to understand all this. Apparently, a lot had happened since she left. All she could do was nod. She put the lemonade down as the thought of it was making her sick.

"Ouch!"

She looked up at Emma's screech. The woman held her side as her face contorted.

"What's wrong?"

The answer came as water pooled around her feet.

"Mama!" Cerisa shrieked.

November 1st

ONE THING WAS FOR sure. It was never cool here in the South. Pierce pulled on the reins and took off his hat, rubbing his forehead with a handkerchief. November and he was sweating.

It truly hadn't taken much to get reassigned to southern Louisiana. With Tennessee more secured, once they'd driven Bragg's men back across the Georgia line, Grant's view was on tackling Lee and he focused on that entirely. Pierce, a brevet general and one with political connections, found it best to play that card. As he recalled, there were Colored troops in the west. He'd push to try to train them, thus giving him the pathway to Louisiana and Cerisa.

Shoving the hat back on his head, he urged his beast on. Heading into the small town before him, he walked into the only hotel for a drink. The man in charge glared at him but poured him a whiskey once he pulled the silver bit out and onto the table.

A dark-haired beauty, dressed somewhat scantily, came and sat right next to him. "Hello, General," she greeted with a sultry tone.

A prostitute. Last thing he needed. "Just stopping through for a drink. That's all."

She sniffed. "And perhaps a bath?"

That line threw him. He probably was a mess, having been in battle and then onto the road without a stop. He snorted. "And you got one?"

"What's you in town for, again?"

"Look, I'm here to find the Fontaine place."

"As in Jack Fontaine?"

He downed the drink, letting the burn of the whiskey settle the nerves that were frayed and burned. She was irritating him. "No, for my wife. Cerisa."

The whore gave him a surprised look. "Well, she won't want to see you, stinkin' like a pig in a bog like you are now." She went behind the bar and pulled the whiskey out from behind the bar to pour him another. "Bring that, soldier-boy. You need a scrubbin' something fierce before you head to Bellefontaine."

"You know them?"

"Yes sir, mighty well indeed. All the Fontaine boys know Delilah. So if you want in their door, better come with me to a tub."

He grabbed his hat and tossed the barkeep another coin. Guess seeing her clean would be better and he followed the whore to a house across the street. A bath and nothing else!

CHAPTER THIRTY-EIGHT

"[he seemed] confused and stunned like a duck hit on the head."
—Lincoln's description on Rosecrans, as he became a beaten man psychologically after the defeat of Chickamauga.

The Next Day

PIERCE TOOK THE WAY Delilah told him to go. He did feel immensely better having shaved and cleaned up. The whore had offered her services but he'd declined. Not that she wasn't attractive enough to give any man a delight or two, but his heart was set on Cerisa and trying to win her back, after the bad news he had to give her about Abraham. And trying to mend the wrongs his father had done. He'd spilled the story out to Delilah as she masterfully scrubbed him. Why he told her he wasn't sure, but she listened and gave him advice on how to get to the house. Despite her telling him about the family, he wasn't prepared for the large and wealthy estate called Bellefontaine Plantation. From what he'd seen of Cerisa, she must've come from a good family with some money to afford a buck the size of Abraham, but this large house with the land was bigger than what he thought.

And his father thought he'd married low again.

He rode to the front, swung his leg over the saddle and slid off the horse, still favoring his left side. The wound was

almost all healed and the pain gone but a twinge every once
and a while reminded him, he wasn't totally over it. A black
boy came out and took the reins, not saying a word and took
the horse away. Pierce had never owned a slave, nor actually
seen one in action. It seemed surreal, because from the look
of Bellefountaine, it looked like it had escaped the war.

By the time he got to the door, another dark-skinned
servant, dressed well as a butler would, let him in and took his
card then walked off. He wasn't sure what to do except wait.
At the top of the stairs, he heard a baby crying and footsteps
above. Babies. He'd never been around one of those either.
His brother never married and he himself was the baby in
the family.

"General Duval?"

He looked over and found another Union officer. "Yes, sir."

"Good, come in. Major Jack Fontaine, at your service."
Jack pointed to a chair in front of his desk. He sat and waited.

Pierce inhaled. "I've come to see my wife. Cerisa Walker, I
mean, Fontaine. Well, truly Duval."

Jack gave him a surprised glance. "Good God, sir, which
one is it?"

"Cerisa."

The major laughed. "Apologies, sir. Just in a celebratory
mood here. My wife gave birth yesterday to a son and both
are well, so I'm rather pleased."

"Congratulations, Major."

"Thank you."

"How good it must be for you to be home when this
joyful event." He stared at the man. Most of the men in the
field hadn't seen their wives in years.

"Yes, it is." His tone wasn't as jovial. "I am a lucky man to
be stationed here." He sat back. "And yes, my sister, Cerisa,

is here. She returned home after years up in the North, very upset and in ill-health. Why should I allow a man, claiming to be her husband, access to her again when it is painfully clear, you couldn't provide for her in the first place?"

Pierce sat dumbfounded. She wasn't well? What happened? His heart raced at the thought of her hurt, but then, that hurt might not have been physical, he reminded himself. How many times had his father taken verbal shots at him and the pain was as real as a knife?

"There is a war. I hadn't meant to bring her with me—"

"You took her to the front?" Jack pushed back out of the chair and lunged forward, leaning on the desk. "General or not, I should shoot you!"

"No, Major, you don't understand." Apparently, he gathered, she didn't tell them of her life in New York City. "I couldn't leave a Southern lady up north, in New York or anywhere. Us Yankees can be a cruel sort to those who are not one with us, if you get my meaning."

Jack drummed his fingertips on the desktop. "I'm not sure she'll see you."

Pierce's heart stopped. "Major Fontaine, I need to speak with her. I have vital information for her ears only. Please." He stuttered a moment, exasperated at this point. "I have traveled a distance to see her. I love her so much, I've veered from my course to try to set things right. You know the war can easily kill, so grant me this wish before I go to see the Grim Reaper and test myself again."

Jack pursed his lips, his mind mulling over the words the man said. He, too, recalled when he had to find Emma and beg her to accept him, that he loved her. Charles, her brother, stated it'd be hell to win her back and it was. But Cerisa was like him and this man, general or not, might have a harder time. The girl was stubborn and resourceful enough to run away years ago and survive, even flourish, carrying this man's child, but would she accept him back now? Jack had heard part of her story, knew better than to push for all now, after seeing the moods Emma had been in for the last few months, so what he heard wasn't a glowing recommendation for the man here, but it didn't condemn him either.

"General Duval, my sister has been through hell. She arrived at my door sick and hungry and in a battered state. Your love may not be enough for her. She deserves more than a brevet general arriving with flowers and promises, especially after dragging her through the pits of hellfire of a battlefield with some wild theory it'd keep her safe."

He witnessed the man nod his head. "I agree. But I do offer more. My heart and all that entails. I just need to get a chance, just one, to try to prove to her I do love her."

Jack hesitated. Emma would kill him for this, then again, she might for not doing so. And Cerisa? What did she want? She was his younger sibling but she had lived on her own. She deserved the chance to decide her future.

"All right. I will let you have your chance. But, General, I will tell you, if you so much as hurt one hair on her, I will kill you."

"I wouldn't dream of it."

He looked sincere and even hurt Jack suggested that. "Then best of luck, General. You'll need it."

Cerisa found happiness in her brother's baby. The child was perfect and Emma and Jack were both so happy. It made her envious and fearful she'd never have the chance to tell Pierce of their child. As she sat on the settee in the study, a flutter in her womb made her think her baby agreed. She closed her eyes and fought against the growing tears.

"Cera." It was a whisper, very quiet, barely audible, enough so she wondered if she'd just heard it. Perhaps Francois changed his mind and in hopes, she turned and opened her eyes to find Pierce, standing on her veranda, dressed in his uniform, though his hat and gloves were in his hands. She blinked, not believing. She'd never told him her real name or where exactly she came from. How had he found her?

"Pierce," she replied, gathering her skirts in a nervous gesture. "What a surprise to see you."

He must've taken that as an invitation because he was by her side in an instant.

"You have no idea how I have missed you. One minute, I have you by my side and in an instant, you are gone, no good-byes, no farewells, nothing."

She inhaled. Half of her wanted to throw herself into his arms. The other half wanted to hit him. "Yes, well, I met your father. Very forthright man, told me everything I needed to know about you, including a fiancée you left behind." The words came out with a snarl, as the anger she thought she hid well sneaked out. *How dare he accuse her of adultery in consideration of this?*

"Charlotte is not my fiancée," he quickly replied. "She was my brother's. When he died, my father hoped I'd take her for wife but I had married Margaret and my parents loathed her because she was Irish." He shook his head. "Charlotte's father owns one of the largest shipping companies in New York and would be a valuable ally for my father, politically speaking. I hardly knew the girl."

"So you married Margaret to rebel against that? And after her death, I was the next ruse to hide behind?" Her fury flung out fast. Red hot fire coursed through her veins, mostly at his father but at him as well. "This marriage is a lie!"

"Cerisa, no—"

"No, that's all right," she said, pacing. "I have a husband. He's a freedman. Off to the war, but from what your father dug to find out, Abraham's still my husband!"

Pierce watched her, saw the anger in her eyes as she spat at him with her words. True, she was married to Abraham, but that was the sad part. *Was*. He inhaled sharply.

"I have news," he started.

"I don't believe you!"

He knew she'd say that. He pulled out the newspaper clipping on the latest deaths, his military report that also said it and handed them to her. The look she shot him meant she didn't trust him but she looked over both and he watched her jaw drop.

"No!"

"Cera," he started.

"Don't call me that!" she stormed off, yanking out her lace hankie as the tears fell. "Not Abraham. No…."

He pulled out the letter and offered it. "You dropped this the last time we were together in Nashville. I couldn't return it because *you* ran off."

Wiping her eyes, she opened it and said nothing about the seal being cracked. Instead, he watched her read every line and he could feel the jab every time she hit a word that more or less told her to go to him and he could tell she wanted to refuse.

"You made him write this!"

He stopped. "That's a wild accusation. I didn't know the man well enough to tell him to do anything of the like."

"You were his commander!"

"Cera, stop. You're not making sense." He ran his hand through his hair. This wasn't going well. He came closer to her and kneeled before her, preparing himself for her to kick him but when she didn't, he breathed. Taking her hands, even as clenched up as they were and wet with tears, he tried to calm her. "Shhh, please, my darling. Shhhh. He's with the angels now."

"This terrible war! You men created it!"

She was right, but now wasn't the time to discuss this. "Shhhh. I agree. No one wanted to agree to stop it. Neither side. But that's not why I've been searching high and low for you."

With a gulp for air and a sniffle, she glanced up at him. Inside, he cheered.

"Why would you come looking for your white trash wife? The one you even accused of sleeping with the surgeon?"

The first part was his father. He could hear the man say those words. Unfortunately, he did the other half. He cringed. "You are not white trash. Good grief, my father thinks Lincoln is white trash! Forget Senator Duval. He has his own desires and that is more power. Me? I want you! I realized I was in love with you and the mere thought of that snake being close, while I was doing my job on the battlefield, drove me mad with jealousy! I love you Cerisa! I told you that right after our marriage. Why don't you believe me? Why didn't you come to me after my father's accusations? I would have told you how he is and you'd see it wasn't true!" Every word came out fast and furious, like a waterfall he couldn't stop. His heart hurt. If she told him to leave, how could he convince her his love was real?

Cerisa listened. Even in the midst of the words he said, she wondered. He was right. He had told her before. He had shown he wanted to protect her, by taking care of those vermin in Washington, the one who attacked her in New York City, had saved her from the mob at the riots and married her so his name could protect her. Truth was Abraham was dead. The official reports and the newspapers had to be right. The letter rang in her head. She feared he went to the war to die so she would be with Pierce. She prayed she was wrong, but he loved her enough to do that, to set her 'free'.

Her mind spun. So did her stomach. She swallowed the bile that started upwards. That would be the deciding factor, she thought. What would he do if he knew she carried his child?

She never got a moment to ask. Her swallowing didn't stop it and she had to yank her hands out of his and race to the chamber pot. It was such a vile thing to do, but she couldn't stop it. It took him a moment but he was there, a towel in his hand.

"Here."

"Thank you." She dabbed her mouth and as quickly, grabbed a peppermint leaf. "Sorry."

He seemed to loom over her. "How long?"

"Pardon me?"

"How long have you known you were carrying?"

"Not long," she admitted. "Doc McElroy confirmed it just before your father arrived." She wondered if he'd accuse her of carrying Abraham's or Peregoy's child, since he'd accused her of infidelity before. But this time, she watched his gaze turn warm and even a bit watery.

"Are you happy to be a father?"

He didn't answer in words but picked her up and spun

her around in his arms and laughed. "Yes. This is the best news you could give me! Well," he lowered her to the floor. "Loving me would be better, but this is a step there." He gave her a huge, warm grin.

"Despite it all, Yankee, I do love you." She reached up to kiss him.

He pulled her into his embrace and kissed her back with a fierceness that rocked her on her heels and made her heart sing. He kissed her deep and then stopped, dropping to the floor on one knee. He took her hand.

"Marry me, Cerisa."

She laughed. "I did, silly."

He grinned. "I love you."

"And I love you."

He stood and bent to kiss her. She reached up around his neck and pulled him closer. She loved him. Probably had from the first time she'd met him. The world tried to keep them apart, by war, by family, by other men, but she decided, those trials were just tests, and they'd passed them all. She hugged him tighter—and prayed she'd not get sick again.

EPILOGUE

"It was badly planned and we were the sufferers."
—Chaplin Bunting, CSA on General Wheeler's Cavalry, 1863

2 weeks later

IT WAS A QUIET moment at the mansion and for that second, neither one said a word. It was the middle of the afternoon and she truly felt decadent, lying naked in bed with her husband. They'd made love with an intensity she wasn't sure she'd ever had but with Pierce, it took her to new heights and made her love him even deeper. But there was something driving him today and she feared what he might say.

"I love you," he whispered, tugging at her earlobe.

"I know." She snuggled closer.

The quietness didn't last. He leaned forward and kissed her neck as his hand splayed over the slight bulge of their child. "Do you feel him yet?"

"Oh, he? What if he is a she?"

"That's not what I meant."

She laughed. "I know. Yes, I think so. It's a slight flutter. Mama says that is the quickening."

"Good." He nuzzled under her ear. "I'll remember this always."

The shoe fell. The beautiful moment shattered by that statement. "What do you mean?" She tried to sound lighthearted but knew it didn't come across that way.

He bit his lower lip. "I have to return to the war. Orders found me."

"Please, Pierce, don't!"

He rolled her on her back so they could see eye to eye. "I have a job, Cera. I've no choice."

"Take me with you," she begged. *No, he couldn't leave her now!*

"I won't and you know it. Look," he kissed her nose. "I'm to report to New Orleans. It's close. There hasn't been any fighting there in months."

She snarled. "I hoped you'd get out."

"You know, I can't just up and leave. Your brother is here, though he too is still serving." He brought her closer. "I love you. And I promise to come home to you."

"Swear on your life you will!" She knew that sounded ridiculous but she was desperate. He was going to leave her and their child for this hell?

"I swear to God above, I will always love you and return to your arms." He kissed her.

She held him tight and returned the kiss with a magnitude she didn't know she possessed. She'd leave a mark on him that he could never forget her, just as she could never forget him.

She loved him. That was all that mattered.

THE END

AUTHOR'S NOTES

Life in the Victorian Age, especially during the American Civil War, is a fascinating and complex time period. The War itself has shaped this nation, verified that democracy and the republic we formed here can exist. While Cerisa and Pierce are fictional characters, many others in this story are not. General Rosecrans did lead the Union army against General Bragg's Confederates at the Battle of Chickamauga and Chattanooga. Garfield was also true to form. These men helped shape the course of the war, along with many more.

Because of the intricacies of the battle and the players involved, research was required. As a historian by education (I hold both a BA and MA in History from the University of Missouri) and career (I have been both a museum educator, Park Guide for Interpretation and Curator), I needed to have this story be written as closely as possible to the actual events. For instance, interracial marriages in New York were legal during the time of the 1860s, though not encouraged or considered socially acceptable. In the Irish settlements, several of the lasses married freedmen, irritating the Irish community and adding more fuel to the fire against freeing the slaves, allowing them to come north for jobs.

Were there women, particularly officer wives, with the Army of the Cumberland? Yes, records record there were and their camp was set up just outside the army camp. They were asked to move just before the battle began. Women nursing had been established by Dorothea Dix in the Union Army but her regimen called for ladies of bland to ugly appearance, for fear the pretty ones would make the male patients too excited and possibly rupture a repair or surgical suture trying to get the lady's attention, though some surgeons needed more than help and if they could have volunteers, male and female, they'd use them. Of course, there were many who wanted no outsiders in their hospitals.

Some resources I used for this novel, on top of the usual historical sources (please view Books 1 & 2 of this series), for the Battle of Chickamauga, a smattering of sources include –

This Terrible Sound, The Battle of Chickamauga by Peter Cozzens

The Chickamauga Campaign, Vol I-III by David A. Powell

The Maps of Chickamauga by David A. Powell & David A. Friedrichs

"The Medical Support at the Battle of Chickamauga, Chapter Five" and *"The Medical Support Following the Battle (of Chickamauga), Chapter Six"* from an Army thesis for Office of Medical History

For more, please contact me or visit
www.ginadanna.com.

NOVELS BY GINA DANNA

Her Eternal Rogue
The Wicked Bargain
Great & Unfortunate Desires
This Love of Mine
To Dance With A Lord
To Kiss A Lady
A Merry Wicked Christmas

THE GLADIATOR SERIES:

Love & Vengeance (Book I)
Love & Lies (Book II)

HEARTS TOUCHED BY FIRE (CIVIL WAR) SERIES:

The Wicked North (Book 1)
The Key To The South (Book 2)
Rags & Hope (Book 3)
The Better Angels (Book 4)

THE BETTER Angels

HEARTS TOUCHED BY FIRE, BOOK 4

Gina DANNA

CHAPTER ONE

"My plans are perfect and when I start to carry them out, may God have mercy on General Lee for I will have none!"

—General Joseph Hooker, The Battle of Chancellorsville, May 1863

Virginia, November 1863

THE GIGGLE WAS FAINT, *very feminine, and without opening his eyes, he grinned. He had always loved her laughter. Light, airy, the sound drifted and he remembered the first time he heard it. He believed he fell in love with her at that moment, not so long ago, when it was summer in Louisiana.*

"Francois, Francois," she coaxed him.

He didn't want to answer, for that meant he'd have to open his eyes and at the moment, he realized his eyelids were so heavy, he doubted he could. Instead, he'd lounge here on this rattan settee in his mother's rose garden and wait for her to get closer.

"Francois, darling," she whispered into his ear. "It's time to wake up."

"No, ma chère, non." He'd snuggle into the cushions more if they weren't so hard. That confused him. His mother never allowed sturdy furniture frames out on the balcony…Plus the birds were overly chirpy, starting to grate on his nerves. He refocused on her.

"Francois, my love," she cooed again, singing into his ear. "You'd better wake, darling."

"Non, ma chère, come back to me," he begged. *He'd put out his arms to take her into his embrace but he discovered he couldn't. It was like he was far under water, trying to build a house, as sluggish as he was. He frowned.*

"Francois…." Her voice faded. No! She couldn't leave him again! The birds around him seemed to multiple, busily squeaking louder and louder. He tried to get up, to go after her but the world began to swirl and he stopped, still feeling trapped and realized he'd gone no where. In his mind, he searched for her but his vision filled with smoke and the acid taste of gunpowder and sulfur burned his throat and clouded his vision.

"Francois! Wake up!" She screamed with a panic tone.

He twisted. In a split second, a stabbing pain shot into his foot, at his ankle, as if he was on fire. He roared in agony, reluctant eyelids splitting wide open. The shock of what he saw made him want to flee. He was lying with other men moaning and groaning. The men upright walked about at a hurried pace, their white coats stained in red along with more men in blue hauling some in and taking others out. The whole area smelled of blood, urine, sulfur, sweat and vomit, wafts so overwhelming, he held his breath, despite his own agony.

The commotion drowned out his pain for the second until two rough hands yanked his wounded leg to the side and repositioned it, the movement set off another cycle of pain. Another man walked up, his white coat not as dulled by red splatters as the rest. He wore a pair of spectacles on his nose and a weary look across his face. He yanked out a long metal rod, the end coated in white.

"Let's see what we got, shall we?" the man said, taking Francois's foot and twisting it.

Francois couldn't stop the cry of agony evoked by the manipulation of his foot. The dull hurt of before turned drastically sharper. Confused, Francois tried to retrace where he was and how he was wounded when another series of lightning bolt pains shot up his legs to his hips, back, shoulders and head, settling into his ears. Unfortunately, the sheering sting didn't stop the man in the white coat from prodding his ankle.

"Reed! Bring me that bag," the man called. "Need to amputate this…"

Amputate? Francois blinked hard, the scene around him blurred. They'd take his foot?

"Emma!!!"

Available Now at Amazon

Made in the USA
Columbia, SC
16 October 2022